The Murder of Emily Fisher

Holly Copella

In loving memory of
Smokey Snyder

ACKNOWLEDGMENTS

Copella Books: First Paperback Edition 2017
Cover Artist: Daniela Owergoor
Dani-owergoor.deviantart.com
Printed by CreateSpace, An Amazon.com Company

PUBLISHER'S NOTE

Chapter One

Thursday, September 24th, 1981.

"I can't do it," Trisha Allister said with a sigh as she leaned on the old, gray stone bridge facing the stream. "Not another day of school. Mr. Malcolm is going to push me right over the edge. I can't stand him."

Fifteen-year-old Sidney McBride looked at her raven-haired friend and rested her back to the bridge. "No one likes Mr. Malcolm," she replied dryly.

Trisha turned sideways and smiled deviously. "Let's skip school."

Sidney frowned and rolled her eyes. It was always the same story with Trisha. "And go where? If my father hears I cut class, I'm grounded for a week."

"He'll never know," Trisha said and leaned on her elbow.

"Of course he will," Sidney replied with a moan. "Nothing escapes the town gossips. Mrs. Cooper and Mrs. Randall make it their business to know everything."

It was a crisp, fresh September morning. The trees were starting to change colors, giving the woods between the development and town an almost scenic appearance. Sidney admired the tall trees as the branches gently swayed in the breeze.

Trisha groaned and struck the bridge with her palm, returning Sidney to reality. "I don't wanna go to class today," Trisha whined childishly.

Sidney looked at her friend and laughed mockingly. "Didn't do your report for Mr. Malcolm's class, did you?"

Trisha moaned again and rolled her eyes. The two girls had been best friends since kindergarten. Trisha had always been the adventurous one while Sidney liked to play it safe. Sidney admired her friend for her spirit and her daring ways. Trisha was often expressing her opinion, which ruffled a few feathers in their small town, especially coming from a teenage girl. Her latest verbal debate was over the recently appointed Sheriff Drukard and his lack of leadership.

The historic stone bridge was located in the woods between the town of Marilina itself and the new development to the north. The vast forest and the bridge was the quickest route to town for most of the schoolkids. The bridge also became a popular hangout for teenagers after school. It was built back in the late eighteen hundreds along with the stone house, which was just a short walk from the bridge and town.

"Billy Randall will be at football practice after school," Sidney said while grinning. "You wouldn't want to miss that, would you?"

Trisha lifted her head and forced a smile. "No, I suppose not," she said gently. "But I'm sure you want to leave right after last period."

"Well, not today," Sidney said and heaved herself onto the bridge, sitting casually, and looked at her friend. "I need to use the school typewriter."

"For what?" Trisha asked.

Sidney looked away as the color rose to her cheeks and a slight smile crossed her face. "I want to type something," she announced then hesitated and spoke almost timidly, "for Harlan."

Trisha chuckled lowly while grinning. "Don't let your father hear that," she replied. "If he knew his fifteen-year-old daughter had a thing for a twenty-five-year-old man, particularly his employee, he'd ground you for life and kill Harlan."

"Come on," Sidney replied dryly at her friend's dramatic comment. "My father isn't *that* bad."

Trisha sharply raised her brows and stared at her.

Sidney frowned and looked away. "Okay, so he's a little protective. It's not like I'm going to sign the letter."

"A secret admirer?" Trisha teased with delight. "I like the sound of that."

"Harlan is everything I've ever wanted in a guy," Sidney said with a dreamy sigh. "He's handsome, smart, mature--"

"Older, experienced," Trisha added with a giggle.

Sidney smirked and shook her head. "He's English," she announced. "What more could a girl want?"

"Someone her own age," Trisha replied. "Someone she could seriously consider dating. You're wasting your time."

"And like Billy Randall, super jock, would ever consider dating a ninth grader?" Sidney snapped.

"Am I detecting some hostility?" Trisha remarked then cast a sly look at Sidney.

Sidney smiled and sighed deeply while sinking into her own fantasy. "I feel so good when I'm around Harlan. Every time I see him, my heart skips a beat." Sidney turned her head and looked at Trisha. "He has the sexiest voice I've ever heard. I love his accent." She inhaled deeply and sighed. "He calls me love."

Trisha rolled her eyes with a low moan. "Oh, please. He's completely plain. You're so weird. Every girl in school faints at Billy Randall's feet except you. Only you would have the hots for an old geek with a camera."

Sidney raised her brow and glared at her friend. "He's not a geek, and I think he's very handsome," she announced boldly. "Far better looking than Billy."

Trisha burst out laughing.

Sidney frowned her disapproval. "We'd better go, or we'll be late," she said with a depressed sigh and slid off the wall.

Sidney grabbed her books and folders and held them against her chest. Trisha moaned and reluctantly walked beside her friend. They walked across the bridge and through the path in the woods toward town.

Trisha eyed her friend with a curious stare. "Does Harlan know how old you really are?" she asked.

"Yeah, my father happened to mention it," Sidney said lowly with a frown.

"Too bad," Trisha said then cast a sly look at her friend. "You could easily pass for eighteen."

Sidney knew it to be true. She'd been mistaken for eighteen many times. Sidney was five-foot-five and had the body of a mature woman. She wore little makeup since her father was against it, but he hadn't noticed the eyeliner she'd been wearing, nor the neutral colored lipstick. She was grateful her mother wasn't as big of a prude as her father. Her long, dark hair was pulled back into a ponytail, which was the only time she looked her age. The September afternoons were still too warm to leave her hair down.

"Mr. Malcolm is going to yell about my report not being done," Trisha said with a soft groan. "I still think we should skip school."

Sidney laughed at her friend. "I'm sure you'll think of some unique and wildly imaginative story to tell Malcolm. He'll give you another day."

"The stories are becoming more difficult than if I'd just do the work," Trisha said simply.

Sidney shook her head.

Chapter Two

The sound of falling books echoed through the hallway as two boys started a fight between sixth and seventh period. Several students cheered them on while teachers ran from their classrooms and attempted to break them apart. Sidney and Trisha flattened themselves against the lockers to avoid the nearby fight. A young, attractive female teacher with her long hair in a French twist approached the fighting students.

"That's enough," Miss Emily Fisher shouted.

It was almost inconceivable that such a harsh voice could come from such a sweet looking, raven-haired beauty. One of the students was thrown against Miss Fisher. She hit the lockers with a loud, metallic crack. Several students gasped with surprise. Two boys in football jerseys stepped forward, pulled the fighting boys apart, and slammed each against the lockers on opposing sides of the hall.

"No one shoves Miss Fisher," Denny, a stocky, dark-haired boy shouted above the student murmur as he held one of the boys to the locker.

Miss Fisher straightened and refused the help of Ms. Persha Palmer, the math teacher.

"I'm okay," Miss Fisher said firmly.

The other teachers escorted the two boys to the principal's office as Miss Fisher approached Billy Randall and Denny Phillips.

"Thank you for your assistance," Miss Fisher said with a polite smile.

"The football team has your back, Miss Fisher," Billy Randall announced. "Just give the word." Billy was an impressive looking senior who stood six feet two with a muscular body and light brown, feathered back hair.

A stout man in his early forties approached Miss Fisher. He shook his head with disgust.

"You were taking a risk getting between those two," Mr. Malcolm said lowly in an annoyed tone. "You could have been hurt."

"But I wasn't, was I?" she replied simply while offering a tiny, knowing smile. "If you'll excuse me, Mr. Malcolm, I have a class to teach."

Sidney watched Miss Fisher return to her classroom just as the bell rang. No one could deny the courage of Miss Fisher. She was the most respected teacher in the entire school--and the most beautiful. Her figure was her most noticeable feature. Most of the boys studied her large bust and toned buttocks to great lengths. Some of the female students were envious toward their overly attractive teacher, but even the girls couldn't deny she was a great teacher with enthusiasm for journalism. Miss Fisher treated all her students with respect, kindness, and as if they were adults. Sidney and Trisha had to rush to their history class. They entered the room a few minutes late along with the other students who were caught in the hallway delay. True to form, Mr. Malcolm marked them all late for class.

"There could be an earthquake, and he'd still mark everyone late," Sidney muttered lowly as they walked toward their seats in the back of the classroom.

"I bet none of the other students were marked late," Trisha said softly as she sat at her desk. "Mr. Malcolm gives the teaching profession a bad name. That's why I adore Miss Fisher. I can tell her things I can't even tell my own mother, and she'd never pass judgment on anyone."

"She's a real lady, that's for sure," Sidney replied.

They looked at Mr. Malcolm as he wrote on the blackboard and seemed to share the same opinion.

"He's had it out for her since she started here," Trisha whispered.

"He's against anyone who treats kids like adults. He has a God complex," Sidney remarked.

Mr. Malcolm was a stern man with dull, brown hair and small, beady eyes set too close together. He had a thick mustache in need of a trimming, and he often smelled of old cigars. His patience was limited with the entire student body and extended toward most of the staff as well. He was difficult to follow while teaching and his drone voice made paying attention almost impossible.

Mr. Malcolm turned toward the class and cleared his throat loudly. "Reports are due today. Pass them to the front of the class."

Trisha frowned and sank in her chair. Everyone else passed their reports to the front. Mr. Malcolm collected them, counted them, and then looked at Trisha.

"Your report appears to be missing, Trisha," he said firmly while glaring at her.

Trisha straightened in her chair and attempted a smile. "It's not missing," she replied simply. "I was proofreading it this morning over coffee when I realized it would be so much better if I'd first tell about his childhood a little." Trisha casually tilted her head. "And maybe even discuss his first true love."

Mr. Malcolm sat on the edge of his desk and folded his arms across his chest. "Trisha, I don't think we want to know that much about Attila the Hun. Just bring the report in tomorrow, or it's a failing grade."

Trisha lowered her head and nodded. She looked at Sidney and winked with a tiny smile.

§

The bell sounded signaling the end of the last period for the day. All the students rushed to their lockers to deposit their books and ran out of the building. Trisha and Sidney were in no particular hurry while returning to Miss Fisher's class to use her old, electric typewriter. Trisha stopped Sidney in the hall and nodded toward the classroom. Miss Fisher was standing behind her desk talking to a man in a black, leather trench coat. He had short, spiked, dirty blonde hair with a sturdy jawline and wore a diamond stud earring in his right ear.

"Who's that?" Sidney asked softly.

Trisha raised an arrogant brow. "That's Miss Fisher's boyfriend, Alex. He bartends at Sam's Tavern."

"He doesn't look like her type," Sidney remarked simply. "He looks like a rock star."

"Bartenders are so romantic, don't you think?" Trisha said with a dreamy smile while admiring Alex.

"I couldn't say. I've never really met one." Sidney sharply eyed her friend. "Have you?"

Trisha tilted her head then sighed with defeat. "No, I suppose I haven't."

They waited for the man to leave before entering the room. He gave them a look as he passed them in the hallway. He was a fairly good-looking man, despite his unshaven face. Both girls hurried into the room. Miss Fisher appeared cheerful; though it was evident something was bothering her by the distant look in her eyes.

"I was wondering where you girls were," Miss Fisher announced. "There's paper in the closet."

"Thank you, Miss Fisher," Sidney said and uncovered the typewriter.

Miss Fisher sat on the edge of her desk and studied Trisha. "Have you been thinking about what I'd said, Trisha?"

Trisha smiled lightly and lowered her head. "Yes, I have. I'm not much of a writer though."

"You don't have to be. This is just for you. Writing can be a way of expressing your feelings to yourself," Miss Fisher said warmly. "You'll have a better understanding of who you are and what you want. If you go back and read what you've written a couple of years down the road, you just may learn something you didn't know about yourself."

"Maybe I'll try it," Trisha replied.

Miss Fisher stood and appeared pleased. "Good," she announced cheerfully. "I'll see the two of you in class tomorrow afternoon. Cover the machine when you're finished and close the door."

Both girls nodded and watched Miss Fisher leave the room.

Sidney stared at Trisha while giving her a strange look. "What was that all about?"

Trisha shrugged and turned toward the windows. "She suggested I keep a journal to help collect my thoughts."

Sidney returned to the typewriter. "You spend too much time alone," she remarked. "You should spend more time at my house when your mother works."

"I spend more than enough time cleaning out your parents' refrigerator," Trisha said then sat on the window ledge and stared outside. "Things haven't been the same since my father died."

"As protective as my father is, I wouldn't want to be without him," Sidney said gently.

They were silent for several minutes before Sidney began to type. Ten minutes had passed when Trisha straightened and stared out the window with great interest.

"There he is," Trisha gasped then sighed. "Oh, he looks so good in his uniform."

Sidney joined Trisha at the window and watched the guys practice on the football field in the near distance. The junior high could be seen just beyond the field. "How do you know which one is Billy?"

Trisha pointed to the moving uniforms. "That's him; number fourteen."

Sidney stared a moment longer but could barely make out the number let alone a face under the helmet. "Can't even tell it's him," she said simply.

"It's him, trust me," Trisha replied while grinning.

Sidney shook her head and returned to the typewriter to finish her letter. She finally removed the paper from the typewriter and stared at it. Trisha snatched it from her and read it.

"Dearest Harlan," Trisha read. "With each passing day I wait for the day I can be with you. Oh, my heart how it aches. You are my dream, my love so true. I can only hope you love me too. Eternally yours.

Trisha lowered the paper and looked at Sidney.

Sidney frowned as if reading her friend's thoughts. "Too much, huh?"

"It's perfect," Trisha said as a smile appeared on her face. "It sounds as if an adult wrote it." She then pointed to the paper. "What's with the 'H'? It's higher than all the other characters in every line."

"It's that ancient fossil of a typewriter. The 'H' is messed up," Sidney replied and inserted an envelope into the typewriter. She typed Harlan's name on the envelope then removed it from the machine.

Arguing voices could be heard in the hallway. Trisha turned her head toward the classroom door.

"That sounds like Miss Fisher and Mr. Malcolm," Trisha announced.

Sidney strained to listen to their conversation.

"You're being completely ridiculous," Miss Fisher said curtly. "This isn't the eighteen hundreds. You're as prehistoric as the class you teach."

The girls looked at each other and held back their laughs.

"I always knew she'd be the one to sock it to Mr. Malcolm," Trisha said.

"You're completely out of line, Emily. You're a bad influence on the kids," Mr. Malcolm said sternly.

"Oh, I am, am I? Look who's talking," Miss Fisher lashed out. "I don't think you have the right to tell me how to treat my students nor how to run my class."

"I wasn't trying to tell you how to run your class. It's your behavior I find appalling," Mr. Malcolm shouted in anger.

"I suggest you deal with it, Paul, because I'm not going away, and I will continue to do what I do. Good day," she snapped.

They could hear her walk down the hallway and away from the classroom.

"I think it's safe to assume Miss Fisher won that round," Trisha teased with a soft laugh then folded the letter and handed it to Sidney.

Sidney slipped the letter into the envelope and sealed it. "I don't think Miss Fisher loses too many arguments," she replied simply.

Chapter Three

Sidney and Trisha walked to McBride's Press in the center of town. They had to pass the old, brick library where Mrs. Randall, Billy Randall's grandmother, volunteered to assist the librarian. Mrs. Cooper spent much of her time there as well. The two local gossips rarely traveled apart. As they passed the front of the library built in the eighteen hundreds, they could see Mrs. Randall peering out the large window. The sixty-year-old woman was about five-foot-three with long, gray hair worn in a bun. She had deep, sagging wrinkles, giving her an older appearance.

Mrs. Cooper could be seen to the corner of the window, talking as usual. Mrs. Cooper was a youthful sixty-three. She had shorter, dark gray hair with silver throughout. She didn't seem to have as many wrinkles as Mrs. Randall, and she stood two inches taller. Mrs. Cooper couldn't remain silent for longer than ten minutes and was rarely, if ever at a loss for words.

"There they are," Trisha moaned as they passed, making sure to look at them. "They should have cards printed up. It's our business to know your business."

"My father said they stop in just about every day to get the fresh gossip. He won't tell them anything that's not already in the day's paper," Sidney said.

They reached the center of town. In the small circle was a park of sorts with an old cannon next to the flagpole. There were also some park benches and shrubs. They saw Trisha's mother in the restaurant across the street from the press and waved to Mrs. Allister while she served coffee to the town preacher and his wife.

Sidney handed Trisha the envelope. "You know what to do, right?"

Trisha nodded and stuck the envelope inside her math book. "You distract him, and I'll plant it somewhere."

"Not where my father might see it," Sidney chirped. "He may suspect it was me."

Trisha nodded.

Sidney pulled the band from her hair and gave her long hair several shakes.

Trisha giggled and shook her head. "You're too much."

They entered the small press with its four aisles of paper supplies, magazines, and books. Sidney's father was behind the register counter with the candy display beneath it. Herb McBride gave old man Taylor some change and thanked him. Mr. Taylor took his crossword puzzle and nodded to both girls as he left the press. Sidney watched Mr. Taylor leave the shop. She swore he never smiled. The man had to be at least a hundred years old. Fortunately, his clothing matched today. Herb grinned and placed his hands on the counter.

"If it isn't my two favorite girls," he announced cheerfully. He removed two candy bars from the display behind the glass beneath him and placed them on the counter. "How's school?"

Trisha leaped at the candy bar, but Sidney wasn't interested. Her stomach was already tied in knots thinking about Harlan in the back of the shop by the press. She just wanted to get the letter to him and get it over with.

"You know, school's school," Sidney replied nervously and cast several looks to the back of the shop. Her heart pounded with anticipation of just catching a glimpse of Harlan. She could barely see the counter in the back through the rows of shelves.

"Is that the new Teen Magazine?" Trisha asked and leaned over the counter.

Herb nodded.

"I'm going to the back and say hello to Harlan," Sidney announced while Trisha kept Herb occupied.

Sidney felt a nervous pang every time she walked to the back of the press to see Harlan. He'd only been in Marilina for two months, but she was infatuated with him from the first moment she'd met him. She slowed her pace when she heard his voice. He had the most seductive accent and low, mellow voice. She paused at the end of the row of paper supplies and saw Miss Fisher standing before the counter. Harlan made photocopies for her on the deluxe copy machine on the other side near the press. Harlan gathered the papers and handed them to her with a pleasant smile while they talked like old friends--old, *close* friends.

"I really must remember to bring my film in tomorrow. You will develop it for me, won't you? You do better work than the place outside town," Miss Fisher said and leaned on the counter while casting her charm upon him.

Sidney thought Miss Fisher looked like a fox on the prowl. She frowned, removed a pack of pens from the shelf, and pretended to look at them while eavesdropping on Miss Fisher's conversation with Harlan.

"Of course I will. Anything for a fellow photographer," Harlan announced with a charming, schoolboy grin.

Miss Fisher giggled and placed her hand on his hand propped on the counter across from her. "We really must get together for a photo session," she announced. "There's this romantic place in the woods where you could photograph me."

Sidney cast a glance at them over the box of pens. She suddenly felt a strong resentment toward her beloved teacher. Harlan's eyes strayed to Sidney as if noticing her for the first time. She looked away and replaced the pens to the shelf.

Harlan looked back at Miss Fisher and remained cheerful. "Uh, perhaps when I have some free time."

"I'm available anytime," Miss Fisher announced then collected her papers. "I'll be back tomorrow with that film."

The attractive teacher gave a little wave then turned and walked down the middle aisle. She didn't even notice Sidney in the third aisle. Sidney approached the counter and watched Harlan's eyes follow Miss Fisher, as many men did. Harlan looked at Sidney and smiled pleasantly.

"Well, hello, stranger," Harlan said then laughed softly in his throat. "What can I do for you today?"

She shook her jealous image of Harlan and Miss Fisher from her mind and insecurely looked down at the counter with some embarrassment.

"I thought you might be interested in a photo opportunity," Sidney said then looked up.

"Always interested in that," he said with a soft laugh. "What am I photographing, love?"

"It's a surprise." Her cheeks immediately reddened. "Do you have your camera?"

"Never leave home without it," he replied with a slightly crooked smile.

"Then we have to hurry before we lose the lighting," she said with a little more confidence.

Harlan raised a suspicious brow. "What? Now?"

"We have to," she insisted. "Dad won't mind."

Harlan chuckled lowly, finding humor in her comment. "You say that a lot, but he always does."

"Please, Harlan."

He groaned softly and rolled his eyes. "I do hate when you beg," he said with a sigh. "All right. I'll get my camera; you get your father's permission."

Chapter Four

The wooded area to the stone bridge was a five-minute walk from town and directly past Mrs. Cooper and Mrs. Randall's houses. Thankfully, neither were home to see her with Harlan. The gossip would surely fly then. Once they entered the woods, Sidney led Harlan along a path just before the stone bridge. It was another ten minutes through the woods before they reached a clearing. The old, gray, stone house had been abandoned for nearly twenty years. The overgrown driveway appeared to be more of a path anymore. The house was well secluded and mostly used by teenagers as a party site. Sidney walked toward the large, stone well and sat on it. The wooden posts on either side of the well were half rotted, yet remained sturdy. She looked around the area and sighed softly.

"This must have been a quiet place to live," she announced with a dreamy sigh.

Harlan snorted a soft laugh and studied the house. "A little too quiet," he replied and adjusted his camera lens. "I've never seen this place before. Where are we?"

Sidney pointed down the overgrown driveway. "That's Cressman Road just beyond the woods. The driveway entrance has a chain across it to keep traffic out."

He looked in the direction she pointed then back at the house and the darkening sky. "There must be a storm coming," Harlan announced with a frown. "The lighting is getting bad already."

Sidney admired Harlan while he walked the area, apparently searching for the best angle. She gently bit her lower lip and held back her sigh. Harlan had a clean-shaven, baby face, beautiful green eyes, and thick, dark hair that touched his collar. He wasn't very muscular or very tall, but he did have broad shoulders and the most handsome smile. Thunder rumbled in the distance and interrupted her fantasy. She looked up to the sky and studied the darkening clouds with great interest. Her lips parted slightly as she admired the almost black sky. She loved a good thunderstorm. She then heard the click of a camera. Sidney looked back at Harlan as he lowered the camera and grinned.

"Sorry," he said timidly. "It's a bad habit of mine. Most people put on a false smile when a camera's pointed at them."

"I really hate having my picture taken," she said simply with embarrassment.

"Me too," he said with a soft chuckle and walked closer to the house.

"Harlan," she said almost in a whisper.

"Yes, love?" he responded without looking back.

Sidney looked down to her feet while nervously rocking them. "Do you think I'm mature enough to make my own decisions?" she finally asked.

"About what?" he asked simply and moved to the front of the house.

She looked up and saw him step onto the half-rotted porch. It creaked, forcing him to back off and make a face.

"About whom I can date," she said simply.

Harlan looked at her with a knowing smile and let out a throaty laugh. "Do you honestly think your father will ever allow you to date?"

She chuckled with some embarrassment. "My father's not that protective."

He walked toward her and sat on the edge of the well just near the post and crank. "Yes, he is," he replied simply with a grin that mocked her. "But I suppose I can't blame him. He has a fifteen-year-old daughter who looks eighteen and acts twenty. It's his job to protect you from--" his brows raised evilly, "the elements of nature." He added a low, throaty laugh.

Sidney stared at him with some surprise and embarrassment. "You think I act like I'm twenty?"

He leaned against the post and placed one foot on the well ledge. "You don't act like any fifteen-year-old I've ever met."

She smiled and felt her cheeks redden. Sidney swiftly stood up on the well ledge and leaned against the opposite post. Harlan's eyes followed her with some disapproval.

"Be careful," he warned. "It would look bad for me if you'd drown."

"I won't drown," she said with a teasing smile. "There's no water at the bottom. I'd just break my neck."

Harlan raised a cocky brow. "Yes, that would go over much better," he muttered.

She laughed softly and walked along the ledge while continuing the conversation. "Think my father would flip if I dated a guy a couple of years older than me?"

"Your father would bloody well flip if you dated period. Maybe you should come down," Harlan announced with a concerned look on his face.

Sidney teetered along the edge and eyed him. "I'm serious, Harlan."

Harlan set his expensive camera down and slowly stood on the well ledge while keeping his left arm securely around the post behind him.

"If you're thinking about dating a senior, I suggest you forget it," he lectured firmly. "Typically they only have one thing on their mind."

Sidney looked at Harlan and frowned. "Yeah, seeing who has the fastest car. They drag race on the road near here."

Harlan chuckled lowly and shook his head. "Not what I was referring to," he remarked. "I think you'd better hold off dating for a couple of years."

Sidney tilted her head and smiled deviously. "Aren't you the prude?" She laughed softly. "I was just kidding," she said and stood still on the ledge halfway toward him. "I knew you were talking about sex. I know all about that already."

His dark brows rose sharply with noted surprise and possible horror. "Oh?"

She folded her arms across her chest and glared at him. "Not like that," she scolded. "I'm not that kind of girl. Guys don't want what they know they can have."

Harlan appeared relieved and laughed aloud. "You're quite unique, Sidney."

The thunder cracked more loudly, getting closer. Both looked to the sky.

"We'd better get you home before that storm hits," he announced and extended his hand to her. "Anything happens to you, and it's my ass."

Sidney stared at his hand a moment as her heartbeat quickened. She couldn't refuse actual, physical contact. She'd never touched him before. Sidney nervously accepted his hand as her heart skipped a beat. When their hands touched, she swore she felt something magical. She walked toward him, now feeling somewhat dizzy and off balance. As she teetered on the stone, her foot slipped, and she nearly lost her footing. Harlan leaped forward to catch her. In his attempt to keep her from falling, he threw her off balance. She fell forward, throwing him backward, and they crashed separately to the ground. Sidney attempted to brace her fall with her hands with little success. She lifted herself to her hands and knees then sat back on her feet. Harlan scrambled to his knees, appeared concerned, and hovered over her.

"Are you okay?" he asked with some fear while holding his elbow.

She looked at him and laughed from their tumble. He groaned and rolled his eyes. Sidney looked at her scraped elbows and palms then brushed the dirt from her clothing. When she looked back at Harlan, he was also brushing the dirt from himself as he stood. He had several scrapes on his lower arms and a scratch on his forehead above his left brow. He helped her to her feet then studied her face with noted concern.

"You have a nasty scrape on your cheek," he said and pointed to it.

Sidney touched her cheek, cringed, and then looked at the blood on her finger. She shrugged with little care. "I've done worse falling from the bridge."

Harlan rolled his eyes.

Chapter Five

Friday, September 25th, 1981. Sidney ran toward the woods to catch up to Trisha. Trisha shook her head with annoyance and hugged her books.

"I can't believe you're late," Trisha said with a huff. "Only I'm allowed to be late." She then looked at Sidney. Her mouth opened slightly, and she stopped just before the path in the woods. "My God, what happened to your face?"

Sidney frowned and touched her make-up covered bruise and scrape. "I fell off the well by the stone house," she said softly. "My father flipped. He thought I'd been attacked."

"Of course he did," Trisha remarked lowly as they continued to walk. "You'll be lucky if any guy ever asks you out on a date. Your father has quite a reputation."

They headed through the woods and approached the bridge at a quick pace.

"So what's the plan for after school?" Trisha asked and cast a look at her friend. "Do we go to your father's press or not?"

Sidney gently bit her lower lip. "I want to, but I'm a little nervous." She looked at her friend. "Do you think he knows it's me?"

"No," Trisha said bluntly without looking at her. "He probably thinks it was Miss Fisher."

Sidney glared at her friend while feeling a jealous pang. "Don't say that!"

Trisha shrugged as they crossed the bridge. "You told me last night on the phone that she had been flirting with him at the press." She immediately frowned with distaste. "Though I can't understand why. She already has a boyfriend. Alex is certainly better looking than Harlan."

Sidney lightly smacked Trisha's arm while frowning her disapproval.

Trisha yelped slightly then laughed. "It's just an opinion," she said. "Don't be so touchy."

"I can't help it," Sidney whined softly and placed her free hand in her jacket pocket. "I can't compete with Miss Fisher." She moaned and looked across the bridge as they nearly reached the other side. "What's the use? He'll be married long before I'm allowed to date."

Trisha smiled and brushed her shoulder against Sidney. "Can't hurt to dream, can it?"

Sidney frowned feeling her heart ache. "Yes, it can," she muttered.

§

After the first couple of classes, Sidney was tired of hearing about the mark on her face. She heard every comment thinkable from her unfeeling, fellow classmates. She entered Miss Fisher's class and collapsed into the desk next to Trisha. Trisha looked at her and smirked, knowing the torment she'd received most of the day. Sidney looked at the front of the class while Miss Fisher took attendance. Sidney felt another pang of jealousy while studying her attractive teacher. Miss Fisher wore a white, lacy blouse that showed her incredible figure, and her black pants weren't tight, but they showed her curves, displaying the round butt the teenage boys adored. Her long, raven hair was French braided in the back. Miss Fisher was dressed to kill. Sidney frowned and looked back at the book on her desk.

The class seemed to drag on forever, giving Sidney too much time to brood over the possibility of Miss Fisher moving in on her would-be boyfriend. Near the end of class, there was a knock on the classroom door. Miss Fisher looked at the door along with every student. Sidney immediately recognized the man in the black, leather coat through the window on the door. It was Alex Trexler, Miss Fisher's boyfriend. Miss Fisher frowned then looked back at the class and forced a nervous smile.

"Would you excuse me," she said then walked toward the door and stepped into the hall.

Some of her classmates began to talk and throw things the moment their teacher had left the room. Sidney and Trisha watched the couple through the glass in the door with great interest, since it obviously wasn't a friendly visit. They could see an explosive argument, though they couldn't hear their words, just murmurs. As the argument became louder, the other students became silent and watched the door with great interest as well. Miss Fisher threw her hands in the air then pointed at him. Alex raised his hands and shook them with anger. He pointed a warning finger at her. She harshly pushed it away and yelled something back. Alex became silent then walked away. Miss Fisher entered the room with a flushed look on her face, and she no longer smiled.

"I'd like everyone to read chapter five in your text," she said curtly then turned toward the blackboard and stood motionless for a moment. She was undoubtedly attempting to pull herself together after the major blowout with her boyfriend.

It was apparent the couple had broken up in the heated argument. Sidney knew it meant Miss Fisher was now free to pursue Harlan, but she couldn't help feeling sorry for her teacher.

The last class of the day seemed to linger on forever. Ms. Palmer had the class read from their textbook nearly the entire period while she talked with a distraught Miss Fisher in the hallway. Persha Palmer was a thin woman in her early thirties with straight, light brown hair, and clay-colored skin. She never wore make-up nor styled her hair. She wasn't much to look at and not very entertaining as far as teachers went. She had never been married and insisted upon being called 'Ms'. Ms. Palmer hated men, and it reflected in her attitude toward the male students as well. Everyone knew she was unfair toward the guys in the class.

She placed a hand on Miss Fisher's shoulder and said something. Sidney wished she could hear some of their conversation. She then looked back at her book with some concern. Was she the future busybody of Marilina? Sidney needed to shake that image as she sank down in her chair and concentrated on the pages before her.

Ms. Palmer entered the classroom and loudly cleared her throat, getting everyone's attention. "I hope everyone's finished reading the assignment. We're going to have an exam on it now."

There were several moans around the room.

Ms. Palmer looked down her nose at the students. "It'll be an essay."

Chapter Six

"Thank God that's over with," Trisha muttered and threw her books into her locker. "I know I failed that test."

Sidney didn't seem to hear a word her friend said. "I'm concerned about seeing Harlan," she announced gently and leaned against her locker while facing Miss Fisher's classroom. Sidney looked into Miss Fisher's room and saw her teacher unfold a piece of paper and read it.

"We'll have to stop next door at the junior high first," Trisha said drearily, practically withholding her moan. "I have to pick up my cousin's homework."

Sidney looked at Trisha and frowned. "Did he play sick again? I swear that's the third Friday in a row."

"I wonder what the little twerp did while alone all day," Trisha remarked.

Sidney felt compelled to look back into Miss Fisher's room. Miss Fisher carefully folded the paper several times and put it in her pants' pocket.

Sidney looked back at Trisha. "I'd like to get to the press before Miss Fisher gets there. She's supposed to be dropping off a roll of film today."

"Relax. We will," Trisha said and closed her locker door with a disgusted sigh. "Let's get this over with."

They walked to the junior high, which was along a private road just past the senior high school. Woods surrounded the entire senior and junior high. There was a steep, treacherous path in the woods that eventually came out on Cressman Road, though it was rarely traveled.

§

Sidney paced the junior high hallway while the teacher insisted upon explaining to Trisha the entire work assignment in great detail. By the time Trisha was able to break away, they had been there nearly an hour. It was already after four o'clock by the time Trisha entered the hallway. Sidney hurried behind Trisha, attempting to keep up with her friend's fast pace.

"That took forever," Sidney snapped, irritated that they were now running late.

"If Steve paid closer attention in class, he wouldn't have felt the need to explain everything to me. He said my cousin has a problem following directions," Trisha snarled. "Now I get to go to his house and explain the entire assignment to him, and when he doesn't do it, Mr. Orloff will blame me."

They hurried from the junior high through town, past the library, and to her father's press. As they entered the press around ten after four, they saw Sidney's father busily stocking some new merchandise.

He straightened and smiled at them. "A Friday visit? This is unusual," Herb announced cheerfully. "What are the big plans for this weekend? Where am I carting you?"

"I was thinking about seeing the horror film festival," Sidney informed him.

Her father frowned, displaying his disapproval. "Doesn't that last until midnight?"

Sidney hesitated and immediately fidgeted. "Well, usually, but Trisha's mother picks us up. It's not like we'd be walking that time of night or anything."

Herb looked at Trisha then back to Sidney and sighed. "I suppose it'll be all right with your mother. Will you be staying overnight?"

"That's the best part, Mr. McBride," Trisha announced cheerfully then swiftly changed the subject to distract him. "Do you know when the next copy of 'Teen Girl' is coming out?"

"I'll check," he said and turned toward the counter.

"I'll just go chat with Harlan," Sidney said softly while feeling butterflies in her stomach.

"He's gone for the day," Herb informed her simply as he walked behind the counter. "You just missed him. He left about twenty minutes ago. Said he had plans."

Sidney's heart sank.

Her father found a notebook, skimmed through it, and then looked up. "I didn't realize that was your teacher in here yesterday," he said dryly. "Very young."

"Miss Fisher," Sidney replied simply.

"Yeah," Herb said appearing tense then looked back at the folder. "She was here about three-thirty. I believe she left some film for Harlan to develop." He looked at Trisha and managed a smile. "That'll be in around Tuesday."

Sidney felt her heart sink. Miss Fisher stopped by after school, and Harlan just happened to leave fifteen minutes later. She sank into her own, depressing world.

Trisha nodded then looked at Sidney, reading her mood, and then offered a timid smile. "What do you say to an ice cream float at the diner? My mother's treating," she said.

Sidney sighed softly. "Why not."

It was five o'clock when Sidney and Trisha left the diner and walked toward the woods for their long, depressing journey home. Sidney's mood hadn't improved any despite her excessively fattening ice cream sundae.

Trisha sighed as they passed Mrs. Cooper's house. "Doesn't appear to be anyone home at the house of local gossip."

They passed the house in between then passed Mrs. Randall's house. "No one home there either," Sidney remarked. "Must be something more interesting happening somewhere else."

Trisha laughed softly. "Nothing happens in this one horse town." She looked at the woods and sighed deeply. "I'm getting out of this place as soon as I turn eighteen."

Sidney laughed at her friend. "Yeah? Where do you intend to go?"

"New York or California. Don't really know. Some big city, I'm sure," Trisha replied.

"Not me," Sidney said simply. "I'm staying right here. I like this little town--gossip and all."

They entered the woods and walked in the direction of the stone bridge. They heard something move in the woods ahead, which wasn't too surprising, although most of the students would be home by now. As they approached the bridge, both saw a man in a black, leather coat scale the wooded hillside just opposite the bridge. They stopped and stared at the vanishing man with some confusion.

"Wasn't that Alex Trexler?" Trisha asked with a curious stare.

Sidney nodded.

"What was his big hurry?" Trisha snapped as she stared up the hillside.

They could hear a car burn out in loose gravel on Cressman Road, which was beyond the hillside. The sound of squealing tires and a blowing horn followed.

"Must be late for work or something," Sidney reported.

They walked onto the bridge with a moment of silence between them. The teenage mind was complicated, and both had their own issues with which to deal.

"What time will you be over tonight?" Trisha finally asked. "You are coming over tonight?"

"I need something to take my mind off Harlan," Sidney announced. "Right after supper, I suppose."

They paused on the bridge and leaned on the wall overlooking the stream to their left as they always did on their walk to and from school. Both simultaneously froze and stared at the woman lying face down on the bank near the water. Sidney immediately recognized the raven-haired woman in black pants. They straightened without hesitation and ran across the bridge to the other side. Trisha fell behind, unable to get any closer. Sidney slowed as she neared Miss Fisher. She paused a couple of feet away and stared at the large amount of blood surrounding Miss Fisher's limp body and on a nearby rock.

"Oh, my God," Trisha cried out as her eyes widened with horror.

Despite what she saw, Sidney realized she might not have been dead. Sidney hurried to Miss Fisher's body and kneeled alongside her, being mindful of the blood.

She nervously touched her shoulder and gasped softly, "Miss Fisher?"

There was no response, and Sidney knew instantly that she was dead. Trisha realized it too and began to scream hysterically. Sidney turned on her knees to her panicking friend.

"Go get help!"

Trisha vigorously nodded her head, backed up a couple of steps, then turned and ran across the bridge. Sidney sat back on her feet while feeling her heart pounding in her chest. She couldn't seem to look away. Tears welled in her eyes, and she bit her quivering lower lip. It seemed like a lifetime, although it was only a matter of minutes before she finally looked past her dead teacher and fought her tears. Her eyes strayed to the blood-covered rock near Miss Fisher's outstretched hand. Sidney let out a soft gasp at the sight of the double vertical lines drawn in blood on the rock then to the blood on Miss Fisher's finger. She'd left a message!

Sidney slowly stood and backed away from the body. She felt oddly cold throughout her trembling body. The reality of the situation dawned on her. Sidney turned and hurried across the bridge. She could hear leaves rustling all around her now. The image of Alex Trexler scaling the hillside repeatedly flashed through her mind. Sidney hadn't even realized she was running along the path through the woods toward town. Tears filled her eyes and blurred her vision to the point where she could no longer see. She heard a sound before her and collided with someone. Sidney cried out and struggled while blinking away the tears. Harlan held onto her arms and nearly dropped his camera.

"Sidney, what's wrong? I heard screaming," he demanded while searching her eyes. "What happened?" He touched her tear streaked cheek. His concern quickly turned to anger. "Did someone hurt you?"

She shook her head and held her breath. "It's--it's Miss Fisher. She's been killed."

Harlan's color drained from his face as his mouth fell open. "Emily Fisher?"

Sidney nodded and grabbed his arm. "Come on," she gasped and pulled him toward the bridge. Harlan ran behind her and stopped on the bridge as soon as he saw the dead woman on the bank. His mouth opened with an apparent look of shock.

"Are you sure she's--?"

Sidney stared off the bridge and nodded. She turned toward him and searched his eyes while nervously biting her lower lip. "Trisha went for help."

Harlan looked away from the body and raked trembling fingers through his hair. He then looked back at the dead woman and held his breath. A strange realization swept over Sidney as she realized he was more worried than upset.

"Are you okay?" she asked softly.

Harlan looked away, set his camera down, and supported himself against the bridge with both hands. Sidney studied his profile while he stared across the stream at the body. A flood of emotions swept through Sidney.

"Trisha and I saw her boyfriend leaving here. He took off in his car right before we found her," Sidney said timidly and softly sniffed. "They had a terrible fight today at school."

Harlan's head snapped in her direction. His eyes rolled shut as he held his breath then looked at her and straightened. "I saw her less than two hours ago. I know how this town feels about outsiders. It wouldn't look good for me. I hope you understand," he said gently.

Sidney continued to search his eyes even though her body trembled from the shock. She could tell he was genuinely scared. She rubbed her chilled arms, looked back at the body, and fought her tears.

Harlan shut his eyes, placed his arms around her, and held her against him. "I'm so sorry. I didn't mean to sound insensitive," he whispered softly to her. "You've had a terrible shock."

Sidney clung to him and began to sob uncontrollably. She realized Miss Fisher wasn't coming back. Even in Harlan's arms, there was no comfort to be found.

Chapter Seven

Sidney lay on her bed and stared at her dresser across the room. She could hear her mother and father arguing downstairs. Although she couldn't hear what they said, she knew it involved her. Sidney hadn't left her room the entire weekend and barely ate anything. She sat up in bed and reached for the discarded newspaper folded to the article on Miss Fisher's murder. Sidney read it nearly fifty times.

The headline read, "Teacher raped and murdered in Marilina." Sidney drew a shaken breath and again read the entire article. It went into gory detail about how the beloved teacher had been beaten and stabbed once in the abdomen. The police determined she had deliberately placed two lines in her own blood on the rock just near her head before dying, although they still hadn't figured out the significance of it. The article mentioned two teenage girls witnessed Alex Trexler fleeing the scene of the crime, and how Mr. Taylor claimed he nearly hit Alex's blue car on Cressman Road just moments later.

A pack of matches had been found on the side of the road with Sam's Tavern printed on them, and Alex's fingerprints were found on the matches. Alex was arrested an hour later at Sam's Tavern.

When questioned, Alex admitted having consensual intercourse with Emily at the old stone house but insisted he didn't kill her. He left her at the stone house immediately afterward, claiming he had to go to work. He insisted he returned at quarter till five, a half an hour later, to give her an engagement ring he had purchased the previous day. He claimed she was already dead when he found her on the bank just before the bridge. Out of fear, he fled the scene. The murder weapon, possibly a pocketknife, wasn't found.

Sidney lowered the paper and drew a deep, shaken breath. The tears once more began to flow freely. She collapsed on her bed and buried her head in her pillow.

§

It was a week later before Sidney finally left her room and went downstairs. She hadn't heard from nor called Trisha since they'd found Miss Fisher's body. Her mother washed breakfast dishes and immediately turned when she saw Sidney.

"Morning, baby, would you like something to eat?" she asked while beaming cheerfully.

Sidney swallowed dryly and nodded. "Yes," she said timidly.

Her mother's mouth opened with surprise then she smiled with a slight gleam in her eyes. "What would you like?"

"Toast," Sidney replied in a weak tone.

Sidney ate one slice of toast and felt sick immediately following. She slowly rose from the table and looked around the kitchen while rubbing her cold arms beneath her sweatshirt.

"I'm going for a walk, okay?" she said softly.

Her mother cleaned up her dishes and nodded. "Would you like some company?"

"No, I want to go alone," she whispered.

Sidney left the kitchen and passed her father's gun cabinet. She paused and stared at the guns, rifles, and knives through the glass. Her eyes focused on one of the knives. She drew a shallow breath and walked out the front door. The sun was shining brightly although it was cool that morning. Somehow, Sidney felt different now. She walked along the street and approached the woods. Something made her stop just short of the path. She turned and walked along Cressman Road then onto the main road into town. Cressman Road was dangerous to walk. It had sharp curves, steep banks, and limited shoulder along thick woods. It took nearly twenty minutes longer to arrive in town, but Sidney couldn't force herself to walk across the bridge in the woods.

Sidney shoved her hands in her pockets and shivered slightly from the cool October air. She walked into town. Everything looked so different in just one week. As she approached the library, she saw Mrs. Cooper and Mrs. Randall rush down the steps and hurry toward her.

"Oh, Sidney," Mrs. Cooper cooed. "How are you?"

They fussed over her for a few minutes before Sidney was able to escape with little more than a 'hello' and 'I'm fine'. She continued on her journey down the sidewalk through the exceedingly small town and could hear both women talking about her as she walked away. Trisha's mother hurried from the diner and rushed across the street. She was nearly hit by a passing car to reach Sidney. Sidney paused and waited for her.

Mary Allister stopped just before her with a strange look on her face. It was hard to say if it was relief or concern. "Hi, Sidney," she said gently with a sympathetic look in her eyes. "It's good to see you up and about."

Sidney forced a tiny smile. "How's Trisha? Did she go back to school?"

Mary's expression faded, and she shook her head. "She hasn't left her room. She won't even talk to me."

That explained Mary's emotional state. Sidney already knew what Trisha's mother was thinking. Sidney drew a deep breath and took her cue.

"I'll stop by later today when I've had time to get myself together," Sidney announced.

Facing Trisha wasn't going to be an easy task. They were bound to discuss the death of Miss Fisher, but it was the last thing Sidney wanted to talk about. Mary unexpectedly hugged Sidney then returned to the diner. Sidney continued her journey to the press. She paused outside the shop and watched her father through the window. She took a deep, shaken breath and entered the store. When he saw her, her father's mouth fell open and a smile quickly followed.

"Sidney, it's good to see you out of your room," he said gently, obviously attempting to keep from making a big deal of it.

She forced a tiny smirk. "I've stared at those four walls long enough." She held her breath and felt a dull pang in her chest. "Is Harlan in the back?"

Her father's expression dropped, and he looked down at the desk. "Harlan left town," he said gently then looked back at her. "He won't be coming back."

Sidney's mouth opened slightly as surprise flooded her. "He quit?"

Her father cleared his throat. "Just moved on."

"Without saying goodbye?"

He looked down and shifted uncomfortably. "It's best that he didn't, Sid. You weren't up to having visitors anyway."

Sidney lowered her head and closed her eyes. "I'd better go see Trisha," she said softly and hurried from the press.

§

Six months later the paper read, "Verdict is back on the murder of Emily Fisher. Her boyfriend, Alex Trexler, was found guilty of murder and sentenced to life in prison."

Chapter Eight

June 1989. Eight years later. Sidney walked through the lavishly decorated lobby of the ritzy hotel. She wore a black skirt suit and her hair up in a French twist. She had a fast, determined walk with her head held high, conveying an air of self-confidence. She examined the fresh flowers on the oak tables with a pleased look as she approached the elegant, sculpted front desk. A bellman walked past and gave a nod.

"Morning, Ms. McBride," he announced cheerfully.

"Good morning, Stan," she replied in a lively tone then paused before the stylish registration desk.

"Morning, Ms. McBride," all three women in neatly ironed uniforms chimed almost simultaneously.

"Good morning. Did I miss much?" Sidney asked with a tiny smile.

"The Brodricks didn't have any towels last night and the woman in room 927 claims she saw a cockroach," Tessie replied pleasantly.

"Not in my hotel," Sidney said firmly then laughed. "I'll call an exterminator when I reach my office. Anything else?"

"Someone called for you early this morning while you were in the cafe," Tessie informed her. "Said they'd call back."

Sidney groaned. "I hope it's not going to be one of those phone days. I hate being tied to the phone."

"You should have let the company give you one of those cellular phones," Tessie remarked. "You could carry it with you and make calls from just about anywhere in the city."

"Yeah, that's all I need," Sidney remarked, "being tied to my phone twenty-four seven." She then waved her hand. "Besides, those phones won't catch on. It'd just be a waste of money. I'll stick with my pager." Sidney never understood why so many people were interested in carrying a portable phone on them anyway. "Is the champagne basket in room 2740?"

"Ready for our important guest," Tessie replied with a wink and a knowing smile.

"Great. Alert me when he arrives," Sidney said. "I'll be in my office--on the phone."

She walked past the front desk to a door marked 'General Manager' and entered her office. She closed the door behind her and sat in the swivel chair behind the large mahogany desk. As Sidney reached for the phone, it rang before she touched it. She groaned lowly.

"It's starting early today," she muttered and picked up the receiver. She leaned back in the chair and instinctively crossed her legs. "Sidney McBride speaking."

"Sidney," came the faint, familiar female voice.

Sidney leaned forward and banged her knee on the desk. She cringed a moment then gasped, "Trisha? Is that you?"

"You have to come home. It's important," Trisha said in a whisper.

"Home? Where? To Marilina?" Sidney asked and frowned at the thought. "Why would I want to do that?" She fiddled with the fresh tear in her stocking.

"You just have to come here. Please, Sidney, promise you'll come right away. I need your help. Promise you'll come," Trisha whispered into the phone with a sound of desperation. "If you don't come, I don't know what'll happen."

"Trisha, I can't just--"

The phone went dead.

"Trisha?"

§

After a plane ride and an hour's drive, Sidney pulled up to McBride's Press in her rental car and stared at the shop. Her heart pounded with nervous anticipation. She took a deep breath and reluctantly got out of the car. Now changed into a pair of jeans and a black blazer, she looked around town. It looked even smaller than she had remembered. Sidney hadn't been to Marilina since she went away to college. She hadn't even been home for Christmas in five years. Her parents were forced to travel to see her once a year, though they were out of place in New York. She closed the car door and smelled the fresh summer air. It was a smell she'd forgotten over the years. Sidney approached the press with its recently painted siding and newly hung sign. As she entered, a young man with acne on his youthful face stood behind the counter and greeted her with a smile.

"Good afternoon," he said.

Sidney gave him a pleasant look. "Is Mr. McBride in?"

"He's in the back," the young man said as his eyes swept over her.

Sidney nodded her thanks and walked through the recently remodeled store. Her father had more items for sale than ever before. She approached the back and saw her father working with a new press. He allowed his frustration get the better of him then cursed and tossed down the manual. When he looked up and saw her, his mouth fell open. A smile immediately crossed his face, and he rushed to her from behind the counter. His hair had thinned and grayed since their visit to New York six months ago. He hugged her happily and didn't let go.

"Oh, Sidney," he practically cried out. "Can it really be my little girl, or am I just seeing things?"

Sidney returned the embrace and had to force him to release her after several minutes. "It's me," she said with a tiny laugh. "Against my will, I have returned."

He gave her an odd look. "They didn't fire you, did they?" He attempted to hide the grin that crept over his face. "You can always work here."

She shook her head, although his enthusiasm for her losing her job was a little creepy. "No, nothing like that." Sidney managed a tense smile. "Trisha called me early this morning."

Herb stared at her with a look of surprise on his face then turned and adjusted some shelves. "Trisha, huh?"

His reaction surprised her. "What's that look about?"

He spun to face her with a sparkle in his eyes. "Does Mom know you're here?"

"No, I came here first," she said.

"We have to get you home before she hears it from someone else," he said with a soft chuckle.

"Dad, why did you make a face when I mentioned Trisha?" Sidney asked sternly.

He frowned and again looked away. "Trisha hasn't been playing with a full deck the last few years," he reluctantly informed her. "She's really acting strange these days."

Sidney drew a deep breath. "Trisha hasn't been right for the past eight years," Sidney pointed out. "Even counseling didn't really help her."

"Let's not talk about that right now. We have to get home and see your mother," he announced cheerfully and waved off his own tears. "She'll cry for hours."

"I need to see Trisha first," Sidney insisted. "Where can I find her?"

"She works at the library."

Sidney was momentarily set back. "The library?" she practically gasped. "She went to college for her teaching degree."

He nodded but didn't offer anything further. She handed him her car keys.

"I'll meet you at the house," she said simply. "Take my car. I'll walk back."

Sidney left the press and immediately headed toward the library, which remained in immaculate condition. It was quite an adjustment getting used to few people, no taxis, and limited traffic. She entered the library and saw Mrs. Randall at the front desk. She still appeared the same as she had eight years ago, except a little shorter and rounder than Sidney had remembered. Sidney decided it was best to look for Trisha herself rather than get caught up in a conversation with Mrs. Randall. She slipped passed unnoticed and walked down the hall of the old, converted house, and passed a door that seemed out of place.

There appeared to be doors all over the converted home. She never realized how much detailed woodwork lie behind the bookcases. It must have been an impressive house in its day. She found the stairs in the back that led to the basement. Somehow, she suspected Trisha would be working in the library archives. She walked down the old, rickety stairs covered with a new carpet. She wandered through rows and rows of reference books, historical magazines, and newspapers. When she reached the back, she saw Trisha sitting behind a desk staring at a computer monitor.

"Trisha," Sidney announced almost timidly.

Trisha turned her head and looked at Sidney. She was thinner and far paler than Sidney had remembered. She had dark circles under her eyes, indicating she wasn't sleeping in addition to not eating enough. Sidney barely even recognized her own friend. She looked at least five years older than her actual age. Trisha sprang to her feet and ran to Sidney, hugging her with giddy delight. Trisha finally pulled away and studied Sidney with amazement.

"You look fabulous!"

Sidney smiled gently and raised her brows while looking over her friend. "You look as if you haven't slept in days," she announced candidly. "What in the world is going on?"

Trisha's expression dropped slightly. She turned toward her desk, removed some papers in a folder, and spun back to Sidney.

"I knew you'd come," Trisha said while grinning. "Let's take a walk."

Trisha took Sidney's arm and practically pulled her from the basement.

Chapter Nine

They walked through town at a leisurely pace and talked about Sidney's job, but it was obvious there was more on Trisha's mind. When they approached the woods, Sidney hesitated. Trisha turned toward her and grinned.

"Come on. It's okay."

Sidney took a deep breath and entered the woods with her friend. They walked a short distance before reaching the bridge. When they walked across, Sidney's eyes strayed to the rock on the bank and felt alarm sweep over her. Someone had painted red lines on the rock after Alex was convicted and sentenced to life. Sidney shivered slightly when she realized it was just red paint.

"I spoke to him," Trisha announced timidly.

Sidney turned her head and gave her a puzzled look. "With whom?"

Trisha raised a sagging brow. "With Alex Trexler," she said and handed Sidney the folder.

Sidney opened the folder and shuffled through the various papers. Every paper had something to do with Emily Fisher's murder. There were copies of old newspaper articles from the murder and the trial, photocopied pages from Trisha's journal, a copy of the police report, and notes from her conversation with Alex.

Trisha sat on the bridge wall and smiled proudly. "Pretty detailed, if I may say so."

"Trisha," Sidney said firmly and looked at her friend. "They tried and convicted Alex Trexler for her murder. He's served eight years of a life sentence. Just let it go, okay?"

Trisha cocked her head to one side. "No, it's not okay. He didn't do it."

Sidney's mouth fell open with shock and surprise. "Trisha, his semen matched what they found on her body," she insisted firmly. "We testified seeing him running from the scene of the crime." Sidney violently shook the papers in the folder. "We helped send him to jail! How can you forget? How can you sit there and claim he's innocent?"

Trisha didn't flinch. Her brows rose confidently. "You have to read those papers to understand," she said simply. "I'm not crazy. For the first time in eight years, I'm not crazy." Trisha slid off the wall and turned toward the bank. She pointed toward the painted rock. "Right out there a woman was murdered," she said and looked at Sidney. "You explain three things to me, and I'll let this entire thing rest."

Sidney glared at her friend and frowned with irritation. "What three things?"

"What's the significance of the lines drawn on the rock? Why would she purposely put two vertical lines in blood on that rock?" Trisha demanded while cleverly raising her brows. "If she didn't do it, why would someone else?"

Sidney closed her eyes and drew a deep breath. The image was still burned into her mind. She opened her eyes and studied her psychotic friend.

"They found nothing on her body," Trisha said simply.

Sidney stared at Trisha without understanding the significance of that statement. "What does that prove?" Sidney asked sternly. "What should they have found?"

"A folded piece of paper," Trisha informed her. "You said yourself that she placed a folded piece of paper in her pocket. Possibly a note of some sort."

"That doesn't mean anything," Sidney snapped. "You're being completely ridiculous. She had plenty of time to throw that away. It was just a stupid piece of paper."

"Not a stupid piece of paper," Trisha snapped with a cocky smile. "It was a note which she took time to fold carefully and place in her pocket. That could be the answer to this entire case right there."

Sidney rolled her eyes and groaned. "You mentioned three things. What else?"

Trisha casually leaned against the wall and raised an evil brow. "Why did your boyfriend disappear just one week later?"

Sidney's mouth opened slightly with surprise. "Surely you're not suggesting Harlan--?"

Trisha bolted upright. "That's precisely what I'm suggesting!" She pointed demandingly. "He was here, in the woods, when she was murdered. I believe he claimed he was photographing in the area when he heard me scream. He arrived five to eight minutes after I screamed. He knew nothing; saw nothing. Yet Miss Fisher stopped at the press to see him around three thirty-five, just after leaving school--looking very fine. Fifteen minutes later, lover boy leaves with his camera."

Sidney raised a cold brow and frowned. "And I suppose that makes him a murderer? They didn't find his semen on the body, Trisha."

"Alex Trexler admitted having sex with her by the stone house between three forty-five and four o'clock," she announced. "He claimed he left her in the woods at four-fifteen and rushed to work, returning just half an hour later. At four forty-five, he found her dead when he panicked and ran."

Sidney shook her head and rolled her eyes. "No, Trisha. He's playing you for a fool," she insisted. "Why are you letting this consume you?"

Trisha dropped her arms to her sides with a surprised look. "Consume me," she cried out. "I don't sleep, Sidney! You ran away. You wanted to forget!"

"You're damned right I wanted to forget," Sidney shouted in anger. "She's dead, and her killer is in jail. It's over! Destroying yourself isn't going to bring her back. Don't you get it?"

Both stared at each other with fire in their eyes while breathing heavily. They relaxed after a couple of minutes.

Sidney placed her hand against her forehead and groaned lowly. "I never should've come back," she muttered.

Trisha drew a deep breath and exhaled softly. "You read those papers and read them very carefully. Keep an open mind. Pretend you saw nothing," she remarked. "But before you leave, let me tell you a story."

Sidney sighed with disgust and folded her arms across her chest while clinging to the folder. She leaned against the bridge and glared at Trisha.

"September twenty-fifth, eight years ago, Sidney McBride writes a love letter to Harlan Brendan, a stranger to Marilina. A young, horny man, who enjoyed visits from an exceedingly beautiful, raven-haired beauty. He reads the love poem and assumes it has to be from the lovely schoolteacher, so he responds with his own letter," Trisha informed her. "Perhaps he asks her to meet him in the woods. In turn, she thinks it's from her boyfriend, wanting to make up. Meanwhile, the real boyfriend intercepts her in the woods, knowing which way she went home. Everyone knew she went home that way. Harlan stumbles across the couple engaged in intercourse. When she's alone, he kills her in a fit of rage. He removes the letter from her pocket and discards the murder weapon down the old stone well."

Sidney continued to glare at her friend. "You're blaming me for Miss Fisher's death?"

Trisha ignored the comment. "One week later, lover boy skips town and is never heard from again." She raised a brow and smirked. "Rumor has it he moved to California. I hired a private detective out there to locate him."

"I can't believe you," Sidney gasped.

"Just read those papers," Trisha announced then turned and headed back to town.

Sidney watched her friend leave then looked at the folder in her hand. She drew a deep, nervous breath then looked back at the stream. Every memory came rushing back in a tidal wave. Her thoughts strayed back to Harlan. He *had* been in the woods that day. Trisha had an interesting point, but she was wrong. Sidney heard voices from within the woods. She spun around and saw some teenage kids approaching the bridge. It was early June, and school was just about over for the summer. One of the boys was wearing his football jersey, although the football season had been over long already. The boy with a huge number fifty-two on his jersey approached her and leaned his back against the wall. Sidney remained facing the stream.

"Haven't seen you around Marilina before," he announced with a bold smile.

Sidney looked at him and attempted to be polite. "I've been out of town the past five years."

He turned to face the wall also. "Really? Did you go to school here?"

"Graduated five years ago," Sidney replied.

One of the girls from their group approached and joined their conversation. "Then you probably remember that teacher who was murdered here."

Sidney took a deep breath and shivered. "I've tried very hard to forget."

"You, uh, friends with Miss Allister?" the jock asked with a hint of a smile.

Sidney looked the boy directly in the eyes. "Yes, we're friends."

The girl moved closer to them. "Did Mr. Malcolm kill her? Or was it that photographer?"

Sidney glared at the girl, surprised by the question. "Her boyfriend murdered her," she said sharply. "What makes you think Malcolm killed her?"

The girl shrugged. "Miss Allister said--"

"Miss Allister is under a lot of stress," Sidney snapped lowly then straightened. "I used to love this place when I was your age, but anymore, it just smells of death. If you'll excuse me--"

Sidney walked past them and headed in the direction of her parents' house on the other side of the woods. Sidney hurried all the way home, but no matter how fast she went, the voices followed her. Every memory from that night returned. It was Trisha's fault for planting the evil seed.

Chapter Ten

After a joyful reunion with her mother, Sidney went to her old bedroom, shut the door, and sat on the bed. She stared at the folder beside her and frowned. As gruesome and unpleasant as it was, she felt the need to read the articles. Sidney started with the police report, though she didn't know how Trisha got her hands on a copy of it. The report didn't tell her anything she didn't already know. There was the location of the sexual assault by the old, stone house, the location and position of the body near the bridge, the condition of the body, and how long she had been dead when they arrived.

Miss Fisher had been punched several times in the face, leaving several bruises and lacerations, before being stabbed with a pocketknife of some sort. She died a few minutes after being stabbed. By the position of the body and the blood on the rock, it was evident that the markings were deliberate, either by the victim or the assailant. The reason behind marking the rock remained unknown. Witnesses reported the fight between Alex Trexler and Emily Fisher in the school just hours before her death. She read about her and Trisha witnessing Alex leaving the scene in a hurry, and old man Taylor nearly hitting him on Cressman Road. The tire tracks left behind matched the tires of both old man Taylor and Alex's cars. There was a matchbook from Sam's Tavern alongside the road with Alex's fingerprints on it. Semen samples proved Alex had intercourse with Emily before she died. Sidney shivered at the thought of what Miss Fisher had gone through prior to and after being stabbed.

Sidney set the paper aside, collected her emotions, and then read copies of newspaper articles that told the same story with a little more drama. They were the same articles she'd read shortly after the murder eight years ago. She read her own statement, Trisha's statement, and Harlan's statement to the police. Harlan's statement was rather vague. He was just a passerby with nothing significant to add to the case. Alex's statement told more of what she'd already known. He claimed to have caught up with her in the woods, knowing which way she went home, and apologized to her from their earlier fight. He stated they had made up, and Emily willingly had intercourse with him by the stone house. Just after, he hurried back to his car on Cressman Road. His story seemed to fall apart when he admitted he'd returned half an hour later to ask her to marry him. Who did that? When he found her dead by the bridge, he panicked and ran.

Sidney read the notes from Trisha's prison interview with Alex from just a couple of weeks ago. He insisted he never killed Emily Fisher, though he had been jealous of other men. He professed his undying love for her. Trisha asked if he had given Emily a letter that afternoon in the school. He denied ever giving her a letter. It was a lengthy interview, but it didn't really support his innocence. The last couple of pages were from Trisha's journal. She started writing a journal the day after the murder but started with the events that unfolded the day preceding the murder. She wrote in detail about Sidney's love letter to Harlan, Miss Fisher's relationship with everyone, including students and teachers, and her own relationship with Miss Fisher. Sidney never knew how close Trisha had been to her.

She wrote about Miss Fisher's fight with Alex, the note on the desk, and then great detail about what happened until the time they found their teacher murdered. The journal entries in Trisha's handwriting read, "Three o'clock. We left school. Went to the junior high to pick up homework. Three thirty. Miss Fisher took her film to the press. Left five minutes later. Three forty-five. Miss Fisher met with Alex Trexler in the woods. Had sex. Three-fifty. Harlan Brendan left the press with his camera. Four-ten. We arrived at McBride's news press. Four-twenty. We had ice cream floats at the diner. Four-twenty. Alex left Miss Fisher at the stone house. Four-fifty. Alex returned to the woods to find Miss Fisher dead. Five o'clock. We left diner. Five-ten. Found Miss Fisher murdered."

Trisha again went into great detail about everything they saw, heard, and even smelled. She wrote her experience while running back to town. How she stopped at Mrs. Randall's house, thinking she saw a vehicle in the garage even though she was certain she hadn't been home earlier. No one was home. She went to the house between Mrs. Randall and Mrs. Cooper's houses. A boy they knew from school lived there. They called the police, her mother at the diner, and Sidney's father at the press. Sidney and Trisha never actually discussed the events following the murder. They barely discussed the murder at all.

The last paper was dated last week. Trisha spoke to Mrs. Randall about the day of the murder. Mrs. Randall hadn't been home from four-thirty until nearly seven o'clock the day of the murder, but she did remember seeing a man with a camera enter the woods around four o'clock. She was almost positive it was Harlan. Sidney set the papers down and stared across the room. If Alex really hadn't murdered Miss Fisher, it would look bad for Harlan. Sidney frowned. She knew what she saw eight years ago. It was a long time ago, and second-guessing now would only cause confusion. Her brows knitted in spite of her insistence what they saw was accurate. Why *had* Harlan left without saying goodbye?

§

After dinner, Sidney and her father took a walk along the ever-expanding neighborhood. Sidney couldn't believe how the development had grown since she'd left. They talked about current events, the press, the hotel in New York, and about some relatives. After a moment of silence, Sidney glanced at her father with a curious look.

"Dad," she said boldly. "Why did Harlan Brendan leave town eight years ago?"

Her father looked at her with some surprise then looked back at the area they passed through. "No one really knows. He just up and left."

"He never gave a reason?" she pressed.

Herb placed his hands in his pockets and drew a deep breath without looking at her. "I really don't want to discuss Harlan. That's in the past," he said curtly.

Sidney was slightly surprised by his tone. She wondered if something transpired between him and Harlan.

"Would you prefer to discuss Emily Fisher?"

"No," he snapped coldly. He stopped on the sidewalk and turned to face her. "That's over. It's already caused enough strain on this family."

Sidney folded her arms across her chest and studied her father. "I realize you're trying to spare me some pain, but I'm an adult now. I need to talk about it."

Her father's expression was stern and bothered. "Talk about it? Sidney, have you seen what had happened to Trisha?" he practically demanded. "She's a basket case. I don't want you becoming obsessed with this as well."

"I'm not becoming obsessed with this," she insisted. "I just want some things answered, that's all. Miss Fisher was a well-loved teacher. It was a difficult thing finding her like that. The scars will always be there."

He frowned and continued to walk. "I know how traumatic it was for you, baby. Your mother and I felt all the pain you did. We were grief-stricken that you'd never be right again. Thankfully, you recovered. We thought Trisha was finally getting over it when she went to college. About two years ago, she went off the deep end. No one really knows what set her off."

Sidney lowered her head with sadness to her dear friend. "There's something I'm curious about, Dad."

"I don't want to discuss Harlan," he said lowly without looking at her.

"What about the film she dropped off that afternoon? Whatever happened to that roll of film? What was on it?"

Herb shook his head. "I don't know what she photographed. Harlan developed the film and turned it over to the police. He never said a word to me." He was silent a moment. He didn't look at her when he spoke. "Don't let her get to you, Sid."

Sidney looked at him with some confusion. "Who?"

"Trisha," he replied and turned his head. "The entire town knows that she's borderline psychotic. It's no secret that she believes Alex didn't kill Emily Fisher. But when she went to see him in prison, a lot of people became very angry."

Sidney nodded. "And I know why too."

"Because she's causing trouble, Sidney. She's practically accused Paul Malcolm of murder."

"That's not it, and you know it," Sidney remarked simply. "This is a small town. No one here wants an unsolved murder in their happy little community. Their feathers get ruffled when they hear talk about a man being falsely sentenced, and the possibility of a murderer running free all these years."

"As far as I'm concerned, Alex Trexler killed Emily Fisher. He's in jail, and nothing's going to change that," her father insisted. "They've got the right man."

Sidney stared across the development and sank into her own thoughts. "I hope so."

Chapter Eleven

Sidney tossed under the covers of her childhood bed. She woke with a gasp and felt her heart pound from the nightmare she'd had. She looked at the clock. It was nearly four in the morning. Sleep wasn't worth the nightmares. She got out of bed, changed, and went for a walk in the cool, early morning air. Sidney hadn't realized how much she missed the quietness of a small town and the fresh air. Before she even knew it, she was standing on the old, stone bridge. She shivered slightly while watching the dark stream. She looked beyond the stream and stared at the bank. She could still see Miss Fisher lying face down with dirt and leaves in her mussed, braided hair.

She took a deep breath and rubbed her chilled arms. She then heard a faint voice behind her. Sidney spun around and looked into the dark woods. There wasn't anyone there. Sidney held her breath and stared at the path that led to town. She crossed the bridge and turned onto the path that eventually led to the stone house. Sidney walked at a leisurely pace then entered the clearing and stared at the familiar house and the old well. She hadn't returned to this spot, not after what Alex had done to Miss Fisher. It was a disturbing thought. Sidney approached the old well and walked around it. There were so many fond memories attached to this place, yet the few bad ones seemed to taint the good. She looked down the well and stared at the water that now filled it.

"Hello, love," came a familiar voice from behind her. "I didn't expect to find you here."

Sidney spun around and stared helplessly at Harlan as her heart pounded with excitement and fright. He looked just as she had remembered him. His handsome face was still baby smooth, and his dark hair just nearly touched his collar. He didn't appear to have aged at all.

"Harlan," she gasped breathlessly as her heart pounded. "What are you doing here?"

His dark brows raised as he approached her. "Since you went to all the trouble of having a private detective locate me, I thought I may as well see what you wanted in person."

She shook her head and hid her enthusiasm. "It wasn't me. Trisha hired him to find you."

Harlan smiled warmly as his eyes traveled her body. "I'm disappointed."

Sidney stared at him as he paused a couple of feet before her. "I didn't think you'd even remember me."

"It would be difficult to forget after all that's happened here." His smile brightened considerably. "I'm really glad to see you again, Sidney."

He gathered her into his arms and held her against him. Sidney melted in his warm embrace and clung to him.

"I missed you, Harlan," she whispered near his ear while feeling his body against hers. "I'd never admit it to anyone, but I never stopped thinking about you."

She pulled away from him and met his gaze then saw the knife in his hand. Sidney gasped as he thrust it forward and into her abdomen.

Sidney shot up in bed, clutched her stomach, and felt the sweat drench her body. She breathed heavily for several minutes and looked around her dark bedroom. The shadows of her nightmares still filled the room. It was difficult to convince herself it was just a dream. She could still see Harlan standing before her with a knife in his hand. Is that what Emily saw right before the knife was driven into her body? Had she felt that horror before the agonizing pain? When her mind cleared, she realized the phone was ringing. Sidney grabbed the phone by her bedside.

"Hello?" she practically gasped into the phone and felt her heart pounding from her nightmare.

"I found him, Sidney," came Trisha's enthusiastic voice.

"Found who?" Sidney asked and raked her fingers through her mussed hair, damp with sweat.

"Harlan Brendan. The detective called me just ten minutes ago," she announced through the phone. "I'm going to California to question him."

It took a moment for Sidney to rationalize what her friend was saying. "Trisha, you're out of your mind," she remarked sternly as her entire body tensed.

"Are you coming or not?"

"No, I'm not going to California in the middle of the night," Sidney snapped lowly.

"Suit yourself. Gotta go. My flight leaves in an hour," Trisha said simply and hung up.

Sidney groaned and slammed down the phone. There was a faint knock on her door.

"Everything okay, Sidney?" came her mother's weary, concerned voice through the door.

Sidney ran her trembling fingers through her hair while leaning forward and sighed. She gingerly rubbed her abdomen and the phantom pain from her nightmare.

"I'm fine, Mom."

§

Sidney entered the skyway just before the gates closed, practically running the entire way. She boarded the plane while attempting to catch her breath then headed down the aisle and paused beside Trisha's seat. Trisha looked up at her with innocent blue eyes. Sidney glared back at her.

"I was afraid you'd miss the flight," Trisha said smugly.

"You knew I'd show, huh?" Sidney asked and tossed her overnight bag into the overhead storage then collapsed in the seat alongside her.

Trisha nodded and didn't give it a second thought.

"This is absolutely insane," Sidney snapped lowly, attempting to keep from raising her voice. "Traipsing completely across the country to talk to a man about a murder that took place eight years ago. I can't believe I'm going. But someone has to keep you from making a fool of yourself."

Trisha laughed softly and placed a piece of candy in her mouth. "Admit it," she announced cheerfully. "You're curious to see him after all these years."

Sidney frowned. "That was a long time ago. I won't allow you to start accusing him of something."

"The detective said that Harlan's been living in California for the past six years. Apparently, Brendan isn't his real last name," she informed her friend. "It's his middle name. His real last name is Vassily. The bastard's Russian."

"He's English, not Russian," Sidney pointed out then shook her head and snatched a piece of candy from her. "You've gone a little too far, Trisha. What do you really expect? A confession? Be serious. You can't just storm into his life and accuse him of killing someone." She placed the candy in her mouth and glared at her friend. "Judging by your recent behavior, I assume that's your big plan."

"That's where you come in," Trisha announced and looked at her with a smile. "You were friends with him. He'll talk to you. Picture this. An accidental meeting, a joyful reunion, and some old conversation."

"I don't know," Sidney said with some concern.

"Someone has to ask him what he knows, or this trip will be for nothing," Trisha proclaimed softly and turned in her seat. "You have to do it."

"What else did this detective tell you? Did he give you a home address?"

"His home address and his usual hangout," Trisha replied casually. "He goes to the same club every Friday and Saturday night. If we don't catch him at his home, we can find him at the club tonight."

Sidney drew a deep breath and sighed. She was annoyed with her friend, but she only had herself to blame for hopping on the plane with her.

"It'll be about five in the morning when we land," Sidney remarked. "What do we do when we get there?"

"Go to his house, of course," Trisha replied.

"At five in the morning?" she exploded while glaring at her friend. "Are you demented?"

"Yes, or so I've been told," Trisha replied with a soft laugh.

They had to switch planes in Chicago, but their connecting flight was laid over for four hours due to a thunderstorm. By the time they finally reached California, it was nine o'clock in the morning. The duo went straight to the detective's office. Detective Bruber was a pleasant, heavyset, older man with a thin mustache and graying hair. He shook their hands and offered them a seat in his small, cluttered office.

"I have to admit; he was a bugger to track. You gave me his middle name as his last. When I discovered that wasn't his real name, he wasn't as hard to find. I took the liberty to check his police record for you," Detective Bruber said and located a piece of paper on his cluttered desk. "He was arrested once for trespassing and disorderly conduct, which was related to his profession, but the charges were dropped."

"Do you know where he is now?" Sidney asked and wondered if she should ask about his current profession.

"Well, when you said you were coming out here, I checked on his home address," he informed them. "He left early this morning, so there's no telling when he'll be back."

"Couldn't we go to his place of work?" Trisha asked while practically wiggling out of her seat.

"He splits his time between writing articles as an investigative journalist and freelance photography," Bruber told her. "He could be anywhere."

"So we have to wait for him to return?" Trisha asked impatiently. "What if he's gone the entire weekend?"

Bruber shook his head. "Not a chance. He has reservations at the Starlight Club for tonight with his usual crowd," he informed her. "It's a classy club and restaurant. The reservations are for dinner at seven with access to the club. Without reservations, one could wait outside all night and never set foot in the club."

"Is it too late to get reservations?" Trisha asked while wringing her fingers together.

He leaned back in the chair. "Under normal circumstances, it would be too late." He then smiled cheaply. "But I have friends all over the city. I can pull some strings to get you into the restaurant." His look turned serious. "I will warn you, though. It's an expensive, classy place." He looked them up and down. "They probably won't even let you in the door without the proper attire. If you don't have anything suitable to wear, you'll just be wasting your time."

Sidney sighed and looked at her friend. "I suppose we'd better do a little clothing shopping before tonight. You're lucky I have a lot of room on my credit card."

Bruber smiled cheerfully and chuckled in his throat. "You're going to need it if you intend to order anything to eat. I'll arrange the reservations with Michael, the host. Make certain you ask for him and mention my name. Don't be late or they'll cancel your reservations."

Chapter Twelve

Sidney and Trisha arrived at the Starlight Club at six forty-five after a grueling afternoon of dress shopping. Sidney bought a black dress that went just below her knees. It was rather simple with thin straps, a low cut neckline, and a long slit up the right leg. She paid two hundred dollars for the dress and another fifty for the shoes. It wouldn't have bothered her so much if she didn't already own similar dresses collecting dust in her New York apartment. Trisha wore a short teal colored dress that only went halfway down her thighs. It was a light, satin dress with thin straps and a matching jacket. Her dress tipped the scales at a little more than two hundred dollars, which was the topic of conversation the entire ride to the restaurant.

Trisha looked spectacular with some make-up to cover her pale skin and dark circles. Sidney helped her do her hair in the hotel room, which cost another two hundred dollars for one night. Sidney was used to the inflated cost of living since she'd moved to New York, but Trisha couldn't get over the prices of everything.

"I really appreciate your putting the room and my dress on your charge card," Trisha said softly while they waited outside the restaurant. They had to wait just to get in the door to ask about their reservations. "I'll pay you back just as soon as we get home."

"There's no rush, Trish," Sidney announced, knowing her friend didn't have enough money for the dress let alone to contribute toward the room. "Let's just get a little enjoyment out of this dinner, for what it's costing."

They entered the restaurant section of the club and watched several spectacularly dressed people being turned away. Trisha was already nervous that Bruber hadn't been able to get them reservations. They approached the middle-aged man at the podium dressed in a tuxedo. With his size, he could easily double as a bouncer. Trisha fidgeted and seemed to lose her nerve in the ritzy atmosphere. She was uncomfortable outside her small town.

"I believe we have reservations for seven o'clock," Sidney said with an air of confidence, being used to dealing with wealthy city dwellers. "Detective Bruber made the reservation with the host, Michael."

"Ah, yes. I'm Michael," he announced pleasantly. "We have a 'special' table for you ladies. Please follow me."

They followed their host through the restaurant past several wealthy looking people dining on lobster tail and caviar. He led them to a corner table near the back of the restaurant that only allowed them to see one table and the bar and was located right next to the bathroom. It was a terrible location, but at least they were in. The host handed them their menus and smiled slyly.

"It may not be the 'choice' table, but the party you're looking for is directly to your right just before the bar," Michael announced while offering a sly grin. "You'll be able to see and hear them just through the plants, and they'll never know you're here."

Michael winked and headed back to his podium in front. Sidney chuckled softly and shook her head.

"That Bruber is a clever fellow," Sidney remarked.

Trisha hid her smile. "He should be for what his services cost."

They both looked toward the empty table near the bar then glanced at their menus.

Trisha let a slight gasp escape. "Look at what they charge for a bowl of soup!"

"You're paying for atmosphere," Sidney remarked simply.

"Atmosphere never cost this much in Marilina," Trisha snapped softly.

Four men dressed in suits were seated at the table near the bar. Both woman nearly jumped out of their seats and observed the men. There were two men with their backs to them, and the other two faced their direction. Both men facing them wore sunglasses, which would have seemed odd anywhere else, but it seemed to be customary in the Starlight. One was a heavyset man with curly brown hair wearing a brown suit. The hair color was right, but there was no way Harlan could have let himself go to that extent. The other man wore a black suit and had short, dark hair, darker than Harlan's. He had a short, thin goatee with some gray on the chin. The man was possibly in his late thirties. One of the men with his back to them, also wearing a black suit had blonde hair, so he was out. The other wore a dark blue suit and had light brown hair. Though the hair color was a little lighter than she had remembered, out of her four options, she knew it had to be Harlan.

"That has to be him on the left with his back to us," Sidney whispered as her heart fluttered slightly. "Go to the bar and make a positive ID."

"Me?" Trisha whispered back. "Why should I go? You knew him better than I did. Besides, you said you were going to do the talking."

"He might recognize me, and I won't talk to him in front of his friends," she insisted. "I have a plan, but I need to be certain that's him first."

Trisha inhaled deeply and nodded. "I'll do it."

She stood and nervously approached the bar just past their table. Trisha casually sat on one of the stools and ordered a drink. Sidney watched through the plants then removed a pen from her purse. She began scribbling on one of the beverage napkins. She looked up every couple of seconds to watch Trisha. Trisha was now positioned sideways at the bar with her legs neatly crossed, and scanned the area casually, as if barely interested. Her eyes fell on the man they suspected to be Harlan. By her reaction, he must have made eye contact. Trisha smiled with some embarrassment and turned toward the bar when her drink arrived.

The man with the longer, light brown hair stood and approached the bar with his back still to Sidney. Sidney groaned lowly, wishing she could catch a glimpse of him. He paid for Trisha's drink, despite her apparent protests and talked to her. Sidney wished she could hear their conversation. Had he recognized Trisha after all these years? It would appear his friends could hear their conversation at the bar. Both men facing Sidney's table turned their heads, watched the bar with great interest, and laughed. The man with Trisha pointed toward the club with its loud music just off the restaurant.

"No, Trish," Sidney mumbled softly, realizing he wanted to take her into the club. "Don't go with him."

Trisha appeared embarrassed, set her drink down, and reluctantly linked onto his arm. He led her past his table and the plants. Trisha looked through the plants. Her eyes were now wide with anxiety, and she made a gesture. Sidney could now see the man's profile and realized it wasn't Harlan. Sidney frowned as her friend disappeared into the nightclub. Had Bruber been mistaken? Had he been following the wrong man? The waitress approached her table.

"Can I get you something from the bar tonight?" the attractive waitress asked with a pleasant smile.

"Iced tea, please," Sidney replied then gave the waitress a curious look. "Can I ask you something?"

"What can I help you with?"

Sidney cleared her throat. "There are three men sitting at that table near the bar," she said gently.

The waitress glanced toward the bar through the plants then looked back and nodded. "Yes, they're here just about every weekend."

Sidney felt some anxiety but held it back. "Does one of them have an English accent?" Her heart now pounded and she didn't even know why.

The waitress appeared humored and let out a slight laugh. "That would be Harlan," she announced.

Sidney raised her brows with some confusion then smiled warmly. "Do you know him?"

"Yes, I know him," she replied with a tiny laugh. "Why? Would *you* like to know him?" The waitress raised a suggestive brow while grinning.

Sidney was set back a moment then leaned back in her chair. "I'm thinking about it." Sidney placed a ten-dollar bill along with the folded napkin on the table near the waitress. "Would you give him this from me?"

The waitress glanced at the money on the table then the napkin beneath it. She took the napkin but left the money.

"Keep your money," the waitress announced with a soft laugh. "I'll give him the note, but don't expect a big response. He doesn't react big to anything."

Sidney watched the waitress leave her table with the napkin then leaned forward and peered through the plants. She was confident he would react to her note in a very big way. The waitress casually approached their table and paused with a sweet, seductive smile. The three remaining men glanced at her. They heavyset man spoke to the waitress while grinning, obviously flirting with her. She set the note in the middle of the table. Both the blonde man and the heavyset man scrambled for the napkin, almost knocking their chairs to the floor as they sprang to their feet. The man in the beard smirked and shook his head with a laugh. Sidney watched the heavyset man yank the napkin away from the blonde man.

He read the note aloud while grinning deviously. If that was Harlan, she couldn't see him through his new form. She took a deep breath and prepared herself. He only read the first line when the man with the goatee suddenly snapped his head in the direction of the man reading the note. He lurched from his chair and snatched the napkin from the other man. Sidney's heart leaped into her throat. He removed his sunglasses and read the note with wide, green eyes as his mouth opened slightly with surprise. Sidney shot forward and stared at the familiar face beneath the thin layer of facial hair. It was Harlan!

The two other men appeared stunned as he bolted away from the table and approached the waitress. Sidney nervously stood while watching his reaction. She didn't like his aggressive behavior. He needed some time to cool down. Perhaps writing the poem she gave to him eight years ago wasn't such a good idea, especially if he thought it had been from a dead woman. The waitress stared at him with some surprise while he questioned her about the napkin. She uncertainly pointed in the direction of the plants. Sidney held her breath and bolted into the nearby bathroom. She couldn't deal with him in his current state.

Chapter Thirteen

Sidney paced the bathroom's elegant, flower-scented sitting room for nearly fifteen minutes. She knew she had blown it. Trisha was going to be upset about her blunder. It made her ill when she thought about all the money they'd invested in this little manhunt. Unfortunately, if she didn't confront Harlan, Trisha surely would. Sidney knew she couldn't allow that to happen. She was positive Trisha would accuse him of murder. She'd have to go out there and explain herself. She left the bathroom and approached the table near the bar, but Harlan was gone.

Trisha and the other man still hadn't returned either. Sidney then noticed Harlan sitting at the end of the bar. He was alone. This was her chance to rectify the situation. She casually walked toward him and sat on the empty stool beside him. She ordered a drink without looking at him. Out of the corner of her eye, she saw him run his finger along the rim of his glass. The note on the napkin lay open before him. Once she got her drink, Sidney turned toward him and gathered all her courage.

"You look like a man who's just lost his best friend," she announced with a timid smile.

He barely glanced at her, raised his brows, then looked back to the napkin and crumpled it. "No," he said with a sigh and tossed the napkin into the ashtray. "Just a couple of ghosts coming back to haunt me."

Sidney stared at him a long moment with some confusion. Hadn't he recognized her? Was this to her advantage?

"Yes," she cooed softly and looked back at her drink. "The past just never dies, does it?"

Harlan looked at her a long moment, tilted his head, and then offered an all too familiar smile. "Always hanging over my shoulder," he replied then extended his hand. "Harlan."

Sidney's heart pounded as she accepted his hand. "Sindy," she replied.

He maintained his pleasant attitude and released her hand. "Are you here alone, Sindy?"

"No," she replied. "My friend is in the club with your friend. What became of her, I'll never know."

He chuckled softly and raised his glass. "Ah, Lyle," he announced casually. "You'll be lucky if you see her anymore tonight. Lyle's burning some bridges."

Sidney laughed softly and studied his handsome profile. He looked so much older than he had just eight years ago. The goatee gave him a distinguished appearance though.

"He chose an iceberg for his latest conquest," Sidney remarked simply with a humored smile.

A thousand memories came rushing back. Her heartbeat quickened. A low chuckle escaped his throat. Sidney knew she couldn't get any information out of him without revealing her true identity, but she didn't want to do it here. The bar was becoming more crowded. She'd have to get him to take a walk with her, but she wasn't sure she liked the secluded area just beyond the Starlight. She guessed there was no rush. She looked around the bar area with great interest.

"Does this place always get this busy?"

"It's always packed on the weekend," he replied while studying her. "We only come here because Lyle's brother owns the place. Gives us our drinks at cost."

She laughed softly.

"Are you from around here?" he asked while raising his brow and gave her a curious look.

"Actually, I'm from New York. We're just visiting briefly," she replied simply. "We leave on the first plane out tomorrow."

"What do you do in New York?" he asked.

"I manage a hotel on Manhattan Island," she said then chuckled in her throat. "That is, I think I still do. I left without advance notice."

"Pressure getting to you?"

She shrugged and thought about the phone call she'd received from Trisha. "Yeah, something like that. What do you do for a living?"

"For a living?" he asked. "Journalism pays the bills, but I'm a photographer at heart."

"Really," she said and tilted her head as if she had no idea. "Are you any good?"

He laughed softly. "I'd like to believe so." A gentle smile crossed his face. "Would you like to see my work?"

Sidney's heart jumped in her chest. Did she dare take him up on that offer? She had a good idea what was going through his mind, but she needed the opportunity to talk to him in private to discuss her real reasons for being in California.

He stared at her expression then laughed softly. "That wasn't a come-on," he remarked. "I assure you, I'm quite safe."

Sidney forced a smile and relaxed some, though her pulse quickened. "I'd be interested, yes," she replied.

He stood and left a tip for the bartender. "My apartment is just a couple of blocks from here," he announced. "Would you like to tell your friend where you're going?"

"Uh, yes. I probably should."

They entered the club portion together. Trisha was sitting at a table with Lyle. They seemed to be having an in-depth conversation. Sidney pulled Trisha away from the table to talk to her in private.

Trisha looked toward Harlan while they spoke. "Is that him?" she gasped.

Sidney nodded and glanced back at the men. Lyle and Harlan were talking as well. She looked back at her friend.

"I'm going with him to his apartment," Sidney said above the loud music.

Trisha's eyes widened with horror. "That's not a good idea, Sidney. If you confront him in the privacy of his own apartment, he might kill you. Besides," she remarked lowly, "you know why he wants to take you there."

"Don't worry about it, Trisha," Sidney announced. "I have everything under control. The walls in apartments are paper-thin. If anything happens, I'll just scream."

"I don't like this at all. I don't trust him," Trisha protested. "Don't go, Sidney."

"You want me to ask him about the murder? I have to get away from here if I want him to talk freely," Sidney said firmly.

Trisha held her breath. "One hour, Sidney. If you're not back at the hotel room in one hour, I'm coming with the SWAT team."

"If I'm not at the hotel, I'll call," Sidney replied simply. "I know what I'm doing."

Chapter Fourteen

Sidney attempted to memorize the direction they drove after leaving the club. Harlan drove his newer model car along a dark road just off the main street. The area looked fairly secluded, without any traces of an apartment building. The further away from the city they got, the more concerned Sidney became. They approached a tall security gate surrounding what appeared to be an old warehouse. Sidney sat forward in the passenger seat and stared at the building. Harlan pressed a button, and the gates electronically opened then closed behind them. She shifted nervously as they pulled up to the old warehouse.

Harlan looked at her and laughed at her silent question. "Yes, I live here," he said simply then stopped the car. "It's more impressive on the inside," he teased. "Come on; I'll show you." He opened his car door and got out.

Sidney eyed the warehouse through the windshield and groaned. "I'm dead."

They entered through a locked door at the bottom and walked toward an old, gate style elevator. When he pushed the button, the doors opened, and she uncertainly entered with him. The gate on the elevator sounded like a prison door closing. They rode to the fourth floor. When the elevator doors opened, they stepped out and he unlocked the apartment door, allowing her to enter the dimly lit studio apartment. He turned on the lights and closed the door behind them. The apartment encompassed the entire fourth floor of the warehouse with large, exposed metal beams throughout. Windows lined the entire wall facing the street with vertical blinds along them. There was a living room with a large screened television, a bar, and a pool table in the right corner. The large kitchen had an island counter, and there was a dining room to the left side. The bedroom was beyond sliding wood doors. The floors were all finished hardwood with large, oriental rugs throughout. There were ceiling fans above each section within the studio. Sidney noticed the large, framed photographs throughout the apartment.

"Do you like it?" he asked while grinning.

"It's amazing," she said and looked back at him. "Who decorated it?"

"I converted the entire studio myself." He walked past her toward the bar while briefly glancing at her. "Can I get you something to drink? I'm afraid I don't have much besides brandy and soda. I don't entertain often."

"I'm fine, thank you," she announced and continued to study the place. "Do you mind if I look around?"

"No, go right ahead," he replied and poured himself a brandy. "My best photos are on the walls. I can't see putting them in albums where they're forgotten."

Sidney wandered around the huge apartment and examined the framed photos. Her heart sank when she saw the photo of the old stone house.

"Where was this taken?" she asked in an attempt to sound casual.

He approached and looked over her shoulder at the framed photo. "I don't remember," Harlan replied.

Sidney knew that was a lie. She continued on her journey around the apartment, examining each photo. He was an amazing photographer. Of course, she knew that years earlier.

"Would you excuse me a minute?" he asked then went toward the bathroom on the opposite side of the apartment from the bedroom.

Sidney paused near his bedroom door and turned on the light. The ceiling fan came on, startling her. On the wall beside the king-size bed was a large, framed photo of her sitting on the well. Sidney's eyes widened with surprise, and her heart pounded. She uncertainly entered the room and approached the picture. She stared at herself a long moment and swallowed dryly. Despite her surprise to see herself in a photo within his apartment, she was astonished at how well he'd captured that day. She couldn't believe how much older she looked in the photo and the seductive way she stared up at the sky. Her hair had been frumpy and wild from the quick shake she'd given it when she had earlier removed the hairband. The ceiling fan stopped causing Sidney to gasp and spin around with surprise. Harlan casually leaned against the doorframe and raised his brows with a curious expression. She nervously glanced back at the photo.

"I'm not very good at photographing people, but that turned out rather well," he remarked simply as he walked across the bedroom. "My friends love that one. They couldn't believe you were just fifteen when that was taken."

Sidney turned and met his stare with some surprise. She didn't know what to say, having been caught in her lie.

"So why are you really here?" he asked sternly with an arched, raised brow.

She fidgeted and fumbled with a response that at least sounded plausible. "I heard you were in California, so I decided to look you up."

He snorted a laugh and shook his head with disbelief. "That's bullshit, and you know it," he remarked lowly as his look turned cold. "You wrote that note, didn't you?"

"Yes, I sent the note with the waitress," she informed him reluctantly and stared into his green eyes.

"Why?"

Sidney stared at him then looked past him toward her only escape.

"Just get it out of your head, Sidney," he growled coldly. "You won't even make it to the door."

She looked back at him with some concern then raised a cocky brow. "Trisha's expecting a phone call from me any minute now," Sidney remarked. "If I don't check in, the police will be knocking at your door."

"Oh, spare me the dramatics," he snapped lowly and folded his arms across his chest. "I want to know what you're doing here, and you'd better tell me now."

Sidney drew a deep breath and stared at him a long moment. The truth seemed to be the easiest lie. "I'm looking for some answers to the murder of Emily Fisher."

Harlan's brows knitted with confusion. "What does that have to do with me?" His head then tilted to the side as his eyes narrowed. "Unless you think I had something to do with it."

Sidney didn't respond.

Harlan rolled his eyes with a groan then shook his head as he glared at her. "I don't understand any of this," he remarked with annoyance. "Eight years ago you were convinced I wasn't involved. Now you show up on my doorstep and practically accuse me of murder."

"I was stupid enough to believe anything I was told," she remarked sternly. "You ran off one week after the murder. Do you have any idea how that looked?"

"I had personal reasons for leaving. It had nothing to do with the murder," he remarked firmly.

"So you're not going to tell me why you left?"

"No," he snapped then appeared curious. "How did you know about that poem? I didn't show it to anyone."

Sidney bit her lower lip nervously and looked away. "Because I wrote the first one eight years ago," she said then looked back at him. "I was a teenage girl with a crush on an older man."

Harlan stared at her with some surprise as his arms fell to his sides. He was silent a moment then sighed and shook his head. "I know what happened was hard on you, Sidney, but the police put her killer behind bars. I had nothing to do with her death."

"If that's true then you shouldn't mind discussing the day of the murder with me," she announced with a renewed arrogance.

Harlan raked his fingers through his hair and groaned. "I'll tell you what I can if that's what you want."

She cast a look around his bedroom then hesitated. "Could we talk somewhere else?"

"Yeah, sure," he announced then removed his jacket and tossed it onto a nearby chair. "I think I'm going to need another drink for this conversation anyway."

Chapter Fifteen

Sidney sat on the sofa while Harlan sat in a plush chair in the living room and discussed in great detail the day Emily Fisher was murdered. Harlan was surprisingly accommodating and volunteered information without any prompting. After the first hour, Sidney looked at her watch and gasped.

Harlan sat forward in his chair. "Is something wrong?"

She sprang from the sofa. "Can I use your phone?" she asked with concern. "I have to call Trisha before she calls the SWAT team."

"Sure, it's on the end table."

Sidney lunged for the phone and dialed the hotel number from the piece of paper she had on her.

Harlan stood and approached the bar with his empty glass. "Can I get you a drink?"

She nodded then listened to the operator. "Could you connect me with room 302?"

"May I ask who's calling, please?" the operator asked in a dull tone.

"Sidney McBride," she replied.

"I have a message for you from Trisha Allister," the woman announced.

"What's the message?"

"She can be reached at 555-7021," the operator informed her.

Sidney wrote the number down with a pen she'd found and repeated it for accuracy. She thanked the operator and hung up the phone. She collapsed on the sofa with confusion.

Harlan handed her the glass and smiled deviously. "Problem with the cavalry?"

Sidney stared at the number and shook her head. "She's not there," she remarked. "The lady at the front desk gave me another number."

"So I heard," he remarked and sat on the sofa near her. "It would appear Trisha is spending some time getting to know Lyle." He offered a sly grin. "That's his phone number."

Sidney's expression dropped as she stared at him where he sat beside her. "You can't be serious," she gasped.

"She abandoned you for Lyle, that horny bastard," he remarked with a humored chuckle then drank from his glass.

"It's not funny," Sidney growled and turned to face him. "She hasn't been right since the murder. There's no telling what will happen to her if she has another traumatic experience." Sidney grabbed the phone and dialed Lyle's number. She groaned when she got his answering machine. "I got his machine."

"Hang up," Harlan announced simply. "He always puts the machine on when he's entertaining."

Sidney slammed the phone down and glared at him. "You think this is amusing, don't you?"

"I wouldn't put it that way," he replied with a timid smile. "But you can't do much about it anymore tonight. Let them enjoy themselves. Would you like to finish our conversation?"

Sidney couldn't believe Trisha abandoned her for a fling with some handsome playboy. She reluctantly sighed and nodded. "I believe you were telling me what happened when Miss Fisher came into the press."

"It was right after school left out. She must have come directly from class," he announced. "The teachers were always out by three-thirty. She brought her film for developing, talked to me for a minute or two, and then left."

She found it hard to believe that was the extent of their interaction. "When did you decide to go into the woods to take photos?"

"I wanted to take pictures of that house since the day before when you took me there," he informed her. "I had your father's permission to leave early from the press. I intended to wait for you since I wasn't sure where I was going, but you didn't show up after school. I had to go when I did, or I'd lose the lighting."

"What time did you get to the stone house?"

He shrugged. "Maybe around four-thirty," he replied. "It was a long time ago."

"You left the press at ten of four but didn't reach the stone house until nearly four-thirty?" she suddenly questioned. "That walk should have taken ten minutes. You must have done something else in between."

"No," he replied sternly. "There were so many paths, and I wasn't sure where I was going. I must have taken the wrong trail." Harlan casually shrugged. "I eventually got there, but it wasn't the way you had gone."

"I suppose it can be difficult to find if you're not familiar with the area," she agreed. "How long were you there?"

He appeared to consider the question a moment. "I'd say about forty-five minutes. I was walking back when I heard Trisha screaming. That's when I ran into you."

Sidney considered the times then took a deep breath and sighed. "So what had Miss Fisher photographed? I was told you developed the film and gave the photos to the police."

"Yes, but I kept a copy for myself," he informed her simply then stood and entered the bedroom.

"Why?" she called after him.

"I suppose so I wouldn't forget," he replied from the bedroom.

She could hear him opening and closing drawers. Sidney noticed a stack of photo albums under the coffee table. She slid onto the floor and flipped through the one on top.

"Do you still have the pictures you took that day?" she called to him without looking toward the bedroom area.

"They're in there somewhere," he replied from where he now stood over her, startling her.

He joined her on the floor and handed her the pack of pictures. She accepted the photos and sorted through them. Miss Fisher had taken pictures of her boyfriend, a face Sidney would never forget, some of the school, some of the senior boys tossing football, and one of herself with Trisha. Sidney was surprised to see them in the photo together. Despite spending the last two days with Trisha, she really missed the girl in the photo. The best friend she used to know was possibly gone forever. The rest of the photos were scenery from the woods and around the school. Harlan sorted through the photo albums and handed her a thin one.

"This contains all the photos I took while in Marilina."

He retrieved his empty glass and returned to the bar for another drink. She could tell the alcohol was starting to affect him by the way he walked. He wasn't intoxicated, but he was somewhere near it. Sidney paged through the thin album, then set it down and retrieved the one she had been flipping through previously. They were pictures from his childhood. She recognized England in most of the photos.

"Harlan," she asked almost timidly. "What did you think when you got that letter?"

He laughed softly from the bar while pouring his drink. "Naturally, I assumed it was from Emily. She was always a bit of a flirt." He chuckled. "I suppose when a woman looks like that, she's entitled to be."

When he returned from the bar, she exchanged albums once more then looked up at him. He sat alongside her with his back against the sofa. Sidney looked through the familiar pictures of her hometown.

"Were you attracted to her?" Sidney asked simply without looking at him, though she felt a jealous pang.

"I noticed her," he remarked with a slightly dirty smile. "It would have been difficult not to."

"Yes, she was rather beautiful," Sidney remarked softly. "Did you say anything to her about the letter?"

"Nah," he announced simply.

"Why not?"

"That would have taken all the fun out of it. Women like to pursue," he replied. "Why spoil it?"

"I don't pursue," she snapped lowly without looking at him.

"I'm pretty sure that's the definition of a secret admirer," he remarked then chuckled. "Although, with the way your father acted, I'm surprised you even date."

Sidney sharply turned her head and stared at him with some surprise. The irony of his statement was almost frightening. He caught her look.

"What's that look about?"

She looked back at the photos and shifted uncomfortably. "I don't date," she replied firmly.

Harlan was silent a moment, but she could feel his eyes on her. "Ever?" he practically gasped.

"Emotional scars run deep," she said timidly and tensed. "Miss Fisher was murdered by her boyfriend, a man who supposedly loved her."

"That's just an excuse, Sidney," he announced. "Your father was overly protective. He's turned you against men."

She glared at him. "Leave my father out of this, Harlan. You wouldn't know what I went through after Miss Fisher's death. You ran away," she snapped. "My father's always been there when I've needed him."

He stared at her only a moment then shifted uncomfortably. "I suppose I deserved that," he remarked and finished his drink without looking at her.

Sidney pointed to one of the pictures. "Are these in order?"

"They should be. Those were the ones taken on the day of the murder," he informed her.

She looked at one of the pictures of the stone house. In the woods to the side, she could see something but couldn't make out whether it was an animal or human.

"What's this in the woods?" She pointed to the shadow in the background.

Harlan leaned closer and studied the picture. "Just shadowing, I guess."

Sidney removed the picture and held it at a different angle. "Are you sure?"

Harlan leaned over her shoulder and examined it more closely. "I can't be positive, but I keep all my negatives. I could enhance it for you. It'll only take a few minutes."

Sidney could smell the fading scent of Harlan's cologne then realized how close he was to her. She turned her head and looked at him. His eyes met hers and her heart pounded in response.

"Would it be much trouble?" she managed to ask.

"None at all. I just need to find the negative. They're all in order according to dates. I have a darkroom just to the side of the bathroom. You can help look for the negative."

He stood and extended his hand to her. Sidney uncertainly placed her hand in his and allowed him to help her to her feet.

§

Sidney peered over Harlan's shoulder while he enlarged the image in the background. He was skilled at his work. The darkroom was fairly small, but she couldn't say she minded the closeness. She watched him enlarge the picture then put it through the tray of chemicals. Once the picture developed, he turned the light on and studied it more closely.

"I can't tell what it is," he said with a sigh. "Enlarging it further will just distort it."

Sidney studied the picture a moment and was certain what she saw. "It's a person, Harlan," she said firmly while holding the eight by ten photo by the corners. "I'm sure of it."

He squinted at the photo. "How do you get a person out of that blob? Looks a little like bigfoot to me. Maybe I can sell this to one of the rag sheets," he muttered lowly, tossed it aside, and walked out of the darkroom.

Sidney followed him from the small room. He washed his hands and poured himself another drink. Sidney collapsed on the sofa and sighed with defeat. Harlan joined her on the sofa.

She frowned and cast a look at him. "Trisha thinks someone saw Miss Fisher and Alex together at the old stone house, became enraged, and killed her out of jealousy."

Harlan snorted a laugh although he obviously wasn't humored. "And Trisha thinks that person was me, huh?"

"She has a couple of theories going," Sidney replied simply.

Harlan turned to face her. "I'm going to tell you this only once," he announced firmly with a moderately serious look on his mostly drunken face. "I had no interest in Emily Fisher, apart from the fact that we both enjoyed photography. Several times, she tried to persuade me to photograph her in the nude, and I turned her down each time. She just wasn't my type."

Sidney stared at him with some confusion. It would seem the alcohol was making him more defensive. "But you said you were attracted to her."

"I never said I was attracted to her," he announced defensively. "I said I *noticed* her. What man wouldn't look twice at a woman with a body like that," he replied simply. "But she had a terrible personality and an even worse disposition."

"I thought she was a lot of fun," Sidney remarked.

Harlan drew a deep breath and stared at her. "She was different outside the classroom, Sidney." He frowned and shifted uncomfortably. "She was a slut, okay," he blurted out. "She'd go to Sam's while Alex tended bar, get pissed up, and beg for it from every man there. She played around on Alex all the time. The woman had no shame."

Sidney stared at him with a look of horror. "Not Miss Fisher!"

"I'd seen her in action," he said firmly. "I went to Sam's on occasion. I heard the things she'd say to the guys. I'd seen her drink

74

herself under the bar. I swear the woman had eight hands. I had a difficult time keeping her off me on more than one occasion." He held his breath then shook his head. "She even had an affair with that teacher, Malcolm."

Sidney's eyes widened at the suggestion. "Mr. Malcolm? But they hated each other!"

"Of course they did," he proclaimed. "The guy was married. He was probably terrified she'd tell his wife about the affair."

Sidney looked away and raked her fingers through her hair. "Everyone knew she went home that way," she whispered. She closed her eyes then groaned. "This is terrible."

"Are you all right?"

She opened her eyes and looked at him. "Please, Harlan, tell me where Lyle lives. I have to get Trisha. We really have to go home. I've had enough of this detective bullshit."

Harlan stared at her a long moment without a word then finally spoke. "I'm sorry, love. You wanted to know the truth. Now I've told you. There's no reason to disturb Lyle and Trisha tonight." He looked at his watch. "It's three o'clock in the morning. Why don't you take the bed, and I'll sleep on the sofa. I'll call Lyle tomorrow morning and take you and Trisha to the airport."

Sidney felt ill from her new discoveries but remained polite. "That's kind of you, but I'll sleep on the sofa," she replied. "It's your bed."

"Don't argue with me, Sidney. I'm tired and half smashed," he insisted. "It's not going to matter much where I collapse. If you want something more comfortable to sleep in, you can help yourself to a shirt."

She smiled warmly and stood. "Thank you, Harlan."

Chapter Sixteen

Sidney woke to sunlight on her face then moaned softly as she glanced around the unfamiliar bedroom then looked at the clock. It was ten o'clock. Sidney shot up in bed with a gasp and threw the covers off her. She hurried into the living area wearing one of Harlan's dress shirts as a nightgown. Harlan was sleeping peacefully on the sofa. She rushed to his side and shook him firmly.

"Harlan, wake up. I'm going to miss my flight," she insisted firmly.

Harlan woke and looked around with some disorientation, possibly hungover then sat up. "What happened?"

"Nothing. You promised to take me to the airport. We have to hurry, or I'll miss my flight," she said and rushed into the bathroom.

Harlan muttered something. When she came out of the bathroom, Harlan was sitting on the sofa with the phone in his hand. He ran his fingers through his hair and sighed.

"Yeah," he moaned into the receiver. "She's here, Lyle. We were just leaving now. Meet us at the airport."

Sidney hurried back into the bedroom and removed her dress from the back of the chair in the corner. She had no choice but to change back into her dress since it was all she had to wear, and rushed into the living room. Harlan appeared from the bathroom looking only a little fresher.

"We have to stop at the hotel for my things," Sidney announced and searched the floor for her shoes.

"I talked to Lyle on his cellular phone," he informed her. "They're at the hotel. Trisha's getting your bag." He then eyed her as if she was holding things up. "Are you almost ready?"

Sidney nodded and found her shoes then looked at him. "He has one of those cellular phones?" she finally asked. "If you were able to reach him through that phone, why didn't you give me that number instead?"

He stared at her a moment then grabbed his car keys from the coffee table. "I didn't want you disturbing them," he insisted. "Do you want to make your flight or not? I'm not driving you back to Marilina."

§

Harlan drove over the speed limit the entire way to the airport. Fortunately, they weren't pulled over. He parked the car at one of the drop-off metered spots in front, and they hurried into the terminal. The plane was already boarding. Thankfully, it wasn't a big airport, and there wasn't a long line through security. Lyle stood alongside Trisha and the woman collecting tickets at the gate.

Trisha saw her and waved the tickets. "Sidney!"

Harlan hurried her to the gate. Trisha gave Sidney her ticket, waved to Lyle, and then boarded the plane.

Sidney turned to Harlan and responded warmly. "Thanks for everything, Harlan."

"It was good seeing you," he announced while offering a gentle smile.

"We have to board the plane now, ma'am," the attendant at the gate announced.

Sidney waved to Harlan and approached the woman before the gate door. As she handed the woman her ticket, Sidney paused and considered something. She turned and hurried back to Harlan, surprising him.

"Did you forget something?" he asked.

"Yes," she replied.

Sidney placed her hands on Harlan's shoulders and kissed him quickly on the mouth. She pulled away, backed up a step, and smiled while blushing.

"Just something I was unable to do eight years ago," she replied then turned and hurried for the attendant at the door. The woman hid her grin, although obviously touched by the sediment. Sidney claimed her ticket and hurried into the skywalk without looking back. Sidney rushed through the plane and collapsed in the seat beside Trisha. Her heart pounded, and she felt hot and flushed. She sighed softly and closed her eyes. When she opened her eyes, she realized Trisha was staring at her with an angry look.

"I can't believe you went back to his apartment with him," Trisha growled lowly. "What if he had killed you? Do you even care that I was worried half to death?"

Sidney straightened in her seat and snorted a laugh while glaring at her friend. "Yeah, you were so worried," she scoffed. "That's why you were at Lyle's when I tried to call you and let you know I wasn't dead."

"I had no choice. I didn't know where to find Harlan's apartment," Trisha snapped hotly. "I called the hotel from the club. When there was no message from you, I went with Lyle to his apartment. He promised he'd call Harlan when we got there."

Sidney cocked her head and raised a suggestive brow. "So why didn't he ever call?"

"He did," Trisha launched with hostility. "He called twice, and I called at least ten times. I kept leaving messages on his stupid machine. Why didn't you pick up?"

"The phone never rang," Sidney insisted and knew she didn't imagine it. "Lyle must have given you the wrong number. When I called Lyle's apartment, I got his machine. Harlan said Lyle always put the machine on while he was entertaining." She gave her friend a demanding, dirty look.

Trisha suddenly gasped while staring at her with wide eyes. "We've both been had!"

"What are you talking about?"

"Lyle said the same thing about Harlan. Both bastards turned off their phone ringers so the phones wouldn't ring." Trisha shook her head with disgust and folded her arms across her chest. "Perverts were just trying to get us in their beds."

Sidney chuckled at the irony. "Well, it worked."

Trisha glared at Sidney as her eyes widened. "You didn't!"

"I slept in Harlan's bed, and he slept on the sofa," Sidney replied with a cheap smile then eyed her friend. "What did Lyle pull?"

Trisha sank into thought then looked back at her friend. "Nothing, actually. He kept trying to convince me you were safe with Harlan. Between phone calls, we talked," she said then grinned as some color entered her cheeks. "He was rather nice." She then frowned and became embarrassed. "He must think I'm horrible after the way I acted."

Sidney noted her friend's interest in something other than her obsession with Emily Fisher. She leaned on the armrest between them and hid her smile. "So what did you talk about?"

Trisha turned halfway in her seat and appeared eager to talk. "Nothing important," she announced while swiftly changing the subject. "What did Harlan have to say?"

Sidney felt her heart sink. She had hoped Lyle sparked some feelings inside Trisha, but her friend seemed to have a one-track mind. It was no use.

"He was very vague," Sidney replied, losing her interest in the topic. "He really didn't tell us much more than what we knew before."

Trisha continued to glare at her. "You'd better tell me what he said, or I'm telling your father you spent the night in Harlan's apartment."

Sidney rolled her eyes and groaned. "Oh, all right," she snapped lowly then drew a deep breath and held it a moment. "Harlan said Miss Fisher was a slut." She saw the shocked look on Trisha's face and forced herself to continue. "He also said she was having an affair with Mr. Malcolm."

"What!"

Sidney turned with embarrassment and placed her hand over her eyes as several heads turned toward them.

"I don't think the pilot heard you," Sidney muttered and looked at the staring passengers.

They eventually minded their own business.

"I don't believe that for one minute. She hated that man with a passion," Trisha snapped hotly. "It's obvious Harlan was lying to cover his own suspicious ass."

Sidney turned to face her friend and pointed a demanding finger at her. "Look, you started this, Trisha," she snapped. "If you want to play detective, then you'd better be a little more open-minded.

You need to listen to what people are saying, weigh the facts, then make an intelligent deduction, but so far you've been completely closed minded." She drew a deep breath and held it a moment. "If she were sleeping with Mr. Malcolm that puts him in a very awkward position with his career and his home life. He could very easily be a suspect. Mind that word, Trish. A suspect is suspected not accused. You have absolutely no grounds to accuse anyone of anything, and you'd best remember that in the future or no one will tell you anything."

Trisha stared at Sidney in silence then turned and looked out the window. "I think I understand," she replied timidly then eyed her friend. "What's our next move?"

Sidney raked her fingers through her hair and sighed. "Why can't you just let it go?" she asked softly.

"I can't," Trisha whispered while staring at her friend. "At first I was just traumatized by the brutality of her death and the way we found her. But after the trial, I kept asking myself why he'd do such a thing to someone so special." She tensed then fidgeted. "About two years ago, I started investigating the murder; I mean really investigating it. I gathered information and studied the articles and reports. When I discovered Alex may have been innocent, I nearly went to pieces. I helped put him behind bars. I sent him to prison for life. I don't know about you, but I can't live with that burden. I think he's innocent, and I just can't live with the thought of him being in prison while the real killer was allowed to simply walk away."

Sidney drew a deep breath. "If Alex is innocent, I don't want to see him rot in jail either. We can question some of the others involved and see what they remember. We'll start with Mr. Malcolm. But if you want my help, you'll have to promise to let me handle it my way. You already have everyone on the defensive."

Trisha nodded. "Yes, I know I've stepped on some toes. They wouldn't listen, so I made them."

"Now it's my turn," Sidney replied simply.

Chapter Seventeen

When they reached the airport terminal, Sidney stopped in the bathroom to change out of the evening dress and into something less conversational. By the time they reached Marilina, both were hungry from the long flight, since neither felt like eating during their layover. They stopped at Sam's Tavern for something to eat since it was the first place they reached. Trisha's mother was working at the diner that evening, but Trisha didn't want to hear another lecture about her actions. Sam's was never very busy on a Sunday evening. Around noon, the church crowd roamed in for lunch, and it was a respectable place until ten o'clock.

The newly added dance club portion brought more income for Sam, but it also drew in some undesirable people from neighboring towns. Sam had the night off, so they wouldn't be able to ask him anything about the day of the murder. None of the regulars were there on Sunday evening, at least not any of those who were allowed to drink eight years ago. Most of the people at the bar were barely twenty-one.

After a leisurely dinner, Trisha leaned back in her chair and groaned. "I suppose I should go home. If I'm lucky, I'll be asleep before my mother gets home," she remarked. "She was upset about the trip to California."

"My parents were still asleep when I slipped out," Sidney remarked. "I assume they got the note I left. I'll probably be grilled on where I went."

Trisha stared at Sidney and appeared interested in something other than the murder for a brief moment. "So what did you think when you saw Harlan for the first time in eight years?"

Sidney studied her friend's expression then shifted uncomfortably. "He's a little rougher than I remember. He lost his boyish charm, that's for sure."

"Like most men, he's become too serious," Trisha said simply. "What's he now? Thirty-five?"

Sidney pretended to think about it. "Yes, I suppose he's around that."

"Any old sparks?"

She shifted uncomfortably in her chair. "That was a long time ago, Trish. I had a childhood crush," Sidney replied dryly.

"Say it enough times, and you may even convince yourself it's true," Trisha muttered then eyed her friend. "Think you'll ever call him?"

"No," Sidney stated firmly. "We both have our own lives, and they certainly don't involve each other."

Trisha stared at the table and played with her spoon. "You know what I miss most about our childhood?"

Sidney tilted her head and listened.

"I miss you and me," she said softly. "We used to tell each other everything. Now we're lucky if we call each other twice a year just to say hello." Trisha looked up with tears in her eyes. "We were robbed of our best years. When Miss Fisher was murdered, a small piece of us died with her."

Sidney knew it was true. Nothing had really been the same after that day. They remained friends throughout high school, but they were both distant and withdrawn. It wasn't the same.

§

Sidney drove Trisha home, although neither spoke on the short drive. They said their goodnights, and Sidney returned to her parents' house. As she walked to the porch, she could hear her parents arguing from inside. Apparently, they hadn't heard her pull into the driveway. Sidney remained on the porch and listened to their heated discussion when she heard her name mentioned.

"It's all Trisha's fault," Herb proclaimed in anger. "She's a bad influence--with the way she's been acting lately."

"I'm just happy to have Sidney home," her mother scolded. "I don't want you shooting off your mouth, keeping her away another five years. She's a grown woman now. Did you expect her to return home and not think about it ever again?"

"You make it sound as if it's my fault she left in the first place," Herb snapped harshly.

"I never said that but you can't be playing the overly protective father anymore," her mother remarked. "She can do as she pleases without answering to you."

"Do as she pleases?" her father gasped. "Everyone in town thinks Trisha is completely mad. I don't want them saying the same thing about my little girl!"

Sidney had heard enough for one evening. She left the porch and took a walk around the surrounding development. The streets along the residential area were well lit with street lamps on each block. The evening was pleasantly warm, so there were several others with the same idea. She was a couple of blocks from her house when she saw Mrs. Randall and a much younger man approaching from the opposite direction. Mrs. Randall waved to Sidney as they drew near. She then realized the man was Billy Randall with his grandmother. He looked a little older, but he was still the handsome, quarterback heartthrob she'd remembered. He stood an impressive six-foot-two with broad shoulders, a big chest, and massive arms, though his light brown hair was now shorter with a more professional look.

"Sidney," Mrs. Randall announced cheerfully. "I'd heard you were back in town. It's been a long time."

Billy Randall's eyes swept over her, and a bright smile crossed his face. "You've certainly grown up. You look fantastic," he marveled while studying her. "I never should've gone away to college."

Sidney felt herself blush with embarrassment.

Mrs. Randall clung to her grandson's strong arm. "My Billy's a doctor now," she announced proudly.

"You're a doctor?" Sidney gasped with some surprise.

Billy nodded. "I'm doing my internship at the hospital in Brighten. I traded my football jersey for a scrub suit."

Sidney forced a tiny laugh. "That's wonderful. I never knew you were interested in medicine."

"When my knees began to give out on me, I realized I'd never go pro," he said with a soft laugh. "I had to make Grandma proud somehow." He swiftly changed the subject to her. "I heard you went away to college also. What do you do?"

"Not much in comparison, I'm afraid."

"Listen, I have to get Grandma home before the nine o'clock movie," he announced while grinning. Mrs. Randall patted his arm and smiled thoughtfully. "Grandma and I just moved to this development last year. I'd really like to talk to you some more. Why don't I give you a call sometime tomorrow, and we can go to Sam's Tavern one of these nights."

"Sure. Trisha and I were there tonight, but it was kinda dead," Sidney announced. "I'm told it can get pretty wild most nights."

"Trisha?" he asked with a note of concern then managed a smirk. "Yes, I forgot you two were close friends."

"Still are," Sidney added gently.

"Of course," he said while attempting to remain cheerful. "It's just that Trisha's been on some crusade lately. She hasn't been acting normal."

Mrs. Randall elbowed Billy. "I don't like hearing that kind of talk about that sweet child, especially from you."

"Sorry," he replied gently to his grandmother. He looked back at Sidney. "I didn't mean any disrespect, Sidney."

Sidney knew she couldn't defend Trisha's behavior herself. "She'll be fine in a couple of weeks. She's already coming around," she easily lied.

"That's great. Perhaps I could get Denny Phillips to join us," Billy announced. "The four of us will have a great time. I'm sure Trisha could use a night on the town."

Sidney knew that was the truth. "Yes, I think that would do her a world of good."

She knew Trisha had a crush on Billy several years back. Maybe an evening with him would stir some emotions.

"Billy, I'm going to miss my movie," Mrs. Randall said firmly.

He patted her hand linked onto his strong arm. "We won't miss the movie, I promise." He raised his brows to Sidney with mockery. "Would you like to join us at Grandma's house? We could rehash old times and talk about school."

It would have been the perfect way to find out more on Mr. Malcolm, but she was too tired even to consider being clever.

"I'd love to some other time," she said gently. "I've had an extremely long, tiring day, but I'd love to hear your thoughts on Mr. Malcolm sometime."

He laughed at the comment. "Malcolm, now there's a work of art. That'll be a marathon conversation in itself," he teased. "Let me know when you have a couple of hours."

"I'll do that," she said with a soft laugh.

Mrs. Randall began to pull on her huge grandson. "It's a really exciting movie, Billy."

"I guess I'd better get Grandma home or she'll have a coronary. Wouldn't want to practice my CPR tonight," he teased. "I'll call you later."

Sidney nodded and watched Mrs. Randall practically drag Billy along the sidewalk. Sidney laughed softly. She wondered how he lived with that woman all those years. It was a known fact that his grandmother practically raised him after his parents were killed in a fire when he was just ten years old. She watched them a few minutes longer then turned and headed back home.

§

Sidney clung to her pillow while she slept. Harlan was in all her dreams, allowing her to relive that scene in the airport several times. Sunlight invaded her pleasant dreams, forcing her back into reality. When she woke, she groaned and rolled onto her back. She stared at the ceiling for several minutes while the night's dreams still flooded her thoughts. It had been a long time since she'd hungered for a man. Unfortunately, it was the same man. She was supposed to meet Trisha at her house by nine-thirty, but she didn't think she'd be able to get herself together so soon. She forced herself out of bed and took a lengthy, hot shower. She was unable to shake Harlan from her mind. In her dreams, Harlan had kissed her back. The sensation of his lips against hers was overpowering.

By the time she reached Trisha's house, it was ten o'clock, and her friend had been impatiently pacing the porch. Trisha jumped off the porch and hurried to meet her halfway.

"You were a lot more punctual when you weren't so old," she remarked sternly. "We have to hurry if we want to catch Malcolm during his prep period at ten-fifteen. That'll give us about forty minutes to extract the affair from him."

Sidney shook her head while they walked. "You're not to say a word," she snapped lowly. "He's not going to confess to having an affair with Miss Fisher in the first five minutes, and if you put him on the defensive, he won't tell us anything. He doesn't have to talk to us at all if he doesn't want to."

"If the police in Marilina weren't so damned lazy, they would have done a better job while investigating the murder," Trisha snapped. "They didn't even want the Brighten Police getting involved until they were given no choice."

"They didn't have a reason to suspect anyone other than Alex," Sidney reminded her. "All the evidence and the motive pointed to him. The only thing missing was the murder weapon."

Trisha frowned. "I suppose Alex did look suspicious at the time."

Sidney rolled her eyes and wondered if Trisha even remembered what they had seen that day or if her memories were so distorted, she only remembered what she wanted.

Chapter Eighteen

Trisha and Sidney entered the school between classes. The hallway was congested with students visiting their lockers to exchange books for their next class. Sidney didn't know how Trisha knew Mr. Malcolm's schedule since they changed each school year. Trisha was a rather clever girl, but no one gave her enough credit because of her attitude. The kids talked with one another and horsed around in the halls. Some boys even threw football. Sidney immediately recognized the hefty boy who caught the ball. It was number fifty-two from the stone bridge the day she'd arrived. He smiled when he saw her and hurried to greet her.

"Hey, I didn't expect to see you here. Just couldn't live without me, huh?" he teased then eyed Trisha. "Hello, Miss Allister."

"Hi, Tim," Trisha muttered softly then looked away.

"We just came to visit some old teachers," Sidney remarked to the teenage boy.

The boy again looked at Trisha then grinned at Sidney. "You wouldn't happen to be McBride's daughter, would you?"

Sidney was slightly set back by his question. "Yes, I am. How did you know?"

"A lucky guess," he replied with some humor. "You were the one who found that teacher in the woods. You and Miss Allister. You didn't say anything about it the other day."

"I'll meet you there," Trisha remarked while frowning and walked down the hall.

Sidney watched her friend filter into the crowd of students. She focused her attention back on the boy. "It's not something I like to boast about," she replied simply.

"Are you kidding?" he asked as his eyes widened. "You were part of a historical event in this otherwise boring, little town. The old biddies have been thriving on that gossip for eight years. I did a report on the murder last year. Ms. Palmer helped me with it. I wanted to interview Miss Allister, but Ms. Palmer was totally against it."

Sidney studied him a long moment, surprised to hear that. "Really?"

"Yeah, I told you before; Miss Allister doesn't think the boyfriend did it. Some of the teachers have mixed feelings toward her because of that. They think she's a nutcase."

She frowned from his comment then forced a tiny smile. "Do you still have that report?"

"I think so, but I don't know where it'd be. If I find it, I'll drop it off at the press," he announced cheerfully. The bell rang for class. He laughed at himself. "Looks like I'm late again. Catch you later."

Sidney watched the boy run through the empty hallway. She wondered why Ms. Palmer had a problem with Trisha. Was the entire town so narrow-minded, that they couldn't bear to think the wrong man was convicted?

Sidney continued to ponder the credibility of the people she thought she once knew as she approached Mr. Malcolm's classroom. She could hear Mr. Malcolm's voice through the open door, forcing her to pause outside his room. She looked above the door and stared at his room number. Number eleven. Two vertical lines. Was there a connection? What was Miss Fisher trying to tell them by marking the rock? When she peered into the classroom, she saw Mr. Malcolm talking to Trisha in a firm, annoyed tone. Malcolm was a bit heavier than she'd remembered, mostly in the midsection. His brown hair was thin and graying.

Sidney knocked lightly on the door then entered. "I hope I'm not interrupting anything," she announced with a pleasant smile then glared at Trisha, threatening her with her eyes.

Mr. Malcolm saw Sidney and appeared enthusiastic. "Well, if it isn't Sidney McBride. How have you been?" he asked cheerfully. "Last I heard you were living in New York."

Sidney didn't expect such a warm response from a teacher she'd never liked. He'd always seemed so unfeeling while she was in school.

"I'm just home for a short visit," she replied pleasantly. "This place hasn't changed much in eight years."

Mr. Malcolm chuckled softly. "Marilina never does. What brings you to my classroom?"

"Just a little trip down memory lane," she replied with a warm smile then looked at Trisha and raised her brows. "Could I speak to Mr. Malcolm alone?"

Trisha frowned, appearing scolded, and left the room. Sidney closed the door behind Trisha then turned toward Mr. Malcolm and shook her head.

"I was so distraught when I discovered the strain she's been under," Sidney said gently then forced a nervous smirk. "She's really had a tough time since the murder."

Mr. Malcolm sighed deeply and sat on the edge of his desk. "Yes, I'm afraid she's having some sort of delusional fantasy about Trexler not being the killer. One day someone will have to lock her up if she keeps going at this rate."

Sidney sighed sadly. "I hope it doesn't come to that," she said. "She has this feeling that the entire town is pitted against her. Of course, we know that isn't true. I'm sure everyone just wants what's best for her."

"Of course."

"I've also been told you've been forced to suffer some indignities as well," Sidney remarked sympathetically.

He groaned then shook his head. "She believes I was involved in Emily's death." He snorted a laugh. "What possible reason would I have to kill that woman? She was a wonderful and brilliant teacher. All the students loved her."

"I'm inclined to believe you," Sidney said and sat on one of the small desks. Sidney remembered several feuds between Mr. Malcolm and Miss Fisher. It was odd his opinion had changed since the murder. She sighed and shook her head. "Simply tragic." She forced a light smile. "How's Mrs. Malcolm these days?"

Mr. Malcolm hesitated then sighed. "We're divorced nearly eight years."

"Oh, I'm sorry to hear," Sidney replied. "I suppose she found out about you and Miss Fisher."

Paul Malcolm stared at Sidney with a shocked look on his face. "What are you talking about?"

Sidney smirked and tilted her head to one side. "Come now, Mr. Malcolm. Everyone knew you and Emily Fisher were having an affair," she said casually despite her trembling body. It was a risk, but she decided she had to take it.

"I--I don't know what you're talking about," he snapped lowly. "There was nothing between Emily and me. Who told you such a ridiculous story?"

Sidney hesitated a moment wondering if Harlan had been mistaken then smiled with confidence. "Several people witnessed your friendly behavior at Sam's Tavern." She then pretended to consider something. "I wonder? Did Alex Trexler know about the affair? I mean, he was tending bar around the same time you left with her, wasn't he?"

Paul continued to stare at her with astonishment. He lowered his head then looked away. "Alex wasn't the type who noticed much. The fool believed anything she told him. She had that effect on most people." He looked back at Sidney with a defensive look. "My involvement with her was a short-term thing. I saw her three, maybe four times before I realized she was playing the entire field. It wasn't worth my wife finding out."

"Too bad she did anyway," Sidney remarked sympathetically while shaking her head, though she didn't have anything to back up her assumption.

"Yes," he said with a soft sigh. "I could never prove it, but I think my wife told Alex about Emily's indiscretions with me. When I heard them arguing in the hallway, I had the impression it was about me, though I couldn't be positive. It didn't matter," he announced and groaned. "Emily was not the type of woman any man could ever have for very long. She was sleeping around with two others apart from Alex and myself. She had her eyes on that guy that worked for your father. You know--the foreign fella. But I don't think he took to her. At least, he never left Sam's with her."

"Yes, Harlan, right? What else do you remember about him?" Sidney asked although it didn't have any pertinence to the case at hand.

He shrugged with little interest. "He left town shortly after the murder. It was rather suspicious. There was talk that he may have been involved, but I don't pay much mind to gossip," Mr. Malcolm informed her. "If you want gossip, you'll have to talk to Mrs. Randall and Mrs. Cooper."

"I'm aware of their reputations," Sidney remarked with a warm smile. "I don't really remember much about the day Miss Fisher was killed, and my father is reluctant to talk about it. Was there anything about that day that seemed unusual or out of the ordinary? Did she give any indication that she was meeting Alex or anyone else that afternoon?"

"Apart from her fight with Alex, she was her usual, perky self. I do remember she left school just as soon as all the students had left," he informed her. "She seemed in a bit of a hurry. I believe she talked to Ms. Palmer before she'd left. I thought she might have had a date by the way she flew out of here. I just figured she was looking for another conquest."

Sidney managed a polite smile. "It's been good talking to you, Mr. Malcolm."

"Oh, please, call me Paul. You're not my student anymore," he remarked with a tiny laugh. "If you're leaving, please take Trisha with you, okay?"

She nodded. "I will."

Sidney gave a slight wave and returned to the hall where Trisha paced. Sidney grabbed Trisha's arm and pulled her down the hall and away from Malcolm's room, out of earshot.

"Well, what did he say?" Trisha demanded to know as they left the school.

"He admitted to the affair and collaborated the story Harlan told about Miss Fisher having several affairs."

"So what do we do now?" Trisha practically gasped. "If he had an affair, he could have murdered her as well, right?"

"We're not doing anything with that information right now," Sidney remarked simply. "We really need to visit with Mrs. Randall and Mrs. Cooper. If anyone in this town knows anything, it has to be them."

"Mrs. Randall is doing her usual volunteer work at the library. She'll be walking to Mrs. Cooper's house in about an hour for tea and her usual dose of gossip," Trisha replied. "Do you want to talk to them alone or together?"

"I think they'll say more if they're together. I've always noticed how they feed off each other."

"Yes, they encourage each other rather well," Trisha muttered under her breath. "We'll escort Mrs. Randall to Mrs. Cooper's house."

"We have time for an early lunch," Sidney informed her friend. "Let's stop at the diner. We can intercept Mrs. Randall when she passes."

"That's a good idea. I am kinda hungry," Trisha replied.

"You're hungry because you don't eat enough," Sidney remarked bluntly. "You'd better start taking care of yourself."

"I shower every morning," Trisha stated. "What more do you want?"

Sidney glared at her friend. "A little color to your skin, less dark circles under your eyes, and a little more meat on your bones." Sidney looked away and groaned. "Honestly, you look like a poster child for some third world country."

Trisha became unusually silent as they approached the diner. Sidney looked at her and gently bit her lower lip.

"I'm sorry, I didn't mean it," Sidney said softly.

Trisha paused just outside the diner and forced Sidney to look at her. "I do look as if death warmed over, don't I?"

Sidney held her breath. "You've looked better. I'm a little worried about your health," she said honestly.

Trisha forced a tiny smile. "If you'd move back home, you could get on my case more often. I'd probably get tired of hearing you nag and eventually listen."

Sidney laughed softly. "Now that's the Trisha I remember."

Chapter Nineteen

The two, young women entered the diner and received a warm reception from Mary Allister. Despite her mother's enthusiasm to see them, Trisha purposely sat at a booth so her mother couldn't listen to their conversations.

"Mrs. Randall knows you better than she knows me, so I suggest you do most of the talking," Sidney informed her. "Just keep it casual."

"Oh, come on," Trisha remarked lowly. "They both know my views on the murder. We just need to give them a topic and watch their tongues wag."

"Then it shouldn't take much to coax them onto the subject," Sidney announced. "I'll bring up something about the murder and allow them to take it from there. That boy in the hallway said it's one of their favorite topics."

Trisha gave her a surprised look. "They never say much about it to me."

Sidney let out a slight laugh. "That's probably because it's you they're talking about."

"There's nothing funny about that," Trisha muttered. "I'm not thrilled about being the topic of gossip. This town doesn't take kindly to views that aren't their own."

Mary brought their sodas to the table. "Why don't you two sit at the counter so we can talk while I work?"

Trisha gave her mother a tiny smile. "Those chairs aren't the most comfortable, but thanks for offering."

Trisha's mother gave them a suspicious look then returned to the counter. Sidney leaned back in the booth and studied Trisha while she drank her soda.

"Have you ever considered the possibility that Alex may have killed her?" Sidney asked while raising a curious brow. "I mean, I will admit there are some unanswered questions and some possible suspects and motives, but the facts are stacked against him."

Trisha played with the straw in her soda without looking up. "I need to be sure," she said simply. "It's just something I feel needs to be done."

Sidney nodded and leaned forward. "But after we've interview everyone who possibly knows anything about the murder, will you give it up if there's nothing to prove his innocence?"

Trisha looked at Sidney and tilted her head. "If you can prove beyond a shadow of a doubt that no one else could possibly have killed her, I'll give it up."

Sidney knew that wasn't as easy as it sounded.

§

Sidney and Trisha no sooner finished their sandwiches when they saw Mrs. Randall enter the press just across the street from the diner. Sidney left some money on the table, and both hurried out the door without a word to Mary. They crossed the street, slowed their pace, and casually entered the press. Mrs. Randall was already in the back speaking to Sidney's father. As they approached the back counter, Herb smiled when he saw them.

"What brings you ladies here this afternoon?" he asked pleasantly.

"Just taking a walk and catching up on gossip," Sidney casually replied then beamed with delight. "I heard the most fascinating thing today, Dad. You just won't believe it."

Mrs. Randall turned her head slightly and listened with great eagerness.

Trisha elbowed Sidney with a stern look. "You can't repeat what you've heard. It wouldn't be right."

Mrs. Randall no longer appeared interested now that she wouldn't get the juicy gossip.

Trisha took Sidney's arm and smiled at Herb. "If you'll excuse us, Mr. McBride, we have some things to discuss."

Sidney and Trisha left the press and walked along the sidewalk at a leisurely pace.

Sidney glared at her friend. "You didn't even give her time to respond," she announced lowly. "That wasn't what we rehearsed. What if she doesn't care?"

"Just wait and listen," Trisha said confidently.

They didn't even get beyond the press building when Mrs. Randall called to them.

"Trisha, Sidney, wait up," Mrs. Randall called out. "I'll walk with you."

They turned as the short, elderly woman hurried to catch up with them. She moved like a penguin. Neither had seen the woman move so fast before. Mrs. Randall squeezed between them and linked onto each of their arms.

"I was just thinking about you as I entered the press. It'd be lovely if the two of you would join Mrs. Cooper and myself for tea this afternoon," she announced sweetly. "If you want to catch up on local gossip, we've got some for you."

"Oh, that sounds terrific, Mrs. Randall," Trisha announced. "If you're sure Mrs. Cooper won't mind."

"Don't be silly," Mrs. Randall boldly stated. "Mrs. Cooper loves visitors for tea. Why just the other day we had Mrs. Lamont over. She told us a fascinating story about a fight that broke out at Sam's Tavern on Friday night. Even my Billy won't tell me when something exciting happens there." She frowned. "I have to hear about it from others."

They walked to Mrs. Cooper's house while Mrs. Randall told them everything they never wanted to know about Mrs. Lamont, sparing few details.

"Well," Mrs. Randall gasped dramatically as they walked onto the porch. "When I found out she'd had an affair with a priest, I nearly went through the floor. They're supposed to be above physical pleasure. Not to mention what Mrs. Lamont must have been thinking. She's a married woman." She cried out dramatically. "Her husband comes and goes so often with his truck driving job.

Though I don't doubt that he's getting a little on the side as well. You know how those men are."

Mrs. Randall paused before the door, knocked once, then opened the door and entered. "Hello, Ester? It's me. I brought some friends for tea."

Mrs. Cooper approached from the kitchen while wiping her hands on her apron as her smile broadened. "Oh, Trisha and Sidney. What a lovely surprise!"

They were ushered into the formal living room with its old, Victorian furniture and tacky carpeting with large, printed shapes. Tea was wheeled into the room on a decorative cart by Mrs. Cooper. Trisha attempted to help, but Mrs. Cooper wouldn't hear of it. Mrs. Cooper was an extremely independent woman. She boasted about her health and how she had been better since they had removed the cyst from under her arm. Sidney and Trisha sat in complete silence while the two women sipped tea and talked about nearly everyone in town. Sidney never heard so much gossip in her entire life. They had to fake interest before they could enter with their own gossip and get the old women started.

"I also heard from a very reliable source," Mrs. Randall started the new topic with her usual line, "that Mrs. Peters' granddaughter is pregnant."

Mrs. Cooper exaggerated a gasp. "I always knew she'd be pregnant before she was eighteen. Who's the father?"

"You'll never guess," Mrs. Randall announced while raising her thin, gray brows.

Sidney wasn't going to last through much more. She nervously began to tap her cup until Trisha nudged her.

"Who?"

"The Shetler boy," Mrs. Randall replied with a brilliant smile.

"No," Mrs. Cooper gasped. "He was dating some colored girl from the city."

"No, no, dear. They broke up because her father didn't approve," Mrs. Randall said.

"Really? How did I miss that one?" Mrs. Cooper asked.

When Mrs. Cooper brought a notebook out from under the sofa cushion, Sidney thought she'd drop her teacup. Trisha looked away and fought her laughter. Mrs. Cooper jotted something in her little book then replaced it. Sidney set her teacup on a coaster on the end table and gently cleared her throat, creating her own opportunity to end her torture.

"I heard the most interesting story about Paul Malcolm," Sidney announced.

Both older women looked at Sidney with great interest. "Paul Malcolm? What have you heard?" Mrs. Cooper eagerly asked as her eyes widened with glee.

"He was having an affair with Emily Fisher just before she was killed," Sidney remarked, hoping to spark an interest in the conversation about the murder. Trisha would need to help keep the conversation going.

Both women waved their hands. "Oh, that's old news. Mrs. Malcolm told us that one right after she'd left him," Mrs. Cooper said simply. "Emily was fairly easy, from what I've heard. That's why her boyfriend killed her. He was enraged with jealousy."

Mrs. Randall turned to Mrs. Cooper. "Did you hear that Paul was at Sam's again Saturday night? I heard he was so drunk that he had to sleep on the floor."

"I also heard Emily had been seeing that photographer from the press," Mrs. Cooper added.

"He left only a week after the murder," Trisha prompted.

"No one really ever knew why he'd left," Mrs. Cooper remarked and leaned back on the sofa.

"Some speculate he was indirectly involved in her death," Mrs. Randall said firmly. "Why else would he just up and leave?"

Mrs. Cooper shook her head. "I don't believe that for a moment. I think he was heartbroken, and that's why he left."

"He was always such a womanizer, that one," Mrs. Randall remarked simply. "Sam said he saw Emily crawling all over him one evening. It was nearly pornographic."

Mrs. Cooper nodded her head vigorously as if either of them had actually been there and saw it.

Sidney shifted uncomfortably. "That entire day is just a blur to me," she said simply while prompting the conversation along. "What do either of you remember about the day Emily Fisher was murdered?"

"The only thing I remember," Mrs. Randall responded promptly, "was seeing Emily enter the woods. About twenty minutes later, that horny photographer passed my house in the same direction. I remember it very well because I was thinking they were probably going to meet somewhere and do the dirty deed."

"I remember seeing him walk past my house, but I can't say I saw Emily that day. Obviously, she'd been past," Mrs. Cooper replied.

"I took Billy to the mall for some new sneakers. His were all worn," Mrs. Randall announced simply. "The mall was crowded that day because of the approaching storm I suppose." She tilted her gray head and appeared curious. "Why do you suppose people like to shop in the rain?"

"Something to do," Mrs. Cooper replied. "No one wants to sit home on a dreary day. Although, I hate walking with packages in the rain." Mrs. Cooper raised a thin, gray brow. "But it didn't rain that day, dear. I was grocery shopping. I wouldn't have gone if there was a chance of rain."

"Of course, you're right," Mrs. Randall said after only a moment of reflecting. "But speaking of malls, I saw Persha Palmer at the mall yesterday."

"Persha?" Mrs. Cooper asked with a sly smile and raised her brows knowingly. "Was her girlfriend with her?"

"Of course," Mrs. Randall replied with a tiny laugh.

Trisha bolted forward. "Persha Palmer? The schoolteacher?"

Both women looked at her and nodded knowingly. "After all these years, we finally know why she'd never married. They moved in together just last week," Mrs. Cooper whispered and slyly pointed toward the woods. "Right next door. They have that tacky, pink flamingo mailbox."

Trisha slowly sat back in her chair. "Well, I'll be--"

Sidney rolled her eyes and nudged Trisha. "I think it's time we took our leave," she said simply and stood.

She'd had enough gossip for one day. Trisha took her cue and stood as well.

"Thanks for the tea," Trisha said.

"Anytime," Mrs. Cooper announced.

They showed themselves to the door. It was a little after five o'clock already and the entire afternoon was wasted on idle gossip that told them little more than Ms. Palmer was a lesbian. Sidney opened the door and saw Billy on the other side about to open it himself. He smiled with enthusiasm when he saw them and paused in the doorway.

"What an unexpected surprise," he announced warmly. "What brings two young women to the old henhouse?"

Sidney laughed softly. "Just some tea," she replied.

"I guess I won't have to call you now," Billy said simply. "Denny is excited about the four of us going out. How does tonight sound? There's this really great Italian restaurant just off the interstate. After dinner, we could go to Sam's for some dancing in his new club. You do like to dance?"

Trisha looked at Sidney with some confusion.

Sidney continued to smile and ignored the look she'd received. "That sounds great, Billy. Why don't you pick us up at Trisha's house?"

"How does seven o'clock sound?" he suggested. "That'll give me just enough time to tear Grandma away from Mrs. Cooper, make reservations, and shower."

Sidney nodded. "That's fine. We'll see you and Denny then." She slipped out the door and pulled Trisha behind her.

"I don't want to go on a double date with Denny," Trisha protested just out of earshot and turned to face Sidney.

"It'll give us an opportunity to question some of the regulars at Sam's," Sidney said simply. "I'd also like to talk to Billy about Mr. Malcolm."

Trisha muttered under her breath. "I don't like this, Sidney. I never liked Denny, and I've outgrown Billy Randall."

"I'm not asking you to marry either of them," Sidney remarked. "It's just a couple of hours. You may even enjoy yourself."

"I doubt it," Trisha muttered under her breath. She then sighed. "But I suppose you won't let me out of it."

Chapter Twenty

Billy and Denny arrived a few minutes after seven o'clock that evening in Billy's brand new sports car. Trisha was still complaining about being forced on a date with Denny, but she put on a false smile when they arrived at the door. The restaurant was rather expensive, though the dress was casual. They had a great meal with a bottle of moderately expensive wine. Sidney didn't like wine, but she drank it anyway. The dinner conversation was mostly about their current careers, leaving Trisha silent for nearly half an hour.

After dinner, they went to Sam's and found a table in the club portion of the tavern. There weren't many people at the club that particular evening. Most of the crowd came on a Friday and Saturday night. Sidney had noticed Mr. Malcolm was at the bar in the tavern area. Billy and Denny went to the bar for their drinks, leaving Sidney and Trisha alone for the first time all evening. Trisha played with the ashtray on the table without saying a word.

"Are you okay? We won't stay long if you don't want to," Sidney said gently.

"I'll survive," she said softly.

The guys returned with their drinks and joined them at the table. "Bill tells me you've been gone for five years, Sidney. Why'd you stay away so long?" Denny asked, seeming curious.

"Too many bad memories," she replied with a faint smile and studied Denny. He was a fairly attractive man with dark brown, almost black hair, small eyes, and a cleft in his chin.

Denny's eyes then widened with realization. "Oh, that's right. You were with Trisha when she found Miss Fisher. I forgot. I'm sorry."

"It was quite traumatic," Sidney informed him simply and shifted uncomfortably.

"I can't blame you for wanting to stay away," Denny said simply.

Sidney then cocked her head to one side and raised her brows. "You were a senior at the time, weren't you? What did you think about the murder?"

"Naturally we were all shocked," Denny replied. "The entire football team adored Miss Fisher."

"She was the best teacher," Billy said while leaning forward. "If you ask me, they should have strung Alex Trexler up by his--" Billy appeared tense and sat back. "Sorry."

"There were all sorts of stories surrounding her death," Denny continued. "But I didn't buy into them."

"What sort of stories?" Sidney asked with great interest.

"You know," Denny began. "That Mr. Malcolm killed her. Even rumors about that photographer from your father's press. But the evidence against Alex was overwhelming."

Trisha suddenly straightened in her chair. "The murder weapon was never found," she stated firmly. "The entire case is based on circumstances and our eyewitness accounts of Alex being at the murder scene. Just because he was there, that doesn't necessarily mean he did it."

"She was raped," Denny snapped and leaned halfway across the table toward Trisha then pounded the table with his finger. "It was conclusive that Alex raped her."

"No," Trisha hissed with irritation. "It was never proven she was raped just that they had been together, which he admitted they had."

"Sure, Trisha," Denny snorted and gave her an irritated look. "If I held a knife to your throat and threatened to kill you, you wouldn't struggle either."

"I'd fight you to the death," Trisha snapped.

"Okay, kids," Billy announced firmly. "Let's just give it a rest. What's done is done. I'm sure the evidence spoke for itself. Can we just enjoy this evening?"

Trisha looked back at the ashtray with narrow, evil eyes. Denny leaned back in his chair and glared at Billy.

"Maybe Trisha and I should go home," Sidney said softly, feeling the tension.

Denny lifted his eyes in gesture to Billy. He was obviously onboard with the idea.

Billy sighed and reluctantly nodded. "I'll give you and Trisha a ride home."

Sidney stood and offered a timid smile. "Thanks anyway, but I think we'll walk."

Trisha sprang to her feet with a sigh of relief.

"Just one dance?" Billy asked charmingly and extended his hand to Sidney.

Sidney politely nodded. Trisha frowned and fell back into the chair. She crossed her arms over her chest and sneered at Denny. Billy took Sidney to the dance floor where they danced to the slow song with a little space between them.

"I'm really sorry, Billy," Sidney remarked. "I didn't think she'd react like this."

"It's okay, Sidney. I know how Trisha has been since the murder," he replied. "I had hoped the subject wouldn't come up. I honestly didn't think Denny would mention it. Guess I shouldn't have given him any credit for intelligence."

Sidney groaned softly and looked over Billy's shoulder while they danced. "It's just killing her, I can see it, but I don't know what I can do."

"You can't save her if she doesn't want to be saved," he replied gently.

Sidney met his gaze and stared into his eyes. She couldn't deny he was quite handsome and understood why Trisha had a crush on him all those years ago.

"I just wish I could believe she's completely wrong about the murder," Sidney remarked.

Billy stared at her with some confusion. "You don't think Alex did it?"

"I don't know what I think anymore," she said with a soft sigh. "I'm getting so disoriented about the whole thing. There are too many stories, but none of them seem to match."

"There was a time I believed that photographer may have had some involvement. I mean with the way he ran off as soon as the dust had settled. It was just odd."

"I don't understand the reason behind that thinking," she announced. "I'd like to think I knew him better than anyone else in this entire town, and I'm sure he didn't have anything to do with what happened to her."

Billy shook his head as his eyes narrowed. "You were just fifteen. You couldn't possibly see him for what he was," he informed her. "He was a nasty son-of-a-bitch to me, but I'm sure you didn't know that."

Sidney was taken aback by the comment. "Did something happen between the two of you?"

"I don't want to upset you because I know how close you were at one time, but he had it out for me," Billy informed her. "He'd give me dirty looks all the time when Denny and I passed the press. Then there was the evening we ran into him as he was coming out of Sam's. He was drunk and smelled of whiskey. He said several obscene things to this girl we were with. Naturally, I stepped in and told him to leave her alone. He got mad and hit me. I tackled him to the ground," Billy said then grinned. "It was a great tackle--" He then cleared his throat, knowing he had gotten off subject. "I guess I knocked him out or he passed out because he was so wasted. That was it. Then we left."

"He hit you?" Sidney asked with some disbelief.

"He most certainly did," Billy said with a slight groan. "Right in the face. Lucky for me he was intoxicated and didn't swing very hard."

"Why do you think he'd want to kill Miss Fisher?" she asked boldly.

"I think he wanted her and she wanted no part of him. He did follow her into the woods that day. My grandmother saw him," Billy admitted. "I'd love to know what happened in the woods. I mean, what could he really photograph in there? A couple of trees and a rundown house?"

Sidney held her breath a moment and remembered the pictures Harlan had taken that day. They were rather good. The quality of the pictures told her he had taken his time when he took them.

"So what was between you and him anyway?" Billy asked, taking Sidney off her guard.

She stared at him a moment and felt her cheeks redden. "Nothing that I was aware," she replied. "I mean, he worked for my father at the press, and we'd sometimes talk." She raised a brow and a mocking smile. "As for anything else, you must remember he was ten years my senior, and I was just a kid."

Billy now looked embarrassed. "I'm sorry. Sometimes you hear things. It was stupid even to ask," he apologized. "It's just that I heard many different stories after he'd left town. Some thought he knew something about the murder, some thought he had a fight with your father, and others insisted he got some girl in trouble. We assumed that girl was you. Obviously not."

Sidney was stunned while staring at him. "People actually thought Harlan and I were messing around? I can't believe someone would make up a story like that. Don't people in this town have anything better to do?"

He chuckled and appeared humored. "No, I don't think so." Billy didn't release her when the song ended. "Sidney, would you consider going out with me, just the two of us?"

Sidney considered it a moment then offered a pleasant smile. "Give me a call sometime. We'll talk about it then."

"I'll do that," he said.

Sidney and Trisha left the club through the tavern. Both looked at Mr. Malcolm where he sat at the bar with his back to them as they passed. He sounded as if he'd had a few too many already. Sam poured Malcolm another drink, while he spoke about the problem with kids today. They left the tavern and started on their long walk back to their homes.

§

Sam's Tavern was down the road from the school in the opposite direction of town along the main road. By taking Cressman Road back to the development, the trip may have been a couple of minutes shorter than by traveling through town, but Cressman Road was always dark, and they would risk being hit by passing cars. They passed the motel just fifty yards from Sam's Tavern. Sidney was surprised to see a car parked before the rooms. It was rare for anyone to rent rooms during the week. Most of their customers stayed on weekends and seldom longer than an hour or two. The high school was just across the street from the motel. There were several automatic lights on in the parking lot, but the school itself was dark and quiet.

The night was warm with a gentle breeze. It was almost full moon, so their walk to town was well lit. Once in town, there were streetlights along the main street.

"I'm sorry, Sidney," Trisha finally spoke. "I didn't mean to lose my temper with Denny. I didn't want to spoil your good time with Billy."

"You didn't spoil anything, Trisha," Sidney remarked. "You're scaring me, that's all. You just have to accept that no one here wants to consider what you're saying."

Trisha turned toward Sidney and walked sideways. "But you believe me, don't you?"

"I'm forming an opinion," Sidney replied simply as they passed the many shops closed for the night. The diner remained open until ten o'clock.

"What do you think of *Dr.* Randall?" Trisha asked with a tiny smile as she now faced forward.

Sidney laughed softly. "That sounds funny, huh?"

"It's pretty amazing if you ask me," Trisha muttered. "He's a doctor, and he's got the body of an all-star quarterback." She sighed with defeat. "So why don't I want him?"

Sidney inhaled deeply and sank into thought. "I was wondering the same thing myself," she said softly while frowning.

"Really?" Trisha asked and looked at her with some surprise. "I thought you were interested in him."

Sidney shrugged then forced a weak smile. "He's really nice, though. Isn't he?" she asked and looked at her friend for her approval.

"Don't look at me. I'm a certifiable nutcase," Trisha replied simply.

They didn't talk the rest of the way home. Sidney left Trisha at her house then continued to her parents' home. The lights were on, but she didn't hear any sound from the inside. She entered the house and found her parents sitting at the kitchen table. Both looked at her when she entered. Her father stood and appeared concerned.

"Are you all right, baby?" he asked while putting his arms around her.

She tilted her head and looked at him with some confusion. "Of course I'm all right. I was just out on a date. I don't see the need for you to worry."

Her father pulled away but held onto her shoulders. "A man called for you tonight. He sounded *strange*. When we asked who was calling, he hung up."

Sidney laughed softly and waved off their concerns. "That was probably someone from the hotel. I left Jim in charge," she informed them. "He gets a little hyper when things go wrong. I'll call him in the morning."

Her father didn't appear satisfied. "I just didn't like the way it sounded. I was worried you and Trisha had upset someone," he remarked. "I hope you two haven't been harassing Paul Malcolm. I don't trust that man when he's drunk."

"I'll be fine, Dad. We haven't harassed anyone, I swear," she said and kissed him on the cheek. "Now, if you don't mind, I'm going to bed." She then raised her brows with a mocking smile. "Oh, by the way. If the police come around looking for me, you haven't seen me."

Her parents glared their disapproval then smirked at the joke. Sidney laughed softly and headed for the stairs.

Chapter Twenty-one

Sidney was up at dawn's first light. Unfortunately, lack of sleep was becoming a way of life for her. She was showered and taking a walk by six in the morning. The days could be rather hot, but the mornings remained cool in their slice of the country. She eventually entered the woods. Breakfast at the diner sounded like a good start to a bright, sunny day. She saw Trisha standing on the stone bridge looking toward the stream. She was a little surprised to see her up so early. Sidney walked toward her and leaned her back against the wall.

"Since we're both up, would you like breakfast? My treat," Sidney announced cheerfully.

Trisha appeared distant. "Did you ever feel as if it was you against the world?"

"Sometimes," Sidney replied and studied her friend.

Trisha continued to stare off the bridge toward the stream. Sidney thought Trisha was acting a little stranger than usual this particular morning. Sidney didn't take her eyes off her.

"It's kind of funny," Trisha remarked softly with a slightly morbid smile. "Before you came to town, people thought I was crazy. Now, it would appear as if I've placed my neck on the chopping block, so to speak." She then straightened but didn't look away from the stream.

"I suppose we've ruffled a few feathers. It's not hard to do in this town," Sidney replied gently.

Trisha appeared to have gotten very little sleep again last night. The circles under her eyes were darker than usual.

"Oh, I'm quite certain we struck a chord somewhere," Trisha said with conviction in her voice. She then turned her head toward Sidney and stared at her a brief moment. Despite her calm disposition, Trisha's eyes revealed a deep fear. "Someone called me last night while we were out. He didn't leave his name or a message just said he'd call back. At two in the morning, he called back and said, you're going to die, bitch."

Sidney's eyes widened, and her mouth dropped open. Her heart pounded with fear while she attempted to speak. "Someone threatened to kill you?" she finally gasped.

Trisha raised her brows and nodded. She must have been in a state near shock, which was the only rational explanation for her behavior.

"Someone in this town wants me dead, so we must be onto something," Trisha remarked.

"Yeah," Sidney gasped. "The next bus out of town. You have to get out of here, Trisha. You can't stay, not after that."

Trisha snorted a laugh and smiled with a sinister look. "You must be kidding. We're close to the killer now."

"Closer than either of us wants to be," Sidney scoffed with fear. "Be sensible. You have to leave town. We'll go to my hotel in Manhattan."

Trisha's brows suddenly lifted with humor. "I'm not going anywhere."

"Trisha! Aren't you scared?" Sidney demanded to know. "I sure as hell am!"

"Oh, I'm frightened all right. I'm terrified out of my insane mind, but I'm not about to give up now." Trisha looked at Sidney and raised a suggestive brow. "We have caller ID on our phone. The phone company traced the number to a pay phone on the corner near the high school."

Sidney's eyes were wide with fear. "The school!"

"I have no choice but to stay, Sidney. Being scared has nothing to do with my decision," she insisted. "Whoever killed Emily Fisher stole a piece of my sanity, but I'll be damned if they're going to frighten me out of my home. This is my town and my life, and they can't have either."

Sidney was set back by Trisha's decision. Trisha again leaned on the bridge then pointed toward the bank.

"Then, of course, there's that little calling card," she announced simply.

Sidney turned and looked over the bridge toward the bank. A dead rabbit lay near the rock where they had found Miss Fisher eight years ago. A smiling face was painted on the rock with the animal's blood. Sidney gasped in horror and placed her hands over her mouth in an attempt to hold back her scream. Trisha turned and casually walked across the bridge heading toward town. Sidney tore her eyes away from the dead rabbit and ran to catch Trisha.

"You have to go to the police, Trisha!"

"The police?" Trisha scoffed with a slight laugh. "That fat, lazy, so-called sheriff isn't going to do anything. I have to go to work now."

"Work!" Sidney felt her entire body tremble as she briskly walked alongside her. "How can you possibly go to work?"

"I have to earn a living somehow," Trisha remarked simply.

§

Sidney walked around the library basement and sifted through several magazines and newspapers for the first couple of hours. She then paced the aisles. Trisha spun away from her computer and glared at Sidney.

"I think you should take a long walk, Sidney. You're starting to get on my last nerve," Trisha remarked lowly.

Sidney looked at her with the same concerned look she wore all morning. "And leave you alone?"

Trisha forced a smile and nodded. "Yes, please. Go get something to eat, talk to my mom, talk to your dad, talk to a wall, just go--anywhere."

"All right," Sidney said with a defeated sigh. "I'll be back in an hour."

"Take your time," Trisha muttered. "And bring me some coffee when you come back."

Sidney left the library and walked around town for a little while then finally ended up at her father's press. The same young man stocked some shelves and looked at her as she entered.

"Sidney, right?" he announced cheerfully.

"Yes," she replied, humored he knew her name already. "Is my father in the back?"

"No, your father went home," the young man announced. "He said he'd be back later to close. I think something needed to be fixed at the house."

"Did he seem upset?" Sidney asked with some concern.

"No more than usual when he has to run home unexpectedly," the young man replied. "I never got a chance to introduce myself. I'm Gerald."

"Nice to meet you, Gerald," she said and offered a tiny smile. "Anything exciting happening in the world today?"

"Found some woman hacked to death in her apartment," he replied simply. "They're going to do an autopsy to see what killed her. Have you ever heard of anything so ridiculous? Hello? The woman was chopped up. I think you can safely assume that's what killed her."

Sidney grinned at Gerald then sank into thought as her expression faded. "Autopsy?" she said softly.

"Yeah, you know; when they cut a person open." Gerald stared at her a moment. "Are you okay?"

Sidney's mouth opened slightly as she remained in thought. She then realized he'd been talking to her and looked at the young man.

"Uh, yeah, I'm fine," she replied then gave him a curious look. "Do you have a plastic bag I can borrow?"

Sidney walked down the corridor of the hospital clutching her plastic bag and darting concerned looks at the workers. She cringed at the smell of disinfectant and the flowery fragrance to disguise it. Sidney saw Billy Randall at the other end of the hall, and her heart nearly leaped into her throat. She was glad she'd caught him on duty. She hurried toward him while he talked to one of the nurses and took in an eyeful of him. She had to admit; Billy looked good in his green scrub suit. He then saw her, smiled, and excused himself. He walked toward her while wearing a boyish grin.

"Sidney, I didn't expect to see you here," he said cheerfully. "What brings you all the way out here?" He then looked oddly at the plastic bag in her hand. "Ah, you brought me lunch. How sweet."

A tiny, embarrassed smile crossed her face. "Not exactly. I need to ask you a favor."

"Sure. What's the favor?"

"Can you do an autopsy?"

Billy's eyes widened as he tilted his head. "A what?"

"An autopsy," she casually announced to lighten the mood. "It's when they cut something--"

"I know what it is," he remarked and shook his head with some surprise. "I just don't know why you're asking."

"Can you do them?"

"Well, I've seen it done before, but I'm not into forensic medicine," he explained simply.

Sidney gently bit her lower lip. "Would you be able to do an autopsy on a rabbit?" she asked and raised the bag.

Billy's expression dropped, and his mouth fell open as he looked at the bag. "A rabbit? You want me to do an autopsy on a rabbit?" he asked in a low whisper while nervously looking around the hall, making sure no one heard.

Her smile faded, and her eyes pleaded with him. "I have to know what killed the rabbit."

Billy stared at her then tilted his head with a concerned look. "That didn't sound good."

Sidney frowned. "I'm not referring to an old-fashioned pregnancy test, Billy. It's just something that's really important to me," she insisted. "I'll pay you for your time. I'm certain it's been shot, but I couldn't convince myself to cut it open."

He searched her eyes then groaned lowly. "How can I refuse that face?" He looked around the hall. "But not here. Meet me down in the morgue in half an hour. It's usually pretty dead down there."

Sidney groaned and rolled her eyes. "Doctors should be forbidden to practice humor."

"I thought I had a fairly good bedside manner," he replied with a chuckle. "My humor may be a little corny, but I didn't go through eight years of med school to do stand-up."

"You do this for me, and I promise I'll laugh at all your corny jokes," she said gently.

"Huh, wait until you get my bill," he teased.

"Thanks, Dr. Randall," she said with a teasing grin. "I really appreciate this."

§

Sidney waited outside the morgue and stood guard as a lookout while Billy performed his illegal autopsy. Thankfully, no one came anywhere near the hall. A short while later, the door opened, and Billy handed her the plastic bag while cringing.

"You can dispose of this," he announced then held a bullet between his fingers. "Here's the culprit. I don't know my guns, but I'd guess this came from a rifle."

She uncertainly accepted the bullet and grimaced. He laughed softly.

"It's clean," he teased then closed the door behind him. "So why did you want to know how a rabbit died? It's just a wild rabbit."

Sidney had taken considerable time to invent a lie that would satisfy him. "Someone killed this rabbit and left it on my porch. I hoped I'd be able to identify the person who did it," she informed him. "I really appreciate the risk you took for me. How much do I owe you?"

He smiled and waved his hand. "You don't owe me anything. I just dug the bullet out. I didn't exactly open her up. Besides, I was hoping to impress you with my doctor like abilities," he teased warmly. "I'll consider us even if you promise to have dinner with me some night this week."

She laughed softly and nodded. "You're on. Give me a call."

Chapter Twenty-two

Sidney returned to the library at three o'clock and hurried down the stairs to the basement archives. Trisha looked up from her computer and gave her a puzzled look.

"I was expecting my coffee a little earlier," Trisha remarked sarcastically.

"I forgot your coffee anyway," Sidney teased.

"So where were you all day?"

Sidney exposed the bullet between her fingers and smiled. "This is what killed the rabbit. I'm going to turn it over to the police and see if they can find the shooter. They may be able to find who threatened you."

"Doubtful. Sheriff Drukard isn't very useful, and that would probably match a hundred rifles in this hick town," Trisha remarked then sighed. "I have some bad news of my own. I'll have to work late tonight to make up for the day I missed."

Sidney nearly gasped with horror. "No, Trisha, you can't work late."

"Don't worry about me," she insisted. "I intend to lock the doors after the library officially closes. It'll just be until eight o'clock."

Sidney groaned while leaning against one of the bookcases. "I'll stay with you and keep you company."

"No," Trisha snapped sternly. "I won't get anything done with you pacing around. If you really feel the need to protect me, come back around eight o'clock. We can have a late dinner and walk home together."

"All right," Sidney said reluctantly with a sigh. "I'll be back around eight."

§

Sidney entered the municipal building just a block from the library. She walked through the empty building and approached the back office where she found Sheriff Drukard behind his desk. His feet were propped up while he slept. Sheriff Drukard was a plump man with a large, double chin, short, slicked-back hair, and a thin mustache. His beady eyes were small in comparison to his pudgy face. His mouth was open as he snored while his head tilted forward to the side, resting on his double chin.

"Sheriff," Sidney announced in a firm voice. He didn't rouse. "Sheriff!"

Sheriff Drukard's feet hit the floor, and he looked around with surprise. "What? What?" He looked at Sidney and moaned softly. "What can I do for you, darling?"

First off, he could start by not calling her darling. Sheriff Drukard wasn't very quick on his feet nor half as intelligent as he pretended to be. Thankfully, there wasn't much crime in their sleepy little town. Sidney set the bullet on the middle of his desk and straightened proudly.

"Last night, someone called Trisha Allister's house and threatened to kill her. This morning we found a dead rabbit as a warning to her," she announced then indicated the bullet. "This is the bullet that killed the rabbit."

He picked up the bullet, studied it, then set it down and looked at her. "This is the same bullet used by every hunter for miles. It could match any number of rifles. Where did you find the dead rabbit?"

Sidney inhaled deeply wishing she didn't have to give up that information. "On the bank by the stream. It was at the same place where Emily Fisher was murdered."

The sheriff groaned and rolled his eyes. "Missy, that rabbit could have been put there by anyone. There's no way to prove it was meant for Trisha Allister."

"Well, what about the threat she'd received?" Sidney demanded. "The phone call was made from the pay phone by the school. You could dust it for fingerprints."

He rolled his little eyes with their red, swollen lids and shook his head. "That phone is used by every student in the high school and people staying at the motel across the street. There wouldn't be one identifiable fingerprint on the entire booth. Even if there was, we can't fingerprint the entire town."

"So you're not going to do anything about it?" she demanded to know.

"There's nothing I can do. I have nothing to work with," he remarked simply.

Sidney frowned, left the office, and walked into the empty corridor. Trisha had been right. Sheriff Drukard was completely useless. She then heard his voice calling her. Sidney turned in the hall as he approached. He was panting from his short jog to catch up with her.

"There's something I'd like to discuss with you, darling," he announced sternly. "There's been talk around town that you and Trisha have been poking around in the Emily Fisher murder. You heed my warning, young lady. That case was solved eight years ago. If I hear any more about you harassing the good people of Marilina, I'll find something to charge you with." His look was threatening. "Do I make myself clear?"

Sidney tilted her head and folded her arms across her chest. "I have a New York lawyer," she announced sternly. "He'll slap you with a lawsuit so fast; you won't even be able to get work giving parking tickets."

Sheriff Drukard stared at her with a concerned look in his eyes then pointed a warning finger at her. "You just watch yourself, missy."

"It's *Ms.* McBride," Sidney snapped lowly and gave him a stern look. "I'm no longer a child, and I will not permit you to treat me as such."

Sidney proudly raised her head, turned, and walked out of the municipal building. She couldn't deny it felt good telling off the lazy sheriff. Sadly, it also meant she was no closer to getting any help from the local law either.

Chapter Twenty-three

Sidney headed into the woods and paused before the path leading to the old, stone house. Apart from that night in her dream, she hadn't been there since that day with Harlan eight years ago. Sidney traveled the path and eventually found her way to the stone house. She studied the house and old well from a distance. A tiny smile crossed her face as she approached the stone well. She walked around it and gently ran her fingers along the edge. She remembered the day she brought Harlan to this place. Sidney subconsciously climbed onto the well and teetered along the edge while her thoughts remained on Harlan. She walked the length of the well then paused by the post and hugged it insecurely behind her, remembering how Harlan extended his hand to her, and the first time she'd ever touched him. She drew a deep breath and sighed with sadness. She wished she could get Harlan from her mind.

"Don't fall," came a familiar, male voice.

Sidney's heart leaped in her chest. She spun around on the wall and stared at Billy. Her heart sank, but she was polite despite her disappointment.

"Sorry, didn't mean to startle you," he said and walked toward her with a pleasant smile.

Billy paused before her and extended his hand to her. She placed her hand in his, but the fireworks weren't there. He helped her to the ground and stood unusually close. Sidney backed up a step to put some distance between them then proceeded to walk around the well.

"Do you come here a lot?" she asked while avoiding looking at him.

Billy looked around the area then looked back at her. "Hardly ever. Unfortunately, for you, the two busybodies saw you walking past Mrs. Cooper's house. I hate labeling my own grandmother that way. I tried calling your house." He chuckled nervously with some embarrassment. "Your father answered in his usual polite tone and said you weren't home. I don't know why, but I figured you had to be here."

Sidney looked around the area and the fading light. "This place has some very fond memories and some very horrible ones."

"I played here as a young boy myself," he said simply. "Denny and I used to sneak into the basement of the house and smoke my father's cigarettes."

Sidney tilted her head and managed a tiny smile. "How old were you?"

Billy laughed. "Nine."

She rolled her eyes and hid her grin. "You smoked cigarettes at nine?"

"Yeah," he said with a soft chuckle. "Thankfully I outgrew that. Can I walk you home? Or drive you home? I have to pick up Grandma. We'll be heading that way."

"Why don't you walk me as far as the stone bridge," Sidney suggested. "I'll walk home the rest of the way myself. It'll be late until you tear those two apart."

"It's a deal," he replied.

They walked through the woods at a leisurely pace as Billy joked around about their day at the hospital. Halfway back to the bridge he took her hand in his and gave it a playful pat.

"I'll never forget the sight of you standing there with that plastic bag," he said and laughed softly. "You're full of surprises."

He held her hand the rest of the way to the bridge. Something stirred inside her, but it wasn't necessarily in a good way. She anticipated his next move with some anxiety then realized it wasn't that she didn't like Billy Randall; she just had a problem with men. There was absolutely no reason why she shouldn't desire this man. He was almost perfect in every way. Sidney stopped him before the bridge and gently removed her hand from his with some embarrassment.

"Thank you for walking me back."

"Anytime, Sidney," he said with a warm smile. "I'm on call for you twenty-four hours a day."

Sidney hoped to slip away without a confrontation, but before she'd even realized what had happened, his hand slipped behind her neck, and he kissed her passionately on the mouth. He pulled away just as quickly, grinned, and walked back toward town. Sidney was stunned a moment then watched him leave and exhaled with confusion. She didn't understand what her problem was with men.

"Was that as disgusting as it looked?" came a male voice from the bridge.

Sidney whirled around and saw Harlan leaning against the wall of the bridge with his hands casually in his pockets. Harlan had a sickened look on his face while staring in the direction Billy had headed. Sidney gasped softly with surprise at the sight of him. Her heartbeat quickened.

He met her gaze, straightened, and walked toward her. "Daddy won't like that one bit," he informed her bluntly.

"What are you doing here?" she gasped as her eyes widened.

"You mean other than becoming violently ill?" he muttered lowly and again stared down the path.

Once her heart had returned to its regular beat, Sidney managed a smile. "Oh, that's right. Billy said you two didn't get along," she remarked then raised a brow. "That must be one hell of a feud to hold a grudge after all these years."

"Ah, yes," he snorted. "Billy Randall, star quarterback. Mister high school spirit himself." He cast his back against a tree and sneered. "I have nothing but admiration for the little bastard," he growled lowly.

Sidney eyed him with a humored look. "He's a doctor now."

Harlan glared at her with a surprised look. "Doesn't that just figure for this town," he muttered lowly and looked around the woods. "I can smell the ignorance as it blossoms."

"You didn't answer my question," Sidney said gently. "What are you doing here?"

His eyes swept back over her, and a frown crossed his face. "I came back to prove something to myself."

"And what might that be?"

"That it's this town that had the problem and not me," he remarked lowly. "I can't believe a town can be so bloody proper yet have absolutely no morals."

"Did you just come back to insult my hometown?"

Harlan straightened and stared directly into her eyes. "I've decided to write an article on the murder of Emily Fisher. It seemed

119

like a good way to piss off everyone and maybe help dig up some information for you."

Sidney felt all the anger drain from her body. A warm smile crossed her face. "You came here to help me?"

He rolled his eyes and groaned lowly. "Not one of my more brilliant ideas."

Sidney sighed as relief filled her entire body. She fought the urge to throw her arms around him with gratitude.

"Just make sure you keep the good doctor away from me," he grumbled under his breath.

She remained overjoyed. "Wait until my father sees you after all these years," she said with anticipation.

Harlan's eyes widened as he stared at her. "I have no intentions to go to your parents' home," he said sternly.

Sidney was slightly taken back. Her shoulders sagged as disappointment swept over her. "Okay, so my house is out of the question. What if we go to Trisha's once she's out of work? She won't be out until eight o'clock."

"Where are you meeting her?"

"At the library."

"Why don't I meet you here at seven-thirty? We can go there from here," he suggested. "We can either talk at the diner or go back to my motel room."

Sidney's heart skipped a beat when she thought about going back to his motel room. She gently bit her lip and smiled lightly. "Okay. We'll meet back here at seven-thirty. Unless--"

"Unless what?" he asked.

"I was just going to suggest going with you, but I really need to get home and shower." She felt unusually dirty after handling the dead rabbit even though she had washed her hands.

"I need to make some calls anyway," he replied.

"I can appreciate that. I should make a couple of calls myself." Sidney fidgeted slightly. "I'm really glad you came back."

"Just do me a favor, and don't tell your father we spoke," he said simply.

Sidney became confused. "Why?"

"Just save us both the aggravation, okay?"

"Okay, Harlan," she replied softly. "I won't say a word to them, but will you tell me what happened between you and my father?"

"Maybe later," he replied. "Now's not the proper time."

Harlan turned and walked across the bridge then down to the stream. She watched him walk through the woods and scale the hillside to Cressman Road. She wondered what he was up to. Why was he being so mysterious? Who was he really trying to avoid? She held her breath and debated her own safety.

Chapter Twenty-four

Sidney ate very little that night at her parents' house since she was supposed to go to dinner with Trisha once she got off work. Her thoughts continuously strayed to Harlan. She picked at her food then realized her parents seemed unusually quiet. She wondered if they had been fighting a lot since she had moved away. It was odd that no one even spoke about what happened that brought her father home early from work. Sidney's father said he would help clean up after dinner. Sidney didn't mind bowing out on dishes then left the kitchen. As she headed toward the stairs, she could hear her parents talking quietly.

Were they talking about her? Her own parents? She shook her head and attempted to listen, but their voices were too soft. Sidney looked at her father's gun case just alongside the stairs. She found the key in its usual spot on top of the case. Her father didn't think anyone knew he kept the spare key there. She unlocked the case and removed a small revolver. She stared at the gun then thought about Sheriff Drukard. He'd love finding her in possession of a gun without a permit. He could make that one stick. She returned the gun and removed a six-inch stiletto dagger from the case in its sheath. With little forethought, Sidney attached the sheath clip to her pants and locked the case. She hurried to the nearby closet and removed one of her father's old blazers. She slipped into it to conceal the dagger attached to her pants. As she turned around, her father approached from the kitchen. Sidney's heart leaped into her throat as she nervously faced him. Had he heard her in the cabinet?

"Are you going out, Sidney?" he asked with a concerned look on his face.

"Yes," she said quickly. "I'm meeting Trisha at the library. We're going to hang out at the diner for a while, or maybe go to Sam's for a drink."

Her father frowned. "Before you leave, we need to have a talk."

Sidney knew something was bothering him, but she really didn't have the time to stop and discuss it now.

"What is it, Dad?" she asked while standing near the door.

"Your mother got a phone call today from Mary Allister," he said gently.

Sidney's heart sank. They knew about the death threat! She attempted to remain calm but didn't offer any information.

"She said Trisha received a death threat last night," he continued. "Someone called here last night for you as well."

Sidney drew a deep breath. "It's under control, Dad. I'm meeting Trisha at the library. We're going to stay together. It'll be all right."

"Yeah, more convenient for someone to kill you both," he remarked sternly. "I don't think you should go out tonight. I'll call Trisha's mother and tell her to pick Trisha up at the library. It's for your own safety."

"I'll be fine," she insisted. "I don't understand why you're so worried. You've told me you're convinced Alex Trexler murdered Emily Fisher. So this is just some hollow threat, right?"

Her father wasn't amused. "I'm almost positive he's the real killer, Sidney. But I'm not about to gamble with your life on my belief." He inhaled deeply. "There's something I think you need to know."

Sidney tilted her head slightly. Was he going to confess something he'd refused to tell her for eight years? Was there some piece of evidence he'd never told before?

"Your mother and I had a visitor today," he reluctantly informed her. "Harlan stopped by the house early this afternoon. He was looking for you."

Sidney's heart began to pound. She hadn't expected Harlan to stop by the house. It was no wonder he didn't want her mentioning she'd seen him.

Sidney forced a surprised look. "Harlan? You mean Harlan Brendan? Did he say what he wanted?"

"No," Herb replied sternly. "I told him to stay away from you. I didn't want to tell you this the other night because I know how close you two were at one time, but it was Harlan who had called here looking for you. He didn't leave his name, but there was no mistaking his voice. Around the same time, Trisha received a phone call as well. Later she received the death threat."

"It could be just a coincidence, Dad. No one called me later," she remarked simply.

"That's because I disconnected the phone before we went to bed," he insisted. "I didn't want him calling back looking for you."

Sidney stared at her father with some concern and surprise. Was it possible? "I'll take my car if it'll make you happy, but I am going to meet Trisha."

Her father suddenly groaned. "You're out of your mind, Sidney. What if you run into Harlan? You have to promise me you'll avoid him if you see him and come directly home."

Sidney inhaled deeply. "I'll keep an eye out for him, okay? I really have to go." She turned and hurried out of the house.

§

Sidney drove her car along Cressman Road then pulled to the side and looked toward the wooded area across the street. Where she parked would have been about where Alex had parked his car when he returned to the bridge and found Emily Fisher dead. Sidney took a deep breath, got out of her car, and crossed the street. She found the small path that led down the wooded hill to the stone bridge. She approached the bridge at seven-thirty, but Harlan wasn't there. She paced the bridge several minutes and studied the area with great caution. She waited twenty minutes longer without a trace of him. She had to meet Trisha at the library on time. She didn't want her waiting outside or doing anything as stupid as what she, herself, was doing right now. She could hear the sound of thunder in the distance. They were in for one hell of a storm tonight. Sidney was about to leave when she saw Harlan approaching from the direction of town. He hurried across the bridge and smiled with some embarrassment.

"Sorry I'm late," he announced as he approached. "I had to wait for a return phone call."

Sidney felt uneasy and shifted nervously. "Why didn't you tell me you stopped at my parents' house first?"

Harlan frowned. "It wasn't a very joyful reunion." He hesitated while studying her. "So what did he say?"

"He said I should avoid you," she snapped. "He also told me you had called my house last night as well."

"Yes, I called your house last night when I arrived in town," he replied. "I guess I need to work on my American accent, huh?"

Sidney's eyes widened in alarm as she stared at him. "You arrived last night?"

"Around nine o'clock," he replied simply. "I called from my motel room. You weren't there, so I tried Trisha's house."

Sidney's heart pounded with concern. Was it really a coincidence? She then remembered Trisha at the library.

"We'd better meet Trisha. My car's just up the hillside," she announced gently.

Harlan walked alongside her as they crossed the bridge then followed her up the hillside. Sidney felt very uneasy with him behind her. She no longer knew what to think about Harlan. There were too many unanswered questions. He always seemed to be at the wrong place and the wrong time.

Chapter Twenty-five

Sidney drove her rental car into the library parking lot after a very brief, but nerve-racking drive. Harlan and Sidney got out of the car and walked around the side of the building to the main entrance. The thunder rumbled loudly nearby causing both to look to the dark sky. Harlan tried the front door, but it was locked. It was five minutes before eight o'clock. Sidney leaned against the railing, folded her arms across her chest, and couldn't help saying what was on her mind.

"Don't you think it's time you told me what happened between you and my father?" she demanded to know.

"It's not something I really want to talk about," he replied with an uneasy look. "I'll tell you sometime, okay?"

Sidney glared at him with some anger.

He smiled warmly then laughed at her. "Come on, love. Don't look at me like that. Show a little trust here," he announced. "I'm not the enemy."

Sidney studied his handsome features and felt her cold heart melt. She couldn't help wanting him despite her suspicions. Perhaps she didn't have a problem with men after all. What was it about him that captivated her so? She again raised her defenses and placed her hands on the railing behind her.

"You want me to trust you, yet you won't explain the things I need to know," she said coldly.

"A little blind faith never hurt," he replied gently.

"A little blind faith can get a girl killed," she snapped then tilted her head and raised her brows suspiciously. "Last night Trisha received a death threat. The phone call was made from the pay phone next to the high school."

Harlan stared at her a long moment with a concerned look in his eyes. "Across the street from the motel?" he asked with a surprised look.

Sidney raised her brows and nodded her head. "Think you might be willing to work with me a little here?"

Harlan drew a deep, nervous breath then shook his head. "I didn't threaten Trisha. I don't even know Trisha well enough to want her dead."

"This isn't a joke, Harlan," she snapped. "Someone is making death threats. It must mean we're on to something."

"I know it's not a joke," he retorted lowly. "I also don't like the way suspicion always seems to point back to me. It's like this town is cursed or something."

"Just be honest with me," she said with a soft sigh. "Tell me what I want to know."

Harlan stared at her a long moment then looked at his watch. "I thought you said you were meeting her by eight?"

He turned toward the door and knocked with the old, brass knocker. Sidney groaned and shook her head. He'd never tell her what she wanted to know. He was very good at changing subjects in order to keep her in the dark.

"She won't hear you," she informed him. "She works in the basement archives."

"Is there another door?" he asked while giving her a curious look.

"There's a back door near the basement. She might hear you knock on that one," Sidney replied.

Harlan walked down the steps and headed around back with Sidney following. They approached the back door near what used to be the old garage. Harlan turned the knob.

"It's locked," Sidney replied with a smug smile. "She locked all the doors at closing."

The door opened. Harlan looked at her with a raised brow. "She forgot one."

Sidney became alarmed and bolted into the library ahead of him. The basement lights were still on, indicating Trisha hadn't left.

Sidney hurried toward the basement steps. Harlan grabbed her arm just before she reached the steps and pulled her back, proceeding down the steps before her. Sidney hurried behind him and strained to look over his shoulder. When they reached the bottom of the steps, Sidney slipped past him in the direction of Trisha's desk. Harlan once more grabbed her arm and forced her behind him as he walked down the aisle. They reached Trisha's desk, but she wasn't there. The computer monitor was turned off.

Sidney looked around the basement with some concern. "Where is she?" she asked more to herself.

"I'll check upstairs," Harlan announced then gave her a firm stare. "Wait here."

Sidney watched him leave then walked around the desk and collapsed into the chair with some confusion. She moved a couple of papers then noticed a plain envelope with her name typed on it. Sidney opened the envelope, removed the folded paper, and read the typed note aloud. 'Sidney, I can't handle the pressure anymore. Please don't be disappointed. I'll call when I reach my destination. Trisha.' Sidney stared at the typed note as horror crossed her face. She leaped up from the chair.

"Harlan!"

Only a minute passed before she heard thundering feet running down the old steps. Harlan rushed across the basement and stopped before the desk while scanning the area.

"What is it? What happened?" He then looked back at her with confusion. "What's wrong?"

She handed him the short, typed note. He briefly read the note then lowered the paper and looked back at Sidney.

"She left town?" he asked with surprise.

Sidney shook her head and remained frightened for her friend. "I'm positive she didn't. Look at the 'H's' in that note," she said while pointing at the paper. "This was typed on the same machine I used to write that poem to you."

Harlan studied the note more carefully then looked back at her. "What's so odd about that?"

"That particular typewriter is at the high school," she replied firmly. "Trisha didn't type this."

"You're telling me someone typed this letter at the school?" he asked. "That doesn't make any sense."

"Something's happened to her, Harlan," Sidney gasped softly. "She's been abducted or--"

Harlan set the paper down. "I think it's time we called the police."

"Sheriff Drukard? Do you really think he's going to do anything about this?" she practically demanded. "He'd be thrilled if he thinks she's gone. Besides, once he sees this letter, he'll deduct that she left town with no further investigation."

Harlan stared at her in silence for a long, uncomfortable moment. Sidney slowly sat in the chair and placed her head in her hand.

"I'll search the library in case she's here somewhere," Harlan said softly then left the basement.

Sidney ran her fingers through her hair and stared at the note. She knew Trisha hadn't left town. Earlier she vowed she'd never leave her home. There was no sign of a struggle and nothing to indicate a forced entry. She wasn't sure how long she sat there before she heard Harlan calling her from upstairs. Sidney bolted from the chair, grabbed the note, and ran up the steps. She found him in the front area with most of the non-fiction books and the checkout desk.

Harlan stood before a typewriter near the desk and inserted a piece of paper. He typed a couple of words then sighed softly. "This was the typewriter used to type that letter. The school must have donated the typewriter to the library. "

Sidney stood beside him and noted the position of the 'H'. She frowned and shook her head. "No. I'm telling you, Trisha didn't type this," she insisted. "She never left town, leastwise, not willingly."

"I believe you," Harlan announced simply and looked at her. "Why would she come up here to type a letter then go back downstairs to leave it on her desk, when she has a perfectly good computer and printer downstairs? It would have been far more convenient to type it on the computer."

Sidney studied Harlan. "Why bother typing a short note at all?" she asked sternly. "The only reason it wasn't handwritten is because she didn't leave it in the first place." She stared at him with concern. "We have to find her Harlan. She may be in serious danger."

As Harlan stared at Sidney, his eyes narrowed in thought. "Put that note in your pocket," he said firmly.

"Why?" she asked.

"You said the sheriff won't investigate her disappearance as long as that note is here, so we'll just get rid of the note. We'll call the sheriff and report her missing."

"That won't work," Sidney snapped irritably. "He's not going to do anything about it for at least twenty-four hours. I know he'll pass it off as her taking a walk or going out somewhere. He doesn't care much for either of us."

"Sounds like he wouldn't be able to find her even if he wanted to," Harlan replied and raked his fingers through his hair. He considered their next move then sighed. "Just hold onto that note. If she had been abducted, it's obvious we're supposed to believe she left on her own free will. Whoever took her may be hesitant to kill her if the town thinks she's missing."

Sidney nervously folded the note and stuck it in her jacket pocket. "What are we going to do?" she said softly with a pleading look in her eyes. "How can we find her?"

Harlan appeared to sink deep in thought then looked at Sidney. "Call her house," he instructed. "Make sure she didn't go home early."

"The door was unlocked," Sidney insisted. "She wouldn't leave without locking up. It's her job."

"Humor me," he remarked.

Sidney nodded then approached the phone on the desk and dialed Trisha's number. Mary answered on the second ring. Sidney jumped with anticipation.

"Hello, Mrs. Allister? Is Trisha there?"

"No, Sidney," Mary replied from the other end. "She's working late tonight. I'm expecting her home soon."

"Would you ask her to call me when she gets in? It's rather important," Sidney said while fidgeting. They exchanged goodbyes and Sidney hung up the phone. She fidgeted nervously while eyeing Harlan. "She's going to be a wreck when Trisha doesn't show up tonight."

"We can't worry about her mother right now. If Trisha had actually left town, I'm sure she'd notify her mother as well. By tomorrow morning, she'll call the police," Harlan said simply. "Until then, we'll just have to review all the people she'd discussed the murder within recent days. We'll go back to the motel. You have to tell me everything that's happened since you arrived in town. First thing tomorrow morning, we'll search her room. There could be an answer there."

"She kept a personal journal," Sidney interjected with a glimmer of hope.

"That could prove useful," he replied, seeming tense himself. "I think we should go."

They left the library, locking the door behind them. It had started to rain quite heavily while they were inside. They ran to Sidney's car and jumped inside. Sidney fumbled with her keys and started the car with trembling hands. She took a moment to collect her emotions then pulled away from the library and drove to the motel. Sidney pulled into the motel parking lot and stopped near the rows of rooms. Harlan gave her a puzzled look.

"Aren't you going to park?" he asked curiously.

She looked at him with some concern. "If my father sees my car parked outside the motel, he'll tear the place down looking for me."

Harlan rolled his eyes and groaned. "Your father can't dictate how you live your life forever. Either you want my help or you don't."

Sidney bit her lip then looked to Sam's just down the road. "I'll park my car there and walk back."

Harlan looked out the window at Sam's Tavern through the pouring rain then looked back at her. "Daft bird. You're going to be soaked."

"Just get out," she snapped lowly. "I'm not afraid of a little rain."

"No, just your father," he replied and opened the car door. "Room seven."

Sidney waited for Harlan to move away from her car before she pulled back onto the road. She parked her car in Sam's parking lot closest to the motel and ran the entire way. She approached room seven and knocked on the door. She was completely soaked from her brief run through the rain. Even the insides of her shoes were wet. Harlan opened the door and shook his head while staring at her. He then handed her the towel in his hand. She accepted the towel and entered the room with some apprehension. He closed the door behind her as she dried her hair and face.

"I'll get you something to change into," he remarked simply and removed one of his shirts from his suitcase. He handed her the shirt. "Here. At least it's dry."

Sidney wasn't about to argue with him. She took the shirt into the bathroom.

§

Sidney entered the bedroom from the bathroom while drying her hair. Harlan sat on the bed with his feet extended and crossed at the ankle while scribbling something on a notepad. Sidney didn't notice any chairs in the room, forcing her to join him on the bed. She put aside her insecurities and sat uncomfortably on the bed, tucking her legs beneath her. She felt a little less than comfortable in just his shirt and her underwear in his motel room despite that he didn't even look at her.

"I need a complete list of everyone the two of you spoke with since you arrived in town," he informed her without interrupting his writing.

Sidney shifted nervously. "Uh, well, we talked to you first. Then there was Paul Malcolm, Mrs. Cooper, Mrs. Randall, Billy Randall, Denny Phillips, and Sheriff Drukard."

He looked up from his notepad. "And with whom did Trisha discuss her views?"

Sidney groaned and rolled her eyes. "Just about the entire town knew her view on the murder. Trisha's always been very outspoken," she informed him. "She created quite a reputation lately, the way I'm to understand it."

"Did she upset many people?"

"Just about everyone," she replied then frowned. "Even my father was irritated by her recent behavior."

"That doesn't narrow the field any," he remarked while sighing as he tapped his pen on the pad. "Do you recall any one person being more upset than the others?"

"Denny was the most irrational. They got into a heated debate about the murder while we were at Sam's Tavern," Sidney announced. "It was so bad, Trisha and I left early."

"Who's Denny?"

"Billy Randall's friend from high school."

Harlan rolled his eyes then sighed. "What about Paul Malcolm?"

"I did most of the talking," Sidney replied. Her eyes then widened. "But I remember Trisha was talking with him about something before I joined them in his classroom. I think they were arguing. I heard she and Paul Malcolm were on very bad terms. Do you think he was holding a grudge?"

"It seems too convenient an answer," he replied. "But it'll be a good place to start after we search Trisha's room. In the meantime, where do you suppose he could stash a grown woman without causing suspicion?"

Sidney leaned on her elbow and thought about what he said. "I'm not sure. I don't even know where he lives," she announced. "He and his wife divorced, so he obviously moved."

Harlan continued to write on his notepad. "I'll look into that tomorrow."

They talked straight into the early hours of the morning. Sidney made herself comfortable and rubbed her tired eyes while Harlan continued to talk. His sexy voice was low and comforting. She closed her eyes only a moment to rest them.

Chapter Twenty-six

Sidney tossed beneath the covers and clutched the sheets just before she cried out, shooting upward in the bed. Her heart pounded from her nightmare. She held her chest while breathing heavily and stared into the darkness of the motel room. For a moment, she had forgotten where she was.

"Sidney?" came Harlan's tired, concerned voice. "Are you all right?"

"No," she gasped while feeling slightly disoriented then trembled. "I had a terrible dream that Trisha was dead."

Harlan sat up and placed his arms around her, comforting her. "We're going to find her," he said gently as he pulled her against his warm body.

Sidney turned, sank against his bare chest while fighting her tears then lost control, and sobbed softly. Harlan gently rubbed her back and held her head to his chest. Sidney finally relaxed in his arms and sniffed.

"What if she's dead?" she whispered.

"Don't think like that," he said sternly. "Whoever took her went through a lot of trouble to make it look as if she ran away. That tells me there's a strong possibility she's still alive."

"I'm scared," she said softly into his chest.

He gently rocked her while rubbing her back. "We'll tear this town apart if we must," he informed her firmly. "But you won't be any good to Trisha or me if you don't get some rest."

Sidney sniffed once more. "Promise me you won't leave me," she whispered.

He groaned as his arms tightened around her. "I'm not going anywhere, Sidney. I'll see you through this, I promise," he said gently. "Will you get some sleep?"

She nodded and nuzzled his bare chest, smelling the fading scent of his cologne. At that moment, she realized the intimacy of their moment together. Despite the ache in her body for him, she couldn't get Trisha off her mind, unable to shake the horrible dream. Harlan lay back down and took her with him. Sidney clung to him like a security blanket as he pulled the covers over them. He held her against him until she finally drifted back to sleep.

Harlan woke Sidney at seven o'clock the next morning. She stirred tiredly and looked at him where he sat on the edge of the bed, freshly showered and dressed, as he brushed the hair from her face.

"It's time to get started," he informed her.

Sidney sat up and raked her fingers through her mussed hair. "I should go home for some dry clothing."

"You can borrow a pair of my shorts," he remarked simply. "I want to talk to Trisha's mother right away. You can go to your house afterward and change."

Sidney nodded then gave him a curious look. "Do I have time to take a shower?"

"Sure, you have time to take a shower. Where are your car keys? I'll get some breakfast for us at Sam's and bring your car back with me," he announced simply.

She gave a nod, indicating the dresser. "They're on the dresser," she replied, lacking enthusiasm.

Once Harlan left the motel room, Sidney searched through his bag and found a pair of black sweat shorts and a sweatshirt that would hide the fact that she wasn't wearing a bra. The sweatshirt would be fine for a few hours in the morning, but it would quickly become too warm by late morning. Sidney took a quick shower and changed into Harlan's clothing. She had just finished brushing her hair when Harlan returned to the room. He set a paper bag on the dresser and handed her a large, Styrofoam cup.

"I hope you still like tea," he remarked.

Sidney smiled with a soft laugh. "I'm surprised you remember that."

"I remember more than you'd think," he said simply. "Bagels okay?"

"I'm not very hungry," she said and took a sip of tea from the cup.

"You have to eat," he remarked sternly. "We have much ground to cover today." He set his cup on the dresser, handed her a bagel, then retrieved his notepad and placed it in his jacket pocket. He cast a look at her. "Are you ready?"

"I just want to get my things and put them in my car," she said then set her bagel and tea on the dresser.

Sidney retrieved her damp clothing and her jacket from the bathroom. She hesitated when she realized the knife was missing. She returned to the bedroom then looked around with some confusion. She remembered taking it off in the bathroom along with her wet clothing.

"Something wrong?" Harlan asked.

She looked back at him, forced a smile, and shook her head. "Uh, no."

"Okay, let's go then," he announced then eyed her. "We'd better take your car if you intend to stop at your parents later today to change."

By the time Sidney and Harlan reached Trisha's house, Mary Allister was a nervous wreck. She hurried Sidney into the house and only briefly eyed Harlan.

"I don't know where she is," Mary said while nervously wringing her fingers together as she paced the hallway. "She never came home last night. I was hoping she was with you. Then, when I called your house this morning, your father said you hadn't been home either. Where is she?"

"I was supposed to meet her last night, but she didn't show up," Sidney said timidly, hating that she had to lie to Trisha's already frantic mother.

Mary looked at Harlan several times, possibly recognizing him. "What if something happened to her? I told the sheriff about the threat, but he said there was nothing he could do about it. I never should've allowed her to go to work yesterday." She looked at Harlan once more. "Who's your friend?" she finally asked without changing her expression.

Sidney saw no point to deceiving Mary. Her father would soon discover she was in his company anyway.

"This is Harlan Brendan," Sidney replied gently.

"Harlan?" Mary questioned as if attempting to place the name. Her eyes then widened. "Oh, you're that photographer who used to work--" Mary suddenly placed her hand to her mouth, withholding her gasp. She lowered her hand and looked at Sidney. "Does your father know he's here?"

"Yes, Harlan stopped by my father's place yesterday," she replied while conveniently leaving out her father's strong disapproval. "Could we look around Trisha's room? I'm hoping there might be something there to indicate where she went."

Mary continued to stare at Harlan with a look that alarmed Sidney then finally met her gaze. "Yes, of course. Do you think she just went somewhere without telling me?"

"It's possible with Trisha. She gets an idea into her head and follows through with it," Sidney attempted to reassure Trisha's mother although she was positive that wasn't the case.

"I hope you're right," Mary remarked timidly then looked at Harlan with the same, strange look of distrust.

Sidney and Harlan went upstairs to Trisha's room and searched through her things. She found Trisha's journal in the nightstand drawer. She sat on the bed and scanned through the most recent entries since she had copies of the older ones. Harlan went through her drawers and sifted through her clothing.

"She really pissed off a lot of people," Sidney stated while scanning through several pages. "I hadn't seen most of these entries in the papers she gave me. According to this, Malcolm had Sheriff Drukard remove her from Sam's for disorderly conduct. She was fined and spent a night in jail." Sidney studied Harlan's back. "What if her disappearance doesn't have anything to do with Emily Fisher's death? Is it possible she just rubbed someone the wrong way?"

"We'll have to look at her disappearance as a separate issue," he informed her from the dresser. "Keep running tabs on everyone that despised her."

"I don't think they so much despised her as they feared her. She was disrupting what they felt to be their safety zone. She created doubt," Sidney announced.

Trisha's mother paused in the doorway. "Have you found anything?" she asked with some nervousness.

Sidney stood and set the journal on the bed. "Mrs. Allister, is there anyone Trisha feared? Were there any people in town who may have disliked her?"

Mary inhaled deeply and eyed Harlan briefly while his back was turned. "You know what Trisha was up to, Sidney. She angered many people. Paul Malcolm hates her with a passion. Sheriff Drukard thinks she's a nuisance. He even suggested I have her committed," she announced then shook her head. "Trisha isn't crazy; she's just confused. As far as town gossip goes, it's been all over town about what she's been doing the last couple of months. Mrs. Cooper and Mrs. Randall seem to have nothing better to talk about. Then there was that incident with Persha Palmer."

"Ms. Palmer?" Sidney asked with surprise. "What happened with her?"

"There was this kid writing a school report on the murder. He wanted to interview Trisha," Mary explained, appearing bothered. "Ms. Palmer put a stop to it and said some hateful things about Trisha. She told the boy Trisha was insane and didn't have her facts straight. The boy must have told someone what Persha said, and it got back to Trisha."

Sidney gently bit her lower lip and gave Mary a sympathetic look. "Do you believe Alex Trexler is innocent?"

Mary stared at Sidney a long moment in silence. "I'm not sure what I believe anymore. I've heard everything Trisha's had to say about the murder," she replied as she rubbed her chilled shoulders. "We've argued, we've debated, we've speculated, but there was never anything concrete to prove Alex wasn't the killer." She stared at Sidney with concern. "Do you think I should call the sheriff and tell him Trisha's disappeared? I know he's completely useless, but I feel like I should do something."

"I suggest you call him and convince him he has to do something," Sidney said firmly. "You know what he's like. You'll have to be persuasive. If Trisha left town on her own, she'll be calling you soon." Sidney held her breath. "But if someone was involved in her disappearance, we want the sheriff to be looking for her."

Mary nodded with some insecurity. "I'll call right away." She hurried from the room.

Harlan opened the closet door and searched the shelf above the hanging clothing. He then looked to the floor. "Her bag's here," he informed Sidney.

Sidney approached the closet and saw Trisha's overnight bag on the closet floor. It was the same one she'd used for their trip to California.

"She didn't plan to leave town," Sidney said softly.

"Does Trisha have her own car?" Harlan asked as he turned to face her.

"No," Sidney replied and sighed gently. "She used her mother's car to travel any distance. For the most part, she walked everywhere."

"Isn't there a house across the street from the library?" he questioned. "Maybe someone was home last night and saw something."

"Mrs. Lamont lives in that house. She's a younger version of Mrs. Cooper and Mrs. Randall," Sidney explained. "Then there's Mr. Taylor to the right of her house. His house is directly across from the library parking lot."

"We should question both of them," Harlan stated. "We'd better go there right away. If the sheriff does decide to investigate her disappearance, they may not be willing to talk to us if he gets to them first."

Sidney nodded and grabbed Trisha's journal. "Mrs. Allister won't mind if I take this with me."

"As long as you're sure."

They left the bedroom and headed down the stairs. Mary could be heard in the kitchen talking to someone on the phone. Sidney was about to enter the kitchen and tell her they were leaving when she overheard Harlan's name being mentioned. Sidney stopped Harlan and listened to her conversation.

"What do you want me to do, Herb?" Mary asked sternly. "I'm having enough problems of my own right now."

Sidney backed away from the kitchen archway. "We should go," she remarked with disapproval. "Mrs. Allister's on the phone with my father."

Harlan groaned while frowning. "I'm really not in the mood to deal with him right now."

"Me either," she replied and headed for the door. "Especially since I didn't go home last night, and I'm wearing your clothes. I can't stress enough how bad that would look."

"Yeah, you're not kidding," Harlan scoffed.

Chapter Twenty-seven

Sidney parked her car in the back of the library parking lot. She wanted to be sure if her father drove past, he wouldn't see it. From the library parking lot, they walked across the street to Mrs. Lamont's house and knocked on her door. Mrs. Lamont opened the door and immediately smiled when she saw Sidney.

"What an unexpected surprise," she announced happily. "What brings you here?"

Mrs. Lamont was a moderately attractive woman in her early forties with naturally curly, peroxide blonde hair that touched her shoulders. According to Mrs. Randall, Mrs. Lamont frequented the hairdresser once a week. She wore heavy make-up, giving her all the appeal of a streetwalker. Her bright, red lipstick glistened, having been freshly applied. She had professionally manicured nails, and the scent of toxic perfume seemed to linger out the doorway and onto the porch, possibly indicating she was on her way out.

"I wish it were under better circumstances, Mrs. Lamont," Sidney said gently. "But Trisha disappeared from the library last night. Could we come inside and ask you a couple of questions?"

Mrs. Lamont's eyes swept over Harlan. She returned her attention to Sidney then nodded and stepped away from the door, allowing them to enter. Harlan entered behind Sidney. Mrs. Lamont led them into the living room.

"I hope nothing's happened to the poor girl," Mrs. Lamont said with concern.

She offered them a seat on the red, velvet sofa. Mrs. Lamont's house was uncluttered, though there appeared to be a thick coating of dust on everything. Cobwebs dangled from each corner of the living room and off the light fixtures. Apparently, Mrs. Lamont didn't spend much time at home.

"That's what we're attempting to figure out," Sidney announced gently. "You live across from the library, where she was last seen. I was wondering if you saw her leave anytime between closing and eight o'clock."

Mrs. Lamont considered the question a moment and once more eyed Harlan. Sidney shifted uncomfortably. Harlan seemed to attract a lot of attention. Was there more to his leaving then she was being told?

"I'm afraid I left around seven o'clock for a card game with some of the girls in Brighten. I didn't get home until after two in the morning," she said with a sinister smile. "When I was walking out to my car, I did see some cars in the parking lot just as the library was about to close. The only one I recognized was Persha Palmer's car."

There was a name that came up on more than one occasion. "And you didn't see Trisha leave the library at any time?" Sidney asked.

"No," she replied. "Even if I had been home, I don't pay much attention to what happens at the library. Too dull for me," she boasted. "Of course, Mr. Taylor spends much time peering out the window. That man has nothing better to do than sit in front of the window all day. Could I interest either of you in something to drink?" she asked then smiled almost seductively at Harlan.

Sidney noted Mrs. Lamont's come-hither look then shook her head. "No, thank you," she announced a little too quickly. "We've taken enough of your time already."

"Don't be silly," Mrs. Lamont said. "I adore visitors. It gets very lonely with Mr. Lamont gone so much." She then looked at Harlan and raised her brows in suggestion. "What can I get you to drink? I'm afraid I didn't catch your name."

"It's Harlan, madam," he said pleasantly.

She suddenly beamed with delight and let a slight gasp escape. "An Englishman. How exciting," she said with enthusiasm. "I'm afraid this town lacks culture." She seductively leaned closer to him. "So what can I get you, Harlan? Just name it."

"Nothing, really," he announced and offered a moderately embarrassed look. "We have to be going."

Sidney couldn't believe Mrs. Lamont hadn't even remembered Harlan. She swore she had by the way she'd been staring, but it was obvious there was something else on the woman's mind. Sidney then remembered the story of the priest with whom Mrs. Lamont supposedly had an affair.

Sidney suddenly bolted up from her seat. "Yes, it's been good talking to you, Mrs. Lamont," she announced. "Perhaps we'll stop by another time."

Harlan was quick to stand as well. He'd obviously felt the sexual tension the older woman projected toward him. Mrs. Lamont sprang to her feet.

"Must you go so soon," she announced pleasantly and added a swing to her hips as she tossed her blonde hair off her shoulder.

Both nodded, equally eager to leave. Sidney walked toward the door with Harlan practically pushing her from the house. Mrs. Lamont followed them to the door.

"It was good seeing you, Sidney," she announced then made eyes at Harlan. "And it was a pleasure to meet you, Harlan. Stop by anytime."

As they stepped onto the porch, Harlan suddenly cast a look back into the house. Sidney saw Mrs. Lamont smile seductively, wave, and shut the door.

"I can't believe she did that," Harlan snorted and hurried off the porch.

"Did what?" Sidney snapped with a hint of jealousy in her tone.

"She grabbed me when we walked out the door," he said and shook his head.

"She did?" Sidney gasped with a surprised look then immediately frowned. "I'm sure you're not too distraught over it."

"What? You think I enjoy being grabbed by married women?" he asked sternly while glaring at her. "What kind of bloody pig do you think I am?"

"Just the average kind," she said simply.

Harlan and Sidney crossed the tidy yard to Mr. Taylor's small, blue house that was in desperate need of some TLC. The paint was chipped, the porch was starting to rot, and the hedges were out of control. Sidney walked onto the less than sturdy porch and rang the doorbell. They had to wait a few minutes for Mr. Taylor to reach the door. Mr. Taylor was about eighty years old now, though Sidney swore he was eighty back when she was a teen. He was a little thinner than she had remembered, although his taste in wardrobe hadn't changed much. He wore a blue, flannel shirt and red, plaid pants held up to his chest by suspenders. He appeared unshaven for days, his hair was uncombed, and his gray eyebrows were almost as bushy as the hair growing out of his ears.

"Good morning, Mr. Taylor," Sidney announced warmly.

"Who're you?" he asked and squinted through cloudy, thick glasses.

"I'm Sidney McBride, Herb McBride's daughter," she said a little more loudly.

"No need to yell. I'm old, not deaf," he said then looked at Harlan and nodded. "Who's this? Husband?"

Sidney looked at Harlan and raised her brows. "No, his name is Harlan. He's a reporter," she said in a normal voice.

"Speak up, child. I can't hear ya when ya mumble," he practically shouted. He then squinted while looking at Harlan. "A reporter, huh? Looks more like that goddamned photographer fella to me."

Sidney looked at Harlan and gently bit her lower lip while hiding her mocking smile. She looked back at Mr. Taylor. "We'd like to ask you a couple of questions."

He grunted and gave a slight nod.

"Were you home last night?" Sidney asked.

"Where the hell else would I be?" he demanded to know. "I'm too old to chase girls."

"Can we come inside?" Sidney asked, feeling herself becoming slightly impatient.

"Why not?" he groaned and shuffled away from the door without lifting his feet. "Won't go away if I don't."

Sidney looked at his feet and noticed he wore old, pink slippers. Sidney and Harlan followed him into his small, cluttered home. It appeared to be clean, but he had boxes of old magazines, empty soda bottles from twenty years ago, and lawn ornaments setting along the hall and throughout the living room. They followed him through the narrow path between the clutter and into his front sitting room. Harlan looked out the smudged window. The library and its parking lot were in direct line of sight with his sitting room window. Mr. Taylor sat in the easy chair facing the window and reclined his fuzzy, pink feet. Sidney sat in a nearby chair while Harlan moved several crossword puzzles from the sofa and uncertainly sat. As Mr. Taylor picked up his crossword puzzle and pencil, they remained and watched him.

Sidney cleared her throat. "Mr. Taylor?"

He looked across the room at them. "Oh, you're still here," he said louder than necessary. "What do ya want? Haven't got all day."

Sidney shifted in her seat with some embarrassment. "About last night," she asked gently. "Were you sitting in your front room as you are now?"

"Nope," he replied simply and again raised his crossword puzzle.

"What were you doing?" Sidney asked with surprise.

"I was sitting in my pajamas last night," he said without looking at her. "Ugly pajamas with ducks on 'em. The late Mrs. Taylor bought them for me."

Sidney was silent a moment then rolled her eyes and inhaled deeply. "Did you happen to look at the library anytime between three and eight o'clock."

He looked out the window above his crossword puzzle. "S'pose so," he replied.

"Did you notice any cars there after the library closed?" Sidney asked.

"Always cars in the lot after it's closed," he replied.

"Mr. Taylor, do you know Trisha Allister? She works in the library archives," Sidney pressed, attempting to keep his attention focused on their conversation.

Mr. Taylor glared at her. "Of course I know Trisha. She's that sweet child who brings me the morning paper af'er she's finished with it. Every mornin' she brings it over at nine o'clock." He then looked at his watch and frowned. "She's late," he scoffed.

"Did you see her leave the library last night?" she pressed.

"She's usually out by five," he replied and scribbled something in the puzzle.

"She worked late last night."

Harlan shifted while rolling his eyes then uncertainly touched something on the sofa. He pulled a half-eaten cheese sandwich out from between the cushions. Harlan made a face and set it on the arm of the chair.

"Oh," he replied without looking at her. "Didn't see her leave. Saw a couple lurking around just after eight last night. Left a little after eight thirty. Had some sort of blue car," he said simply. "It was raining hard when they left. Probably screwing around in the parking lot."

Sidney looked at Harlan with defeat. At least Mr. Taylor was able to distinguish Sidney's car and that they had been there after eight. She looked back at the old man.

"But before that," she prompted. "Do you remember seeing any cars there after closing and before eight?"

"That lesbian teacher was there," he said simply. "What's a word for distortions of perception?"

"Persha Palmer?" Sidney asked curiously.

Harlan smelled the area beneath him. He grimaced, stood, and approached Sidney's chair. He sat on the arm of her plush chair.

"Only lesbian teacher I know around these parts," Mr. Taylor replied simply then appeared thoughtful. "Psychedelic." He scribbled the word into the book.

"What time did she leave?" Sidney asked.

"Bout quarter after seven," he replied and continued with his crossword puzzle. "A sheath or container for a dagger or sword?"

"Was there anyone else?" Sidney pressed.

"There was a taxicab. Must've made a wrong turn. Pulled out of the parking lot," he announced then pointed with his pencil. "Scabbard," he said and wrote the word in his book.

"A taxi?" Sidney asked with some concern. "Did you get a good look at it?"

"It was yellow," he replied coarsely without looking at her. "Had a huge dent on its front passenger side."

"Are you sure it didn't pick someone up?" Sidney asked.

"Didn't see it pull in. Just saw it come out of the back parking lot and head out of town," he replied.

"Did you notice anyone in the back?"

"Two people," he informed her. "A couple. Sat really close together."

Sidney and Harlan looked at each other then returned their attention to the old man. "Thank you, Mr. Taylor," Sidney said. "You've been a tremendous help."

As they stood to leave, Mr. Taylor looked at them over his crossword book. "Does your father know you took back up with that photographer fella?" he asked and nodded toward Harlan.

Sidney looked at Harlan with some surprise. Mr. Taylor had a fantastic memory for details when it suited his purpose. "If he did," she teased, "he wouldn't approve."

Mr. Taylor laughed softly at the comment. "There's an old bomb shelter in the basement of the school. Door's behind the boiler now." He winked at Harlan. "You can take 'er there. Her father will never find you kids. Wish I knew about it when the late Mrs. Taylor and I were young." He laughed lowly with a wrinkled smile.

Sidney looked at Harlan with alarm. "Bomb shelter," she gasped softly.

Both hurried from the house.

Chapter Twenty-eight

Harlan followed Sidney through the empty hall of the high school while classes were in session. They slipped through the door to the basement without being seen and hurried down the stairs. Sidney and Harlan wandered through the maze of machinery and storage space until Harlan spotted the boiler. They hurried toward it and easily slipped behind it. Mr. Taylor had been right; there was a metal door. They could hear a soft female moan coming from the other side. Harlan forced the door open. A teenage boy and girl jumped into a sitting position from the blankets scattered on the floor. The old bomb shelter consisted of a single, large room, which was lined with shelves and old supplies.

"Don't call my mother," the girl cried softly while frantically buttoning her shirt. "Please don't call my mother."

Harlan eyed the kids while shaking his head and motioned toward the door. "Get dressed and get back to your class," he announced firmly.

Harlan and Sidney left the hidden bomb shelter and walked across the basement with mild disgust.

"So much for that theory," Sidney said with a sigh while rubbing her chilled arms. Her concern for Trisha was tearing her apart.

"Since we're already here," Harlan announced with defeat. "Why don't we talk to Persha Palmer?"

"She's all yours," Sidney muttered, dreading the thought. "I could never talk to that woman. She's cold and unfeeling."

Once they returned upstairs, they approached Ms. Palmer's class and waited until she had a free minute. She gave the class a reading assignment then joined Sidney and Harlan in the hallway. Harlan immediately extended his hand to her.

"I don't believe we've met before," he announced cheerfully, diving into reporter mode. "My name is Harlan Brendan."

Ms. Palmer shook his hand then raised a sharp brow on her prudish face. "Aren't you that photographer fella?"

Harlan chuckled and nodded. "Yes, I used to work for Mr. McBride several years ago, but now I'm a journalist," he announced, playing up the angle. "I'm doing a follow-up story on the murder of Emily Fisher since I had been in Marilina during that time. I heard from several sources that you were friends with her. Would you be willing to help me get some facts straight on the subject?"

Ms. Palmer folded her arms across her chest. "I'd be glad to give you the correct version of what happened that day," she said sternly. "Not that anyone wants to know the truth. Let's go outside to talk."

They followed her out the back of the building through a nearby door and sat at some tables set outside. Ms. Palmer lit a cigarette and inhaled deeply. She blew smoke across the table and looked sharply at both.

"The day of the murder, her boyfriend, Alec, came to the school. He started arguing with her in the hallway during one of her classes." Her brow rose sharply. "Then he hit her."

Sidney's mouth opened with surprise then immediately shut. Considering she had witnessed the incident, she knew that was inaccurate.

"Of course, I comforted her," Ms. Palmer insisted while practically inhaling her cigarette. "Told her men were rotten pigs." She gave Harlan a wry smile. "No offense."

Harlan shifted uncomfortably but remained polite. "Did she tell you what they had been arguing about?"

"Naturally," Ms. Palmer replied then immediately lit a second cigarette off the first. "They had a fight over his infidelity. The man was a real womanizer. Emily would stay at home and cry herself to sleep while that barbarian was out skirt chasing." She took a long drag on the second cigarette again and blew smoke past Harlan. "But getting back to the story. We talked about the fight, and she seemed convinced he was no good for her. She met up with him on her walk home. That's when Alec beat, raped and killed her right there on the bridge."

Sidney groaned to herself and looked away. Her story wasn't accurate with any of the facts. She wondered if they were even talking about the same case. Without looking at him, Sidney gently nudged Harlan's thigh under the table.

"Fascinating story," Harlan announced with a pleasant smile, ignoring the false facts, and then flipped through his notebook. "If you wouldn't mind, I'd just like to ask you a couple of quick questions. Points of interest, if you will."

"No, I don't mind," she replied then puffed on her cigarette and lit another from it. She crushed the old cigarette and lined the second butt alongside the first.

"What was on the letter Emily Fisher received the day of the murder?" he asked simply and stared at her for her reaction.

She stared at him a moment with a look of surprise. "Letter? What letter?"

"She had received a letter the day of the murder. Two witnesses saw her read a letter and place it in her pocket just before she left school for the day," Harlan explained.

Ms. Palmer shook her head. "I don't know anything about a letter."

"She didn't mention the letter to you when she spoke to you after school?" he asked with surprise.

"No, we didn't talk after school the day she was killed. She left here in a bit of a hurry," Ms. Palmer announced then hesitated. "Although when I went out in the parking lot, I saw her around the back of the school talking to Paul. At least I think it was Paul. They were around the corner of the building, and his back was to me. No, I'm quite positive it was Paul."

It would make an interesting theory, Sidney thought, except her recaps of the murder were less than accurate. It would seem they'd be asking Mr. Malcolm a few more questions.

"Yes, you're probably right. My facts have been a bit sketchy from the start, but you're helping clear up a lot for me," Harlan said with a smile that mocked her. While studying the notes he had written from Trisha's journal on his pad, he let out a slight laugh and scratched his temple with the back of his pen. "On a more personal note," he announced and looked at her. "There's quite a difference between your story and the version I heard the other day." He skimmed his notes. "Sidney's friend, Trisha, insists the real killer is still free."

150

Ms. Palmer groaned lowly and rolled her eyes. "That little parasite has been spreading that rumor for nearly two months." Ms. Palmer then eyed Sidney as well. "Forgive me. I know she's your friend." She leaned across the picnic table toward Harlan and motioned him closer with thin fingers pinching her cigarette. He leaned forward. "She actually went to the prison and talked to that murderer. If you ask me, I think she has feelings for the bastard. She's half psycho. I feel a little sorry for the child." She shook her head and leaned back. "I know she went through a lot, but the murder was traumatic on all of us. I adored Emily. She was like a sister to me."

"So you're certain there couldn't have been anyone else responsible for her death?" Harlan asked while tilting his head with a curious stare.

She leaned on the picnic table, laughed softly, and waved a hand at him. "Not unless you killed her, Mr. Brendan. You were the only other suspicious person in town."

"Suspicious? You mean a stranger?" he asked with raised brows and sarcasm in his tone.

"Well, it was no secret Emily wanted you," Ms. Palmer remarked simply and added a knowing smirk. "Young, good-looking, and European. She said she loved an English accent. If you ask me, I think she enjoyed the uncut member."

Sidney was confused by the comment, not sure she understood. The way Harlan shifted uncomfortably and avoided looking at her, Sidney immediately figured it out. She looked away and held back her embarrassed smile. Harlan scratched his goatee with the back of his pen then looked to his notepad.

"I'd like to hear your version of what happened last night at the library. Since it sort of involves the murder," he said bluntly then looked at her.

Ms. Palmer stared at him with some confusion. "The library? What version?" she practically gasped. "Nothing happened at the library last night."

Harlan's brows knitted in confusion as he flipped back in the notepad. "I could have sworn--" He pointed to the page with his pen. Sidney stared at the blank page over his lower arm. "Yes, here it is. According to Miss Allister, you approached her in the library archives and said to her, 'This town isn't interested in the truth. No one will ever believe you. They will never know the truth. I'll make sure of it." Harlan lowered the notepad. "Just what did you mean by that?"

Sidney held her straight face. Harlan deserved an award for the role he was playing.

"Well, well." Ms. Palmer fumbled as the color rose to her cheeks. "That's all a lie," she exploded. "I never said any of that. It's obvious she's lying!" Ms. Palmer was breathing rapidly and puffed nervously on her fourth cigarette. "That little bitch! It's obvious she's trying to turn everyone against me or use me to make others believe her ridiculous stories!"

Harlan scribbled something on the notepad.

"You just wait until I see that little bitch," Ms. Palmer scoffed in anger and shook her head defensively. "I'm going to set her straight for ever saying those things!"

Harlan's eyes narrowed, and he leaned forward on his elbows. "What was your conversation with her last night?"

Ms. Palmer frantically shook her head. "Very casual. We don't get along."

"Would you mind telling me exactly what had transpired? We should get the facts straight," Harlan remarked simply without looking at her and literally began to scribble on the notepad to convey the illusion of writing.

"That little bitch," Ms. Palmer snapped and crushed her fourth cigarette. She blew out the smoke and lit another with angry, trembling hands. "I went into the archives to look at some old yearbooks. I've been helping with the school paper. One of the teachers is retiring, so we wanted to find a picture of him from his first year as a teacher here at Marilina. I asked Trisha about that particular year. I couldn't even find the damned yearbooks. It's her job to know where these things are. She found the book I needed and even photocopied the page for me. Nothing happened between us. Neither of us ever says more than we have to. I just can't believe she'd stoop that low."

"I see," he replied then eyed her. "What time did you leave the library?"

"About seven fifteen," she replied sternly and inhaled on the cigarette. "I also checked out another book for my personal reading, but that wasn't anywhere near the archives."

"Did anyone else happen to hear your conversation with Trisha? Was there anyone else in the archives with you?" Harlan asked while raising a brow.

"No, not a soul," she remarked. "But I assure you, what I've told you is the truth."

"Was there anyone else in the library at that particular time? Perhaps someone coming in when you left?" he asked.

"No one else came in. The library closes at seven, but they don't rush you out if you're looking for something in particular," Ms. Palmer informed him. "In fact, after closing is when they're the most helpful."

"Who was working that night?" Harlan asked.

"Just Trisha. At least, she was the only one there from six until seven while I was there," Ms. Palmer remarked then pointed at Harlan with realization. "Now that I think about it, there were a couple of kids doing some research for Paul's report due today. Damned kids wait until the last minute. I remember seeing some guy in the back corner of the self-help section, but I didn't see who it was. I'm not the type to mind other people's business--like some. But I didn't see anyone after seven."

"Did you recognize any of the cars in the parking lot?" he pressed.

She shook her head. "Mine was the only car in the lot. I don't believe there was any parked out front either."

Sidney gently nudged Harlan's foot with hers.

Harlan cleared his throat and smiled. "You've been incredibly helpful, Ms. Palmer," he announced then stood. "I hope we haven't disturbed you too much."

Sidney stood also.

"No, not at all, Mr. Brendan," Ms. Palmer replied with a slight smile. "Glad I could help with your article."

He thanked her again, and they walked away from the table. Harlan then paused about ten feet away, surprising Sidney. He turned toward Ms. Palmer as she crushed her last cigarette and pointed his pen from his temple to her.

"I'm sorry, Ms. Palmer. There's just one more question I really think I should ask," he said and looked back at his tablet. "I hope you don't mind."

"Of course. What would you like to know?" Ms. Palmer asked with a slightly flustered look about her as she stood.

He lifted his head and met her gaze from several feet away with a serious look. "When did your romantic relationship with Emily Fisher end?"

Ms. Palmer's face drained of all its color, and her mouth fell open. Harlan stood his ground and maintained his straight expression. Sidney shot a stare at Harlan with disbelief as her mouth fell open with surprise.

"I--I don't know what you're talking about," Ms. Palmer gasped softly. "We were just friends."

"But you did have romantic feelings for her?" he pressed sternly.

Her stunned expression didn't change, and she remained nearly speechless. "Well, I--"

Harlan walked toward her and paused by the table. "In Alex's interview from prison, he said Emily told him you had romantic feelings for her."

Ms. Palmer stared at Harlan a long moment and placed a trembling hand to her eyes as a tear rolled down her cheek. "We were just friends," she said softly then looked back at Harlan. "I had nothing but respect for Emily."

"I'm really sorry," he said gently. "I didn't mean to upset you. I never should've brought it up in the first place." He managed a smirk. "I'll just write that you were an admirer of hers as a teacher and a friend."

Ms. Palmer sniffed and smiled warmly. "I appreciate it. Thank you."

Harlan turned and entered the school with Sidney, who linked onto his arm. She playfully slapped his forearm.

"You are smooth, Harlan Brendan. I've never seen anyone handle Ms. Palmer that way in my life, especially a man." She looked at him while they walked and met his eyes. A cheap smile crossed her face. "You *are* good at what you do."

"It's my job to get as much information from people as possible. Though it's usually about some animal attack or weather condition," he said with a soft laugh. "Her story was full of holes."

"She didn't even get Alex's name correct," Sidney replied while groaning. "I think she just doesn't remember much about that day. She's not the most intelligent teacher in the building. Either that or she has a bad memory for detail."

"Not details--just facts," he replied simply. "So what was that about Paul Malcolm? It would appear he lied to you in your previous interview. Would you like to give me a shot at him while we're here?"

"I'm not so sure we should be concerned about Miss Fisher's death at the moment. Trisha's our priority right now," Sidney remarked gently and released his arm.

"We are working on Trisha's disappearance. Someone in this pathetic town must have seen something at the library," he insisted. "If Persha Palmer is right, there was someone in the back of the library last night before closing time. It could have been an abductor."

"What we really need are the names of the kids who were doing the reports last night," Sidney stated. "They were in Malcolm's class. It's a start."

"Let's talk to Malcolm while we're here," he announced. "Someone in this town saw something. Usually, it finds its way back to someone else."

"Then I suggest we talk to Mrs. Randall and Mrs. Cooper when we're finished with Malcolm," she insisted. "Between those two, they know everything about this town."

Harlan groaned with annoyance. "Precisely why I left. Too many damned busybodies."

"Just two," she teased.

"Two too many, if you ask me," Harlan snorted.

Chapter Twenty-nine

Sidney and Harlan found Mr. Malcolm in the auditorium watching over a study hall class of nearly seventy students along with two other teachers. When Sidney asked him if he could talk for a minute, he was surprisingly cooperative. They went out into the empty hall where Sidney introduced him to Harlan. Both men shook hands.

"Ah, yes, Harlan. The photographer fella who worked for Herb." He then looked at Sidney while grinning. "Dating his daughter now, huh?"

Harlan smiled and chuckled softly in his throat. "We've been seeing quite a bit of each other," Harlan teased.

Harlan then explained how he was working on a feature story for his newspaper about the murder of Emily Fisher. Mr. Malcolm appeared impressed and accommodating.

"I'll make this brief, since I have notes from Sidney's earlier discussion with you," Harlan remarked. "After school left out that day in September, did you recall seeing Emily Fisher leave the building? Maybe you would have noticed Alex's car around the area?"

"No, I hadn't seen either after school let out. As I told Sidney, Emily ran out of here as soon as we were dismissed," Mr. Malcolm replied. "She only spoke to Persha before she'd left."

"You're sure she only spoke to Ms. Palmer?" Harlan questioned with a raised brow.

He nodded. "I heard their voices in the girls' lavatory. Why women prefer talking in the bathroom is beyond me."

"When was that?" Harlan asked.

"Just before we were dismissed at three-thirty," he replied simply. "Half an hour after the students are dismissed."

"Where did you go after school? Do you remember seeing either Emily or Alex as you left?" Harlan asked in a casual manner without looking up from his notepad.

"I didn't see either of them on my way to Sam's," he informed him. "It's a short trip."

Harlan looked up and pointed with his pen. "Sam's, huh? That's perfect," he announced and wrote on his notepad. "So you must have seen Alex at some point. Do you remember what time you reached Sam's?"

"Of course I remember," Mr. Malcolm announced. "I left here at quarter till four. I caught Billy and Denny hanging out after school smoking in the boy's lavatory. Once I was finished yelling at them, I walked to Sam's. I usually walk. The walk back helps clear my head," he said with a slight laugh.

Harlan added a throaty chuckle, understanding his reasoning for wanting to walk.

"So I reached Sam's around four o'clock. I stayed there until six, and then I walked back for my car."

"What time did Alex arrive at the tavern?" Harlan asked. "He was late, wasn't he?"

"He showed around five-thirty, which was half an hour late. Sam would have been upset, had he not been in the back watching the game. Alex seemed nervous about something. At the time, I thought it was just because he was late for work. After the police questioned us, I realized the real reason."

"Was there anyone else at the tavern that you remember?" Harlan continued.

"Just one or two others, but no one I usually socialize with," he replied. "So I don't recall who they were anymore."

Harlan wrote something on his notepad then studied it a moment with a curious look before glancing back at Malcolm. "See, now I'm a little confused. I was told you did speak to Emily Fisher just after school left out that day," Harlan corrected then offered a tiny smile. "Someone had seen you. Would you care to tell me what you talked about?"

Mr. Malcolm became tense and fidgeted. "It didn't seem important enough to mention," he replied almost timidly. "We spoke briefly."

"What about?" Harlan asked.

"Nothing much, really," he replied.

"Did the conversation have anything to do with your affair with Emily?" Harlan pressed casually.

Mr. Malcolm frowned and drew a deep breath. "She mentioned she was getting back together with Alex," he announced with a groan. "In her best interest, I tried to talk her out of it."

"Did she mention anything about a letter?" Harlan asked and glanced at him.

Mr. Malcolm nodded and seemed surprised by the question. "Yes, she'd received a love letter from Alex. That's what made her decide she was going to make amends."

"Did she show it to you?" Harlan asked.

"Yes. Although, I found it strange that it was typed," Mr. Malcolm replied. "It looked as if a child typed it. Some of the letters were higher than the others."

Sidney held back her gasp and shifted looks at Harlan, who didn't even flinch at the comment.

"It said something about meeting him at three forty-five or something like that," Mr. Malcolm said simply.

"How can you be sure it was from Alex? Was it signed? What did she do with the note?" Harlan pressed.

Mr. Malcolm was silent a moment. "Well, I, uh--?" He then considered it a moment longer. "Actually, no, it wasn't signed. She said it was from him, so I just assumed he gave it to her. She put the note back in her pocket."

"Did you tell the police about the note," Harlan asked while giving him a curious look.

"No," he said with some embarrassment. "It didn't seem important. I mean, they already had the evidence against him. I assumed they found the note on her."

"I understand," Harlan replied then tilted his head. "There's just one more thing I'd like to ask you. A reliable witness overheard you arguing with Trisha Allister last night at the library just before it closed. It was something to do with Emily Fisher's murder. Would you care to tell me the details of that argument?"

Mr. Malcolm stared at them a long moment with a surprised look on his face. "I wasn't anywhere near the library last night. I got that Internet access on my computer. I haven't been to the library since." He laughed softly. "But there are plenty of people who have a grudge against Trisha. It could have been anyone with her."

Harlan frowned. "Hmm, I guess my source isn't so reliable after all. Were you anywhere near the library?" he asked.

"Nowhere near the library. I was at Sam's, where I usually hold up," he said with a timid smile. "I was there from the time school left out until nearly eight-thirty. Sam's nephew was tending bar until eight o'clock last night. He'd verify I was there. I had a couple of drinks with Denny as well." Malcolm laughed softly. "Though we did talk about Trisha briefly. I really do have better things to do than talk to that girl."

"Thanks for your help, Mr. Malcolm," Harlan announced and extended his hand.

Sidney watched the two men shake hands then followed Harlan down the hallway.

"Do we believe him?" she asked.

"As far as Trisha's concerned, I think we have to believe both of them for now. Neither appeared nervous that we supposedly spoke to Trisha this morning. Had they been involved in a kidnapping plot, I think they'd be more surprised."

"If we don't find her soon, I'm afraid it'll be too late," Sidney said as her nervousness increased. A thousand horrible scenarios played in her mind. "We're not getting anywhere."

"We're narrowing down her suspect list," Harlan corrected. "Malcolm was her biggest rival. I think it's safe to concentrate elsewhere."

"Where do you suggest we look next? Maybe we should call the local taxi service," Sidney suggested.

"That would be admitting she may have left town on her own," Harlan said simply.

"I don't care," she snapped. "We have to find her. I could care less about this entire murder case right now. All I want is Trisha home alive."

"All right. We'll go to Sam's," Harlan replied. "You can use the pay phone there while I talk to Sam. He was always full of information."

"Yeah, tons of the useless kind," Sidney remarked lowly and allowed her irritation get the better of her.

"Do you have a better idea?" he asked sternly as they walked into the school parking lot.

"No," she moaned softly.

He stopped her halfway to her rental car and forced her to face him. "I'm doing the best I can to find her."

Sidney stared into his green eyes and held her breath. "I'm sorry, Harlan. I know you're only trying to help," she replied in a timid voice then became frustrated. "I just feel as if I should be knocking on doors demanding to search homes."

He placed his arm around her shoulder and guided her toward the car. "We'll stop at Sam's then check with the local busybodies," he announced in a soothing tone. "If we don't learn anything after that, we'll start tearing the town apart, okay?"

Sidney managed a nod and smiled. She believed him too.

Chapter Thirty

Harlan sat at the bar talking to Sam while Sidney argued with the taxi service over the pay phone in the corner of the smoke-filled room. She could see Sam smile and laugh at something Harlan said. She wondered what they were talking about.

"I'm telling you," Sidney said into the phone with a groan. "There was a taxi here in Marilina last night around seven-thirty. Yours would be the only company that would possibly come this far. There are no others."

"I have the roster in front of me, ma'am," the man on the other end said firmly. "There were no pickups, no drop-offs, and no calls to that area. I assure you none of my guys even went there by accident."

"A woman's life is at stake here," Sidney almost shouted.

"I'd really like to help you, lady, but there wasn't anyone there last night or any night," he informed her. "We sold some of our cabs a couple of weeks ago. Maybe someone bought one. It's possible you saw someone with one of them."

"Do you have a list of buyers?" Sidney asked with a spark of enthusiasm.

"Somewhere in this mess. I can call you back, but it'll be a couple of hours," he said simply.

"This is really important. I'll call you back in an hour," Sidney said firmly. "Would that be okay?"

"I'll try to have that information for you by then," he said while sighing.

She thanked him, hung up the phone, and joined Harlan at the bar. Both Harlan and Sam were laughing like old buddies. Sam was a tall, lean, muscular man with sandy blonde hair parted on the left side. With his bronze tan, he had the appearance of an old surfer. Sidney always had the impression that he was a womanizer, although she had nothing to support that theory.

"I've caught kids fooling around in the tavern basement already," Sam announced while hiding his grin. "But I didn't know that bomb shelter even existed."

Sidney sat beside Harlan and glared at the cranberry colored, mixed drink before him. It seemed a little early in the morning to start drinking.

"How many of those have you had?" she asked sternly.

"Two," he replied simply with a pleasant smile.

Sam laughed at her apparent nagging and attended to a man in a business suit at the opposite end of the bar.

"No luck?" Harlan asked, noting the defeated look on her face.

She shook her head and sighed. "I have to call him back in an hour. He said they sold some of their cabs last week." Sidney took his drink from him and took a swallow. She made a face and looked at him. "This is cranberry juice!"

He laughed at her surprise. "Yes, I know. What did you think I'd be drinking before noon?"

Sam returned to Harlan's end of the bar and dried some glasses. "So what brings you back to this hick town?" he asked with a humored grin.

Sidney observed all the gold jewelry Sam wore. He had a gold ring on each ring finger, a thick chain link bracelet, a gold watch, and a solid gold necklace around his thick neck.

"I'm doing a story on the murder of that schoolteacher," Harlan announced casually.

Sam nodded and raised his brows. "Yes, I know the story well. Possibly the only really big thing to happen in this little town," he remarked. "Shouldn't be too hard to get the entire story. Mrs. Cooper and Mrs. Randall will tell you everything you never wanted to know about everyone in this town."

"Actually," Harlan said boldly. "I had been interviewing this young lady's friend." He pointed to Sidney. "Then, last night, she disappeared."

Sam looked at Sidney then back to Harlan. "Are you talking about Trisha Allister?"

Harlan nodded and appeared curious. "Yes, had you heard something about her disappearance?"

"I wasn't aware that she'd disappeared," Sam remarked. "If she has, the word hasn't gotten around yet."

"We were supposed to meet her at the library last night, but she wasn't there. Vanished without a trace," Harlan announced and drank some of his juice. "Did you hear about anything suspicious happening last night?"

Sam's brows knitted a moment. "Don't really recall anyone mentioning anything involving Trisha," he replied. "But there was another stranger in town last night. He came into the bar around eleven o'clock and started asking all sorts of questions." Sam paused and tilted his head. "Come to think about it, he was asking about the teacher's murder also."

Sidney's heart pounded harshly.

Harlan leaned forward on the bar with a suspicious look. "Did he give a name?"

Sam shrugged. "If he did, I wasn't paying attention. He was talking to some of the other guys."

"What did he ask?" Harlan questioned with great interest.

"He only asked me a few questions about the murder," Sam informed him. "He wanted to know if I'd been here that day tending bar."

"Were you?"

"I believe I was in the bar area until nearly six o'clock. After that, I went to my living room just beyond the kitchen and watched the game until nearly six-thirty. That's when the police came and arrested Alex right here in the bar," Sam replied. "It was about an hour and a half after they found the body."

"Was Paul Malcolm here that night?" Harlan asked with a curious look.

"That was a Friday. He's always here on a Friday," Sam remarked. "Though that particular Friday he just had one beer then left."

"Are you sure?" Harlan asked with some confusion.

"I'm positive. He left around four o'clock. I remember because I thought it was strange for him to leave so early on a Friday night," Sam reported. "I think he and his wife were having problems. He burned out in the stones in the driveway."

"He drove that day? I thought he always walked here," Harlan remarked.

"Usually does, but not that day," Sam assured him while drying the same glass repeatedly.

The older man in the business suit staggered toward them and placed a hand on both Sidney's and Harlan's shoulders. "I was here last night," he announced with the smell of whiskey on his breath. "I talked to that stranger about the murder."

Harlan looked back at the man then made a face and turned his head away. Sidney could smell the whiskey without looking at the intoxicated man.

"What did he ask about the murder?" Harlan asked while attempting to avoid his whiskey breath.

"Buy me a drink, and I'll tell you all about it," the man said while leaning heavily onto Sidney's shoulder.

Harlan requested a drink for the man. Sidney moved to another stool so the man would sit down and stop leaning on her shoulder. They listened to his story of the prior evening and discovered the man had asked many questions about the murder. He didn't tell them anything that would help them identify the stranger.

"I also saw something odd last night," the drunken man remarked from where he sat on the stool between Harlan and Sidney. "I saw a taxi pass the tavern around seven-thirty. Don't see many of them around here."

"A taxi?" Harlan asked with great interest. "Did you notice anyone in it?"

"Looked like a man. Must have made a wrong turn," the drunken man informed him. "Damn near ran over me in the parking lot."

"Are you sure there was only a man in the back?" Harlan asked suspiciously.

The drunken man shook his head and nearly fell off his bar stool. "Not in the back. He was driving the cab," he announced. "There was no one in the back. I'm positive."

Harlan bought him another drink. "Thanks, you've been a big help."

The drunken man took his drink and returned to the other end of the bar, allowing Sidney to return to the barstool beside Harlan.

"What do you suppose that means?" she practically gasped. "Trisha called a cab that doesn't even exist and left with some boyfriend I know nothing about?"

Harlan shook his head and finished his cranberry juice. "No, it means there was one guy at the library and another who drove up with the cab." He left a tip for Sam then stood. "I want to separate for a while," he said as he guided her to the tavern door and outside into the parking lot.

Sidney stopped him short of her car. "Separate? Why?"

"I need to make a few calls from my motel room then do a little snooping," he said simply.

"Why can't I go with you?"

Harlan groaned lowly. "Because I'll need someone to bail me out of the clink if I get caught."

Sidney's eyes widened. "You're going to break into someone's home?"

"That would depend if the doors are locked or not," he remarked and forced her toward her car. "Just go to Mrs. Cooper's house and talk to the old biddies. See if they know anything."

Sidney attempted to protest, but Harlan was persistent.

Chapter Thirty-one

Sidney drove to the library since she knew that was where Mrs. Randall would be at that time of day. She entered the library and headed for the basement archives since she'd most likely find the local snoop there. It was a stroke of luck that she found both busybodies within the archives. Mrs. Randall saw Sidney and hurried toward her.

"Sidney, Mary Allister called me and said that Trisha is gone," Mrs. Randall gasped while clutching Sidney's hand with both of hers. The older woman's hands were unusually cold despite the warm weather. "What happened? Where is the child?"

Sidney saw the concerned look in Mrs. Randall's eyes and knew she was genuinely upset. She shook her head. "I don't know where she is, Mrs. Randall."

Mrs. Cooper approached with a horrified look in her old eyes as she gently rubbed her hands along her chilled arms. She shared her friend's concern.

"She had received a death threat early yesterday morning," Sidney informed them. "She was supposed to wait here for me after work, but when I got here, she was gone."

Mrs. Randall shook her head vigorously with great fear. "No, not that poor child. What if something happened to her?" she gasped. "I just couldn't live with myself if something happened to her."

Mrs. Cooper gently patted Mrs. Randall's shoulder. "I'm sure she's fine," Mrs. Cooper said with certainty then looked at Sidney. "It wouldn't be the first time she's up and left without telling anyone. She's very independent and rather clever."

"No," Mrs. Randall gasped softly and looked back at Mrs. Cooper with horror in her eyes. "Something terrible has happened to her, I know it!"

"Calm down, Maria," Mrs. Cooper said gently and rubbed both her shoulders. "Remember your blood pressure."

"I'm trying," Mrs. Randall said softly and wrenched her trembling fingers together. "I just feel so helpless."

"We do have a lead," Sidney said gently. "Mr. Taylor across the street said he saw a taxi here last night around the time of her disappearance."

"There you have it, Maria," Mrs. Cooper announced firmly. "She left town on her own."

Sidney shook her head, disproving the theory. "No, I called the local taxi service. They said there weren't any cabs in this area last night."

"A taxi?" Mrs. Randall asked with some surprise in her eyes. "Could Mr. Taylor have been seeing things?"

"It was a consideration, but there was this man at Sam's today who claimed he was almost hit by a taxi last night," Sidney remarked. "It had a dented passenger side door."

"Sounds like the car Sam bought last week," Mrs. Cooper stated with a tilt of her head. "Wasted his money, if you ask me."

Sidney's heart skipped a beat as all the color drained from her face. "He what?"

Mrs. Randall suddenly gasped and placed a hand over her mouth. "Oh, my God, no!"

Mrs. Cooper looked at both women without a clue. "Surely you don't think--?"

"I have to go," Sidney announced as her heart began to pound uncontrollably.

Mrs. Randall grabbed Sidney's wrist with a firm, harsh grip. Her icy fingers chilled Sidney's skin. Mrs. Randall's eyes were wide and frightened.

"Have you looked in the old, stone house?" she practically gasped. "Sam and my son, Billy's father, used to hide out there as kids. If he has her, she's there."

Sidney felt a chill sweep through her body. She pulled away from Mrs. Randall and ran for the basement stairs. Sidney thundered up the stairs, ran out of the library, and bolted across the road directly in front of a car. The car slammed on its brakes with a screech, narrowly avoiding her. Sidney didn't even stop to look back. She ran along the sidewalk, causing several people on the sidewalk to stop and watch her. Sidney made it to the woods in under two minutes. She turned the path to the stone house and jumped over several rocks in her way. She reached the clearing in just five minutes. Her heart was racing, and her breathing was rapid. She stopped a moment to stare at the old house then hurried at a brisk walk for the front porch.

Sidney walked onto the porch, the steps creaking under her weight. She paused before the door and noticed the padlock over the front door. It was old and rusted. No one had been through the front door in years. Sidney hurried across the rickety porch and jumped down the steps. She jogged around to the back of the house and paused before the half-rotted wooden cellar door. The padlock was fairly new and unlocked. Sidney's heart raced as she removed the lock and pulled open the heavy door. The stone steps were broken, narrow, and steep. Sidney stared into the dimly lit cellar. Cobwebs seemed to line the walls, but none covered the stone steps. She couldn't see much beyond them. She cautiously walked down the steps. When she reached the bottom, she saw Trisha tied to one of the thick, tree trunk support beams in the middle of the cellar. She had duct tape over her mouth, and her head hung down.

"Trisha," Sidney gasped softly as fear and relief swept through her.

Trisha had a difficult time lifting her head but managed to look at Sidney. She was barely conscious, possibly doped up. Trisha groaned through the duct tape with a drowsy excitement. Sidney's heart pounded, and she ran across the cellar to her friend.

"Trisha! Thank God you're all right!" she cried out and removed the duct tape from her mouth.

"He stuck a needle in me," Trisha gasped softly as her eyes rolled back then shut. "He's going to make it look like I overdosed on drugs."

Sidney then saw the needle, a candle, and a bag of white powder on a small table in the corner. Sidney slipped around Trisha and fumbled with the ropes. There was padding around her wrists to prevent marks from the ropes. It had to look like an overdose and bruising would look suspicious. Trisha was so doped up; she was unable to fight the ropes that bound her anyway. Sidney struggled with the tight knot.

"Sidney," Trisha gasped with fear.

Sidney straightened and saw Sam appear at the bottom of the steps holding a semi-automatic handgun.

"You're a clever girl," Sam announced simply. "After I heard that story about the taxi nearly hitting that drunk, I wondered if someone would mention that I bought one." He walked a few steps closer. "It's a shame Trisha shot you when you tried to stop her from overdosing on cocaine. Friends are funny that way."

Sidney stared at Sam with horror while shielding her helpless friend on the floor. There was a shadow on the steps. Harlan appeared at the bottom of the steps with a tire iron in his hand. Sidney held her breath, and her heart pounded nervously as Harlan crept up behind Sam with the tire iron coiled back. Sam must've heard something and whipped around. The tire iron struck him on the shoulder rather than the back of his head as intended. Sam cried out, and the gun flew from his hand. Harlan coiled back for another swing. Sam lunged for Harlan, and both men struggled for control of the tire iron. Sam whipped Harlan around and cast him against the first support beam just before Trisha. The beam moved, and the ceiling creaked loudly.

Sidney ran for the discarded gun, looking around the dirt floor. She saw it near the wall. Trisha screamed a warning as best she could. Sidney didn't even have time to look behind her. She leaped for the gun, snatched it from the ground, and tossed herself into a sitting position with the gun aimed. The crowbar struck her hand. Sidney cried out in pain as the gun flew from her hand and hit the wall near her. Sam scrambled for the gun while Sidney clutched her hand in agony. She then saw Harlan lying unconscious on the floor near Trisha's feet. Sidney stared at Sam and the gun he now pointed at her.

"Get up," Sam ordered while breathing heavily as blood seeped from the corner of his mouth.

Harlan apparently got a few shots in before he went down. Sidney nervously rose to her feet while keeping an eye on Sam.

"Untie your friend," Sam demanded and motioned wildly with the gun.

She approached Trisha, checking Harlan's condition as she passed, then untied her friend. Trisha dropped to the floor and attempted to pull herself to her knees. She once more collapsed. Sidney made a motion to help her.

"Leave her," Sam ordered.

Sidney straightened and looked at Harlan, who still remained motionless. For a moment, she thought he might be dead. Her heartbeat quickened nervously. She had to do something, or they were all dead, but she didn't know what to do.

"Pick up those ropes and bring them to me," Sam announced firmly.

Sidney picked up the ropes and approached him without taking her eyes off him.

"These old houses are so unstable," Sam remarked simply. "They can collapse at any time." He kicked the weak support beam several times until it creaked and collapsed. The upper level creaked loudly as dirt fell to the basement.

"Sidney!" came her father's voice from somewhere outside the house. "Sidney, where are you?"

Sidney's heart raced with fear, knowing he'd shoot her father. How could she not warn him? She was dead already.

Sam looked back at Sidney with a scowl on his face. "You're coming with me to the top of the steps. You tell him everything's fine and convince him to leave, or I'll shoot both you and him," he growled. "Do you understand?"

Sidney nervously nodded. She feared for her father's life, but mostly she feared what she might do to stop that from happening. Sam forced her to the basement steps and kept the gun on her while remaining out of sight. Sidney stepped partially out of the basement and stared at her father just near the edge of the house.

"Sidney," he cried out with concern in his eyes. "What are you doing here? I nearly hit you with my car. What's going on?"

"I found Trisha," she said with a quiver in her voice. "You can tell her mother she's all right. We'll be along shortly."

"She's okay?" her father asked with a look of relief. "Thank God."

"You'd better go tell her mother. She'll be relieved to hear," Sidney said and held her breath.

Her father's eyes narrowed. "Are you okay?"

"Yes," she replied and attempted to sound confident. "Everything is under control. Trisha doesn't want to talk to anyone right now. Please, just find her mother and give her the message," she almost begged as tears welled in her eyes.

"All right, baby," he said gently.

Her father then tilted his head and pointed to the basement with knitted brows and a question in his eyes. Sidney's heart nearly stopped as her mouth dropped open. He suspected something was wrong without even an ounce of suggestion. Her eyes widened. She made a gun with her left hand against her thigh so Sam couldn't see. Her father nervously straightened and cleared his throat.

"Don't be long," he said simply then walked toward the side of the house.

When he disappeared around the corner, Sidney turned to Sam behind her on the steps near her right leg.

"He's gone."

Sam motioned for her to return to the basement. The ceiling continued to creak. Trisha lay motionless on the ground, possibly unconscious. To both their surprise, Harlan was gone! Sam stared at the spot where Harlan once lie then spun around. Harlan stepped out of the dark corner and kicked the gun from Sam's hand, sending it flying across the cellar. Harlan held the knife from her father's cabinet pointed inches from Sam's face.

"Get Trisha," Harlan shouted.

Sam stared coldly at the knife in his face without a word. Sidney ran to Trisha's fallen side and attempted to pull her to her feet. She wouldn't move or rouse.

"Drop it, Harlan," Herb shouted from the steps.

Sidney heard the familiar sound of a rifle being cocked. She whirled around on her knees with surprise and horror, though she couldn't see her father.

"Dad, no!"

Sam lunged for Harlan and the knife. They wrestled for control of the weapon. Harlan punched Sam roughly in the face. He fell into the support beam where Trisha had been tied. It moved and the ceiling buckled. Sam recovered and tackled Harlan to the floor as both men struggled with the knife. Dirt and wood dust clouded the cellar. Sidney's father hurried into the cellar with his high-powered rifle aimed.

"Daddy, help me!" Sidney cried out and tried to lift Trisha's limp body with her injured right hand.

Her father ran through the debris and gathered Trisha in his arms. She helped steady him as he lifted her friend. The house let out a thunderous crack. Herb sheltered Trisha in his arms and ran to the cellar steps. A plank from the ceiling crashed to the cellar narrowly missing the barely visible men still rolling around on the floor. Sidney sheltered her eyes and ran toward them. Sam seized the knife while beneath Harlan. He slashed at Harlan, who raised his arm for protection. The knife cut Harlan's forearm, causing him to cry out. Sidney violently thrust her foot into Sam's side. He cried out but didn't release the knife.   Sidney grabbed Harlan's arm and pulled him to his feet with all her strength.

There was a loud crack.   Harlan looked up, grabbed Sidney's arm, and threw her toward the steps.   The entire ceiling collapsed in one thunderous crash that vibrated the ground beneath their feet. Harlan and Sidney fell to the concrete steps as debris and dirt flew past them in a rolling cloud and a gust of air.   They coughed and gasped.   Sidney looked up and saw her father grabbing her arm as he pulled her to her feet.   She slowly stood on her own and coughed from the dirt.   Herb extended his hand to Harlan.   Harlan stared at his hand a moment then accepted it, allowing him to help him to his feet.   Once they climbed the crumbled basement steps, they turned to look at the house.   The entire stone structure remained standing.

Chapter Thirty-two

Sidney paced the emergency room while waiting for word on Trisha's condition. Her friend was unconscious when the ambulance brought her to the hospital. Sidney's father remained at the stone house to assist the police with the collapsed interior. It was possible Sam was still alive. Harlan was taken for stitches, which seemed to be taking a long time. When she looked toward the emergency room doors, Billy hurried toward her.

"I came as soon as I heard Trisha was brought in," he announced and gathered her in his arms.

Sidney returned the hug then pulled away and looked at him with some surprise. "You're not taking care of her?"

"She's with Dr. McQuinn. He's an excellent doctor," he informed her then shook his head. "Looks like a drug overdose. What happened?" He noticed her bruised wrist, held up her right arm, and examined her injury. "You're hurt."

"I'm alive," she informed him. Sidney drew a deep breath and collapsed into one of the chairs. "Do you have an hour for the entire story?"

"Not really."

Sidney gave a quick review of what had happened, which left Billy stunned.

"I can hardly believe things like that happen in Marilina," he gasped. "And Sam--" He shook his head with disbelief. "We've

173

known Sam for years. He was my father's best friend. Do you know what motivated him to do something like that?"

"I suppose it had to do with the murder of Emily Fisher," Sidney replied, now feeling weary from her ordeal. "There's no other explanation, really."

Billy continued to shake his head. "Wait until grandmother hears about this. It'll kill her."

"She already knows," Sidney gently informed him.

He shot a look at her. "She knows? How?"

"It's really a long story," Sidney explained. "I'm sure she'll tell you all about it when you get home."

"I'm sure I'll hear about it for weeks on end." He then tilted his head. "She was rather fond of Sam. She may not want to discuss it. I'd better call her and see that she's all right. Do you think she's at home or at Mrs. Cooper's?"

"I really couldn't say," she replied. "I saw her in the library with Mrs. Cooper. I think they're probably together wherever they are."

"Probably Mrs. Cooper's house," he said gently. "I'll check on Trisha's condition for you. I know how slow these doctors can be when you're waiting for news. I'll bring you some ice and a wrap for that wrist when I return. I just have to check on one of my patients first. Came in with a knife wound. Real unruly." He shook his head. "Wouldn't even allow me to look at the cut. The nurse had to take care of him."

Sidney forced a nervous smile. "Uh huh," she said gently. "That would be Harlan Brendan."

Billy stared at her with a look of surprise. "Harlan?"

"Yeah, uh, he came to town yesterday on assignment," Sidney said with some embarrassment. "He discovered Sam's taxi in the garage behind the tavern, became suspicious, and followed Sam. If he hadn't, Trisha and I would be dead right now."

"Well," Billy said while raising his brow. "I suppose I should be thankful to see him, but it appears he still has it out for me."

Sidney shifted uncomfortably. "He's rather stubborn."

"That wasn't the word I was searching for," Billy muttered then managed a smile. "I'll let you know what's happening with Trisha when I return."

"Thanks, Billy," she said timidly.

Sidney stood and paced some more once he had left. She wondered what had happened between Harlan and Billy. She couldn't imagine Harlan simply disliking someone, yet he wouldn't discuss his problems with Billy or her father. Sidney realized she didn't know Harlan all that well. He *was* a man of mystery.

§

It was a little while later when the doors to the emergency room opened, and Harlan wandered out. He saw Sidney and hurried toward her. His right forearm was wrapped in white bandages, but he seemed fine otherwise.

"I spoke with Trisha's doctor," he announced while pausing before her. "She should be fine."

Sidney felt a tremendous weight lift from her then exhaled and closed her eyes. "Oh, thank God," she gasped softly.

"Her mother's with her now. The doctor said she was almost in a coma," Harlan said gently. "It's a good thing we got her here when we did. They don't think there's any damage done that they can tell, but she'll be here a couple of days for recovery and observation. The drugs are still in her system, so there's still a potential hazard."

Sidney nodded understanding, although she remained concerned. "But she's out of danger, right?"

"Immediate danger, yes," he replied. "They wouldn't let me in, but I could see her from the hall. She was still out of it."

The nurse allowed Sidney to visit with Trisha, but only for a few minutes. Mary remained by her side. Trisha had IV lines in her arms and an oxygen cannula in her nose. She woke periodically, appeared to acknowledge them, and then slipped back to sleep. The nurses chased Sidney from the room after a few minutes. Billy joined her in the hallway near Trisha's room. He wrapped her wrist as promised then walked with her to the waiting area.

"I'll see that she's given the best care," he said and offered a warm, reassuring smile.

"I really appreciate it, Billy," Sidney said gently. "How's your grandmother?"

"She's upset about what happened with Sam, but Mrs. Cooper is looking after her until I get home."

They entered the waiting room and saw Sidney's father talking to Harlan.

Billy stopped and frowned. "I'll call you later, okay?"

Sidney nodded, accepting their hatred for each other for the time being, and then headed to join her father and Harlan. Her father gathered her in his arms and held her against him. He pulled away after a long moment then looked at her.

"Harlan says Trisha should be okay in a couple of days," Herb said gently while putting on a brave front. "I'm just so glad none of you were hurt worse."

"What about Sam?" Sidney asked.

Herb shook his head and gently rubbed her shoulders. "They're sure he died instantly."

"Justice be swift," Sidney remarked lowly.

Her father smirked and pulled her to his side. "I should get you home. Your mother is worried sick," he said softly then turned to face Harlan. "Care to join us for dinner, Harlan?"

Harlan looked at him with some surprise then smiled. "I'd love to."

§

They had a friendly conversation over dinner that evening. Harlan and Sidney's father laughed together for the first time in eight years. Sidney listened to them and wondered what caused them to fight in the first place. Was that incident forgotten or just set aside considering Harlan's heroics? After dinner, Sidney helped her mother clear the table while her father and Harlan went onto the porch to talk. Sidney wondered what they were discussing, but her father appeared to want to speak to him alone. Sidney handed her mother the dirty dishes to rinse before placing them in the dishwasher. Her curiosity had gotten the better of her.

"Mom, what happened between Harlan and Dad eight years ago?" she asked her mother bluntly.

Sidney's mother looked at her with some concern then looked back at the dishwasher. She placed the glasses on the top rack and appeared unwilling to discuss it.

"That's something you should discuss with your father," she replied.

Sidney laughed lowly. "Yeah, sure." She handed her mother a plate. "He won't tell me and neither will Harlan. I think if it's a question of Harlan's character, I have a right to know. We've been together for twenty-four hours. I don't like the way you and Dad keep secrets from me."

"They're together now," her mother said simply without looking at her. "Why don't you go ask them yourself?"

It was obvious her mother knew the answer but wasn't about to tell.

"I think I'll do just that," Sidney announced then handed her mother the last plate and walked through the living room.

She could hear low, harsh voices as she walked onto the porch. Harlan leaned his shoulder against the post with his arms folded across his chest while staring at her father with a harsh look. Her father remained sitting in a nearby chair with an equally scathing look.

"Did I interrupt something?" she asked nervously.

Her father forced a tiny smile. "No, of course not. We were just discussing old times."

Harlan's expression didn't lighten.

"The good ones, I hope," Sidney remarked lowly and looked at Harlan with some concern.

"I'd like to finish this right now," Harlan snapped lowly while glaring at Herb then straightened.

Sidney was surprised by his curt tone. When Harlan turned his attention to her, she became concerned.

"Tell your father what happened that day by the well at the stone house," Harlan snapped with anger.

Sidney stared at him a moment with some surprise then looked at her father. "Harlan took some pictures of the stone house, but the lighting was bad." She then looked back to Harlan and gave him a puzzled stare.

Harlan shook his head. "No, tell him about the scrapes on your arm and the cut on your cheek."

Sidney was confused for a few seconds. Her mouth suddenly fell open, and she shot a glare at her father. "I told you what happened. I fell off the well!"

Her father's expression became stern. "I know what you told me."

Sidney's head tilted, and her eyes widened. "Do you mean to tell me you'd believe the gossip of a bunch of old biddies over the word of your own daughter?" She shook her head with anger. "I was fifteen! I can't believe you'd actually think that Harlan and I were screwing around!"

"It wasn't just Mrs. Cooper and Mrs. Randall," her father snapped back. "Persha Palmer told me she overheard you and Trisha talking about some steamy scene by the well."

Harlan rolled his eyes and turned his back to them while groaning.

Sidney angrily folded her arms across her chest. "I had a crush on an older man. Get a life, Dad. It's because of you I don't even date!"

Harlan spun around and glared demandingly at Herb. "Now you're hearing it from your own daughter," he snapped irritably. "Doesn't that tell you something?"

Herb sprang to his feet and pointed a finger at Harlan. "You stay out of this!"

"Bloody hell I will! Not this time," Harlan snapped with anger in his eyes. "Your daughter was the only friend I had in this Godforsaken town. Yet you turned a simple friendship into some dirty molestation. Then, as a last resort to keep me away from Sidney, you cast accusations about Emily's murder, as if I had some fiendish part in it. I don't have to take it from you, Herb. The only person you're hurting is Sidney." Harlan then turned his attention to her. "You know where I'll be if you need me."

Sidney watched him leave the porch and walk across the front lawn. She bolted past her father and ran to catch Harlan. She caught his arm and forced him to face her. She pleaded with her eyes.

"You promised you'd help me, Harlan. You can't just leave me," Sidney said urgently.

"I'm not leaving you, I'm just going back to my room," he remarked with hostility. "Thank your mother for dinner. At least she's decent toward me."

Sidney stared at him for a long moment. "Wait right here," she announced. "Promise you won't leave until I return."

Harlan groaned softly. "I promise," he said with a roll of his eyes.

Sidney ran to the house and entered without a word to her father. She hurried upstairs, threw some clothing into her overnight bag, and then ran back outside. Her mother hurried after her while frantically drying her hands on a dishtowel. Sidney stopped to face her father, who'd been standing near the door, apparently waiting for her.

"Like it or not, Dad," Sidney announced boldly. "I'm staying with Harlan at the motel. I've never lied to you before. I'm a grown woman, and I can do whatever I want. Learn to accept it. When you decide to apologize to Harlan for your accusations, I'll come home."

Sidney ran off the porch and approached Harlan. He looked at her bag then raised a brow.

"Going somewhere?" Harlan asked.

"He needs to accept my word and respect my wishes," she remarked simply. "If it makes you uncomfortable, I can get my own room."

Harlan snorted a humored laugh. "I think I'll survive a couple of nights."

Sidney could hear her mother and father arguing as they walked to his car.

Chapter Thirty-three

Sidney lay across the bed on her stomach and flipped through Harlan's notepad while he sat on the other side of the bed and read the complimentary newspaper provided by the motel. Sidney read Harlan's notes from their interviews and frowned.

"I don't understand why Sam would kidnap Trisha," Sidney remarked simply. "I don't see how he could possibly be connected to Emily's murder."

"I don't think we'll ever really know his motivation. He took that secret to the grave with him," Harlan remarked then glanced at her above the paper. "Perhaps he had another reason for wanting Trisha out of the way."

"What other reason?" Sidney announced boldly and looked at Harlan. "Mr. Taylor confirmed there was a couple in the back of the cab, and obviously there was someone driving."

"Obviously."

"So who was Sam's accomplice?"

"Rumor had it Sam had been into drugs for years. Maybe that's the connection," Harlan said. "Maybe Trisha can supply that information once she's feeling better."

"Trisha wasn't buying drugs from Sam; I can assure you that," Sidney snapped lowly.

"That might be something you wouldn't know. You hadn't even seen Trisha in five years," he remarked. "How do you know what she was doing?"

"Trust me," Sidney said firmly. "She's not into that." She then looked at Harlan with wide eyes.

"What if Sam had been secretly in love with Emily? They could have been lovers also," she said and raised a brow. "Don't you agree?"

"Sam was a little on the old side for Emily, but that's not to say he couldn't have been in love with her," he remarked. "This mysterious typed letter that conveniently vanished must have some relevance on this whole case. Someone sent her a love letter. It wasn't Alex, and it wasn't me. It could have been Sam."

"Or Malcolm," Sidney chimed in.

Harlan frowned and stared across the room. "Or Persha," he said dully.

Sidney looked at him and gasped. "That's right. I can't rule her out as a potential lover."

"It's obvious she had strong feelings for Emily." He drew a deep breath and tossed the paper aside. "I'd like the opportunity to talk to Mrs. Randall and Mrs. Cooper about Sam," Harlan said simply and eyed Sidney.

She cringed slightly. "I don't know if that's such a good idea. Billy's usually close behind his grandmother. I'd like to keep some distance between the two of you."

"I honestly don't know what you see in him," Harlan remarked lowly without looking at her.

"I'd like to know what happened between you two that caused such harsh feelings," Sidney said and rolled onto her right side to study him.

Harlan frowned and shifted uncomfortably on the bed. "I caught him with a girl in a parked car outside Sam's Tavern. Knowing how indiscreet kids can be, I first passed it off," he informed her. "When I heard the girl scream, I knew she was in trouble. The girl was trying to get away from him, but he wasn't letting her go. So I helped him out of the car. We had some words, he swung at me, and I escorted him to the ground. Apparently, the girl never pressed charges, but I'll never let him forget what I know."

Sidney stared at him with surprise. "I can't believe he'd do something like that."

"Well there's my word, and there's his word," Harlan said simply. "You'll have to decide whom you want to believe."

Sidney stared at Harlan a long moment. "I think I'd believe just about anything you told me," she replied simply then smiled. "I suppose it's that blind faith. I wouldn't say I know you much better than I know Billy, but I know Billy had gotten into some trouble when he was younger." She laughed softly. "Of course, you may also have, but I wouldn't know much about that."

"I got into some trouble on occasion, though nothing to warrant an arrest. My mother was strict while I was growing up," he said simply.

"What about your father?"

Harlan drew a deep breath and shifted uncomfortably. "My father died in Russia. He was in the theater when he met my mother. He defected, they were married, and I was conceived. The government caught him, and he was returned to Russia."

"Trisha and I discovered Brendan wasn't your real last name," Sidney admitted. "Why didn't you tell me?"

"I got enough static about being English in this narrow-minded town," he announced with a chuckle then eyed her. "Had they known I was part Russian, they would have hung me as a spy or something."

Sidney managed a humored laugh. "Come on, Harlan. The people of this town aren't that narrow-minded."

"Try being an outsider," he remarked bluntly. "I was always 'that foreign photographer fella'. Your father treated me decent until he thought I was molesting his daughter. You were the only one who was genuinely nice to me."

"You could have been an alien from another planet, and it wouldn't have mattered. You were cute and had a nice butt," she announced then looked back at the notebook. "That's enough for a teenage girl."

Harlan continued to smile. "The reason didn't matter. I was just glad to be accepted. It wasn't easy making friends around here," he replied. "When I moved to California, Lyle and I worked for the same newspaper. He invited me to a poker game at his house. I lost one hundred dollars to him. We've been friends ever since." He chuckled and grinned. "Of course, I've won all the poker games since then."

"Trisha really liked Lyle," Sidney said gently then allowed her thoughts to stray to her friend in the hospital.

"He has that effect on women," Harlan remarked, catching Sidney's attention. "He can be very charming."

Sidney gently cleared her throat. "I suppose we could see Mrs. Cooper tomorrow. We may be able to catch her alone while Mrs.

Randall does her volunteer work at the library. We can avoid Billy, for your sake."

"You never did answer my question," Harlan remarked simply and cast a look at her.

Sidney tilted her head and looked at him with some confusion. "What question?"

"Your interest in the good doctor," he remarked bluntly.

"He's been helpful," she replied then casually shrugged. "But there isn't anything beyond that."

Harlan raised a skeptical brow. "Judging by what I saw at the bridge, I'd say there was something more."

Sidney laughed and looked away with some embarrassment. "Oh, that," she replied and looked back at him with a tiny smile. "Some men are a little more affectionate than others."

Harlan continued to stare at her with little expression. "Some men only have one thing on their mind too."

"It's not like we were really even out on a date," she stated with some concern to what Harlan might think. "Well, sort of like a date."

"So he's interested in you, and you're leading him on?" Harlan asked while raising a curious brow.

Sidney sat up and stared at Harlan with some surprise. "It's not that way at all," she remarked defensively. "I never said I was interested in dating him."

"You don't have to," Harlan replied simply. "Men get their own ideas. I heard him say he'd call you later."

"That was about Trisha," Sidney said lowly.

"Are you so sure?"

"Just stop it, Harlan," she snapped. "I don't need a lecture from you on how to talk to men."

"It would seem to me, Billy hasn't changed much over the past eight years," Harlan retorted. "You lead him on, and it might be you in that car trying to escape."

"He's a doctor. Do you really think he's going to put his profession on the line for something like that?"

"His profession doesn't matter. Professionals have committed crimes," Harlan informed her. "A doctorate doesn't make a man a saint."

"You've got the wrong idea about Billy. Someone could easily say the same thing about you," she snapped with sharply raised brows. "I mean, what's more convenient than having me in your motel room? There was a time when others thought you were a child molester."

"Now that hurt," Harlan muttered lowly while staring at her. "You know me better than that."

"Yes, I do, but there are those who don't trust you. Billy has been very accommodating and helpful, so just lay off him, okay?" she remarked.

Harlan drew a deep breath. "I won't bring him up anymore." He stood. "I'm going to get some coffee from the diner. Do you want anything?"

"No, thank you," she said softly then watched him leave.

§

Sidney thought about her situation while Harlan was gone.

She realized she had become as obsessed with the murder as Trisha had, and it nearly cost Trisha her life. It was a dangerous game they'd been playing, and someone was bound to get hurt. But what about Sam? What was his involvement in Emily Fisher's death? Nothing seemed to indicate he had anything to do with the murder, so why did he want to eliminate Trisha? Who drove the cab? There had to be an accomplice. Her thoughts then strayed to Harlan. After all the years that had passed, her feelings for him hadn't changed, yet she hadn't given him any indication of her feelings. She suddenly realized why she avoided relationships all these years. She was still thinking about Harlan. In her mind, she'd built him up to be her idea of the perfect man. A little older, she now realized that fantasy men were never what they seemed, but Harlan was still the man she wanted.

Chapter Thirty-four

It was nearly nine o'clock when Sidney decided to join Harlan at the diner. He had walked there an hour ago and still hadn't returned, possibly because of their disagreement about Billy Randall. She knew she'd cross paths with Harlan somewhere between the motel and the diner. She was determined to tell him how she felt and finally let it all out. She left the motel room and found herself staring at Sam's Tavern. The lights were out, and the bar was closed possibly for the first time in decades. Sidney rubbed her chilled arms then turned and hurried toward town. Once she reached town, there were some people on the sidewalks, but the night was a little too cool to sit on their porches.

She approached the diner, which was a little busier since Sam's was closed, and looked in the window before entering. Sidney saw Harlan sitting at the counter with Mrs. Lamont occupying the seat beside him. Mrs. Lamont threw her head back and laughed at something he'd said then placed her flirty hand on his lower arm. When she saw Harlan smile in reaction, Sidney immediately frowned. She couldn't believe the nerve of Mrs. Lamont. She couldn't believe Harlan was enjoying the flirting of the shameless, married woman. Sidney stood motionless while watching them. She had half a nerve to go in there and fight for the man she wanted. She suddenly felt defeated. If Harlan had any feelings at all for her, he would have made a move by now. She no longer saw the point in pursuing him. At least that explained why he hadn't returned to the motel.

As she turned and headed back toward the motel, Sidney decided she would go to Trisha's house and see if her mother would allow her to spend the night there. She didn't want to return to her parents' house, not after the scene she had made earlier, and she wasn't about to stay in Harlan's room another night either. He'd obviously found a woman more his speed anyway.

"Sidney," came a familiar male voice.

Sidney turned to her right and saw Mr. Taylor standing by his front door. He waved for her to join him. She wasn't really in the mood to talk to anyone, but she reluctantly walked onto his porch and joined him.

"Heard about Trisha," he announced with a look of concern on his wrinkled, sagging face. "Is she okay?"

It would seem Trisha had a place in more hearts than Sidney had given the town credit. She forced a tiny smile. "She's holding her own," she replied with optimism. "She'll have to stay in the hospital a couple of days."

He shook his head vigorously. "That son-of-a-bitch Sam. I'm glad the bastard's dead," Mr. Taylor nearly shouted. "Never would've believed he'd do such a thing. I suppose they've closed the tavern."

Sidney nodded.

"Huh," he snorted lowly. "Those old boozers will have to go somewhere else for a while. Malcolm will be heartbroken. That was his home away from home. Swear that man didn't have a life. Wife found out he was screwing around with that teacher who was murdered."

Sidney studied Mr. Taylor. It seemed surprising his mind was so sharp, despite his outward appearance. "What do you remember about Emily Fisher's death?"

He lifted a sagging brow and stared at her. "I remember I nearly hit that biker fella she'd been dating. He was fleeing the scene, so they said."

"We witnessed him running away from her body," Sidney added as she insecurely placed her hands in her pockets.

"Ah," he remarked and waved her off with irritation. "I don't believe the biker fella killed her."

Sidney tilted her head with surprise. "You don't?"

"Not after what happened today," he boldly announced. "Trisha kept telling me that biker fella didn't do it. I told her she was young and foolish. But on the day that Fisher woman was killed, I remember seeing Sam speeding through town as if he caught the devil."

"Is there something unusual about that?" Sidney asked without understanding his point.

"Sam never drove through town. If he ever came this way, he'd walk," he insisted. "Something possessed him to get somewhere in a hurry. I doubt that he stopped at the diner. He'd already been serving food at the tavern for nearly a year. Sides, he'd walk if that were the case."

"Around what time do you think you saw him?" Sidney asked then wondered if that was too much to expect him to remember after eight years.

"Don't remember the time anymore, but I was getting ready to leave for my granddaughter's," he informed her. "She'd just had a baby boy a week earlier. That's when I saw Sam speeding past. About twenty minutes later, I nearly hit that biker fella on Cressman Road."

Sidney pondered his comment for several minutes while Mr. Taylor stared at her. "That would've given him enough time to be in the woods while Emily was alone, but if he had killed her, why would he drive to town to establish his alibi?"

"Mrs. Randall has been a family friend for years," Mr. Taylor responded to her question, nearly startling her.

Sidney snapped out of her trance like state and looked at the elderly man before her. "So Mrs. Randall had said, but Mrs. Randall wasn't home that afternoon, so he couldn't have gotten his alibi from her." Sidney's eyes then narrowed as she thought about her conversation with Mrs. Randall in the library. "I wonder if she suspected Sam had something to do with the murder."

"If you talk to her long enough," Mr. Taylor said simply, "she'll eventually tell you everything she knows. That biddy doesn't know how to shut up."

Sidney then looked to her right and saw Harlan leaving the diner. She held her breath a moment then saw him walk in the opposite direction from the motel. Sidney wondered where he was going. He wasn't even heading in the right direction for Mrs. Lamont's house. She looked back at Mr. Taylor and smiled.

"Thanks for your help, Mr. Taylor," she announced then hurried off the porch and followed Harlan from a safe distance.

When he passed Mrs. Cooper's house and entered the woods, Sidney became concerned. She kept her distance and remained hidden within the darkness of the woods. Harlan approached the stone bridge. Sidney could barely see him from where she stood, but she didn't dare get any closer. A man appeared from the other side of the bridge. She couldn't see who it was, but he was slightly larger than Harlan. It could have been her father for all she knew, though she doubted it. They spoke too softly for her to hear. Sidney wondered what he was up to. Why was he meeting people here this time of night? She decided it wasn't a good idea to be where she was.

She turned and hurried out of the woods before she was seen. Sidney walked at a fast pace back to the motel. She wasn't sure what she wanted to do. Should she continue with her original plan and go to Trisha's house? Or should she play it cool and remain in the room until Harlan returned? A small part of her wondered if Harlan was connected with Trisha's disappearance. She shamed herself for even thinking such a thing, but he had left the bridge with the knowledge of Trisha's location. He was also back in enough time to have gone to the library, removed Trisha with Sam's help, and arrive for their meeting by the bridge. He was also in town the night Trisha received the death threat.

Sidney raked her fingers through her hair then shook her head. "No, I will not believe for one minute he had anything to do with it," Sidney heard herself say aloud as she approached the motel room.

Had he and Sam been in on it together, Sam would have said something in the cellar of the old house. They fought against each other. Even if they had turned on each other, something would have been said; she was almost positive. Sidney entered Harlan's room and saw Billy standing by the dresser looking at the notebook that lay on it. Sidney was momentarily startled to see him in Harlan's room.

"Billy, what are you doing here?" she asked while eying him with surprise.

Billy set the notebook down and turned to face her with a look of concern. "I was looking for you. Your mother said you fought with your father, so you came here with Harlan. Are you okay?"

"Yes, of course," she replied but didn't move from the doorway. "You can't stay here. If Harlan finds you here, he'll flip."

"I'm not afraid of him," Billy snapped lowly. "If you need a place to stay, you can stay at my house. I don't like the idea of leaving you alone with him. You shouldn't put so much trust into him."

Sidney folded her arms across her chest. "You think I have a lot of reason to trust you?"

He suddenly turned defensive and cocked his head. "What's that supposed to mean?"

"I heard Harlan's version of what happened outside Sam's Tavern with that girl," she remarked while glaring at him. "Someone's been lying to me."

Billy frowned and shook his head. "I wouldn't lie to you. If you start trusting him, you're going to get hurt. Don't you know what older men want with younger women? He's just going to use you until he gets his way, then he'll discard you and go home. You're smarter than that, Sidney."

She nodded her head and raised her brows. "You said it. Yes, I am smarter than that," she informed him. "I think I can deal with Harlan. I really don't want him to find you here, so would you please leave?"

Billy nodded toward the notebook on the dresser. "You're investigating the murder of Miss Fisher, aren't you?" he practically demanded. "This isn't some game, Sidney. If he was involved, as half this town thinks he was, you could be putting your life in jeopardy. I don't want to see anything happen to you. If you use a man like Harlan, he'll hurt you."

Sidney rolled her eyes and groaned. "Look, I know what I'm doing. I'll talk to you tomorrow when I visit Trisha."

Billy's eyes strayed past her. Sidney turned around and saw Harlan standing behind her. She jumped with alarm then nervously ran her fingers through her hair. Harlan glared at Billy with narrow eyes.

"What the hell are you doing in my room?" Harlan growled lowly.

Billy folded his arms across his chest and returned the stare. "I was making sure Sidney was all right."

Harlan snorted a laugh and raised a cocky brow. "Of course she's all right," he snapped. "She's with me, not you."

"I don't know what lies you've been telling her, but I won't tolerate it," Billy said with anger in his voice. "This entire town knows what sort of monster you are."

"Monster?" Harlan growled. "What an interesting choice of words. Is that what that girl called you when you attacked her in your car?"

Billy's eyes narrowed. "I don't know what you're talking about, Harlan, but it had better stop."

"Get out of my room," Harlan snarled. "Or I'll throw you out."

Billy looked at Sidney then approached the door and Harlan. Billy was at least four inches taller than Harlan, ten years younger, and built more muscular. Harlan showed no fear and didn't take his eyes off him.

"If I hear you've harmed Sidney in any way, I'll make you sorry," Billy snapped coldly.

"She's not being forced to stay," Harlan remarked lowly. "She can leave if she wants to."

Billy glanced back at Sidney with a gentle look in his eyes. "You don't need him, Sidney. Whatever you're looking for, I can help you find it."

Sidney held her breath, looked at Harlan, then back to Billy. "I appreciate your concern, but I'm staying here."

Billy nodded. "All right. I'll talk to you tomorrow." He glared at Harlan then left the motel room.

Harlan slammed the door behind him then locked it. When he turned around, his expression hadn't softened.

"So what was that conversation about?" he asked and gave her a cold stare.

Sidney raised a curious brow. "What conversation?"

"The part about you using me," Harlan snapped with irritation. "What's going on between you two? Is there something you're not telling me?"

Her mouth opened with surprise. "There's nothing between Billy and me. And I'm not keeping things from you."

"Why would you be using me?" he demanded to know.

Sidney groaned and shook her head. "He thinks I'm using you to uncover the truth behind Emily Fisher's murder. He came up with that assumption all on his own."

"If the two of you are conspiring, I think I have a right to know," he snapped hotly.

Sidney rolled her eyes and walked across the room. "We're not conspiring against you, Harlan," she snapped then spun around halfway across the room. "I have little involvement with Billy. You know just as much as I do. What's your problem anyway?"

"My problem?" Harlan launched back with wide eyes. "I've dropped everything to come back here and keep you from getting yourself killed. I was nearly killed by a disgruntled bartender, and a house almost fell on top of me. We won't even discuss the little matter of the way I've been treated by your father. I'm starting to question my reasons for coming here in the first place. I must have been bloody mad to talk myself into it!"

"I didn't force you to come, Harlan," she snapped then held her breath. She stared at him for a long moment. Her expression lightened, and she sighed softly. "But I was grateful that you had. I don't want to fight with you." She walked toward him and stopped a couple of feet away. "If you think there has to be sides taken, then I'm on your side. I thought that was rather obvious." She stared into his eyes. "I don't get it, Harlan. I've been defending you all along. Why have you stopped trusting me?"

Harlan looked away and scratched his bearded chin. "I haven't stopped trusting you. It's just--" He held his breath then sighed. "It's been a long day. Let's just forget it, okay?"

Sidney had to agree with that. If the day had been any more traumatic, she'd be on Thorazine. "Would you like me to leave? I could go to Trisha's house. Her mother wouldn't mind," Sidney said softly.

Harlan looked back at her and searched her eyes with a strange tenderness. "No, don't go," he almost whispered. He moved toward her and pulled her against him. "I'm sorry, Sidney. I didn't mean to take my frustrations out on you."

Sidney felt her heart skip a beat then pound harshly. She placed her arms around his neck and returned the embrace. She sighed softly and rested her head on his shoulder.

"I haven't exactly been the most pleasant person this past week either," she gently replied.

"I think we both need some sleep and pretend this day never happened," he said gently.

"No," she said with a sigh. "I just needed a hug."

Harlan laughed softly. "Me too."

Chapter Thirty-five

Sidney woke the next morning and realized that Harlan had snuggled against her from behind sometime during the night. His left arm securely clung to her waist, and his body was spooned against hers, allowing her to feel his entire body pressed against her from behind. She couldn't deny she enjoyed the way he felt against her. She placed her left hand on his arm and gently caressed it. Her body ached with desire. He stirred slightly allowing his hips to grind against her buttocks. She could feel his morning desire, which only increased the dull ache throughout her body. His mouth touched her neck, and he gently kissed her. She tensed slightly and felt her heartbeat quicken. He abruptly stopped, possibly having awoken from his erotic dream.

"Forgive me, Sidney. I--I didn't mean to--" He pulled away and jumped from the bed. "Sorry."

Harlan hurried into the bathroom and shut the door before she had a chance to protest. Sidney groaned while rolling onto her back and pulled the pillow over her head. She heard the shower running a couple of seconds later. Had he initiated, she would have made love to him without a second thought. Perhaps it was better this way. Once the investigation was over, he'd return to California, and she'd have to morn losing him all over again. Sadly, she still couldn't shake the overwhelming desire he'd stirred within her.

§

Harlan and Sidney stopped by the diner for breakfast that morning. They sat in one of the empty booths with an awkward silence between them. Mary Allister approached their table with a look of relief on her face.

"Oh, Sidney, I'm so glad you stopped here this morning," she announced with a pleasant smile. "Trisha was talking last night. She was still in and out, but at least she knew what was happening around her."

"That's great, Mrs. Allister," Sidney announced cheerfully. "I'll be visiting her later today."

"I'm working until five tonight," Mary reported with enthusiasm. "What can I get you two? It's on me. It's the least I can do for all that you've done for Trisha." She then looked at Harlan. "I owe you so many apologies, Harlan. If there's ever anything I can do--?"

Harlan smiled politely. "You can start by not thanking me anymore. If I was some sort of hero, I think Herb would appreciate me a lot more."

Mary let out a sharp snort. "You wait until I see that grouch. I'll give him a piece of my mind." She then smiled and gave Harlan an approving once-over. "He should be proud to have such a heroic man dating his daughter."

They ordered some coffee and tea then watched Mary return to the counter for their drinks.

Harlan shook his head and looked at Sidney. "What did I do?" he asked and snorted a soft laugh. "I got my ass kicked while your father carried Trisha out of the building. The house took care of Sam."

"Accept hero status for a day," Sidney remarked bluntly. "It may never happen again."

"Damned right," he snapped. "I'm not a fighter." Harlan looked out the window and groaned. "I may have to rethink that last statement."

Sidney looked out the window also and saw her father crossing the street and approaching the restaurant. She jumped from her seat.

"I'll handle this," she announced then hurried from the diner and stopped just outside the door.

Her father paused before her and raised a tiny smile. "Hi, baby," he said softly.

Sidney folded her arms across her chest and glared at her father with limited patience. "I hope you didn't come here to start trouble with Harlan."

"No," he replied softly. "You gave me a lot to think about last night, and I realized you were one hundred percent right for telling me off. I want to apologize for my behavior these past eight years." He drew a deep breath. "I admit I was damned overbearing. Whatever your present relationship with Harlan, you have my complete support."

Sidney was surprised by the comment. Her arms fell to her sides and her head tilted. "Will you apologize to Harlan?"

He nodded without hesitation. Sidney stepped away from the door to the restaurant and followed him inside. They approached the table near the window. Harlan looked up and rolled his eyes. He muttered something under his breath.

"I'm not here to start anything with you," Herb announced gently. "I've come to apologize for everything I'd said to you eight years ago, and everything I'd said to you last night. My insecurities about my daughter are something I'll have to deal with. I should never have taken them out on you. I know you'd never do anything to disrespect my family or me."

Harlan stared at her father a long moment then drew a deep breath. "Care to join us for breakfast?"

Her father sighed with relief then smiled more naturally. "I'd love to."

Sidney sat in the booth alongside her father and across from Harlan. Mary approached with her pad and pen, ready to take their order. She stared at Herb with surprise and then pointed her pen at him with an angered look on her face.

"You, sir, are on my shit list!" Mary proclaimed loud enough for the entire restaurant to hear.

Herb looked at her with some surprise. "Me? Why me?" he asked.

"After all this man has done for both our daughters, and you can't even get beyond whatever disagreement you two had eight years ago," she launched. "That's plain insulting!"

Sidney was slightly embarrassed. "It's okay, Mrs. Allister. He's apologized."

Mary blushed and shifted from foot to foot. "Oh, I'm sorry. I hadn't realized--"

"It's okay," Herb announced warmly and fidgeted. "I deserved it."

Mary took their order without another word then scurried away. Her father leaned on his elbows and studied Harlan while Sidney drank some bitter tea.

"Pauline and I were discussing it last night," he announced and released a gentle sigh. "If you want to marry Sidney, we're proud to have you as a son-in-law."

Sidney gagged on her tea then looked at her father with shock and dismay. Her mouth fell open and her cheeks immediately reddened. She looked back at Harlan and shifted uncomfortably. Harlan stared at her father with his same solemn expression and a timid smile.

"I'll keep that in mind," Harlan announced and didn't bother correcting him.

Sidney stared at Harlan a long moment with surprise. Harlan looked back at Sidney and chuckled softly with amusement.

Chapter Thirty-six

Sidney eyed Harlan as they walked to Mrs. Cooper's house, which was just a short distance from the diner. She shook her head and nervously ran her fingers through her hair.

"I can't believe you did that," she remarked sharply.

He looked at her with a gentle tilt of his head and an arrogant smile. "Did what?"

"Led my father to believe we might get married one day," she snapped.

"Your father already thinks we're lovers, and he's accepted it," he announced. "I didn't see the harm."

"I don't understand the logic behind that," she remarked.

"Why lower his opinion of me? It would just upset him all over again," Harlan replied simply while they walked.

Sidney rolled her eyes. "You're something else." She then entertained the thought of being married to Harlan. She looked down the street toward Mrs. Cooper's house and the woods. A feeling of defeat swept over her. It was useless to dream something so outrageous. She frowned and placed her hands in her pockets. They approached Mrs. Cooper's house, walked onto the porch, and knocked on the door. Sidney then realized Harlan was staring at her.

"What's with you?" he asked while sharply raising a brow. "You look annoyed about something."

Sidney forced a tiny smile and shrugged. "It's been a rough week."

They waited a couple of minutes before the door was finally opened. Mrs. Cooper appeared happy to see Sidney and ushered them into the front room where she offered them some tea. Both declined. Mrs. Cooper sat in the chair across from them, wrenched her fingers together, and shook her head.

"I'm worried about Maria," she said while looking at both. "She was so upset last night; I was afraid to leave her. When Billy came home, he had to give her a sedative."

"I'm sure she'll be fine," Sidney replied. "Billy will take care of her."

"Sam was a close friend of the family. He was best friends with her son since high school. When Mrs. Randall's son died, Sam was there to comfort her and Billy. I just can't believe he'd do something so underhanded." She looked at Harlan then back at Sidney. "I mean, I know he tried to kill Trisha and both of you as well. I'm not that naive. I just don't understand why."

Sidney nodded sympathetically. "I understand your confusion, Mrs. Cooper. We're equally stumped about his motive," she replied. "We're almost positive it had something to do with the murder of Emily Fisher. Trisha was investigating her death when she received the threat." Sidney tensed slightly. "Do you think you could answer a few questions about that day? If you can remember."

"Of course I can. My memory is very good," she replied almost offended. "A lot better than Mrs. Randall's, but don't tell her I said that."

Mrs. Cooper told her accounts of that day. Her story coincided with the original version she had told Sidney and Trisha earlier that week. Once she had finished, with as little speculation as possible, Harlan began to ask his questions.

"Where did you go that afternoon?" Harlan asked with great interest.

Mrs. Cooper looked at the ceiling and appeared to consider the question. "I left for the grocery store around four-thirty. Mrs. Randall usually goes with me on a Friday. They have discounts on all their canned goods on Friday," she informed them as if it mattered. "Mrs. Randall had to take Billy shopping at the last minute for some things. That boy hated to shop."

"So you wouldn't know if Sam had been this way the day of the murder," Harlan remarked with a depressed sigh.

"Oh, yes," Mrs. Cooper declared with enthusiasm. "I didn't think much about it at the time. It was nearly six o'clock when I returned from the store. Sam drove past me in town with his dirty, old pickup truck."

Harlan's brows knitted. "Six o'clock? Are you sure?"

"Of course I'm sure, young man," she remarked sternly. "I was home in time to watch my game show. It came on at six, though it's not on anymore," she remarked then pondered the comment. "They canceled it nearly three years ago. I hadn't even known about the incident in the woods. The police must've driven right through the path to the bridge."

"Where do you suppose he had been?" Harlan asked while leaning forward.

"Wouldn't have been at Mrs. Randall's. She didn't come home until seven or so," Mrs. Cooper said simply. "I suppose he could have been to her house, realized she wasn't home, and returned to the bar."

"Actually, Mrs. Cooper," Harlan began, "Sam was seen heading this way around ten to five. He was somewhere for an hour if your story is accurate."

"Of course it is," she proclaimed with offense. "I know what I'm talking about. Your other source must be mistaken. There's nowhere Sam would have been on this side of town except at Mrs. Randall's place."

Harlan was silent a moment then shifted uncomfortably before exchanging looks with Sidney. He then looked back at Mrs. Cooper. "Did you see Mrs. Randall return at seven?"

"Well, no," Mrs. Cooper replied simply. "I don't know what that--?"

"Did you talk to Mrs. Randall that evening?" he interrupted, not letting her control the conversation.

"Only briefly. She was exhausted after her shopping trip," Mrs. Cooper said. "Why would you ask--?"

"The next morning, did she seem her usual self?" Harlan pressed sternly.

"Well, I, uh, don't really remember," Mrs. Cooper said and placed a hand to her temple. "We, uh, had a conversation about shoes, I think. She had a terrible headache that day. I remember that well. I gave her some of my special pills." She appeared confused. "Why all the--?"

Harlan took Sidney's arm and pulled her up with him as he stood. "Thank you for everything, Mrs. Cooper. You've been a tremendous help."

"But, wait," Mrs. Cooper announced and stood more slowly. "Why all the questions about Mrs. Randall?"

"We'll show ourselves out, Mrs. Cooper," Harlan announced and practically dragged Sidney out the front door.

Once they left the porch, Harlan hurried toward the woods. Sidney had to jog to keep up with his fast pace.

"Why are we in such a hurry? Mrs. Randall isn't going to run away," Sidney announced.

"Don't be so sure," Harlan replied. "I'd like to get there before Mrs. Cooper forewarns her of our visit. I don't want to give her any time to perfect her story for that day."

"But if our theory is correct, and she knew about Sam's involvement, that would mean Billy knew as well," Sidney remarked sternly.

"An accessory after the fact," Harlan announced firmly. "It wouldn't have been too difficult for Sam to leave the tavern, park along Cressman Road, intercept Emily by the bridge, kill her, then drive back to Mrs. Randall's before Alex returned to find her dead."

They crossed the bridge at a brisk walk.

"But Trisha said no one was home at Mrs. Randall's when she went for help," Sidney protested. "Certainly if Sam was looking for an alibi, he'd leave his truck in plain sight."

Harlan stopped at the woods' edge just before Cressman Road and the development and stared at her with some confusion.

"If she wasn't home, wouldn't he have returned to the tavern right away?" Sidney asked. "He was taking a greater risk being gone so long. I mean, he claimed he was at the tavern during the time Emily Fisher was murdered."

"But we've established he wasn't," Harlan said softly and looked at the ground deep in thought. "I'm almost positive she was there," he said and looked at her. "If he didn't use her as his alibi, then he must not have done it." Harlan's eyes widened. "We have to hurry. I just had a terrible thought."

Sidney and Harlan ran the rest of the way through the development. Sidney could hardly believe it of Mrs. Randall. They hurried onto the porch of the large home, where she lived with Billy. Harlan rang the doorbell. They waited impatiently, but there was no response. Harlan approached the large, bay window and looked between the separations in the curtains. Sidney knocked on the door with the brass knocker. Harlan suddenly ran back to the door and pushed her aside. Sidney looked at him with some surprise then watched as he turned the doorknob. It wasn't locked! Harlan ran into the house with Sidney directly behind him. She froze with horror when she saw Mrs. Randall lying on the floor at the bottom of the stairs. She was twisted in an awkward position on her back with her pale hand on her chest. Harlan sank to one knee and checked her pulse.

"I'll call an ambulance," Sidney gasped and hurried down the hall to the phone.

"Don't bother," he announced and straightened.

Sidney froze and spun to face him as her heart pounded in fear of his words.

"She's been dead a couple of hours. Call the police," he said gently.

Sidney hurried to the phone and attempted to keep her hand from shaking as she dialed the number while tears welled in her eyes.

"And don't touch anything else," Harlan stated firmly.

Sidney suddenly looked at him with surprise at the statement. "Why?"

"It would appear she fell down the steps and had a heart attack," he remarked simply. "But I'm not buying it."

Sidney jumped when Sheriff Drukard answered the phone. She told him what they suspect had happened, and that he should get to Mrs. Randall's house as soon as he could. She replaced the receiver and turned around. Harlan was no longer by the stairs. She looked around with concern.

"Harlan?" she called out and walked toward the stairs.

She peered at Mrs. Randall's lifeless body as she passed. Harlan stood in the living room and stared at one of the older pictures on the wall.

Sidney looked over his shoulder. "Should I call Billy or wait for the police?"

"I'm sure he's aware of her condition," Harlan remarked bluntly, as his eyes narrowed while staring at the picture.

Sidney stared at Harlan's profile with a surprised look. "What are you suggesting?" she gasped softly.

He looked at her and raised his brows. "Sam went to Mrs. Randall's house for an hour, but he didn't admit to being there. Mrs. Randall claims she wasn't home, but she had to be, or Sam wouldn't have risked staying there. The only possible explanation for neither claiming to be together is obvious. Sam didn't need an alibi."

He then pointed to the picture on the wall. "Ever make this connection?"

Sidney looked at the large, framed picture of Billy from high school in his football uniform. There was a large number fourteen on his chest. Harlan placed his finger up to the picture and blocked the extension on the four, leaving two vertical lines. A chill ran down Sidney's spine as she gasped and covered her mouth.

"Oh, my God!"

Harlan raised his brows sharply. "A dying woman's last image is the number fourteen on a young man's jersey, but she's only able to complete two vertical lines."

Her eyes were wide and horror-filled. "The letter from the school typewriter, Sam's involvement, and the eleven--it all makes sense now!"

"Though we're left with a lack of evidence," Harlan remarked lowly.

She stared at him blankly, unable to think straight. "What do you suggest we do?"

"We certainly can't tell Sheriff Drukard what we suspect. It's going to look like an accident, even in an autopsy," he informed her. "Mrs. Cooper said Billy gave her sedatives. They'll assume she was weak from the sedative, fell down the stairs, and had a heart attack from the shock of the fall. Suggesting Billy murdered Emily would be a mistake. We have no proof, and it'll just give him time to perfect his story."

"Oh, Harlan," she gasped softly and rubbed her chilled shoulders while fighting her tears. "He killed his own grandmother?"

Harlan pulled her into his arms and held her against him. "We'll think of something, Sidney," he said gently. "Just keep yourself together, okay?"

Sidney clung to Harlan and sniffed softly. "I will," she whispered into his shoulder.

Chapter Thirty-seven

Sheriff Drukard confirmed what Harlan suspected. It appeared to be a heart attack caused by her fall down the stairs. There was no evidence of foul play, as Harlan suspected there wouldn't be. When Billy was contacted, Harlan insisted they leave. They walked in silence toward the woods. It wasn't until they entered the woods when Sidney spoke.

"Do you really think Billy killed his own grandmother?" Sidney asked and gently bit her lower lip.

"She was upset about Trisha," Harlan reported simply. "I think she would have told us what we wanted to know. Billy probably realized that." He sighed and stared into the woods. "Her fall was estimated around eight o'clock in the morning."

"But Billy's gone by seven o'clock in the morning. Surely someone would have seen him return home or know if he left late," Sidney announced.

Harlan shook his head. "You seem to be forgetting something, Sidney. Billy is an upstanding citizen. He was captain of the football team, and now he's a doctor," he informed her. "Sheriff Drukard isn't about to accuse him of killing his own grandmother. There's no proof. It would be unheard of. Even if they decide to do an autopsy, it'll probably just prove she died from complications due to the fall."

"But why wouldn't Billy and Sam have claimed they were together? He'd have an alibi," Sidney remarked simply. "Why the whole charade?"

"I'm sure Sam suspected someone would have seen him driving through town. It'd be concluded he wasn't at Mrs. Randall's before the murder," Harlan replied. "Mrs. Randall was probably upset, so she called Sam to tell her what she should do. The best solution was to pretend she wasn't home during the murder. Possibly set up just moments after the killing, Mrs. Randall called Mrs. Cooper to establish that they wouldn't be home. Leaving the house may have been too risky, and Mrs. Randall was possibly too upset to drive anyway."

Sidney groaned lowly. "So how do we prove it if there's no proof?"

Harlan sighed deeply. "Let's just hope Trisha knows something useful."

Sidney stopped before the bridge and grabbed Harlan's arm. "Oh, my God, Trisha! He's in that hospital. If she saw something, he could kill her too!"

Harlan stopped Sidney before she could run across the bridge. She spun to face him with a concerned look on her face. His expression was calm.

"Trisha's perfectly safe," Harlan said gently. "I took some precautions in case the cab driver was involved."

Sidney stared at him with some concern and confusion. "What precautions? I want to see Trisha for myself."

§

Sidney hurried along the hospital corridor with Harlan two steps behind her. He attempted to keep her calm, but she didn't want to listen. She was almost certain Billy had left the hospital once Sheriff Drukard had called, so there was no chance of running into him, but she wasn't sure he hadn't already put some devious plan into effect to eliminate a potential witness. Sidney rounded the corner and entered Trisha's private room. She stopped just inside the room, allowing Harlan to run into her from behind from her sudden stop. She stared with surprise at Lyle, who had his feet propped on the foot of the bed. His head rested on his knuckles as he slept peacefully in the bedside chair. He stirred to Sidney's presence. Lyle lowered his feet to the floor and stretched slightly.

"Morning," Lyle announced with a weary smile.

Sidney stared at Lyle, her mouth hanging open. He was the last person she expected to see at Trisha's bedside.

"Everything okay?" Harlan asked as he pushed Sidney into the room and closed the door behind them.

Lyle stood and stretched with some discomfort. "Nothing happening here," he replied. "She's still not aware enough to eat on her own." He tapped the bag that hung from the pole. "The nurse said she's doing much better."

Sidney was still baffled.

Harlan placed an arm around Sidney's shoulder. "Lyle's been occupying the room next to mine at the motel," Harlan explained the situation. "He flew out when he heard Trisha had disappeared, wanting to help."

Lyle smiled lightly and placed one hand in his pocket. "I knew you'd get in over your head. Someone has to keep you out of trouble," he replied simply. "I'm going for some coffee and the morning paper."

"There's something important we need to discuss, Lyle," Harlan announced and nodded toward the door. "I'll tell you about it on the way to the cafeteria."

"It was you," Sidney announced firmly and pointed her finger at Lyle.

He cocked his head to one side. "More than likely. I get blamed for everything."

Sidney spun to face Harlan. "He was the person you met by the bridge."

Lyle laughed and extended his hand to Harlan. "You owe me five dollars. I told you she followed you."

Harlan frowned. "I'll treat when we get downstairs." He then looked back at Sidney and attempted to smooth things over. "We thought, considering Trisha's disappearance, it was best to keep Lyle's presence a secret."

"Even from me?" she demanded to know.

Harlan shrugged and appeared uncomfortable. "I thought it might make you uneasy."

"Why would it make me uneasy?" Sidney asked in a demanding tone.

Lyle looked at Harlan and inhaled deeply. "You haven't told her?"

Harlan shook his head.

"Told me what?" Sidney demanded to know.

Lyle looked at her and smiled charmingly. "I used to be a professional cat burglar a few years back." He looked at Harlan. "I was asked to come out of retirement to search several homes to find Trisha."

Sidney's eyes widened with surprise as she looked at Harlan. "I can't believe you asked him to do that," she gasped. Sidney shook her head, and a tiny grin crossed her face. "You sneaky, little bastard."

Lyle chuckled lowly.

Harlan raised his brows. "You aren't angry?"

"No," she said with a soft laugh. "I just wanted Trisha found. I didn't care how it was done."

"I'm surprised to hear you say that," Harlan remarked then shook his head and smirked. "Though I'm glad you weren't offended." He then turned back to Lyle. "After Mary Allister comes to the hospital tonight, stop by my room. There's someplace I need you to search thoroughly."

Lyle tilted his head and appeared intrigued. "Have you found something?"

"Nothing to warrant an arrest. We need proof from the house," Harlan said softly.

"Will anyone be home?" Lyle asked simply.

"I'll get him out of the house for a couple of hours. We'll work out the details tonight around six," Harlan stated simply. "I don't really want to discuss anything more here."

Sidney knew what Harlan had in mind. He was going to send Lyle into Billy's house to look for evidence of either murder. She watched the men leave the hospital room before sitting at Trisha's bedside. She placed her hand over Trisha's and gave it a gentle squeeze.

"Hey, Trisha," she said softly.

Trisha's eyes opened slightly then shut. "Sidney," she whispered and attempted a tiny smile.

"How are you feeling?" Sidney asked while containing her joy that Trisha acknowledged her.

"Tired," she replied softly.

Sidney attempted to rouse her again, but she wouldn't wake. The older, stout nurse entered the room ten minutes later with a blood pressure cuff. She grinned at Sidney and stood on the opposite side of the bed.

"Trisha," the nurse said loudly, causing Sidney to jump with surprise to the outburst.

Trisha's eyes opened and rolled toward the nurse. "What?" she moaned loudly. Her eyes again shut.

"I don't allow my patients to sleep," the nurse said loudly as she placed the cuff around Trisha's upper arm. "If you want to sleep, you'll have to get your butt out of that bed and go home."

Trisha's head rolled toward Sidney as her eyes opened. "Make her shut up."

Sidney laughed softly and shook her head. "You'll have to tell her yourself."

"So who was the good-looking man with you all night?" the nurse asked loudly as she pumped the rubber ball attached to the blood pressure cuff.

Trisha's eyes opened again then shut. "What good-looking man?"

The nurse listened through her stethoscope then released pressure on the cuff. "I suppose you'll have to stay awake a little longer," she announced. "There was a handsome man at your bedside all night, and I'm sure it wasn't your father."

"He's dead," Trisha muttered softly.

"I'm sorry," the nurse replied gently then managed a smile. "If you stay awake another twenty minutes, I'll try to sneak you some ice cream."

Trisha drifted back out without responding.

"Do you want some ice cream, Trisha?"

Trisha jerked, and her head flopped to the side the nurse stood on. "No," she groaned in response.

The nurse left the room.

Trisha's eyes closed as she groaned. "My God, she's annoying." She opened her eyes and looked at Sidney for a brief moment. "I had the most wonderful dream," she said in a weak voice. "I dreamt about Lyle."

"It wasn't a dream, Trisha," Sidney announced louder than necessary, hoping to keep her awake. "Lyle's here. He's been keeping an eye on you."

Trisha's eyes opened, and her head rolled. "Here? I must look like hell," she muttered.

"You've looked better," Sidney replied. "He's coming back in a couple of minutes. He and Harlan went for coffee. If you can stay awake long enough, you can talk to him yourself."

Trisha clutched the sheets. "Help me up," she said gently without opening her eyes.

Sidney found the remote to the bed and raised the head. Trisha groaned loudly as her head rolled from side to side.

"I'm so tired. Can't stay awake," she groaned. "Where's my hairbrush?"

Sidney found Trisha's brush on her bedside table and ran it through her hair.

Her eyes once more opened. "Do I look better?" She then looked down at herself, touched the hospital gown, and groaned. "What the hell am I wearing?"

"A hospital gown."

"No," she moaned softly and pulled on the covers.

Sidney helped pull them up to her chest and tucked them under her arms. "Better?"

"Much," Trisha replied and struggled to keep her eyes open. She lifted her hand to her forehead. "I feel like shit. What happened?"

"What do you last remember?" Sidney asked as she sat on the edge of the bed.

"It's so fuzzy," Trisha said softly and fought her closing eyes. "I was in the library archives. There was a noise." Her eyes rolled shut then popped open. "I went upstairs. There was a pain in my head."

"Is that all you remember? You don't remember any of what happened in the cellar?" Sidney asked with surprise.

"I can't think," she said softly and allowed her head to roll to the opposite side, although her eyes remained open for a change. "Where's Lyle?"

Sidney was happy Trisha was finally interested in something other than the murder case. "I'll have the nurse page him. I'll just be outside the door," she announced and hurried across the room.

Sidney caught the nurse just outside the door and explained Trisha's request. The nurse smiled and laughed softly. Sidney returned to Trisha's bedside and found her friend holding her head in her hand as she groaned softly.

"Must wake up," she muttered.

Harlan and Lyle ran into the room five minutes after they heard the page.

"What happened?" Harlan asked with some concern.

Sidney grinned while Trisha struggled to keep her eyes open. "She wanted to say hello to Lyle."

Lyle approached Trisha and sat on the edge of the bed facing her. "Hey, how are you feeling?" he asked gently and offered a charming smile.

Trisha smiled warmly despite her barely opened eyes. "I've been better," she replied softly. "What are you doing here?"

"I came looking for you," he announced simply.   "I was told you'd vanished."

Trisha's eyes focused on Lyle and remained open.   "You came out here just for me?"

He nodded and placed his hand on hers.   "I hoped to impress you with something heroic, but I was on the other side of town chasing shadows."

Trisha offered a tiny laugh.   "I'm impressed anyway."

Chapter Thirty-eight

Sidney folded her arms across her chest and glared at Harlan while she stood in his motel room. She was tired of being told what she could and couldn't do.

"Why not?" she demanded to know in an angered tone. "I think it's an excellent suggestion."

Lyle remained sitting on the bed against the headboard with his feet stretched out before him. He too looked at Harlan, demanding an answer.

"Nothing's going to happen to her," Lyle remarked simply, attempting to make her case.

Harlan pointed a finger at Lyle. "You just stay out of this," he snapped. "She's not going to keep Billy busy while you search his house."

"He doesn't suspect we know anything," Sidney launched back. "I'm your best shot at this. He likes me."

"He also liked Emily Fisher," Harlan retorted. "It may have been his jealousy that got her killed. He also thinks we're sleeping together, so that won't go over well."

Lyle was about to speak.

"Don't even think it," Harlan snapped hotly while glaring at his friend.

Lyle placed his hands in the air. "I didn't say anything."

"It's really quite simple," Sidney remarked while groaning. "He's supposed to be grieving the loss of his beloved grandmother. I call to express my sympathies and invite him to dinner at my parents' house. I'm not alone with him, and he's guaranteed to be away from home a couple of hours. If something does happen, I dial Lyle's cellular phone, and he gets out of the house."

Harlan tilted his head and raised skeptical brows. "And what if he suspects something while in your parents' house? He might kill all of you."

"My father has an arsenal of weapons in the house, and he's not afraid to use them. Billy's not going to try anything," she explained simply. "What could you possibly come up with that would be safer than what I've suggested?"

"She has a point," Lyle stated.

Harlan glared at Lyle.

"It's my ass on the line," Lyle announced with an innocent look. "If he did kill his own grandmother, he's not going to hesitate shooting an intruder."

Harlan rolled his eyes and groaned. "I don't like this plan at all."

Sidney's mother eyed her daughter while she set the table for their invited guest. Herb casually sat at the kitchen table and loaded his semi-automatic. When he cocked it, her mother jumped and nearly dropped one of the china dishes. She placed the plate on the table with trembling hands. Sidney turned toward her mother and drew a deep breath.

"Mom, relax a little," Sidney said reassuringly. "Maybe you should go to Mrs. Cooper's and comfort her. It'll seem perfectly natural."

Her mother shook her head with wide eyes, horrified at the thought. "I'm not leaving my family alone with a killer," she announced firmly.

"We don't know he did it," Herb announced sternly. "There's nothing to support it. If you can't put on a good front, then you'll have to leave for a while."

"I'll be fine," her mother remarked with a crackle in her voice. "I just don't know why we had to invite him over here."

"It's the only way, Pauline," her father said gently. "If there's evidence to be found, someone has to find it. Can't count on that lazy, worthless sheriff."

Sidney watched her father place the semi-automatic in a clip and attach it to his belt on the back of his pants. She knew her father would be extremely cautious and keep his eye on things.

"Where's Harlan?" her father asked as he adjusted the gun in the holster behind him.

"Climbing the walls in Trisha's house," Sidney replied while groaning. "From there, he'll see when Billy comes this way and when he returns home."

The phone rang causing all three to jump. Sidney hurried to the phone and answered it.

"Hello?"

"He's on his way. He'll be there any minute," Harlan informed her. "Be careful, okay?"

"Stop worrying," Sidney remarked then hung up the phone without care.

The doorbell rang two minutes later. Her mother gasped and dropped a glass. It shattered against the tile floor. Sidney and Herb looked at her with their mouths opened. Sidney released a nervous breath and hurried from the kitchen. Her father followed her into the living room, leaving his wife to clean the broken glass. Sidney opened the door and allowed Billy to enter.

"I'm really sorry about your grandmother, Billy," Sidney said gently and looked down to hold back her anger and fear, which she masked as sorrow. She hadn't realized how differently she'd feel now that they were face-to-face.

Herb extended his hand to Billy and gave a sad nod. "Sorry about your grandmother."

Billy forced a tiny smile and shook his hand. "I'm glad you invited me over," he replied gently. "I would have just sat home feeling sorry for myself."

Herb invited him into the house. Sidney's mother entered the living room before they were seated. She appeared unusually tense. Sidney held her breath and watched her mother. Pauline had tears in her eyes, and her hands trembled. Her mother approached Billy, threw her arms around him, and hugged him. Both Sidney and her father nearly fell to the floor.

"I'm so sorry, Billy," Pauline whispered softly. "She was a fine woman." Her mother pulled away, wiped her eyes, and forced a tiny smile. "I don't think I'll be able to join you for dinner. Excuse me," she said and rushed from the room.

Sidney watched her mother hurry up the stairs to her bedroom. She looked back at her father and Billy. "I, uh, suppose I should check on dinner."

She didn't want to leave her father alone with Billy, but she wasn't sure what condition her mother had left the kitchen or how far along dinner had been.

Chapter Thirty-nine

They had a pleasant dinner with little conversation to avoid any unpleasantness. Both Sidney and her father lingered over their meal, although not very hungry. Billy didn't appear hungry either. He talked of his grandmother's heart condition, which seemed natural and yet almost rehearsed. When he mentioned the sedatives and admitted they may have made her weak, Sidney was filled with terror. His story was nearly convincing enough for her to believe he had nothing to do with her death.

"Have you spoken with Mrs. Cooper?" her father asked while picking at his slab of roast beef. "How's she taking it?"

Billy sighed gently. "She's very upset, naturally," he said sadly. "They've been friends for many years. I think her daughter was going to stay with her until after the funeral."

The conversation continued in the same direction for nearly half an hour. All three cleaned dishes after dinner. The phone rang, startling Sidney, though she attempted to hide it. She picked up the kitchen receiver.

"Hello?"

"Hi, Sidney?" came an unfamiliar male voice. "It's Denny. Is Billy there?"

"Uh, yeah," she replied with some confusion then handed the phone to Billy. "It's Denny."

Billy looked puzzled. "Really?" He took the phone from her. "Yeah, Denny?"

Sidney walked toward her father as he rinsed the dishes and looked at her out of the corner of his eye. Both shared the same look of concern.

Billy made few comments in the two-minute conversation. "Thanks, Denny." He hung up the phone and turned toward them with a strange look in his eyes.

Sidney looked back at him as her father dried his hands. "Something wrong?" she asked gently.

Billy frowned and shook his head. "It would appear someone's broken into my house. I hope it's not Harlan. I'm not in the mood to deal with him tonight." He held his breath then attempted a polite smile. "I don't mean to eat and run, but I'd better see what's happening."

"I'll go with you," Sidney said quickly.

She could feel her father's eyes but didn't bother to look at him. She didn't want to hear him lecture. Billy nodded and headed toward the living room and the front door. Sidney's father grabbed her arm before she could follow. She jumped with concern as he stuck the gun down the back of her pants.

"You better know what you're doing," he muttered lowly while staring into her eyes.

Sidney nodded then hurried from the kitchen and grabbed a jacket as she followed Billy out of the house. They walked briskly along the sidewalk, heading toward the development.

"I assure you," Sidney announced simply. "It's not Harlan. He went to the hospital with Trisha's mother."

As they passed Trisha's house, Sidney subconsciously turned her head. Harlan's rental car was in the driveway, which surprised her. When Harlan got out of his car and walked toward them, Sidney thought she'd die. Billy stopped when he saw Harlan.

"Sidney, where are you going?" Harlan demanded to know and glared at Billy.

"Someone broke into Billy's house," she remarked simply.

Harlan grabbed her arm and slung her behind him without releasing her. He pointed a warning finger at Billy.

"Let's get something straight right now," Harlan growled lowly. "She's my girlfriend, not yours. Whatever was between you two is over."

Billy's eyes narrowed with anger. "I don't know who you think you're talking to," he snapped, "but I don't like the way you're treating her."

Harlan raised a cocky brow. "The way I treat her is none of your concern."

Sidney became painfully aware of what Harlan was attempting to do. He was giving Lyle time to get out of Billy's house by picking a fight.

"Harlan, stop this," Sidney gasped loudly and pulled her arm from his hand. She was genuinely concerned for Harlan's health. Billy was bigger, younger, and stronger than Harlan. "I'm not some possession!"

Harlan glared at her but kept Billy in view. "I will not share you with another man, Sidney. You knew that the other night. Either we date exclusively, or it's over."

Sidney stared at Harlan with her mouth open. She wasn't sure how she was supposed to respond. Which answer would provide Lyle the time he needed to escape and also keep Billy from beating Harlan senseless? She folded her arms across her chest and glared at him.

"How dare you threaten me?" she snapped lowly and looked him up and down. "I don't recall exclusive rights being part of that conversation."

"We're about to have a whole new conversation," Harlan snarled and raised his brows. "Wait in my car. I want a word with Billy boy."

Sidney stared at Harlan, uncertain how to react.

He raised his brows sharply. "Wait in the car."

Sidney drew a deep breath. "Fine," she snapped. "We're going to talk all right."

She walked away from the men, uncertain of her next move. She hoped she'd be able to keep Billy occupied while she had it out with Harlan. When she looked back, Harlan and Billy were rolling on the ground, punching each other. A car pulled into the driveway and slowed upon seeing the men fighting on the ground. Lyle got out of his car and watched the two men with surprise. He shook his head with a frown, walked toward the house, removed the garden hose, and showered cold water on both men. They jumped apart and sprang to their feet while breathing heavily. Lyle shut off the hose and cast it aside.

"I don't know who either of you are," Lyle announced gruffly. "But I suggest you get off my aunt's property before I call the police."

Both stared at him while dripping wet.

Harlan approached Sidney. "Let's go," he said firmly and nodded toward his car.

Lyle placed his arm around Sidney's shoulder and pulled her against his side. "Uh, I think you'd better stay with me, Sidney," he announced and glared at the two, soaked men. "I don't trust either of these characters."

Sidney placed her arms around Lyle's waist and hugged him. "I'm so glad to see you, Cousin Lyle."

He laughed softly and returned the hug. "I bet you are. We have some old times to catch up on." Lyle turned her toward the house then glared at Harlan and motioned with his hand. "Go on. Get out of here. You're wrecking the lawn."

Chapter Forty

Sidney entered the house with Lyle and watched as he closed the door behind them. Once the door was closed, both looked out the separation in the curtains. Harlan backed out of the driveway, and Billy continued in the direction of his house.

"What happened?" Sidney asked Lyle with a concerned look in her eyes.

Lyle smiled and laughed, humored at the snafu. "One of the neighbors must have seen me enter the house, though I can't imagine how. It's so much easier at night in the dark," he remarked lowly. "Anyway, the snitch decides he's going to capture me himself."

Sidney's eyes widened. "What did you do?"

"Locked him in the pantry."

"Did he see you?"

"Not with a pillowcase over his head," Lyle remarked simply and cast himself into the reclining chair. "There's a reason why I've never been caught." His smile brightened. "I'm just too damned clever."

Sidney laughed and shook her head. "I'd better call my parents before they worry themselves to death."

Lyle jumped out of the chair. "I'm starving," he boldly announced. "I wonder if Trisha's mother has any leftovers in the fridge?"

Sidney followed Lyle into the kitchen. He was a work of art. She called her parents from the kitchen phone, telling them not to worry and everyone was all right. She watched Lyle remove several packs of lunchmeat. Sidney hung up the phone, leaned against the counter, and watched him build a sandwich. He smelled one of the packages then made a face.

"This one's no good," he announced with disgust and cast it aside. "Should have grabbed lunch at the doc's house. He had fresh turkey in his fridge."

"You looked in his refrigerator?" she asked with some surprise while staring at him.

He looked at her innocently. "I get hungry when I work." He removed some mayonnaise from the refrigerator.

Sidney casually turned and leaned on her elbows to watch him. "Have you ever killed anyone?"

He ate a piece of ham and gave her a surprised look. "No, it's not in my nature to kill."

"Did you steal a lot?" she asked while raising her brows.

He placed the last slice of bread on top of the sandwich and shrugged without looking at her. "Enough." He then looked at her. "When I went straight, I gave most of it back."

Sidney gave him a surprised look. "That's a little hard to believe."

"Didn't say you had to believe me," he replied simply and took a bite from the sandwich. "But I have nothing to gain by lying to you."

He sat at the kitchen table with his thick sandwich. Sidney joined him at the table and sat across from him.

"Why'd you decide to go straight?"

He stood, approached the refrigerator, and removed a can of soda. Lyle returned to the table and sat down. "A woman," he replied simply while sliding his chair closer to the table.

"You fell in love with a woman and went straight?" she asked with a tiny, romantic smile.

He lifted his eyes above his sandwich. "No, she nearly shot me. When I stared down the barrel of that shotgun, I realized it was time to choose a new profession."

"Were you arrested?" Sidney asked with wide eyes.

He smirked. "Uh--no. She wasn't interested in calling the police; just wanted me dead. I disarmed her just before she fired. Shot a hole right through her ceiling. I made a hasty exit out the back door." He opened the can of soda.

"So why give the money back?" she asked.

"I wasn't really in it for the money. I just wanted to prove I could do it," he replied simply. He drank some soda and studied her a long moment. "I know what you're thinking. You think Trisha can do a lot better than an ex-burglar."

"No, I didn't think that at all. You made a couple of wrong choices, but your heart seems to be in the right place," she replied. "Trisha needs something more than what she has right now, and I think you'd be good for her. That is if you want her."

He smiled charmingly and leaned back in the kitchen chair. "Well, that's a fresh opinion. Usually, when I'm honest, decent women get all uptight."

"Are you serious about wanting to see Trisha?" Sidney asked while giving him a curious look. "You weren't just telling her what she needed to hear?"

"No, I was serious."

"You'll have to tell her about your past," Sidney stated simply. "She's really touchy about secrets."

"She already knows," he replied simply and continued to eat his sandwich. "We talked for several hours. I've always found women difficult to talk to, but Trisha was different."

Sidney laughed softly. "Yes, Trisha is very different. The two of you will have entertaining stories to swap."

"What I find ironic is her obsession with this murder," he remarked. "The entire evening we spent together, she never once mentioned Emily Fisher."

"That is strange," Sidney replied.

The front door opened. Sidney sprang to her feet and hurried to the living room. Harlan entered the house wearing clean, dry clothing. He bolted past Sidney and entered the kitchen.

"I suppose you thought that was funny," Harlan snapped angrily at his friend.

Lyle leaned back in his chair and smiled with a childlike innocence. "I could have allowed that ape to beat the crap out of you, but that wouldn't have been very nice on my behalf," he teased. "And, yes, I thought it was funny."

Harlan groaned and shook his head. "At least tell me you found something useful."

"Plenty of useful stuff," Lyle replied. "But nothing to convict a man of murder."

Harlan frowned and collapsed in the kitchen chair Sidney once occupied.

"There was an empty bottle of Thorazine," Lyle said simply. "With the hospital label on it, I might add. I found a phone in the doc's bedroom, one in the kitchen, one in the hall, but none in the grandmother's room. There was an extra phone in the doc's closet, though, which I found a bit strange." Lyle shook his head. "There should have been a needle mark on her arm somewhere. The sheriff should have insisted upon an autopsy after seeing a needle mark, even if he knew she'd been given an injection."

"Sheriff Drukard isn't very observant," Sidney replied simply. "When Emily Fisher was found, they had to call the police from Brighten. Drukard didn't want to admit it, but he didn't even know where to begin."

"As I remember it," Harlan added. "He was traipsing all over the murder scene."

"How did he get that job?" Lyle said while shaking his head in disbelief. "Sounds to me like this town would be an excellent breeding ground for a criminal. Stupid sheriff and no one even locks their doors."

"He was deputy when the first sheriff retired," Harlan stated. "I remember that was a couple of months before I arrived. Herb was complaining about it."

"Trisha expressed her opinion as well," Sidney added. "Even back then, Drukard thought she was trouble." She sighed with disgust and leaned against the wall near the table. "We're never going to prove Billy killed either of them. Sam and Mrs. Randall were the only ones who knew anything, and they're both conveniently dead."

"I could search the tavern," Lyle announced simply. "Sam lived above it, didn't he?"

Harlan inhaled deeply. "I suppose it couldn't hurt, but I doubt if you'll find anything to incriminate Billy." Harlan then looked at Sidney. "What time are visiting hours at the prison?"

Sidney's brows rose with some surprise. "I doubt they're open anymore tonight. Do you want to visit Alex?"

"He's the only one left who might know something," Harlan replied. "After Alex, I'm fresh out of witnesses."

Lyle stood with a sigh. "Well, I have work to do." He smiled deviously and placed a hand on Harlan's shoulder. "Don't you kids wait up for me." He tossed his soda can in the garbage and left the kitchen.

"I suppose I should walk you back to your parents' house," Harlan said gently.

"What do you intend to do?" Sidney asked.

"There's a pub not far from the hospital," he replied. "I guess I'll go there for some dinner and a couple of shots."

"I could use a drink too," Sidney moaned lowly.

Harlan stood and took her hand. "Come on. Let's get sloshed."

Sidney stopped him. "Wait," she announced with a devious smile. "I have a better idea." Sidney opened one of the lower cupboard doors and removed a bottle of brandy. "Trisha's mother is staying at the hospital all night. Why don't we stay here, watch some movies, and kill this bottle?"

Harlan smirked and laughed softly. "There's a pizza place just outside town. I'll pick up a pizza, and you pick some movies. And, please, something amusing. I've had enough seriousness and drama to last me a lifetime."

Chapter Forty-one

Sidney and Harlan sat on the floor against the sofa and watched the movie of non-stop laughter while drinking steadily. Both were fairly drunk by the end of the first movie. Sidney put the second movie in while Harlan replenished their drinks from the bottle sitting on the coffee table. Sidney sat on her feet and attempted to figure out which way the tape should be inserted. They kept the lights off so no one would know they were in the house. Mary wouldn't mind, but she feared Billy might decide to return and cause a scene. The doors and windows were locked, and the shades were drawn so that they could have a quiet, dull evening. She started the tape and crawled back to her spot by the sofa. Harlan collapsed on the sofa and watched her while snickering.

Sidney looked up at him and smiled drunkenly. "What's so funny?"

"I don't really know," he replied with a soft laugh and handed her the drink as she returned to the sofa, collapsing alongside him. "I guess I've just never seen you drunk before. You're so grown up."

Sidney set her drink on the coffee table before them, placed her arm on Harlan's shoulder, and leaned against him to watch the movie. It took her nearly ten minutes to realize his right hand was on her knee. Her heart pounded as a dull ache swept through her body. While Harlan watched the movie, Sidney now watched him. The alcohol seemed to enhance her feelings for him beyond any rationalization. His hand subconsciously moved along her leg. He didn't appear to notice his own actions. Sidney's breathing became rapid and shallow. She placed her right hand on his arm and stroked it affectionately. Harlan laughed at something that happened in the movie and patted Sidney's thigh. Sidney straightened and attempted to watch the movie.

Harlan looked back at her through drunken eyes. "Are you uncomfortable?"

"I'm fine. Just a little cold," she said gently.

He placed his arm around her and pulled her to his side. "Better, love?"

She closed her eyes and exhaled. "Much, thank you," she whispered.

Halfway through the movie, Sidney went to the bathroom down the hall while Harlan again refilled their drinks. Sidney found walking a little difficult on the return trip. She stopped just inside the living room and studied Harlan while he placed their drinks on the coffee table. He turned his head and smiled with amusement.

"I'm surprised you can still walk," he remarked with a low snicker.

She walked toward him despite her unsteady gate. He met her halfway while chuckling.

"Need some help?" he teased and gallantly helped her stumble to the sofa.

They collapsed on the sofa together. Sidney's heart pounded, and she was no longer interested in the movie. She stared at Harlan as every emotion and feeling she'd ever had for him came back to her. Sidney instinctively touched his beard with her right hand and caressed his face. Harlan looked at her with some surprise and searched her eyes. His hand covered hers and gently caressed it. Sidney swallowed dryly. Harlan removed her hand from his face and kissed her palm in a way that sent shock waves through her body. He released her hand and smiled with embarrassment while looking down.

"Each time I look at you I live with a terrible guilt," he said softly.

She stared at him with some surprise. "Really? Why?"

"The first time I saw you, I didn't know you were only fifteen." He then searched her eyes and smirked timidly. "I thought you were the most beautiful girl. Sure, eighteen was a little young but acceptable." He inhaled deeply and shook his head. "Once I found out you were only fifteen, I knew I had to forget any thoughts I had," he said gently. "I had this insane plan to ask you out on your eighteenth birthday. But after the murder and the way your father had treated me, I couldn't stay. He'd never allow me near you again. He said so much."

Sidney stared at Harlan with her mouth open. She couldn't believe he'd been interested in her back then.

"I suppose I had a crush on you as well," he informed her gently. He tilted his head with a timid look. "Do you think any less of me?"

Sidney stared blankly into his eyes. Her hand returned to his beard. She loved the way it felt against her hand.

"I'm not fifteen anymore," she whispered and stared at him with anticipation.

He stared back at her, as if uncertain how to respond. His left arm slipped around her waist, and he pulled her close. Harlan hesitated and seemed apprehensive. Sidney gently bit her lower lip and searched his eyes.

"I wouldn't admit it to anyone, Harlan, but I never stopped loving you," she said softly.

He stared into her eyes. Sidney's heart pounded harshly to the silence between them. He placed his right hand on the side of her neck and lowered his mouth to hers. Sidney shut her eyes and felt his lips gently brush past hers. She trembled slightly as he kissed her tenderly. When he drew away, her eyes opened with some disappointment that he had stopped.

Without warning, he pulled her against him, covered her mouth with his, and kissed her passionately and with some aggression. Sidney was caught by surprise. She tensed slightly then slipped her arms around his neck and returned the kiss. She'd longed for this moment since she was fifteen, and her own aggression told as much. Her head began to spin, and her heart raced. She was barely able to keep up with his wild, passionate kisses, although she didn't back down from the challenge. Sidney pulled her mouth from his and gasped softly. His mouth sought her neck, and she could feel his tongue against her skin. She moaned softly. Her cheeks were now hot and red. When he kissed her throat, she knew she wouldn't be able to take much more.

Harlan slowly lowered her to the sofa and pulled her beneath him. His hands freely caressed her side and thigh causing her to groan with pleasure as his body pressed against hers. His mouth returned to hers, and she returned his urgent, aggressive kiss. Her head was spinning nearly as fast as the room. She wanted the moment to last, but she feared she'd pass out. She wanted him to make love to her. Sidney finally felt things were as they should have been before her world crashed. His kiss was making her dizzy while his body pressing against hers aroused her sexual desire. She felt his hand caress her hip and buttocks just before everything went dark.

Chapter Forty-two

A faint chirping noise woke Sidney around four in the morning. She looked around the living room in a daze and with some disorientation. Harlan lay face down on the floor between the sofa and the coffee table with a throw pillow under his head. The chirping sound continued with a pause in-between. Sidney attempted to remember what happened last night while holding her pounding head. She was still fully dressed so it couldn't have been too exciting. She moaned softly and rolled her eyes. The chirping sound was beginning to irritate her.

She scanned the room, unable to turn her head any faster. She thought her head would explode from the sudden movement. Sidney then saw the cellular phone on the coffee table. She reached for the coffee table and picked up the annoyingly chirping phone. It took her a second to figure out how to use the phone, especially in the dim lighting. She'd never used a cellular phone before, and by all accounts never wanted any part of them.

"Hello," she said softly, almost unable to speak.

"Sidney?" the gruff, male voice whispered.

"Yeah," she replied with some confusion.

"Listen carefully," the voice said. "Meet me at the old stone house in ten minutes."

"Who--?" the line was disconnected.

Sidney lowered the cellular phone and stared at it. It had to be Harlan's phone, which meant it had to be Lyle on the other end. Sidney disconnected the phone and nudged Harlan below her.

"Harlan," she said sternly.

He didn't rouse, so she shook him harshly. He moaned but still didn't rouse. Sidney moved from the sofa, carefully stepping around Harlan. She ran her fingers through her hair, took Harlan's car keys, and grabbed the gun from the coffee table. She placed it down the back of her pants. Sidney's gait was slightly unsteady from being hungover and lack of sleep. She felt as if her blood was rushing through her body at an extraordinary rate. Her heart pounded incredibly fast, possibly from the alcohol still in her system. She hurried into the garage.

Sidney drove Harlan's car toward the stone house on the opposite end of Cressman Road. She had a difficult time seeing the road. Her vision was rather poor in the darkness. The private drive was narrow, dark, and frightening. Sidney began to question the voice on the phone. What if it wasn't Lyle? Was she driving into a trap? She was able to drive straight to the house since the police had taken the chain down when they uncovered Sam's body in the rubble of the house cellar. She stopped the car just before the porch to the house and looked around the dark area. She wasn't sure she wanted to leave the security of the car. She saw something move near the well right before the car door opened. She cried out with surprise as Lyle jumped into the passenger seat.

"Drive," he gasped and slouched in the seat, pinching his eyes shut.

Sidney's heartbeat quickened after her shock of him jumping into the car. She turned the car around and found it just as difficult driving back to the main road. The path from the house was dark and difficult to see.

"What happened?" she asked with concern and turned her head to look at him.

Lyle removed a bloody handkerchief from under his jacket and cringed slightly. "I wasn't the only one interested in Sam's Tavern," Lyle said lowly.

Sidney gasped when she saw the blood. "You're hurt!"

"It's just a scratch," he said and stiffly sat up with some discomfort. "I called the motel. Where were you guys?"

"At Trisha's house," she said and nervously eyed him several times. "Should I take you to the hospital?"

"They ask too many questions," he remarked. "All I need is a first aid kit."

"I'm sure Trisha's mom has one somewhere," she said. They reached Trisha's house in less than five minutes. She pulled into the garage to keep Harlan's car hidden. Sidney closed the garage door and attempted to help Lyle into the house, but he seemed steadier than she was.

She followed him into the downstairs bathroom and helped him with his jacket. Sidney searched the bathroom vanity and found a first aid kit then helped Lyle remove his blood-soaked shirt. She could see the large slice across his side. It was nearly six inches long but didn't appear too deep. Sidney cringed.

"Fill the sink with cold water," he announced firmly and opened the kit.

Sidney did as he instructed then watched him clean the cut with some difficulty. She eventually cleaned it for him. He leaned against the sink and told her how to sterilize the site properly. He had her cut the surgical tape into thin strips and place them across the cut to hold it together. They weren't as effective as stitches, but they seemed to serve their purpose. Lastly, she placed a dressing over the wound and securely taped it.

"Aren't you going to tell me what happened?" Sidney asked while cleaning up the mess she had made with the gauze wrapping and blood from the washrag.

"There's not much to tell, really," he replied simply and looked at his bloody shirt. "I went into the tavern around one o'clock and conducted a search. The place had been closed up, so I took my time. About quarter till three, while I was upstairs, I heard someone else in the tavern downstairs," he announced. "Naturally, I wanted to see who was poking around down there, so I went to investigate. I got a little too close and surprised the guy. He was a nervous fellow. When he turned around, he slashed me with his knife and ran from the tavern, tripping the alarm. I had to leave in a hurry. The deputy arrived just as I made my exit." He gingerly touched the dressing over his wound. "I saw someone outside the motel, so I had to go someplace else. I backtracked around the school, and then found my way to the woods on some steep, rocky path."

"What did the man look like?" Sidney asked with a curious tilt of her head.

"About six-foot. Big guy with dark hair, little beady eyes, and a cleft in his chin," Lyle stated and sighed. "Probably in his mid to late twenties."

"Cleft in his chin?" she asked with some concern. "You've just described Denny, Billy's friend. That's a frightening thought. What would he be doing at Sam's Tavern? Do you think he was robbing the place or protecting Billy's interest?"

Lyle appeared to consider the question. "He didn't have anything to carry stolen goods, not that he couldn't have taken a pillowcase from upstairs. If he was there to steal, he's an amateur." He shook his head while frowning. "He was far too nervous to be a professional. Besides, a smart thief doesn't carry a weapon. If you're caught with a weapon, the severity of the crime goes up."

"I wonder if it would be wise to question Denny about the murder and Mrs. Randall's death?" Sidney said aloud but was talking more to herself.

Lyle sighed deeply and examined the dressing on his side. "Considering my reaction from him, I wouldn't recommend it." He picked up his shirt and frowned at the blood and the large cut. "Never should've worn my good shirt."

Sidney then snapped out of her daze and offered a tiny smile. "I'll see what Mary has in her closet. I don't think she gave all her husband's clothing away. She had kept a couple of his suits, though I don't know why."

"As long as you think she won't mind," Lyle announced.

Sidney was surprised how conscientious he was about other people, considering his previous lifestyle.

"I don't think she'll mind. Trisha's mother is very charitable," Sidney replied.

"Where's Harlan? Why didn't he answer his phone?" Lyle asked as they walked from the bathroom. "I told him to keep it on him for a change."

"He's sleeping," she informed him and hid her embarrassment.

"Sleeping? Didn't he hear the phone?" Lyle asked from just a step behind her.

"He had a little too much to drink," Sidney reported without looking at him.

Lyle followed her upstairs to Mary Allister's room. Sidney turned on the bedroom light and approached the closet.

"You look three sheets to the wind yourself," he remarked simply.

Sidney glared at him then conceded. "I suppose I was drunk as well," she replied lightly.

Lyle leaned against the wall near the closet with one arm across his chest and his right hand to his chin. A devious smile crossed his face.

"Hmm, bet that was an interesting evening," he teased.

"Shut up, Lyle," Sidney growled lowly. "Nothing happened, you pervert." She sifted through the clothing in the closet.

"No disrespect intended," he announced while grinning. "I didn't think his flying across the entire country for a woman was a really good idea. He must've had it pretty bad for you."

Sidney found a white, dress shirt and handed it to him. "He didn't come out here for me," she firmly insisted. "He wanted to know the truth about Emily Fisher's murder, and perhaps clear his own name."

Lyle slipped into the shirt with some discomfort then snorted a laugh. "Sure he did," he muttered lowly. "Harlan's never chased a woman in his life." He buttoned the shirt without looking at her. "But when he told me he was flying out here because of that goodbye kiss at the airport, I knew he was insane or in love. Maybe a little of both." He then looked at her.

Sidney was surprised by his comment.

"He's only been in love once, that he's actually confessed," Lyle remarked. "It was with the young woman in the photo in his bedroom."

Sidney stared at Lyle with surprise as her mouth fell open.

"Did anyone ever tell you that you talk too much?" Harlan said in a drowsy tone while leaning in the bedroom doorway with his arms folded across his chest.

Lyle turned and smiled mockingly at his friend. "It's a gift," he announced cheerfully then looked Harlan up and down. "You look like hell."

"I feel like it too," Harlan snapped. "What are you doing up so early?"

"Up? I haven't been to bed yet," Lyle replied simply. "I've been busy bleeding all over this one-horse town and evading the police." He then turned to Sidney. "Do you think Mrs. Allister would be upset if I occupied her bed for a couple of hours?"

Sidney shook her head. "No, you go right ahead," she replied. "I'll tell Harlan all about your evening rendezvous with Denny."

Chapter Forty-three

Sidney made some coffee and told Harlan everything Lyle said about the incident in Sam's Tavern, including his run-in with Denny. Harlan leaned back against the kitchen counter while Sidney proceeded to wash the dishes they had dirtied.

"I wonder what he has to do with the whole sorted affair?" Harlan grumbled.

"Do you think we should talk to Denny?" Sidney asked and gave him a curious look.

"Absolutely," Harlan replied. "Alex can wait, he's not going anywhere for a while."

Sidney stared at Harlan a moment longer. His eyes met hers. He held his breath and looked away while running his fingers through his hair.

"I think I should take a quick shower before we go anywhere," he said and gently exhaled without looking at her.

Harlan straightened and headed across the kitchen. Sidney hurried after him and cut off his path to the downstairs bathroom. Harlan paused and met her gaze with a slight frown.

"Why did you come back to Marilina?" she asked sharply and placed a hand on either side of the bathroom doorframe. She wanted to get this out in the open once and for all.

Harlan rolled his eyes with a soft groan then stared at her. "I thought Lyle made that perfectly obvious," he remarked then fidgeted while unusually tense.

Sidney gave him a puzzled look. "I can't believe you really came all this way just because I'd kissed you."

He raised a dark brow. "Oh, believe it," he said sharply and stared into her eyes. "Do you remember what I said to you last night?"

"You thought I was older than fifteen."

"I'm not much of an opportunist, and I've never been a womanizer." He sighed and gently scratched his bearded chin. "I've had a tough time getting to know women. After that goodbye in the airport, I knew it was destiny," he said softly.

Sidney felt her heart skip a beat as she stared helplessly into his eyes.

"I've been missing something for a very long time, and I wasn't about to let you walk out of my life forever." He drew a deep breath and proudly raised his head. "I came here to state my position in person, but my timing wasn't very good."

Sidney snorted a soft laugh and nervously folded her arms across her chest. "No, I suppose it wasn't. I pulled you into this whole sorted affair."

"I was glad I came," he said gently. "I don't want to imagine what might have happened if I hadn't shown up when I did." He then studied her a long moment with a timid expression. "Do you remember what you'd said last night?"

Sidney nodded and felt her cheeks become hot and red. "I meant what I said," she said softly and searched his eyes for a response.

Harlan looked down with some embarrassment then met her gaze. "I'm not really sure how I should proceed."

Sidney stared into his eyes and raised a seductive brow. "How would you like to proceed?"

Harlan chuckled lowly in his throat, looked away, and nervously rubbed the back of his neck while hiding his smile. He raised his brows as he met her gaze.

"Like a love-starved bastard," he replied simply. "But I have that beast under control."

Sidney stared at him while every thought imaginable passed through her mind. She gently cleared her throat.

"We could discuss it further," she replied gently, "in the shower."

Harlan's eyes remained fixed on her with a shocked look. He shook his head with a timid smile and some embarrassment. "If we take a shower together, there won't be much left to discuss, love."

"I know what I'm suggesting," she replied gently. "You're the only man I've ever wanted, Harlan, and I think I've waited long enough."

Harlan was perfectly still for nearly a minute while Sidney stared at him and felt her heart pound with anticipation of his response. He stepped toward her, pulled her against him, and kissed her passionately. Sidney felt her entire body tense then relax. She returned the aggressive kiss and clung to his neck. He backed her against the doorframe and firmly ran his hand along her buttocks and down her thigh. Sidney's breathing became harsh as she attempted to keep up with his passionate kisses. She moaned softly. He slowed down as his left hand slipped under her shirt and caressed her bare back while his free hand traveled along the front of her shirt and fumbled with the buttons. They heard the front door open. Harlan pulled away and turned his head while breathing heavily and listened a moment.

"Sidney?" came Mary's voice from the living room. "Are you here?"

Harlan jumped away from Sidney and nervously raked his fingers through his hair. He let out a low groan and a slight laugh. "I guess a shower is out of the question," he remarked softly.

Sidney and Harlan approached the living room and saw Mary looking around nervously. She jumped when she saw them then relaxed. Mary looked at them with tired eyes and large, dark circles just beneath them.

"Oh, Sidney," Mary said softly. "I didn't expect you to be here. I saw a car parked in the garage, but I didn't know whose it was."

"Harlan and I were housesitting. I owe you a bottle of brandy," Sidney informed her with a tiny smile.

Mary waved a hand. "Don't even think twice about it. I'd empty a bottle myself if I wasn't so tired. Your mother is staying with Trisha, so I can get some sleep. I won't be going to work today."

"How's Trish doing?" Sidney asked gently.

"Trisha's doing great. She was alert the first two hours I was there," Mary replied. "I'm a one-woman disaster though. I almost wish you hadn't told me about Billy Randall. With her in the hospital, I'm a complete wreck. Isn't there something we can do? Isn't there some proof?"

Sidney shook her head. "That's why you can't tell anyone what we suspect. It's slander to his good name," she snapped with a frown.

"But you're convinced he's the one?"

"Almost one hundred percent. Though I could be wrong, it seems unlikely," Sidney replied simply.

"I'm going to get a couple of hours sleep, if it's possible, then I'm going right back to that hospital," Mary announced. "I don't want him anywhere near Trisha. Until she's released, I'm not leaving her alone, not for a minute."

Sidney nodded with understanding. She watched Mary leave the living room and walk toward the stairs. Sidney wondered if Billy would dare try anything. Trisha was recovering nicely. She'd probably be out in another day or two. A fatality would be very suspicious. What about her safety once she returned home? Would he consider trying anything then? It wasn't safe for her. She wondered if Trisha remembered anything more about her abduction. She was never fully awake to have that conversation. Sidney slipped back into reality and looked at Harlan with alarm.

"Lyle!"

Harlan stared at Sidney with some confusion. They heard Mary scream. Sidney and Harlan ran upstairs as Lyle ran into the hall from the master bedroom. Sidney was just thankful he was fully dressed. Mary ran out of the bedroom with a baseball bat.

"Get out of my house, you pervert!"

Sidney jumped into Mary's path and stopped her. "Mrs. Allister, wait!"

Mary stared at Lyle, who ducked behind Harlan. She had a wild, half-crazed look in her eyes.

"This is Lyle," Sidney announced nervously while attempting to calm her.

Mary looked at Sidney with knitted brows. "Lyle? That name sounds familiar."

"Trisha's potential love interest," Sidney announced firmly and raised her brows.

Mary's eyes widened as she lowered the bat. An embarrassed smile crossed her face. "Oh, that's where I've heard that name." She looked at Lyle and nervously touched her temple. "I'm terribly sorry. I didn't know what to think. There hasn't been a man in my bed for fifteen years."

Lyle gave a weary wave with one hand while clinging to Harlan's shoulder from behind with the other.

"As long as you're willing to put the bat down, we'll call it even," Lyle announced and grinned.

§

Sidney and Harlan went to town to get something to eat at the diner before visiting the office where Denny worked in the neighboring town of Brighton. Harlan parked his rental car by the curb near the diner and both got out. Mrs. Cooper hurried along the sidewalk and nearly knocked Sidney over, surprising her when she grabbed her arm. The older woman had a look of distress on her wrinkled, tired face.

"Have you heard the news, Sidney?" Mrs. Cooper gasped.

Sidney shook her head with a concerned look.

"The police arrested Denny last night. They caught him breaking into Sam's Tavern," Mrs. Cooper announced with wide eyes. "He's Billy's friend, isn't he? What would possess that boy to do such a thing?"

"I--I don't know. Did the police say anything?" Sidney asked with surprise, although she already heard that news.

"Nothing was missing, so they claim," Mrs. Cooper announced. "I'm very concerned. There was something Mrs. Randall said to me after we heard Sam was dead." Mrs. Cooper's attention shifted to Mrs. Lamont, who approached them wearing a short, leopard skin, miniskirt, and a tight, thin sweater with no bra. She seemed reluctant to talk in front of the prowling cougar. "Stop by my house later today. I'll be at the library for a while, but I should be home by three. We can talk in private." Mrs. Cooper scurried away as Mrs. Lamont paused alongside Harlan.

Sidney looked at Harlan as Mrs. Lamont placed a dainty hand on his lower arm and gave him a long, seductive look.

"So, we meet again," Mrs. Lamont cooed and tossed her long, blonde hair.

Harlan looked at Mrs. Lamont and forced a tiny smile. "Good morning, Mrs. Lamont. I hear there was some excitement around town last night."

Sidney folded her arms across her chest and glared at the painted woman clinging to her recently acquired boyfriend.

"It's too exciting," Mrs. Lamont said with lust in her eyes and glanced over his body. "Denny was arrested for breaking and entering Sam's Tavern, of all places."

"Are there any details?" he asked.

Mrs. Lamont looked toward Sidney then back at Harlan and placed her hand on his chest. "Why don't you come to my place for some coffee, and I'll give you all the juicy details."

Harlan smirked and removed her hand from his chest. "I don't think so. Sidney and I have a lot to do today," he informed her.

Mrs. Lamont pressed against the arm she held. "Perhaps you could stop by later tonight. I have some really exciting stories I could tell you."

"I wasn't interested the other night, Mrs. Lamont, and I'm still not interested," he said simply and casually removed her hand from his arm.

Mrs. Lamont eyed Sidney then looked back at Harlan. "Suit yourself." She turned and walked back toward her house with an added swing to her hips.

"What a tart," Harlan muttered lowly under his breath. "Absolutely no morals."

Sidney watched Mrs. Lamont flirt with the mailman as he approached Mr. Taylor's house.

"She touches you again, and I'll give her something to think about," Sidney growled coldly.

Harlan chuckled lowly in his throat, causing Sidney to look at him with limited patience. He placed his arm around her waist and pulled her against him.

"You're beautiful when you're jealous," he teased warmly while holding her close.

Sidney hid her embarrassed smile and uncertainly placed her hands on his shoulders. "I don't want to lose you, especially to someone like that."

"That's something you'll never have to worry about," he said and sighed softly. "I've invested too much already to give you up without one hell of a fight."

They received several looks from people just inside the diner near the window.

Sidney gently bit her lower lip and smiled timidly. "We're attracting some attention," she said softly.

"Let them talk," he said simply and kissed her passionately in front of the dining spectators.

She returned the kiss without hesitation. When he pulled away, Sidney blushed.

"We have a busy day ahead of us," Harlan said simply. "We'll visit with Denny at the local jail, stop by the prison to talk to Alex, and then see what Mrs. Cooper wanted. It should be three o'clock by then."

Chapter Forty-four

Sidney and Harlan entered the sheriff's office within the municipal building. Sheriff Drukard was sleeping at his desk with his feet propped and his chin to his chest. His snoring sounded like a snarling, wild boar. Harlan frowned and shook his head in disapproval.

"It's a good thing there isn't much crime in this town," Harlan announced.

"Sheriff Drukard?" Sidney announced.

He didn't stir. Harlan went back to the door and slammed it. Sheriff Drukard woke and nearly fell over backward in his chair. He looked around with surprise then stared at them. His lips twisted into a frown.

"Oh, it's you," he announced to Sidney. "What do you want this time?"

"We want to see Denny," Sidney replied lowly.

Sheriff Drukard snorted a laugh. "Of course you do. Should've known you two were friends. You certainly know how to pick them."

"It could be worse," Sidney retorted. "I could've voted you into office."

Sheriff Drukard glared at her as he removed the keys from the desktop. "You watch your tone, missy." He then shot a look at

Harlan. "I'll need to see some identification before you can see the prisoner."

Sidney's brows lifted as she glared at him. "You mean you don't know who he is?"

Sheriff Drukard pointed the keys at Sidney. "With the company you keep, you consider yourself lucky I don't run a background check."

Harlan rolled his eyes and removed his wallet. He flashed his driver's license. Sheriff Drukard compared the picture and examined the license. Drukard glared at Harlan without emotion.

"What country are you from?" Sheriff Drukard demanded to know.

"England," Harlan remarked lowly.

"Let's see the green card, son," Drukard snapped.

"I'm a United States citizen," Harlan replied sternly and replaced his wallet. "Don't harass me; I know my rights."

Sheriff Drukard frowned. They were led into the basement with four cells beyond a large, steel door. Sheriff Drukard left them at the entrance. Denny, the only prisoner, was lying on a cot in the fourth cell.

"Sheriff Drukard doesn't even know who you are," Sidney remarked lowly. "He still hasn't made the connection. I can't believe everyone else in town remembers you except the man who should."

"Amazing he can get himself dressed in the morning," Harlan muttered under his breath.

As they approached Denny's cell, Denny looked at them from where he lay on his cot then sat up. A relieved smile crossed his face.

"Sidney," Denny announced overjoyed to see her as he sprang to his feet. "I didn't expect to see you here." He approached the cell door and clung to the bars. "You have to get me out of here. I didn't do anything, I swear. There was someone else in Sam's house. I thought I'd play the hero and capture him, but Sheriff Drukard doesn't believe me."

Sidney hoped that wasn't true. Lyle seemed convinced Denny was there for reasons of his own and was surprised to find someone else there.

"I even injured the guy, but they couldn't find my knife with the blood on it," Denny said with a concerned look on his face. "I wasn't stealing anything, I swear."

Sidney shook her head. "I don't know, Denny. It doesn't look good."

Denny tilted his head with concern in his eyes. "What do you mean?"

Sidney moved closer to the bars. "When Sam kidnapped Trisha, there was another man involved. Sheriff Drukard may suspect you were the driver in her kidnapping. You know how things are around here. Rumor has it Sam could have been involved in the murder of Emily Fisher as well. That puts you in a very bad position."

Denny's eyes widened with horror. "I had nothing to do with her death."

"Maybe not," Sidney replied. "But you were found in Sam's Tavern. That makes it look very bad for you."

"I wasn't anywhere near the woods the day she was murdered," Denny informed Sidney. "I was late leaving school that day. Malcolm caught Billy and me smoking in the boy's bathroom. He kept us there until nearly four o'clock. I went straight home after that. My mother and two sisters were there; they can vouch for me."

"That still doesn't clear you of any wrongdoing in Trisha's kidnapping and attempted murder. Sheriff Drukard knows you weren't stealing, Denny," Sidney announced in a tone that conveyed concern. "In fact, he's looking for evidence that connects you to Sam. We're trying to help. If you know something, you should come out with it now, before it's too late."

Denny looked from Harlan to Sidney with a nervous look in his eyes. "I was looking for something," he announced quickly. "It's an old, wooden cigar box. Sam had it somewhere on the first floor. Billy asked me to get it," he informed her. "He offered me a lot of money if I'd break into Sam's and find it. I don't know what was in it, but I have a feeling it has something to do with Trisha's kidnapping." His eyes then pleaded with hers. "I think Billy may have been involved. If he finds that box, he could tamper with it, couldn't he? He might attempt to make me look guilty of something."

Sidney's mouth opened slightly as she stared at him. "Why do you suspect Billy was involved?" she asked while her heart pounded with excitement.

"After Sam's death, Billy was upset. He wasn't the sad sort of upset; he was more nervous and edgy. That's when he asked me to get the cigar box for him. I needed the money. I've been on a losing streak at the racetrack," Denny said gently.

"Unlike Sheriff Drukard," Sidney announced, "I believe you, but it's going to be difficult to prove anything without the cigar box or evidence against Billy. Are you sure there's nothing else you can tell us about Trisha's abduction? Is there any reason to believe Billy was involved in the death of Emily Fisher?"

Denny stared at Sidney with wide eyes and a blank expression. He looked at Harlan then back to Sidney. "Billy was in love with her. He typed a letter to her that afternoon in the school while she was at lunch. I don't know what the letter said; he wouldn't tell me."

Sidney remained calm, but her heart was pounding wildly as he told her everything Trisha had suspected.

"I remember telling him he was crazy. There was no way Miss Fisher was going to date him ever, but he was insistent she was in love with him too. More than that, he didn't tell me." Denny inhaled deeply. "He didn't go directly home that day. He took that steep, rocky path that comes out by Cressman Road."

"When you cross the road, that takes you to the stone bridge," Sidney interjected.

Denny nodded. "It's not a popular path, but if he didn't want his grandmother to see him pass her house, it would have been the ideal route. We've gone that way before. We'd smoke some pot on that path without fear of being caught. No one ever goes that way. He seemed to be in a hurry."

"What about after the murder? When did you next talk to Billy?" Sidney asked.

"That evening, after word about the murder got around. I thought he'd be upset," Denny explained. "He didn't want to talk about it. I assumed he was having a difficult time dealing with her death."

"Do you think he could have done it?" Sidney asked with fear in her eyes.

Denny held his breath while staring at her. "He would've had enough time, I suppose. But I don't think he'd kill anyone, especially Miss Fisher. I mean, he was in love with her. If anything, he would have killed Alex."

"Where was he the evening Trisha was abducted?" she asked gently.

Denny shook his head. "I really couldn't say. He wasn't home," he announced. "I would've seen his car parked outside the house like always."

"Weren't you at Sam's that night?" Harlan interrupted.

Denny looked at him nervously. "Well, yes, for a short while, but I went right home afterward."

Sidney clutched the bars near Denny. "I must warn you," she said gently. "Friend or no friend, if Billy is guilty of either Trisha's kidnapping or Miss Fisher's murder, he's about to frame you for it. If he comes here to see you, I suggest you just play it cool. Harlan and I will check into this cigar box, but Billy can't know what you've told us. If he is guilty, he's going to protect himself even if it means sacrificing you."

Denny nodded. "I'm interested in protecting my own ass," he announced firmly. "You just do whatever it takes to get me out of here."

§

Harlan and Sidney left the municipal building and walked toward Harlan's car parked not far from the diner. Both were preoccupied with what Denny had told them.

"That certainly sheds some light on the situation," Harlan announced. "So there's a cigar box somewhere? Do you suppose Billy already has it?"

Sidney shook her head as they reached his car. "I don't think so. I think it's still at Sam's place."

Harlan took a deep breath, removed his cellular phone from his jacket pocket, and punched in a number. He only waited a moment before the call was answered.

"Lyle?"

There was a click. Harlan looked at the phone and frowned. He punched in the number again.

"Lyle, don't hang up on me," Harlan snarled into the phone. "I need one last favor."

Sidney could hear the voice shouting on the other end. Harlan held the phone away from his ear a moment.

"Yes, I'm aware you've only had a couple of hours sleep." There was more shouting. "Yes, I know you were stabbed last night. This is important," he explained. "The man you ran into last night is in jail. He claims Billy paid him to break into Sam's to find a wooden cigar box. There must be some significance to this box." Harlan was silent a moment then smiled. "Thanks, Lyle, you're a real friend."

Sidney waited for him to disconnect the call then eyed him with a humored look. "He won't be your friend much longer," she announced while grinning. "I hope you're compensating him for all he's done."

"Of course I am. I promised to buy the first round of drinks once we get home," Harlan replied simply.

Sidney rolled her eyes and groaned. "I'll never understand the male relationship."

"It's far less complicated than the female relationship," he remarked. "Let's visit Alex."

Chapter Forty-five

Sidney felt very uncomfortable in the dreary, cold prison visiting room. Both sat on the opposite side of the smudged glass and waited for the guard to bring Alex to the area before them. Alex looked much older than Sidney had remembered. His dirty, blonde hair was now streaked with gray, and there were noticeable wrinkles on the outer corner of his eyes. He wasn't much older than Harlan, but he looked to be about forty-five. Alex stared at them with a strange look and uncertainly picked up the phone on his end. Sidney and Harlan did the same. Sidney's heart pounded nervously as she watched him. She was convinced he was innocent, but he still made her feel uneasy after all these years.

"Do I know either of you?" Alex asked gently with some confusion.

"Somewhat," Harlan announced simply. "I'm Harlan Brendan, and this is Trisha Allister's friend, Sidney McBride."

Alex looked from Sidney to Harlan. "Harlan? Yeah, I remember you now. You were the guy Emily had her eyes on." Alex forced a tiny smile and chuckled. "There was a time when I would have enjoyed knocking you senseless, but I'm over that now."

He then looked at Sidney. "So, you're Sidney, huh? You look a lot older than I remember from the trial. Trisha and I talked about you when she visited. How is she?"

"She's fine now," Sidney said gently while studying Alex. "Sam abducted her, and nearly killed her."

"Sam?" Alex gasped with wide, horrified eyes. "Why would he want to hurt her?"

"She was poking around in Emily's murder, and he must not have liked it, not that Sheriff Drukard had made any real connections," Sidney replied bluntly. "Sam was killed."

Alex was silent a moment then nodded. "Damned good thing too," he replied firmly. "You said Trisha's okay? I told her to let it go. No one believed either of us anyway."

Sidney drew a deep breath and held it a moment. "Opinions are slowly changing, Alex," she said gently. "We need to ask you a few questions."

"I've answered all Trisha's questions," he said simply. "I don't really know what more I can tell you that hasn't been told a million times."

"You can start with Sam," Harlan announced. "The day Emily was killed; you went to the tavern for the beginning of your shift. Was Sam there?"

Alex considered the question a moment then shook his head. "No, I don't think so, but that wasn't unusual. He would sometimes sneak off into the back room to catch the score of some game he had money on."

"When did he return?" Sidney asked.

"I'd say he returned around six o'clock, about half an hour before the police arrived," Alex explained. "I reached the tavern about five-thirty."

"Did anyone complain about not being served their drinks on time?" Harlan asked.

Alex had to think. He scratched his head thoughtfully then nodded. "Malcolm complained, now that you mention it. Almost all the glasses were empty," he replied. "Malcolm said Sam gave them a free round about four-thirty or so. That must have been around the time he went into the back room."

"Paul Malcolm was there?" Sidney asked.

Alex nodded. "He was a permanent fixture, especially on a Friday."

"Sam said he had left after one drink," Sidney replied simply. "Of course, Sam lied about everything else. I suppose he wanted to make Malcolm look suspicious."

Harlan gently cleared his throat. "An eyewitness saw Sam driving through town just before five that day. He wasn't in the back room watching a game," he informed Alex.

Alex stared at him with surprise. "I was out of sorts," he said gently. "I didn't think twice about old Sam. Where had he gone? Surely, you don't suspect he killed Emily. Around the time you say he'd left the bar, would have been around the time I found her dead."

"No, we don't suspect he killed her," Harlan continued. "We're convinced he went to Mrs. Randall's house."

Alex nodded. "Yeah, that's a possibility. They were close ever since her son died. She called Sam when she had trouble with Billy. Sam was like a father to Billy."

Sidney wasn't surprised to hear that. It made perfectly good sense that Mrs. Randall would call upon Sam that day, especially if she had nowhere else to turn.

"We think Billy was in trouble," Harlan said and held his breath while staring at Alex through the cloudy glass. "There's a distinct possibility Billy may have murdered Emily."

Alex's mouth fell open while he stared at Harlan. "Billy? Billy Randall?" he gasped softly and shook his head. "That's impossible. Billy adored Emily."

"We think Billy may have been in the woods by the stone house while you and Emily exchanged apologies," Harlan announced delicately and cleared his throat. "We think he killed her in a jealous rage."

"Mrs. Randall met with an accident right after Sam's death," Sidney informed him sadly. "We think he may have silenced her as well."

Alex stared at them with disbelief. "You suspect he killed his own grandmother?" He shook his head. "I just can't believe he'd do something like that. Not his own grandmother. If anyone killed Emily, it was Malcolm. They were having an affair."

"But by your own testimony, Malcolm was at the bar when you arrived," Harlan remarked. "In order for him to have murdered her, you would have passed him on Cressman Road. He'd never have made it back to the bar in time by foot. Cressman Road is the only road between here and there. He would've been seen had he driven through town."

Alex frowned and nodded. "I suppose you're right." He glared at them with a look of anger. "Her affair with him made me so angry." He leaned forward on the counter between them and stared at Harlan. "I mean, I could understand her chasing you, but that Malcolm--?"

"Why didn't you tell Trisha about Malcolm and Emily having an affair?" Sidney asked since it seemed like an important detail to leave out of an otherwise candid conversation.

"Emily's dead, and I'm in jail. Trisha adored Emily. I saw no reason to lower her opinion of her. At least someone would have a fond memory of Emily," he said then sighed with defeat. "Tell Trisha I'm glad she's feeling better and just to give it up. I'm not blaming either of you for testifying against me. It was just a matter of being in the wrong place at the wrong time for all of us. It's not worth getting herself killed over."

§

Once they left the prison, they had plenty of time before they were to meet Mrs. Cooper. They decided to stop at the hospital to check on Trisha's condition. Trisha was roaming around the room in her housecoat while Sidney's mother sat in the bedside chair reading a woman's magazine. When they entered the room, Trisha was excited to see Sidney. She hurried to her friend and hugged her.

"They're supposed to release me tomorrow morning, but I'm pushing for tonight. I just want out of this place," she said happily while pulling away from Sidney.

"That's great Trisha," Sidney said with a relieved smile then fidgeted. "You haven't seen Billy today, have you?"

"No, he hasn't been in since his grandmother's death," she said sadly then turned angry. "It sickens me to think what he's done, and no one can prove any of it."

"We're working on it," Sidney replied gently.

"Poor Mrs. Randall," Trisha scoffed. "A real pain in the ass, but she'd never hurt a fly."

"Do you remember anything more from the night you were abducted?" Sidney asked.

Trisha shook her head. "I wish I did. Maybe I could point the finger at Billy for that much."

Harlan's cellular phone chirped. He removed it from his pocket and answered it. "Hello?" He was silent a minute then looked at

Sidney. "You did? Don't keep us in suspense," he practically cried out. "What's in the box?"

Sidney approached Harlan and listened intently.

"You're kidding," he said with some surprise as his expression dropped. "You didn't remove the box, did you?" Harlan was silent a moment then sighed. "Thanks, Lyle."

Trisha's eyes brightened at the mention of Lyle's name. Harlan disconnected the call and appeared defeated. Sidney, her mother, and Trisha stared at him with little hope.

"The box contained cocaine," Harlan said lowly. "I think Denny lied to us."

"Do you think Denny wanted the drugs for himself?" Sidney asked.

Harlan nodded.

"So why lie about Billy's involvement?" Sidney asked with some confusion.

"We put him in a position where he thought he had no other choice," Harlan informed her. "He didn't want to be connected to Trisha's abduction, so he threw suspicion onto his best friend."

"That's low," Trisha said coldly.

"We're officially back to square one," Harlan muttered.

"How are we going to prove Billy killed Miss Fisher or his grandmother?" Trisha demanded.

"I doubt that we'll ever be able to prove it," Harlan remarked simply then glared at Trisha. "As for you, I don't think you'll be snooping around for quite some time."

Trisha folded her arms across her chest and glared at Harlan. "I'm feeling perfectly fine," she insisted. "I'm not going to allow one little incident stop me from my mission. We're too close to stop now."

"Yes, you're close all right," Harlan remarked sternly while glaring at her. "Close to getting yourself killed. Arrangements have been made for your safe transportation to California, compliments of Lyle Holstead."

Trisha stared at him with some surprise and almost appeared uncertain how to respond. "I'm not going anywhere; not even with Lyle."

"I don't think he's going to give you much choice in the matter," Harlan informed her. "He's stubborn about these things."

"Yeah, well, I'm stubborn too," Trisha remarked.

"I think you'll find you met your match in that department," Harlan replied.

"We'll just see," Trisha scoffed.

When she thought no one was looking, Sidney caught a glimpse of Trisha hiding a tiny grin. Perhaps Lyle could be just what the doctor ordered.

Chapter Forty-six

Sidney and Harlan left the hospital a few minutes later. They were still a little early for their appointment with Mrs. Cooper, so they decided to meet her at the library and walk her home. They entered the library and found a young girl in her mid-teens replacing some books on the first floor. The library seemed unusually quiet with no one around. Sidney approached the young girl while she worked.

"Did Mrs. Cooper leave yet?" Sidney asked the girl near the checkout desk.

"She had been downstairs in the archives," the young girl replied. "But I heard someone go through the back door. She may have left."

Although it seemed unlikely that Mrs. Cooper would leave the back way, since she'd have to walk all the way around the library to head for her house, Sidney thanked the girl and walked with Harlan to the basement steps.

"Yo, Sidney," came an unfamiliar male voice.

Sidney and Harlan turned and saw number fifty-two walking through the front door and down the hall toward her. He was breathing heavily as he extended a folder. Harlan looked down the hallway toward the back door with a raised and curious brow.

"I was on my way to the press with my report. You'd asked to see it," number fifty-two announced with a broad grin. "What a stroke of luck that I ran into you. Ran when I saw you on the sidewalk."

Sidney accepted the folder. "Thank you. I really appreciate this," she said pleasantly.

"Tell me if I didn't deserve an 'A' on that report," he teased while grinning boyishly. "Ms. Palmer gave me a 'B'. What a witch."

Sidney laughed softly.

"Gotta go. We're shooting hoop tonight at Roger's house," number fifty-two announced proudly then turned and hurried from the library.

Sidney sighed and looked at the folder. "This won't do much good anymore," she replied simply. "The case is pretty much solved."

Harlan and Sidney continued toward the basement and walked down the rickety, old steps. The archives appeared to be abandoned as well. They walked through the rows of books, magazines, and newspapers. As they neared the back, Sidney saw a thin hand on the floor just beyond a rack of books.

"Oh, my God!"

Sidney ran toward the bookcase and saw Mrs. Cooper lying face down in the aisle. Her silk scarf was tight around her neck, and she didn't appear to be breathing. Sidney sank to her knees and loosened the scarf. Mrs. Cooper gasped and wheezed once the scarf was loosened from around her neck.

"I'll call an ambulance," Harlan said and removed his cellular phone from his jacket but was unable to get a signal.

He ran to Trisha's desk and snatched the phone from its cradle. Sidney gently rolled Mrs. Cooper onto her thighs and elevated her head. The elderly woman clutched her chest and gasped for her breath. Her eyes rolled as she looked at Sidney.

"You're okay, Mrs. Cooper," Sidney announced and gently rubbed the woman's shoulder.

Mrs. Cooper continued to gasp. She attempted to speak but couldn't find the breath. She wheezed and clutched Sidney's arm with fear.

Harlan approached them from Trisha's desk. "An ambulance is on its way," he announced with a look of panic in his eyes. "Is she okay?"

Sidney shook her head. "I--I don't know."

"I thought I heard someone leave through the back door just before we came down here," Harlan announced. "Watch her. I'll be right back."

Sidney watched helplessly as Harlan ran from the basement. She could hear Harlan's feet running up the creaking, old steps then heard him yelling something to the young girl. Sidney listened to the sound of his footfalls on the first floor as he possibly ran out the back door. Sidney continued to rub Mrs. Cooper's shoulder with concern while attempting to reassure her.

"The ambulance will be here soon," Sidney chanted. "Just relax until they get here. You're going to be fine."

"My purse," Mrs. Cooper suddenly gasped while attempting to catch her breath. "It's in my purse."

Sidney looked around the aisle with some confusion. Her purse lay on the floor partially hidden beneath Trisha's desk. "I'll get your purse," she announced reassuringly. "Don't you worry about your purse. Just relax. You're going to be fine."

Sidney was actually hoping to convince herself that the woman would be okay. The young girl appeared in the entrance between the bookcases. Sidney looked up and saw the look of fear on the girl's face. Mrs. Cooper suddenly clutched her chest with a loud gasp. Her eyes rolled, and she fell limp on Sidney's legs. All color ran from Sidney's face, and her body began to tremble.

"Mrs. Cooper!" Sidney shook her shoulder as fear filled her. "Mrs. Cooper!"

Without a moment's hesitation, the young girl dove to the floor and pulled Mrs. Cooper from Sidney's lap. Sidney stared in complete surprise as the young girl placed her hands on the woman's chest and started performing CPR. Sidney's mouth fell open as she watched the fifteen-year-old push on Mrs. Cooper's chest then breathed into her mouth. Harlan returned and stared at the scene with similar surprise. Mrs. Cooper groaned softly and now breathed on her own. The young girl fell onto her backside and placed a trembling hand on her head. The paramedics arrived shortly after, giving her oxygen and connecting all sorts of monitors to Mrs. Cooper's body. Once she breathed the oxygen, she seemed more alert. Harlan called the young girl's mother to come for her after her trying ordeal. Once the ambulance left, Sidney picked up Mrs. Cooper's purse and the folder number fifty-two had given her.

"I didn't see anyone," Harlan replied gently. "Maybe that boy saw someone when he left."

Sidney sighed and nervously looked around the library. "I just don't understand it. Do you think Billy knew Mrs. Cooper was going to tell us something?" She then shook her head. "That's a huge risk he took. Could he be that stupid to strangle an old woman in a public place?"

"The answer's rather obvious," Harlan replied simply. "That was no accident."

"It doesn't make sense," Sidney said lowly.

"Unless the attempt on her life wasn't related to the murder," Harlan said simply.

Sidney shook her head and sighed. "I'm out of answers," she replied.

Harlan placed his arm around her. "I think we could both use a rest. Let's go back to my room and relax a while."

Sidney nodded. "That sounds like a good idea to me. I could use a little more sleep."

Chapter Forty-seven

Sidney lay in Harlan's arms unable to sleep despite being exhausted. She looked around the motel room and thought about everything that had happened in the past two weeks. It almost seemed amazing what they had been through since her return home. She wondered if Mrs. Lamont had anything to do with Mrs. Cooper's near fatality. Mrs. Cooper had been reluctant to talk in front of her. Was there a connection? Sidney slipped out of Harlan's arms and reached for the folder number fifty-two had so graciously brought to her. She read the five-page report despite her burning, tired eyes. There were many facts taken from the newspaper articles at the time of the murder, and some opinions from Ms. Palmer, Mr. Malcolm, and the principal of the school.

Sidney frowned when she read Mr. Malcolm's comment about the murder. Ironic how much better the sugarcoated truth sounded. Ms. Palmer told what a wonderful woman Emily was and how Alex treated her so poorly. Sidney also knew that wasn't the truth. Ms. Palmer only saw an attractive woman. Since she hated men, she was going to speculate Alex was a rotten son-of-a-bitch. She set the folder aside and looked at Harlan while he slept. There was a harsh pounding on the door. Harlan jumped with surprise and sprang out of bed. For a moment, he was disoriented. He looked back at Sidney then turned to the door. Sidney remained sitting on the bed as he unlocked the door.

Lyle barged into the room with a huge grin on his enthusiastic face. "You are not going to believe what I just heard," he announced excitedly.

Harlan ran his fingers through his hair while attempting to recover from his interrupted nap. "Then why bother telling me," he muttered lowly.

"Denny confessed to assisting Sam to kidnap Trisha," Lyle announced and raised his brows with a suggestive look. "What do you think of that?"

Harlan and Sidney stared at Lyle with some surprise.

"He did?" Harlan asked. "What possessed him to do such a thing?"

Lyle chuckled lowly. "It may have had something to do with the idiot leaving his answering machine on while Sam arranged to kidnap Trisha at the library." Lyle waved the small tape he held between his fingers. "He preferred the kidnapping charge over attempted murder, so he confessed to everything. He knocked Trisha unconscious, and Sam brought the cab around back. He claims he knew nothing about the drugs Sam gave her, and he wasn't aware that Sam intended to kill her. He claims Sam told him he was just giving her a scare to chase her out of town."

"What was the reason for wanting Trisha out of the way?" Harlan asked.

"Sam was protecting Billy," Lyle said simply. "There was circumstantial evidence against Billy in Emily's murder. Sam was afraid Trisha would reopen the case, and Billy would be framed. Sam had been covering for Billy all these years, but Sam confessed to Denny that Billy wasn't involved in the murder. They've taken Billy in for questioning." Lyle continued to smile cheaply and clipped his press badge to his shirt. "Come along cameraman," he announced to Harlan. "We must get first scoop."

Harlan ran across the room, grabbed his camera bag, and hurried to join Lyle by the motel room door. He turned and looked back at Sidney.

"Wait here until I return," Harlan announced.

"Can't I come along?" Sidney demanded to know.

"No, you just wait here," Harlan replied. "I don't want you anywhere near Billy Randall."

Sidney frowned. "Yes, Dad."

Once they left, she flopped back on the bed and picked up Mrs. Cooper's purse. Sidney reached for the phone and called the hospital. They wouldn't report on Mrs. Cooper's condition, so she asked to speak to Mrs. Cooper's daughter. Sidney had called her when they took Mrs. Cooper to the hospital from a number she found in her wallet. Her daughter lived nearly two hours away but dropped everything to be with her mother. According to Mrs. Cooper's daughter, she was recovering from her ordeal and a mild heart attack. Naturally, they would need to do more tests to see if there was any damage to her heart, but she was doing fine. She was somewhat groggy from the medication they gave her, but they expected a full recovery in a couple of days. Sidney reported that she had Mrs. Cooper's purse, but her daughter wasn't concerned about retrieving it at the moment and offered to pick it up tomorrow.

Once she hung up the phone with Mrs. Cooper's daughter, Sidney opened the purse and looked through it, since she had nothing better to do. To her surprise, she saw Mrs. Cooper's notebook that she usually kept under the sofa cushion. Sidney flipped through the small notebook. She flipped to the back and started with the most current entries starting with the date Sam had died. She read the note written behind the date.

June 3rd: Sam kidnapped Trisha Allister. He tried to kill her in the old, stone house. The house collapsed on him, killing him. Mrs. Randall was very upset. Said she had something very important to tell me about the day Emily Fisher was murdered. Billy interrupted our conversation.

Sidney frowned, realizing that was the moment both women's fates were sealed. She shifted uncomfortably then looked at the next entry.

June 4th: Spoke with Mrs. Lamont during my early morning walk. Talked about Sam's death, and how he nearly killed Trisha. We also discussed Denny's drug problem. Mrs. Randall fell down the stairs and died! I can't believe Billy would leave her alone in her condition. Why didn't he call me to watch her? Sheriff Drukard said it was an accident, but I'm not so sure, not after what happened with Sam. I'm going to have a talk with Billy.

June 5th: Ran into Persha on my morning walk. Told me Denny had been arrested last night for breaking into Sam's Tavern. Discussed the murder of Emily Fisher. She believed Billy had some involvement in her death. Said she saw Billy entering the woods near the school, which would bring him out on Cressman Road just before the stone bridge. Paul Malcolm had a completely different story, but I should see him this afternoon when he comes to the diner during his lunch period.

Sidney stared at the last entry with some confusion. Mrs. Cooper seemed fairly upset when they met outside the diner, yet her last entry didn't convey much emotion. Something troubled Mrs.

Cooper between her morning walk and around eleven when she and Harlan ran into her. Had Mrs. Cooper thought of something? Or had she run into someone? Sidney shot upward in the bed. Her father may have seen something. Sidney jumped off the bed and ran from the motel room.

Chapter Forty-eight

Sidney hurried through town, passed the municipal building, and entered her father's press. She found her father behind the counter. When he saw her, he leaned on the counter with wide eyes.

"Have you heard? They took Billy in for questioning," Herb announced almost in disbelief.

"Yes, I heard," she replied.

He groaned and shook his head. "Thank God they're finally making some progress."

"Dad, were you here all day?" she asked.

Her father appeared surprised that she changed the subject so quickly. "Aren't you happy to hear about Billy?"

"They haven't convicted him of anything yet," Sidney replied with little enthusiasm. "Questioning is a long way from being charged with anything. Sheriff Drukard won't even know where to begin or what questions to ask. Billy will be out in an hour."

"You're just a ray of sunshine today," her father scoffed lowly. "At least it's something. Why do you want to know if I was here all day?" He then straightened and rearranged the candy bars under the counter.

"You know what happened to Mrs. Cooper this afternoon," Sidney announced firmly.

Herb nodded and eyed her. "How could I not hear that? Someone nearly kills her, and my own daughter finds her," he remarked. "Everyone in town has stopped by to report that news. No one seems to know why anyone would want to kill her though. The only one seen leaving the library was that high school kid; Murphy's boy. I heard that idiot Sheriff Drukard is starting to suspect Harlan's involvement." He glared at her and raised an arrogant brow. "You two have a bad timing problem."

"Did you happen to see Mrs. Cooper talking to anyone earlier today?" Sidney asked, practically ignoring her father's concerns.

"No, can't say I did," he replied while shaking his head. "But I don't spend all day staring out the window either."

"I saw her," came a female voice from nearby.

Sidney spun with alarm and saw Mrs. Lamont approach the desk from the middle aisle. She cradled her collection of women's magazines in her arms against her chest. Her face was pale and drained of all emotions.

"I saw her talking to Persha. I believe they walked all the way to the school together," Mrs. Lamont said softly. "It took her a while to come back this way. I wanted to tell her how sorry I was about Mrs. Randall. We had coffee at the diner when she returned. She was writing stuff in that little notebook of hers, but she seemed so distant." Mrs. Lamont held back her tears. "While driving from town half an hour later, I saw her outside the school at a picnic table with Paul Malcolm. I'll never know how she got there so fast, but she was there."

Sidney's eyes narrowed with a look of confusion. "Malcolm?" she remarked softly. "That's odd."

"That's the same thing Sheriff Drukard said when I told him. He said she'd also talked with Gladys, the waitress from the diner, shortly before the attack. The young girl at the library said she returned her purse," Mrs. Lamont informed her. "Apparently Mrs. Cooper had left it there this morning. That was very unusual for her to forget her purse anywhere. Like I said, she was unusually distant for some reason."

Sidney attempted to take in all the new information. It would seem that Mrs. Cooper got around town that morning, talking with nearly every suspect on the list. Mrs. Randall's death must have stirred something inside the older woman.

"I appreciate your help," Sidney announced then hurried from the press without saying goodbye to her father.

Sidney hurried through town in the direction of the motel. She passed the municipal building, saw a crowd gathering, and wondered what was happening there. Had everyone heard about Billy being taken in for questioning? She walked a couple of feet past the building when her arm was grabbed, and she was flung around. She stared into Billy's angry eyes. Sidney's mouth fell open, and her eyes widened with surprise.

"What the hell is wrong with you?" Billy demanded to know in a low voice.

His hand gripped her arm, causing her some pain. Sidney winced and stared at him, uncertain how to respond.

"This entire time you thought I was the one who killed Emily Fisher?" he lashed out angrily. "I can't believe you'd even consider something so outrageous. Then to pit Denny against me!"

Apparently, Denny had mentioned her name in his confession. Sidney attempted to pull away from Billy. His grip tightened, causing her to wince in pain.

"They're going to do an autopsy on my grandmother. You started this, Sidney," he growled lowly as his eyes burned into hers. "But I'm going to finish it."

"Get your bloody hands off her," Harlan growled lowly from nearby.

Billy cast Sidney away from him, allowing her to fall into the grassy area just off the sidewalk. He lunged for Harlan. Harlan cast his camera aside and blocked Billy's fist. Sidney scrambled to her feet and watched in horror as the two men punched each other. A crowd gathered outside the building to watch the men fight. Harlan tackled Billy to the lawn and punched him several times before he was thrown off. Sidney was actually surprised Harlan was able to hold his own against the much younger, more muscular former football player. Billy dove on top of Harlan and attempted to punch him, but Harlan blocked nearly every blow. Lyle pushed through the crowd and pulled Billy off Harlan. Sheriff Drukard and his deputy appeared and grabbed both Harlan and Billy.

"How about a night in jail to cool your heels," Drukard announced loudly to both men.

Sheriff Drukard and his deputy escorted both men toward the building. Sidney and Lyle watched helplessly while Harlan and Billy were taken into the municipal building. Lyle grabbed Harlan's discarded camera and approached Sidney. He turned to stare as the sheriff disappeared inside the building.

"Can he do that?" Lyle asked.

Sidney shrugged and frowned. "It's accepted for disorderly conduct and public drunkenness," she replied with a sigh. "He'll release them in the morning. They'll probably have to pay a fine of some sort. Usually, the sort that lines his own pockets."

Lyle rolled his eyes and moaned. "Unbelievable."

"It's a small town with no lawyers," she replied while sighing with defeat. "He gets away with a lot of things that aren't legal in the civilized world."

"I'll work on a plan to get Harlan out of the clink later." Lyle took her arm and guided her in the direction of the motel. "We need to talk."

§

Sidney sat on Harlan's bed while watching Lyle pace and listened while he told her what they'd discovered during their roles as reporters at the municipal building.

"They're going to perform an autopsy on Mrs. Randall tonight, and they're also going to search Billy's house," Lyle informed her. "They questioned Billy in the sheriff's office, so I was able to hear most of their conversation through the door from the hallway. Billy stuck to his original story about the day Emily Fisher died. He also claims he had no involvement in Trisha's kidnapping and attempted murder." Lyle continued to pace the small motel room. "He claims his grandmother's death was an accident. Of course, Sheriff Drukard didn't push the issue any, except the autopsy. If that autopsy shows what we suspected it'd show all along, Billy won't be questioned further."

Sidney frowned and shook her head in disbelief. "So questioning Billy gets us absolutely nowhere," she scoffed. "What do we do now?"

"I'm going back to the jail and see if I can spring Harlan tonight," Lyle informed her. "I don't really want to leave him there overnight. Then I'm going to the hospital to keep an eye on Trisha until she's released tomorrow morning."

"There's something I need to discuss with Paul Malcolm. He had a conversation with Mrs. Cooper earlier today," Sidney announced. "I'd like to know what they talked about. It may have been important."

"Isn't he that alcoholic schoolteacher?"

Sidney mechanically nodded. "I might try calling him on the phone."

"He's probably at the bar just outside of town by the highway," Lyle said simply. "It's a public place. I suppose you could question him there. I'll give you my cellular phone number. If you run into a problem, you can call me."

Sidney smiled gently. "Thanks, Lyle."

Chapter Forty-nine

Sidney entered the barroom located just before the interstate and saw Malcolm leaning on the bar, huddled over his drink. He looked as if he'd been there a while. She approached the bar and took the vacant seat alongside him. It took him several minutes to notice her. He looked at her as if she were the grim reaper then groaned softly and looked back across the bar.

"We've got to stop meeting like this," Malcolm said in a drunken tone. "The rumors are sure to start."

Sidney ordered a rum and cola then focused her attention on Mr. Malcolm. "I thought I might find you here," she replied. "Had you heard about Mrs. Cooper?"

"Poor Mrs. Cooper," Malcolm said and shook his head. "A real pain in the ass, but I can't believe someone would try to kill her." He then turned on his bar stool to face her, barely able to keep his balance. "Does anyone know how she's doing?"

"I heard she was doing better," Sidney replied. "But I don't think she's talking yet."

"It's ironic. I just spoke to her this morning," Malcolm said with a soft moan. "She came to the school and forced me out of my class. For a woman who's usually a fly on the wall, she was very persistent. I don't think I'd ever seen her in such an aggressive state before."

Obviously, the strain of what happened to Mrs. Randall, or something she had heard had gotten the older woman riled.

"What did she want to talk to you about?" Sidney asked while studying the drunken man.

"You and Trisha really opened a can of worms," he said bluntly. "She was asking about Emily's murder."

"Really? What did she ask?"

"She was asking about Billy Randall. She wanted to know what time he'd left the school that day," he replied and suddenly looked at her with a strange realization. "They don't suspect Billy Randall, do they?"

"I heard Sheriff Drukard took him in for questioning," she confirmed. "That's as much as I know. What did she ask about Billy?"

Malcolm shook his head and groaned. "She was interested in which way he went home that day," he announced. "I told her he went through the woods near the school. I saw him walking past the football field as I was walking toward Sam's."

"You're positive he went the back way to Cressman Road?" she asked with some confusion.

"Sure I'm sure," he remarked with a stern look. "Why would I lie about something so trivial?"

"Just something Mrs. Cooper said earlier," Sidney replied. "She thought that you and Ms. Palmer had conflicting stories about the way Billy went home."

Malcolm's eyes narrowed. "Persha?" he practically demanded. "How would Persha know which way Billy went home? She left long before Billy and Denny."

Sidney was confused and attempted to sort out all the information within her head. A strange thought occurred to her. "Had you told Mrs. Cooper that?"

"It came up," he casually replied. "I was the last teacher to leave school that day. I would've been out earlier if it wasn't for Billy and Denny misbehaving. Persha was leaving the building as I went back inside after my talk with Emily. I was heading back to my classroom for my jacket when I caught those two smoking in the boy's bathroom."

Sidney thought about what he said and stared at his profile. "Which way *did* Emily Fisher leave school that day?" she asked with great interest.

"Through town," he replied with little emotion. "She always went through town. She was stopping at the press to drop off her roll of film. You knew that."

"What about Persha?" she asked. "She walks to school, doesn't she?"

Malcolm snorted a soft laugh. "Yeah, she walks. She went the back way. She always walks the back way to avoid the snoops," he remarked then considered the comment. "Of course, back then she was living with her sister in your development."

Sidney sank deep in thought then turned toward Malcolm and leaned on the bar. Her look was serious. "Was Persha having an affair with Emily Fisher?" she bluntly asked.

Malcolm turned his head and stared at Sidney a long moment with surprise. "An affair? No, I don't think so." He chuckled softly. "Although, I suppose Persha liked women even back then. Persha took a liking to Emily, but it was very one-sided."

Sidney jumped from her stool. "Thanks, Mr. Malcolm. You've been a big help."

"Where're you going?" he asked with surprise then eyed her drink on the bar that she hadn't even touched. "Aren't you going to finish your drink?"

"No," Sidney replied.

Without asking, he pulled the drink before him.

"I'd like to ask Ms. Palmer a couple of questions before it gets too late," Sidney informed him. "You don't happen to know where I might find her this time of evening?"

"I don't know," he replied then grinned and chuckled softly. "What time is it?"

"Eight o'clock," Sidney replied.

"Bowling," he replied simply without even hesitating. "She belongs to a women's bowling league. They meet on Fridays. They should be there at the bowling alley by now."

Sidney only knew of one bowling alley locally. It was in the neighboring town of Brighton.

§

The bowling alley was less than a ten-minute drive from the bar outside of town. The lanes were fairly crowded that Friday evening as the sound of toppling bowling pins filled the room. Sidney entered the building and looked around. She saw Ms. Palmer with three other women, who all wore matching bowling shirts. Sidney collected herself before casually approaching the women. She sat on one of the nearby benches and watched them bowl. Ms. Palmer bowled a strike and celebrated her victory. She and another woman slapped hands excitedly. It only took a moment for her to notice Sidney on the nearby bench. Persha said something to the three women then approached Sidney and joined her.

"Sidney, I didn't expect to see you here," Ms. Palmer said cheerfully and leaned on the back of the bench facing her. "Do you bowl?"

"I've tried it once," Sidney replied.

She remembered it well. She was about ten years old and dropped the ball on her foot. So ended her enthusiasm for the sport and her father's dream of a father-daughter champion duo.

"So what brings you here?" Ms. Palmer asked then looked around. "Where's your man friend?"

"In jail," Sidney replied simply. "Disorderly conduct."

Persha snorted a soft laugh and appeared humored. "Typical men," she replied. "Are you interested in bowling a couple of frames?" She raised her brows suggestively and nodded toward the lane with the rest of her league.

"Actually," Sidney announced. "I'm trying to figure out who tried to kill Mrs. Cooper in the library today."

Ms. Palmer shook her head with sadness and disbelief. "I still can't believe that happened to that poor woman. You know what I think, don't you?"

Sidney shook her head.

"Mrs. Randall takes an unexpected fall down the stairs," Ms. Palmer announced with cleverly raised brows. "Then someone tries to kill Mrs. Cooper." Her look turned commanding. "I think Billy was involved. It makes sense if you really think about it."

Sidney stared at Ms. Palmer a long moment, surprised she had come to the same conclusion. "You may not be entirely wrong with that theory," she remarked. "On the day Miss Fisher was killed, I was told Billy was seen leaving the back way from school from two separate witnesses as well."

Persha nodded as her eyes widened. "He did. Eight years is a long time, but I'm fairly certain I remember seeing him leave that way," she insisted. "He would have had more than enough time to meet up with Emily in the woods." She shook her head with disbelief. "Could you imagine the scandal if they discover it was him and not Alec?"

Sidney eyed Ms. Palmer with little expression. "He would have had enough time," she agreed then tilted her head and leaned forward with great interest. "One thing I'd really like to know though. How did you see Billy leaving the school grounds when you had left nearly half an hour earlier?"

Persha's eyes narrowed at the question, and she looked at Sidney with some confusion. "I don't know what you're talking about. I didn't leave school early that day," she insisted. "It was a Friday. I stayed after to grade some papers, so I wouldn't have to do them over the weekend. I always grade exam papers on a Friday after school."

Sidney stared at Ms. Palmer, wishing she could remember what every person did that particular day, but she could barely remember what she herself did. It was tough deciding whom to believe. Mr. Malcolm appeared to have lied before, but that was according to what Sam had verified, and it was more than obvious Sam had been lying all along. Ms. Palmer seemed to have good intentions, but she tended to make things up as she went along. If Sidney claimed she'd seen an alien abduct someone, she was almost certain Ms. Palmer would be able to identify the spaceship. Sidney stared at Ms. Palmer then finally forced a smile.

"I guess we'll never really know," Sidney announced then stood. "Sorry to have disturbed your game."

"You didn't disturb anything," Ms. Palmer replied and took a sweeping look over Sidney. "Are you sure you wouldn't care to join us?"

Sidney suddenly felt uncomfortable. It would appear a few drinks had loosened up her old teacher enough to come across as flirty. It was time to leave.

"Thanks," she announced, "but I really have to go."

§

Sidney left the bowling alley and paused just outside. Her mind was reeling with the new information she'd received. Too many things were going through her head, and she needed someone to help sort them out. She noticed the pay phone near the front door. She removed the piece of paper containing Lyle's cellular phone number from her pocket and hurried to the pay phone. She inserted her coin and punched in his number. Lyle answered on the second ring.

"Lyle," Sidney announced and fidgeted slightly. "What are you doing?"

"Uh, paying some extortion money to Sheriff Drukard," Lyle remarked simply. "Everything okay?"

"I'm not sure," she said with a sigh. "Can you do me a big favor?"

"For you? Anything," he replied with a soft laugh.

"I need you to look around someone's house within the next hour," Sidney said softly so anyone passing by wouldn't hear her conversation.

"Oh, I can do that. Who's house?" he asked.

"Persha Palmer," Sidney announced and looked around to make sure no one listened to her conversation. Fortunately, she was alone outside. "It's next door to Mrs. Cooper's house. The red brick, bi-level."

"The one with the stupid flamingo mailbox?" he asked then laughed. "I know the one."

"You aren't talking in front of Sheriff Drukard, are you?" she practically gasped.

"Nah, I'm at the ATM, stealing my life savings for that worthless boyfriend of yours," he replied simply.

Sidney smiled gently at the sound of his remark, liking that he thought Harlan was her boyfriend. "How much?"

"A thousand dollars. Three hundred for the fine and a seven hundred dollar processing fee," Lyle said with a tiny laugh. "Make sure he pays me back, okay?"

"I'll do what I can," she replied. "Thanks, Lyle."

Sidney hung up the phone and looked around the parking lot. Thankfully, there was no one around. She walked past several cars before reaching hers then suddenly hesitated. She looked around the parking lot with an odd feeling that someone had been watching her, but there was no one there. Sidney jumped into her car and drove back to Marilina.

Chapter Fifty

Sidney paced Harlan's motel room and stared at the clock on the nightstand. She'd been back nearly an hour. Harlan still hadn't returned to his room, and Lyle hadn't called. She suspected Lyle would be calling shortly, but she didn't understand why Harlan was gone so long. Had Sheriff Drukard changed his mind and decided to keep Harlan? Sidney then had a crazy notion that Drukard may have tricked Lyle into paying a fine, took the money as a bribe, and threw Lyle in jail as well. Her mind was too active tonight. There was too much worrying her. She decided it would be necessary to make a trip to the municipal building and see just what was happening.

Sidney walked the short distance to town. It would have been pointless to drive that far. It would take her longer to find a parking space than it would just to walk. She made it to the municipal building in ten minutes. When she entered the building, she found Deputy Hawkins on duty for the evening. She approached his desk and attempted a polite smile.

"Hello, Deputy Hawkins," she announced pleasantly. "I was wondering if I could see Harlan Brendon."

Hawkins gave her a strange look. "He's been released. His friend bailed him out an hour ago."

Sidney raised her brows although her heart sank. "Oh. I'm glad to hear. Thanks." Sidney left the municipal building with an uneasy feeling. If Harlan left an hour ago, did he leave with Lyle? He wouldn't possibly be assisting Lyle in his search of Ms. Palmer's home, would he? Sidney reached the sidewalk and looked across town, staring at nothing in particular as her imagination ran away with her. Her eyes then fell upon the light coming from Mr. Taylor's sitting room in the front of the house. Mr. Taylor had answers on more than one occasion. Perhaps he'd be able to help her again. Sidney hurried across town and stepped onto Mr. Taylor's porch. Mr. Taylor looked out his sitting room window at her.

"Sidney," he announced in a low tone. "What brings you here this time of night?"

Sidney approached the screen window and the old man who peered out it. "I was wondering if you'd seen the gentleman I'd been traveling with."

He snorted a laugh and appeared humored. "The one they arrested this afternoon?"

"Yes, that'd be the one," Sidney replied and fidgeted nervously. "He was supposed to be set free on bail. Did you see which way he went?"

"He and another fella left the municipal building and walked down the street in the direction of the diner. Couldn't say if that's where they went or not," Mr. Taylor announced. "Can you believe what happened to Mrs. Cooper?"

"I'll stop by another time, and we can talk about it," she announced while offering him a warm smile. "It's important that I find my friend."

Sidney hurried off the porch and headed for the diner. Neither Harlan nor Lyle were there either. Harlan must've gone with Lyle to search the house. Sidney continued down the street and turned toward the row of homes just before the woods. She stopped in her tracks when she saw Ms. Palmer's car in the driveway. Sidney's heart pounded with fear. She uncertainly walked toward the house and listened for any sound that might indicate what became of Lyle and Harlan. Mrs. Cooper's house had no lights on. The house to the left, closest to the woods, also had no lights on. Sidney crept around Mrs. Cooper's house and approached Ms. Palmer's house from the side. The downstairs lights were on. Sidney strained to look inside the living room window.

Sidney straightened with alarm when she heard the upstairs window open. She hurried to Mrs. Cooper's house and looked up at the second story window of Ms. Palmer's house. She stared with horror to see a man about to climb through the window. The bedroom light came on, startling her and the man. Sidney ducked behind Mrs. Cooper's bushes and looked back, concerned for Lyle's welfare. She saw the outline of the man, almost certainly Lyle, with his back turned to the window. He'd been caught! She could hear Ms. Palmer's voice as she yelled something. He darted away from the window to escape through the bedroom. Sidney could still hear Persha Palmer's voice as she screamed something else. They'd been caught! Was Harlan with Lyle? Were they both in trouble? Any minute now, Ms. Palmer would be calling the police to arrest them for breaking and entering. Sidney attempted to think of a way to help Lyle and Harlan without being arrested herself. She could hear thundering footsteps within the house, possibly running down the stairs.

She then saw the man who had to be Lyle running into the dimly lit living room. Sidney had a direct view into the room. Ms. Palmer ran into the room with a butcher knife and stabbed him in the back as he attempted to escape.

Sidney's eyes widened, and her mouth fell open. "Lyle," she gasped and straightened from the bushes.

Ms. Palmer looked toward the window. Sidney's heart pounded harshly as panic swept through her entire body. Had she been seen? Persha Palmer looked around the room. Had he survived? Did she give him enough time to escape? Or was Lyle dying on her living room floor? Sidney ran out from behind the bushes and headed to the front of Mrs. Cooper's house. She had to find a phone and call the police, though she was almost positive Lyle was already dead. A chill ran down her spine. She'd sent him there! It was her fault! Harlan was possibly still in the house, maybe hiding. She had to get the police there right away. As she ran past the garage, someone stepped out of the dark tree line in front of her. Sidney attempted to stop but collided with him. She screamed and struggled blindly against the arms that held her.

"Sidney," Harlan cried out with alarm. "Calm down. What's wrong?"

Sidney held her breath as she stared at Harlan. Her heart continued to pound, and her breathing was harsh. "Harlan," she gasped with surprise then threw her arms around his neck and sobbed softly. "Thank God you're alive!"

"Why wouldn't I be?" he asked and pulled her away from him to look into her eyes. "What's the matter?"

Sidney fought the tears in her eyes. "It's Lyle," she cried out in panic. "Ms. Palmer killed Lyle in her house. I saw her do it! We have to call the police!"

Harlan removed his cellular phone and called the police. Sidney listened to his chilling words. He yelled into the phone to the deputy, insisting he go to Persha Palmer's house and investigate a possible murder. He then explained they would be at Sidney's house.

"I'm going to take you to your parents," he said firmly and grabbed her hand. "I have to go back and see what happened to Lyle."

"No," she protested as her eyes widened with fear. "You're not going anywhere without me."

"Don't argue with me," Harlan snapped hotly. "My best friend's possibly been murdered, and you're the only witness. She might come after you."

Sidney pulled her hand from his and jumped back a step with a fire in her eyes. "And I won't allow her to kill you either. I'm going with you!"

Harlan's look was harsh and unpredictable. "Stay right behind me," he snarled coldly.

As Harlan and Sidney hurried around the front of Mrs. Cooper's house, they saw the police car heading for Ms. Palmer's house. The blue and red lights flashed, but the siren remained silent. Harlan grabbed Sidney's hand and pulled her behind him toward the homes and the squad car. Deputy Hawkins got out of the car with another officer. Harlan and Sidney approached the officers, who motioned for them to stay back. They remained near the squad car and watched the men approach the front door to the house. They pounded on the door with some uncertainty and urgency.

There was no response. Both deputies looked at each other. They pounded again and gave a couple of seconds for a response. Sidney bit her lower lip and looked at Harlan, who stared at the door with wide, concerned eyes. Deputy Hawkins walked around the front of the house and peered in through the living room window. He turned his head toward the other officer and motioned with a sense of urgency. By the expression on his face, Sidney knew he saw Lyle's body. The second officer proceeded to break the door open.

Harlan placed his arm around Sidney and pulled her close to him. The shattered look in his eyes as he stared helplessly was almost more than she could stand. Sidney began to sob uncontrollably. Harlan pulled her into his arms and held onto her so tight; he nearly crushed her. Both officers ran into the house. A couple of minutes later, they hurried back out. Deputy Hawkins reached into the car and removed his cellular phone.

"Sorry to disturb you at home, Sheriff, but I think you need to come out to Persha Palmer's house," Hawkins announced. "We found an unidentified man stabbed to death in her living room.

We're going to search the house for the suspect we believe to be Persha herself."

A few people from town appeared to be casually drifting down the secluded, dead-end road. Deputy Hawkins returned to the house and disappeared inside with the second officer. Only five minutes passed before Sheriff Drukard drove along the road past the growing group of spectators. His lights flashed, and he allowed the siren to wail to move them aside. He pulled into the driveway and immediately motioned the crowd to move back. Deputy Hawkins ran from the house and approached the sheriff.

"Sheriff," he said softly, though Sidney and Harlan were close enough to hear. "We found Persha's girlfriend murdered in the upstairs bedroom. She's been stabbed to death as well."

Sheriff Drukard rolled his eyes and groaned lowly. He apparently noticed Harlan and Sidney and became enraged. "What are you two doing here?" he suddenly demanded. "You two always seem to be close by when someone in this town is discovered dead. Get out of here before I haul both of you in for conspiracy."

Deputy Hawkins gently cleared his throat. "Sheriff, Sidney witnessed the murder."

Sheriff Drukard glared at Sidney and placed his hands on his broad hips. "Oh, you did, did you? Always at the wrong place at the wrong time. I can't wait to hear your story, missy."

Sidney pulled away from Harlan and turned angry. "I'm not telling you anything," she lashed out. "I'll wait for the real police to arrive. If you'd been doing your job from the beginning, none of this would have happened in the first place!"

Harlan pulled Sidney's face against his chest to silence her; worried she'd get herself into more trouble.

"I'm not at all convinced the two of you weren't somehow involved in the deaths of these two people," Sheriff Drukard snapped with anger then eyed Deputy Hawkins. "Search the house for Persha. If I'm correct, you'll find her dead also. When you do, I want these two taken in for questioning."

Deputy Hawkins looked from Sidney and Harlan to Drukard. "But, sir, I don't think you understand--"

"Just do it," Drukard shouted.

Hawkins uncertainly turned and walked back to the house.

Sheriff Drukard turned to them and pointed a warning finger. "I suggest the two of you remain where you are until we search the entire house," he snarled as his beady eyes cut through them. "I want you real close when we find evidence."

Harlan rolled his eyes, turned Sidney away from Drukard, and leaned against the squad car. Sheriff Drukard went back to the street and ushered the crowd away.

"Break it up," he announced while attempting a calm tone. "There's nothing to see here!"

"So what's going on?" came a familiar male voice from alongside them.

Both Harlan and Sidney spun toward the hood of the squad car and saw Lyle only a foot away. Sidney felt the color rush from her face. Harlan released Sidney, grabbed Lyle, and hugged him happily

Lyle struggled to free himself. "What's wrong with you?" he demanded to know.

Harlan laughed happily. Sidney darted past Harlan and jumped into Lyle's arms. She kissed him several times on the cheek, overjoyed he was alive.

"We thought you were dead," Harlan said while chuckling softly then shook his head. "I've never been so happy to see your ugly mug before in my life."

Lyle tightened his arms around Sidney and hugged her affectionately. "I ought to die more often," he teased and kissed Sidney quickly on the lips.

Harlan frowned and pulled Sidney away from him. "Okay, that's enough you two," he remarked sternly.

Lyle continued to smile, enjoying the attention. "You have my permission to keep her," he teased then looked at Harlan with a more serious look. "So what made you think I was dead?"

"I saw Ms. Palmer stab a man," Sidney announced. "I assumed it was you. I thought she found you in her home."

"Not me," Lyle replied simply. "I made a hasty exit when her lover unexpectedly came home with a male friend. I've been camping out at Mrs. Cooper's house, raiding her fridge. She had some good leftovers."

Sidney eyed both men. "That must be who she murdered. She caught her girlfriend in bed with someone else."

"Crime of passion," Harlan said simply and inhaled deeply. "I'm detecting a pattern here."

"She had plenty of motive and opportunity," Sidney said firmly. "It's been established Billy went the back way through the woods that day. She claimed to have seen him even though she supposedly left school early. I think she saw him because she was in the woods as well."

Lyle gave both an odd look. "So who murdered the teacher?" he asked and appeared curious. "What's the doc's connection with all this?"

Sidney and Harlan looked at each other with some confusion. Once the police established that Persha Palmer wasn't dead inside her home, Sheriff Drukard had to concede it was possible she was the killer. Harlan and Sidney were taken to the municipal building, where she again refused to talk to Sheriff Drukard. She waited for a detective from Brighton to arrive. The capable detective took Sidney's statement. She told the detective everything she'd suspected, starting with the death of Emily Fisher eight years ago. It was possibly the first time someone took the new theory seriously. Once the detective had finished with her, Deputy Hawkins drove them back to Sidney's house where Lyle waited for them.

Chapter Fifty-one

Sidney's father loaded several rifles and handguns while Harlan and Lyle checked the windows and doors to make certain they were locked. Deputy Hawkins knocked on the door before entering and lowered his flashlight.

"Everything's secure out there," Hawkins announced reassuringly then sighed. "We'll send patrol cars through the neighborhood throughout the night."

Sidney's mother thanked Hawkins and locked the door behind him. Lyle had been pacing while talking on his cellular phone then disconnected his call and frowned.

"Trisha's been released from the hospital," he announced and looked at Harlan. "She and her mother left half an hour ago. I think it's best if I went to her house and waited for them there."

Harlan nodded.

"I'll drive you there," Herb announced sternly and slung a rifle over his shoulder.

"That's quite all right," Lyle said and managed a tiny laugh. "I think I can make it half a block by myself. Besides, the killer's never seen me before. I'm not exactly a target."

Herb extended his rifle to him.

Lyle looked at the weapon and shook his head. "No, thanks. I'd probably just shoot myself."

"Believe me," Harlan said to Herb and raised his brows. "Lyle can take care of himself."

Pauline watched Lyle leave and nervously shut the door behind him. "I don't like this," her mother announced. "Why haven't they picked her up yet? Where could she possibly hide? A brutal murder like that? She must have some blood on her clothing."

"Billy's house?" Sidney suddenly announced, becoming animated. "There's no one home. Sam's place is vacant also." She then shivered. "This town is becoming a ghost town."

"More like a morgue," Herb muttered and handed Harlan a .357 Magnum revolver.

Harlan looked at the massive gun he held, raised his brow, and then looked at Sidney, who smirked. "Just think of it as a dangerous camera," she informed him.

Her father extended a gun to her mother. Pauline stared at the gun then glared at her husband. "You must be joking," she remarked lowly.

"Come on, Dad," Sidney remarked simply. "You're being a little paranoid here. The thought of Mom with a gun is more frightening than Ms. Palmer."

"I'm just trying to protect my family," her father announced. "Is there something wrong with that?"

"No, but don't give guns to people who don't know how to use them," Pauline said firmly. "I'm liable to shoot one of you by accident."

Harlan handed his gun to Sidney. "I've never used a handgun in my life," he informed her. "It's not really a *thing* in England. I'd probably miss."

Herb looked at Sidney and tilted his head in question. "Well, baby?"

"I'll back you, Dad," Sidney announced then smirked. "After all, I am a better shot than you."

Herb placed his arm around Sidney and gave her a firm hug. "That's my girl!" He drew a deep breath and glanced around with a serious look. "Now what do you say we set some traps around the doors and windows?"

"That's a little much, Dad," Sidney remarked while giving him a humored look. "Ms. Palmer knows you have a hundred guns in the house. Honestly, she probably wouldn't consider coming here. She may not even know I witnessed anything. She's probably on her way to Mexico by now."

"Still," Herb announced. "I think I'm going to keep watch tonight."

"Suit yourself," Sidney replied. "I'm going to bed. It's been one hell of a long day." She looked at Harlan and smiled gently. "Would you mind keeping me company?"

Harlan gently cleared his throat and shifted a look at Herb. "Your dad's holding a gun," he muttered softly. "Let's not provoke him."

"Oh, go on," Herb snapped lowly, apparently hearing them. "I'd feel better knowing she wasn't alone tonight."

Harlan gave him a surprised look then nodded. "Well, you do have a point."

§

Sidney closed her bedroom door behind Harlan and set her gun on the bedside table. Harlan sat on the bed and stared at the revolver. He held his breath and looked at her.

"Do you think any less of me, because I don't feel comfortable handling a gun?" he asked gently.

Sidney smiled warmly and sat beside him on the bed. "No, of course not. If you can't pull the trigger, then you're better off not being armed," she informed him. "It's dishonorable to be shot with your own gun."

"Bloody deadly too," he teased then turned serious. "I'm not kidding you, though. I don't know how to use a gun, and I could never shoot a woman."

Sidney placed her hand on his leg. "It's okay. It takes a long time to become comfortable with guns," she insisted. "I've never shot at any living thing, and I don't want to start either."

"That's comforting to know," he said with a soft laugh. "Why don't you get some sleep? I'm going to stay up a little while. I'm not really tired."

"Will you lie with me until I fall asleep?" she asked softly and bit her lower lip. "I feel like I've been to hell and back. I'm tired, but I'm afraid to close my eyes."

Harlan gently kissed her forehead. "I'll hold you all night long if it'll make you feel better."

She smiled warmly. "Yes, I'd like that." She sighed and shook her head in disbelief. "All this time we'd suspected Billy killed Emily, but now it doesn't look that way at all."

Sidney made herself comfortable on the bed and watched as Harlan joined her. He placed his arms around her, and she clung to him, resting her head on his chest.

"We never really had any solid evidence against him," he replied then shut his eyes and shook his head. "Honestly, I don't know what to think anymore."

§

Sidney woke to the faint sound of the doorbell ringing.

When she looked around, she was alone in her bedroom. She sprang out of bed, having remained fully dressed, and hurried downstairs to see what was happening. She discovered Deputy Hawkins at the front door waiting for her father, who was slipping into his light jacket. Harlan stood within the hall, obviously having witnessed what had happened. She approached Harlan, stopped alongside him, and clutched his arm.

"What's happening?" she asked the deputy with concern. "Did you catch her?"

Hawkins shook his head.

"It's okay," Herb informed Sidney. "The alarm at the press went off. Deputy Hawkins thinks Persha may have broken in and done some damage." He zipped his jacket to conceal his handgun. "We're going to check it out. We won't be gone long."

"I don't think I like that," Sidney replied gently. "What if you're running into a trap? She may even double back here. There's no telling what's going through her psychotic head."

"Harlan's here, and there's another car patrolling the area," her father said simply and offered a tiny smile. "Everything will be fine, baby."

Despite her father's reassuring words, Sidney wasn't so sure. She clung to Harlan's arm and glanced at his profile. Judging by his expression, he wasn't convinced either.

Fears of Persha Palmer and her reign of terror diminished with the night. Sidney woke to a beautiful, sunny morning. Harlan was exhausted from remaining up all night, but he reported that her father had returned shortly after she'd fallen asleep on the sofa. Harlan went to Sidney's bedroom to get a couple of hours sleep, while Sidney and her mother fixed themselves some breakfast which neither men would be up early enough to enjoy. Sidney called the police to check on their progress with Ms. Palmer, but they reported she hadn't been seen anywhere in the entire town. Trisha reported in just when they were about to eat breakfast. She was feeling better, though she was still weak and wouldn't be running around today. Mary went to work that morning, but Lyle would be staying with Trisha. Once she hung up the phone, Sidney and her mother ate their semi-cold eggs. After breakfast, Sidney's mother placed the breakfast dishes in the dishwasher and wiped her hands on the dishtowel.

"I suppose I should wake your father," her mother announced. "I don't know if he'll bother opening the press this morning. He never told me what sort of damage was done last night." She eyed Sidney as if concerned to leave her alone for five minutes. "I'll be right back."

Sidney nodded and finished her tea before placing the mug in the dishwasher. She looked out the kitchen window to the day ahead of her. She'd be lucky if she'd be allowed to stray from the house. Sidney decided she'd spend the afternoon in bed with Harlan, not that either of them would consider picking up where they had left off at Trisha's house--not with her father home. The phone rang, nearly startling her. She grabbed the phone with anticipation of Hawkins telling her they had caught Ms. Palmer.

"Hello," Sidney said with a gleam of hope.

"Sidney, it's Mary. Is Trisha there?" came the faint, nervous voice.

Sidney could tell the woman was upset about something. She could just about hear the fear in her voice. "Trisha? No, she's not," she replied with some confusion. "I thought she was with Lyle at your house?"

"No, Trisha didn't answer the home phone. I think I saw her heading into the library," Mary announced with a trembling voice. "I can't leave the diner right now. Could you go to the library and pick her up?"

"Sure, Mrs. Allister," Sidney said with a low sigh. "I swear she's going to be the end of me yet."

"I'd, uh, better go," Mary said in a slightly crackling voice. "There's a morning hen convention here."

Mary disconnected the call without her usual pleasantries, indicating she must have been overwhelmed at the diner that morning. The diner was as good a place as any for the citizens of Marilina to get together and discuss gossip of extreme importance. Last night was front-page news and anyone who was anyone needed to get the details. Sidney leaned against the wall near the telephone and sank into thought.

"Why would Trisha go to the library?" she muttered and considered the comment. Her brows suddenly narrowed, and her mouth fell open. "You stupid girl!" Sidney bolted from the kitchen.

Chapter Fifty-two

"I think you're being just a little paranoid," Harlan said from the passenger side of the car.

Sidney drove her rental car at high speed around the sharp curve on Cressman Road and nearly hit the guardrail. Harlan held his breath and clutched the passenger door.

"Damn it! Slow down," he shouted. "You're going to get us killed!"

"I know what I'm talking about, Harlan," she said while breathing heavily and nervously raked her fingers through her hair. They entered another sharp curve.

Harlan squirmed in his seat. "Two hands! Drive with two hands!"

She placed her hand on the steering wheel and skidded around the curve. Her car approached the stop sign at the end of Cressman Road without stopping and made a left onto the main road into Marilina.

"We should have gone by foot," Sidney muttered under her breath. "It would have been much faster. This damned road is out of the way."

"I'm not taking any chances," Harlan retorted and glared at her briefly then looked back out the windshield with concern. "There's no telling what or who is lurking in the woods just waiting for us to pass by."

"Just trust me, okay?" Sidney said in a nervous tone.

"I trust you, but I'm never letting you drive again," he said and stomped his foot on the floor in an apparent attempt to brake for her. "Bloody hell! Slow down!"

Sidney slowed the car as they entered town and pulled up to the front of the library, which had been closed since Mrs. Cooper was nearly killed. Both got out of the car and looked toward the silent library. Harlan looked down the street at the diner. Sidney noticed Lyle's rental car parked in front of the diner then looked back at Harlan. He inhaled deeply and nodded toward the library.

"Keep close," he said firmly.

Sidney walked beside Harlan to the front doors. He opened the door, which wasn't locked, and entered cautiously. Sidney stepped into the doorway and looked around the wide, empty hallway. She removed her father's revolver from the back of her pants and approached the non-fiction section to the left, which used to be the sitting room when the library was a house. Harlan followed her into the room where the book checkout counter was. Both looked around the rows of bookshelves then returned to the hallway. They crossed into the fiction section on the right. There wasn't a sound from anywhere within the library. The old floorboards creaked beneath their feet, alerting anyone who might be lurking about to their presence and location. The fiction section was empty as well. Harlan looked at the ceiling.

"What about the children's section?" he asked softly and pointed to the floor above them.

Sidney shook her head. "No, we should go to the archives. That's where we're expected to go."

Harlan held his breath then shook his head. "We should've called the police."

"For what?" she asked and glanced at him then looked back at the surrounding area. "Because I'm paranoid? Do you think they'd come out here just to check on Trisha?"

"Hawkins may have," Harlan replied dryly. "He seems fairly intelligent and concerned for the welfare of this town."

She walked into the hallway and looked around. "We already know Trisha is safe at her house," Sidney said softly. "It's Mary I'm worried about. She supposedly called me from the diner in a panic about Trisha's safety, yet she wasn't there when I called back to tell her Trisha was fine. I mean, what if it wasn't really Mary who called in the first place? She was whispering. It could have been anyone on the phone. What reason would Mary have to whisper? Breakfast hour at the diner? She'd practically have to scream." Sidney shook her head. "That's why I called Trisha before we came out here."

"It would make sense that Mary would come here, had she thought Trisha was heading here," Harlan announced then sighed. "We'd better check downstairs."

They approached the back of the library and cautiously headed down the old steps to the archives. Sidney didn't like being behind Harlan, especially when she was the one who held the gun. Each step creaked beneath their feet. Harlan looked back at Sidney and frowned. He stopped her on the steps and took the gun from her hand. He drew a deep breath and looked back at the lower level just a couple of steps below them. Sidney smelled the air and looked around the stairway with concern. Harlan jumped the last couple of steps and hit the opposing wall with his right shoulder. He aimed the gun to the side of the stairs then smelled the air as well. He looked at Sidney with horror in his eyes.

"Gasoline!" he cried out.

Harlan darted away from the stairs. Sidney ran down the last couple of steps and smelled the strong scent of gasoline. She then saw Harlan running through the rows of old magazines and books. Sidney darted after him. Mary was tied to Trisha's desk chair and appeared to be out cold. She had a laceration, which bled freely above her left eyebrow. As Sidney passed the row of old newspapers, she saw the stacks of newspapers burst into flames. Sidney screamed and spun around with alarm. Persha Palmer darted from an aisle of magazines and ran for the stairs. Harlan frantically worked on the ropes that bound Mary to the chair then tossed her the gun. Sidney barely caught it, stunned he had thrown it. She was grateful it was a revolver and not a semiautomatic.

"Don't let her lock us down here," Harlan cried out.

Sidney looked back at the flames then ran past the burning aisle and toward the stairs. She ran up the stairs as the door was shutting before her. She didn't slow despite the closing door. She couldn't allow the door to close. They'd be locked in the burning basement. Sidney plowed into the door with her shoulder. The door flew open, and Ms. Palmer slammed into the opposing wall. Sidney aimed the gun at Persha and hesitated to pull the trigger. Ms. Palmer took advantage of her moment's pause, lurched forward, and grabbed Sidney's already bruised wrist. Both women fell against the wall just near the basement stairs. Sidney's head hit the wall, dazing her. The gun flew from her hand and tumbled down the basement steps. She felt the pain surge through the back of her head and darkness swept past her. She fought the spinning room. The room once more brightened as she narrowly avoided unconsciousness.

Ms. Palmer pulled a gun from her jacket and aimed it at Sidney's head. The back door cracked and splintered just a couple of feet away from them. It flew open and struck the doorstop with a crash as Lyle stood directly behind it. Ms. Palmer spun with surprise and fired at him. He attempted to leap out of the way but caught the slug in his shoulder. He clutched his shoulder as he struck the door, blood seeping through his fingers. He cast himself back outside to avoid the second, deadly shot. He'd given Sidney just enough time to get out of Ms. Palmer's path. Sidney darted into the room to her left and slammed the door behind her while gasping to catch her breath. She could smell the smoke coming from the archives. She hoped Harlan got Mary out of the basement. The door vibrated against Sidney's body, followed by Ms. Palmer's psychotic scream. Sidney fumbled with the lock then bolted away from the door and looked around the dimly lit room.

She was in an old summer kitchen that was now used as an employee break room. There was a door just to the left of the room. Sidney ran for the door and flung it open. Ms. Palmer stood in the doorway and aimed the gun at Sidney's head, forcing her to back into the room. Smoke detectors now wailed their shrill alarm, indicating the building was on fire. Sidney backed until she hit the wall behind her.

Ms. Palmer's eyes were narrow and filled with hatred. "Why couldn't you just let it go?" Persha demanded to know in a low tone. "I didn't want to kill Mrs. Cooper, and I certainly don't want to kill you, but you couldn't let it go."

Sidney's breathing was harsh as she stared at the barrel of the handgun pointed only inches from her face.

"You were jealous of her," Sidney gasped softly. "That's why you murdered Emily Fisher. When Trisha refused to accept Alex was the killer and started poking around the murder, that's when you tried to frame Billy."

"Frame Billy?" she scoffed lowly with disgust in her eyes. "That oversexed boy had his own evil thoughts. Yes, I knew he wrote her that love letter and not Alec. I didn't tell her because she needed to learn her lesson about men the hard way. When I arrived in the woods, Billy had beaten her and taken his letter from her while she cower like a dog on her hands and knees. Even after her ordeal, she still refused my love," Ms. Palmer remarked with rage. "She was really better off dead. As for Billy, he needed to learn his lesson as well. That's why I put an eleven on that rock. His jersey number.

Except no one made the connection." Ms. Palmer shook her head with disgust. "I thought that would be evidence enough against the little parasite. I was rather disappointed when they arrested Alec for her death because I wanted to see Billy punished for the way he treated women."

Sidney could hear the hallway floorboards creak. "Number fourteen," she announced boldly and tore her eyes away from the gun aimed at her to meet Ms. Palmer's gaze.

Ms. Palmer glared at her. "What?"

"His jersey number was fourteen," Sidney informed her. "Not eleven."

The sprinklers came to life and showered them with water. Both jumped with surprise to the cold, foul-smelling water. Unfortunately, it didn't ruin Ms. Palmer's concentration.

"Sorry, Sidney, it's nothing personal," Ms. Palmer said above the hiss of the sprinklers.

"Drop it," Harlan shouted gruffly from the doorway while holding the Magnum revolver in his hand.

Ms. Palmer didn't move nor lower her gun aimed at Sidney's face. Sidney could see Harlan holding her father's .357 Magnum from where he stood just inside the room. Harlan inched his way across the room, keeping the large revolver steady with both hands while aimed directly at Persha Palmer. She looked at him out of the corner of her eye. He stopped halfway across the room to Sidney's left side only about twenty feet away.

"I don't think so, Harlan," Ms. Palmer scoffed as the sprinklers soaked all three. "You miss and Sidney's dead."

"She's dead no matter what I do," Harlan snarled. "You shoot her, and you're dead too. The only solution would be for you to drop the gun. You can't escape."

Ms. Palmer snorted softly and appeared humored. "I'd rather be dead then spend the rest of my life in prison."

"Persha!" came a shrill, female cry.

Ms. Palmer glanced at the doorway to her left while keeping the gun on Sidney. Trisha stood in the doorway and clung to the frame to support herself. With the sprinkler water soaking her, Trisha was barely recognizable. Her usually wavy raven hair now hung straight and wet reaching beyond her shoulders.

Ms. Palmer's eyes widened in panic. "Emily?" she gasped with a look of terror. "It can't be! You're dead!"

She became enraged, aimed the gun at Trisha, and fired without hesitation. Harlan simultaneously squeezed the trigger on the revolver. Gunshots echoed from both corners through the small room only muffled by the hissing sound of the sprinklers. Sidney screamed and crouched to the floor while covering her head, almost afraid to look. Ms. Palmer's head snapped to the side from the impact of the .357 Magnum shell striking her temple, nearly exploding the side of her head. She was thrown to the floor with blood quickly pooling beneath her head, immediately washing away with the water from the sprinklers. Sidney gasped then bolted upright and looked at the doorway. Trisha hugged the doorframe with her forehead resting against it, and her eyes pinched closed. Trisha uncertainly opened her eyes and lifted her head. She looked at her body and felt for a gunshot wound, apparently surprised to be alive. Trisha hesitated then touched the splintered wood just inches from where her head had been.

"Oh, shit," Trisha gasped.

Harlan allowed the large revolver to fall from his hands. It struck the floor with a loud clatter. Sidney straightened and stared at Persha Palmer as the sprinkler continued to wash her blood across the floor. Lyle stepped through the doorway and looked across the room with surprise while clinging to his bleeding shoulder. He looked at Harlan, who remained motionless with the gun at his feet, and then back at the dead woman. Sidney slipped past Ms. Palmer's body and ran to Harlan. She threw her arms around his neck and clung to him. His arms tightened around her waist as he held her in his trembling arms. He drew a shaken breath.

"Are you all right?" he whispered into her neck, refusing to pull away.

"Thanks to your excellent aim and timing," she practically gasped with relief then kissed him on the cheek.

He nervously pulled away from Sidney and gently rubbed his temple with a trembling hand. His eyes met hers with a look of fear. "I, uh, was aiming for her arm."

Sidney's eyes widened with a horrified expression.

Chapter Fifty-three

Sidney looked at the morning sky as she walked alongside Trisha toward the woods. Trisha had more strength this morning, and she appeared particularly happy while carrying her can of spray paint. They hadn't spoken much since they met outside Trisha's house.

"How's your mother doing? I bet she's tired of hospitals, huh?" Sidney asked while grinning knowingly.

Trisha laughed at the comment. "Yeah, but she's being released today. It was just for an overnight observation," she remarked then eyed Sidney slyly. "But she did have some company."

"Really?" Sidney asked with a curious look. "Who?"

"Mrs. Cooper."

Sidney's eyes widened. "Oh, no."

"When Mrs. Cooper heard my mother was being admitted, she insisted they put her in her room." Trisha laughed. "My mother was begging me not to leave her there. I'm glad Mrs. Cooper is feeling better. She's back to her old self. She wanted to know all the gossip and had to tell her story nearly a hundred times of how Ms. Palmer tried to kill her in the library. We're never going to hear the end of that one."

They entered the woods and admired every tree they passed. The day felt like a blessing, and both were happy to be alive. When

Sidney had enough of nature, she felt the need to pry into her friend's personal life.

"So what did you and Lyle do all alone in your mother's house last night?" Sidney asked while grinning deviously.

Trisha blushed and looked away, unable to control her radiant smile. "Use your imagination," she announced then eyed her friend. "I had eight years of pent-up lust."

Sidney laughed and shook her head. "I would have thought he'd be in too much pain after having stitches on his shoulder."

"Remarkable how men forget about pain so quickly," Trisha informed her while giggling. She inhaled deeply and sighed while looking around. "I feel as if a huge weight has been lifted off my shoulders." Trisha then looked at Sidney and turned serious. "Lyle left the house early this morning. Where do you suppose he went so early?"

"I'm sure he's with Harlan," Sidney announced then frowned. "Harlan was a wreck last night after the shooting. He wouldn't even stay at my parents' house. He went back to his motel room around ten o'clock." She shoved her hands in her pocket and sank into thought. "I hope he's not too traumatized after shooting Ms. Palmer."

"That's ridiculous. He had no choice. It was either her or you." She then reconsidered. "Actually it was her or me," Trisha announced then suddenly eyed Sidney. "She tried to kill me, didn't she?"

Sidney nodded and shivered at the thought. "I really thought you were a goner," she remarked.

"Did she call me Emily?" Trisha then asked. "I think I was a little out of it, but I swore she called me Emily. Do you think she was insane?"

"I'll tell you, for a moment there, I almost thought you were Emily standing in that doorway too. It was a little frightening." She then looked at the can of white spray paint Trisha had in her hand. "What's with the paint?"

"You'll see," Trisha said simply and offered a tiny smile. She then tilted her head as her concern returned. "You don't suppose those two went home, do you? I mean, the murder has been solved. What's to keep them hanging around here?"

"Well, us, I hope," Sidney replied. "Harlan asked me to go to California with him."

Trisha stopped Sidney just before the bridge and cocked her head to one side. "You're leaving me?"

"I want to be with Harlan," Sidney said gently then managed a timid smiled. "You can come to California with us. Lyle will be there."

Trisha walked onto the bridge and looked around the surrounding woods. "This is my home," she replied with a sigh. "There was a time when I wanted to leave so badly, but I wouldn't be happy anywhere else. I have family and friends. I know everyone here." She cast a look at Sidney. "You don't have unity in a city, not like in a small town."

Sidney lowered her head now feeling guilty. "I love Harlan," she said gently. "He'd never live in this town." She met Trisha's gaze. "He hates it here. His job's in California, and that's where he wants to be."

Trisha sighed and attempted to remain cheerful. "I'll visit," she assured her.

They hugged happily. Sidney was relieved. She didn't want to lose her friend all over again. Trisha pulled away and raised her spray can.

"I have work to do."

Sidney watched Trisha carry her spray can down the bank of the stream. She leaned on the bridge and watched her friend spray over the red lines on the rock with the white paint. When she was finished, the entire rock was white. Trisha straightened with a satisfied smile.

"Eight years ago, I painted those lines on that rock so I wouldn't forget," Trisha said and looked at Sidney on the bridge. "Emily Fisher has finally been laid to rest in my mind. They'll review the case, Alex will be set free, and I'll be able to sleep at night with a clear conscience."

"Time to finally start living, right?"

"You can say that again," Trisha replied and laughed.

They could hear voices approaching the bridge from the direction of town. When they turned, they saw Harlan and Lyle approaching, talking to each other and laughing. Trisha hurried onto the bridge as the men approached them. Harlan hugged Sidney and kissed her quickly on the lips.

She eyed him with some surprise. "I assume you're feeling better," Sidney said cheerfully.

Harlan nodded while holding her. "Much, thank you. We have the most fascinating news from the local gossip," he announced. "It would seem the autopsy on Mrs. Randall showed she'd been given a massive dose of Thorazine which matched a bottle found in Billy's medical bag. The coroner said she would never have been able to walk to the stairs on her own." Harlan grinned with satisfaction. "Billy Randall confessed to killing his grandmother after the autopsy reports came back."

Lyle placed his arm around Trisha and looked at Harlan and Sidney. "He even gave up some of the story on Emily Fisher after he'd found out Persha Palmer had killed her," he informed them. "Billy approached Emily in the woods after he saw her having sex with Alex. They had a fight about his feelings for her." He frowned and shook his head. "It happened just as Persha said. He beat her and left her by the bridge. He didn't know Persha witnessed the entire incident. When he got home, he realized he was in trouble for beating his teacher. His grandmother called Sam, and they worked on a plan to keep Billy from going to jail. A couple of hours later, Alex was arrested at the tavern for the murder of Emily Fisher. They knew they couldn't allow anyone to figure out Billy had beaten her, or he risked being accused of murdering her as well."

Harlan eagerly jumped in when Lyle paused. "When Trisha started poking around in the murder case, Sam took it upon himself to protect Billy," Harlan informed them. "He bribed Denny with drugs to help him kidnap Trisha and take her to the stone house. Billy claimed neither he nor his grandmother knew what Sam had done until it was too late. Mrs. Randall was so upset by what happened with Trisha; she was about to confess what really happened eight years ago. Billy wasn't going to stand for a scandal, not with his status as a doctor on the line. He took advantage of his access to certain medication from the hospital, doped her, and threw her down the stairs."

Sidney still couldn't believe it and shook her head. "Amazing how some people think," she practically gasped. "Not only has he lost his profession, but he's going to jail for premeditated murder. Had he allowed the truth to come out, his career would have suffered for a while, but he'd still have his freedom."

"What's more," Harlan remarked. "When they searched Persha's house, they found a shoe box with photos of Emily cut apart and taped back together again. Some had threats and curses written on them. We're talking creepy stalker stuff here."

"So it was a crime of passion," Trisha said then shook her head. "Just not as I had envisioned it though."

"It's over now," Harlan announced and sighed. There was a brief pause then his look turned serious. "That was the good news. Now for the bad news."

Lyle laughed and looked at Trisha while grinning. "I've decided to move to Marilina," he announced cheerfully.

Trisha's mouth fell open as she stared at him with disbelief. "You what?"

Lyle then looked at Harlan, who frowned while hiding a tiny smile. "Harlan and I decided to buy Sam's Tavern and go into business together."

Sidney looked at Harlan with astonishment. "You? You're planning to live here? I thought you hated this town?"

Harlan made a face and shrugged. "Lyle gave me little choice. I owed him for all the favors he did for me and for getting him stabbed," he then hesitated and considered, "--and shot. I suppose between you and Lyle, Marilina can be tolerable."

Sidney hugged and kissed Harlan with enthusiasm. "You are wonderful, Harlan."

Harlan returned the hug and hid his grin. "Yeah, I know." His smile then faded. "But we're living outside of town," he insisted. "Lyle's going to live at the tavern for now, and we'll need to find a place for my mother. She hated California anyway."

"Your mother?" Sidney asked with surprise. "I had no idea your mother lived in the states."

"You didn't think I'd just leave her all alone in England, did you?" he practically demanded. "We'll move her somewhere near Mrs. Cooper. They'll have a lot to talk about. If there's one thing my mother knows a lot about, it's gossip. She'll make Mrs. Cooper look like a saint."

Trisha stared at Lyle and could barely contain her grin. "So why did you decide to buy Sam's Tavern? You'd have more success with a bar in California."

"It's a charming town--when people aren't killing one another," he said with a soft laugh. "I grew up in a town similar to this one. I also thought I might pursue a relationship with a certain young librarian, and living here would make that a whole lot easier."

Trisha smiled brightly and threw her arms around Lyle. "We can discuss relationships later. I'd really like to just have a wild affair for now."

Lyle stared at Trisha with a surprised look in his eyes. "Well, I suppose that can be arranged." He grabbed Trisha around the waist from behind and spun her in the direction of the development. He eyed Harlan and Sidney. "We'll catch up with you later next week," he announced simply.

Trisha screamed playfully as Lyle whisked her away despite his injured shoulder. Sidney raised her brows, smiled, and shook her head.

Harlan leaned against the bridge and stared at her. "You don't mind staying here, do you?"

Sidney looked at him with some surprise. "Are you kidding? I'd love to stay here. I've been away too long as it is. Besides," she said with a warm smile and walked closer to him. "I'd follow you anywhere."

"Do you mean that?" he asked gently and brushed his hand along her face while searching her eyes.

Sidney nodded.

Harlan smiled deviously. "In that case," he said and drew a deep breath. "I think I'll be returning to my motel room and stay there for a couple of days."

He eyed her slyly and waited for a response.

Sidney placed her hand in his and laughed softly. "As if this town didn't have enough to gossip about already--"

The End

Other books by Holly Copella!

amazon.com/author/hollycopella

Reviews left on Amazon are appreciated!

"The Battle for Andrea Maria"

A cruise ship attack turns six survivors into overnight celebrities after they take credit for the heroic act of a stowaway who died saving them.

The cruise is just what Jess needed--a bit of harmless fun far from her daily grind. But what begins as a relaxing vacation turns into a desperate fight for her life when terrorists take over the ship and start piling up bodies. Teaming up with a mysterious stowaway, Jess attempts to send out a distress call but knows they cannot wait for help to come. If she or the few remaining passengers have any hope for survival, Jess must act now. The papers dub it "The Battle for *Andrea Maria*," but to Jess it is the moment she fought side-by-side with her enigmatic Romeo, saving the ship--and losing him. She thinks the story ends there, but really, the nightmare is just beginning...

"Insanely Deadly"

When the dead return to life, it's up to an admiral's daughter and a mildly insane, former war hero to save their small town.

Jetta Cross, a Navy Admiral's daughter, is tasked with keeping her father's comrade, a former war hero turned town crazy, grounded in the real world. Capt. John Hunter is still fighting the war in his head, where imaginary dead people are part of his world. When a viral outbreak brings about a zombie uprising, Hunter is left to his own devices. He must resume his role as a one-man commando unit in order to destroy the ravenous undead. With Hunter still fighting his own inner demons as well as the undead, the townspeople fear their zombie neighbors may not be the only threat. Stranded at the island's luxurious resort with a handful of workers, Jetta is forced to live up to her father's reputation and take charge of the deteriorating situation at the hotel. She must wage her own war against the infected before the government declares her hometown a total loss.

"Deadly Institution"

A town recluse suspected of killing his wife teams up with a young woman in order to stop a killer.

After being accused of murdering his wife, Konrad Asher turns his back on the town that once adored him. Ten years later, he still holds his grudge and the title of the most feared man in town. With the reopening of the burned mental institution, where his wife had died, former employees are now murdered one-by-one, throwing suspicion back on Asher. A young local reporter, Jacey, is forced to reveal her long-time friendship with the infamous recluse in order to clear his name not only in the recent murders but to exonerate him in the death of his wife as well. Will Jacey's relationship with Asher invite the killer closer to her? Or is the killer already in her life?

"Screenplays: The Island Collection"
"Jungle Princess", "A.L.F. Resort", "Brighton Island"

Discover how romance and fun in the sun can be downright *chilling*!

"Jungle Princess" is a romantic/thriller that leaves a teenage girl stranded on an island with two male shipmates and a creature of "unknown" origin. She soon discovers the island is home to an abandoned prison with several prisoners roaming free. What really killed over one hundred prisoners? And is it still out there--?

"A.L.F. Resort" is a romantic/thriller set on an island resort with Artificial Life Forms as the main draw. At this resort, all your fantasies come true...until a malfunction removes safety inhibitors on the A.L.F.'s. Zombies, biker gangs, and mobsters run amuck, turning fantasies into nightmares. A young reporter gets more of a story than she anticipates, but will she survive long enough to write the story?

"Brighton Island" is a romantic/thriller set on a private island. When the owner's niece brings her psychic friend to the mansion, his presence awakens the spirits' tortured souls. As the psychic attempts to solve the old murders, the niece is confronted with the possibility that she's next to join the mansion ghosts. Stranded on the island with a crazed killer, her uncle wages his own war to save them. Will his "shock and awe" tactics actually save them or get them killed?

"Death Displacement"

A grief-stricken man travels back in time to seek revenge on the woman who murdered his girlfriend but inadvertently falls in love with her.

Kane is about to marry the woman he loves. His life is perfect. A few weeks before the wedding, a vindictive woman from his girlfriend's past mysteriously arrives and kills her. He learns of a traumatic accident that happened five years earlier, which triggers Riley's hatred for his girlfriend. Distraught over his girlfriend's death, Kane uses an antique time machine to travel into the past in order to find and destroy the woman responsible. When he runs into Riley's younger self, he realizes she's not the monster she later becomes, and he can't bring himself to destroy her. With a little help from his oddball friend from the past, they formulate a plan to prevent the accident that sends Riley down her destructive path. Kane's plan backfires when he falls for the younger Riley. His new tortured existence is further complicated when future Riley, his girlfriend's killer, shows up with her own devious agenda that doesn't include him. Will he be able to stop the time ripple, which ultimately ends with his girlfriend's death? Or will future Riley take him out of the timeline forever--

"Dead Village"

After strange happenings isolate a small resort town from the rest of the world, nearly one hundred residents seek refuge at the closed hotel. Only eight survive the night. And that's just the beginning...

One day after the entire population of Fox Ridge Village disappears, a car wreck forces several unsuspecting crash victims to seek help at the closed summer hotel. Within the hotel, they discover the grisly aftermath of a brutal slaughter. Crash victims Vander and Devon, a reluctant clairvoyant, team up to solve the riddle of the "haunted hotel" and the mass hysteria plaguing the remaining survivors. By the time they discover the hotel's secret, they're already drawn into the hysteria. As the body count continues to climb, it's a race to isolate the source and bring everyone back to reality before they kill one another. Will Devon be able to communicate with the traumatized spirits before their fate becomes her own?

"Misfits, Inc."

A seemingly ordinary, young woman meets four misfits who claim she has given them supernatural powers.

While on a business trip to a remote island paradise, a bored secretary, Hailey, has her world turned upside down when her path collides with a psychic freak, Skyler. He attempts to convince her that they had met in his dreams, and she had chosen him as one of her four mystic warriors. After Skyler foresees a woman's death, they discover an unidentified creature has killed one of the guests. They are joined by a lounge pianist and a rich playboy, who also claim they had met her in their dreams. If Skyler's prophecies are genuine, the evil entity controlling the ravenous creatures needs to destroy Hailey to ensure its survival. Reluctantly accepting her fate, Hailey has to locate the last and most powerful of her chosen warriors, The Guardian. Their fate is in doubt when The Guardian turns out to be a self-absorbed, former cat burglar with a bad attitude. Can Hailey turn her company of misfits into an elite team of mystic warriors? Or will The Guardian's secret agenda destroy them all?

"Basement Dwellers"

A viral outbreak at a hospital leaves a mortician, sheriff, and coroner fighting for their lives against a horde of undead and the CDC.

After a massive car wreck leaves several survivors in critical condition at the local hospital, a surgeon uses experimental drugs on his critical patients and accidentally causes a zombie outbreak. When local mortician, Lexx, receives an infected corpse as her client, she becomes stranded in the hospital basement during CDC quarantine along with the local sheriff and the coroner. The infamous surgeon struggles to find a cure for his infectious blunder by using the other survivors as test subjects. Meanwhile, Lexx and the sheriff attempt to locate his missing sister, who's stranded somewhere in the battle zone that once was the emergency room. It's a race against time and the ravenous undead. Can they survive the undead before CDC sanitizes the hospital of all infection?

"Witness Protection"
Also available in audiobook!

After witnessing an execution, a resourceful young woman attempts to disappear while being pursued by a hitman and a handsome federal agent.

A helicopter pilot, Jackie Remus, reluctantly agrees to go on a date with one of her clients, but her date is unexpectedly cut short when she witnesses a man being murdered. After narrowly escaping with her life, she is placed into protective custody. When the safe house is breached, Jackie makes a daring escape from both the hired killers and the handsome FBI agent, who wants to return her to protective custody. With a little help from her sly and crafty friend, Monroe, Jackie is convinced she can disappear until the trial. While on her journey to meet with her friend, she solicits help from a few shady but lovable characters along the way. Although she manages to stay one-step ahead of the hired killers, the federal agent remains in hot pursuit. Will Jackie reach Monroe before she's captured by the FBI and returned to protective custody? Or will the hired killers silence her first?

"Town Darling"

After surviving a brutal attack that claims the lives of those she loves, a young woman seeks revenge on a corrupt town.

Going back home is never easy, but for Casey, it means returning to her corrupt hometown where she barely survived a brutal attack. Accompanied by two family friends, she seeks justice for the night that destroyed her life. Her physical scars are nothing compared to her emotional ones, forcing the local sheriff to believe that the town darling is back for revenge. As the conspiracy for her revenge appears to be leading up to the coveted town fair, the sheriff is determined to stop her from fulfilling her vengeful scheme...but guilt over his role on that fateful night continues to haunt him. Will his desperate need for Casey's forgiveness be his undoing? Or will Casey's desire for revenge destroy them both?

"Unconditional"

A young woman puts her life on hold to care for an unstable, highly skilled combat soldier, who believes someone is trying to kill him.

A botched military coup leaves a team of elite fighters injured with one clinging to life in a coma. When Harlan wakes from his coma, he's left with no memory of his past life. His commander's daughter, Indy, takes it upon herself to care for the fallen war hero. She's challenged with more than just his physical care as she combats with not only his memory loss but also his newly found desire for her. His infatuation with her becomes the least of her worries when he sinks back into his role of a combat soldier. Believing his life is in danger, his fighting skills surface, turning him into an unpredictable and dangerous man. Will his memory return to him before Indy is forced to commit him? Or will he finally find his nemesis, "the coyote", and possibly claim the life of an innocent person?

"Witness Protection 2"
The Return of Whiskey Tango Foxtrot

Believing she holds the clue to millions in missing laundered money, a young woman is placed into the protective care of a former Navy SEAL team.

Feeling sorry for her recently separated co-worker, Leeann invites Wiley to join her and her friends on their night out. Little does she know that finding her co-worker murdered is just the beginning of her nightmare. Leeann unknowingly holds the key to fifty million dollars in potentially laundered mob money. With hired killers pursuing her, the FBI places her into a different kind of protective custody. Former Navy SEAL team Whiskey Tango Foxtrot reunites to keep Leeann alive at their secret hideaway. What should be an easy assignment takes an unscheduled turn when secrets, lies, and betrayal threaten to derail their mission. Is the team prepared for a war on their own doorstep? Will Leeann's misguided trust endanger the lives of those sent to protect her?

"Deadly Institution 2"

When blackmail turns into murder, a young woman finds herself caught in the killer's crosshairs.

The small town of Stony Ridge is no stranger to scandal and persecution of the innocent. When a brutal killing shakes the town's prestigious country club, Jacey McMurray seeks help from a self-proclaimed vigilante, Konrad Asher. As her professional and personal worlds collide, Jacey fears the stress of the country club killings have finally taken their toll on Asher. Can a stressed out vigilante stop the killer before he strikes again?

"Witness Protection 3"
Alpha Mike Foxtrot

A helicopter pilot risks her life to help a team of retired Navy SEALs rescue two girls from a killer.

When former Navy SEAL team Whiskey Tango Foxtrot asks for a simple favor, Jackie reluctantly offers her air-taxi services. What could go wrong? What begins as a search and rescue for two girls turns into a fight for survival against a heavily armed drug cartel. Wanted by the law with the cartel in hot pursuit and their home base breached, the team is forced to call in a favor from a questionable ally. Unfortunately, their new safe house isn't what it seems. Without knowing who the real enemy is, can Jackie and the team save their young witnesses from the hands of a killer?

"The Pen Pal"

In order to save her friend, she must enter the mind of a serial killer.

When her best friend is abducted, no one believes Jolynn saw it in a psychic vision. With nowhere to turn, Jolynn reluctantly joins Agent Harris Slade and his team on their hunt for a sadistic serial killer known only as "The Pen Pal". Finally confronted with the killer, Jolynn realizes she must enter the mind of the psychopath in order to stop the brutal killings. But when her vision reveals a particularly disturbing death, can Jolynn sacrifice her lover for her friend?

"Awaken the Dead"

A grieving innkeeper struggles to keep her haunted hotel out of foreclosure.

After losing her parents in a suspicious boating accident, Harley Brandon is determined to keep the family hotel out of foreclosure. Unfortunately, the hotel ghosts have other plans. Built with tainted money, the century-old Horizon Hotel thrives on a tradition of murder, scandal, and suicide. As the paranormal activity increases to alarming levels, Harley discovers the truth about the hotel and its residents. Can Harley save her friends from the hotel's frightening hidden secrets?

"Already Dead"
Supernatural Collection

From the already dead to the undead. Three supernatural tales of "things that go bump in the night".

"Bloodletting" - A vampire-themed resort allows guests to *participate* in their Bloodletting Ritual to celebrate the island's legendary vampires.

"Reaper of Souls" - A young woman must outwit an evil sorcerer in order to save her brother or become one of his minions forever.

"Already Dead" - When Flight 220 crashes, ten passengers make it to an isolated island, but only one man lives to tell the lie.

"Witness Protection 4"
O-Dark-Hundred

A simple assignment turns deadly when a retired Navy SEAL team uncovers a plot to kill a notorious mob boss.

When Whiskey Tango Foxtrot embarks on a simple stalking case, they're not prepared for a trip to a private island paradise owned by an infamous mobster. With one of their own suffering from traumatic head injuries, the team is left scrambling to decide what is real or imagined. The situation escalates even further when they uncover an assassination plot where everyone is a suspect. Now targets themselves, can the team survive their trip to paradise?

"Witness Protection 5"
Outside the Wire

After suffering several casualties on their last assignment, a retired Navy SEAL team discovers their misery is just beginning.

When Whiskey Tango Foxtrot returns home after suffering a devastating loss, they're hit with even more bad news regarding the rest of their team. Their grief is cut short when they discover their names are all on the same hit list. Hunted by relentless assassins, the scattered team must decide whether to remain safely hidden or find the man who put the price on their heads. Against the wishes of her teammates, Jackie strikes out on her own in order to save a friend who wants her dead. In a kill or be killed situation, will Jackie's emotions finally betray her?

"Cemetery Stalkers"
Horror Collection

Four tales of horror from flesh eaters to bloodsuckers.

"Night Creatures" − A rescue party stranded on an abandoned cruise ship is hunted by a frightening creature.

"Ravenous" − After surviving a crash, a woman seeks refuge in a mysterious mansion with a terrifying secret.

"The Feast" − A creature on a bloody rampage terrorizes a small town.

"Cemetery Stalkers" − When 'The Reaper' stalks a cemetery, death follows.

"Once Upon a Disaster"

A young homicide detective finds herself at the mercy of a hitman in the aftermath of an earthquake.

While investigating the murder of a hitman, Detective Jade Wesson pursues a lead connecting the dead man to a break-in at a computer programming company. She's drawn into the world of nightclub owner and front man for the mob, Cody Riley. Her investigation keeps pointing to Cody's right-hand man and possible hitman, Vahn Lott. Despite her efforts to keep her investigation on track, Vahn has plans of his own for the attractive detective. When an unprecedented earthquake rocks their east coast town, Jade must put her life in Vahn's hands if she wants to survive. Can she trust a man who might be the killer she's hunting?

ABOUT THE AUTHOR

Holly Copella has been writing since the age of twelve when her frustration at a book's poor plot drove her to author her own story. Over the last decade, she's written a number of screenplays, some of which she's now adapting into novels. Her fascination with zombies and other darker material lends an edge to her writing, which tends to lean toward horror. As a fan of Agatha Christie, she appreciates the craft of a good plot and the importance of creating significant characters.

Hailing from Pennsylvania, Copella lives in the Endless Mountains on a farm with her rescue horses and other animals. In addition to writing and reading fiction, she enjoys riding horses and traveling to Las Vegas and Disney World.